GUILTY

JANE BIDDER

Published by Accent Press Ltd 2014

ISBN 9781909624160

Copyright © Jane Bidder 2014

The story contained within this book is a work of
fiction. Names and characters are the product of the
author's imagination and any resemblance to actual
persons, living or dead, is entirely coincidental.
Please note that I have tried to be as accurate as
possible, regarding prison and legal protocol. However,
prisons vary and rules are constantly changing so I
apologise if there are any mistakes. On a small number of
occasions, I have bent certain facts slightly to fit in with
the plot.

Dedications

I dedicate this book to that little voice inside us all, that tells us what is right and wrong.

Also in recognition of the extraordinary skill, talent, dedication and hard work that goes on in prison – on both sides of the law

Acknowledgments

I would like to give thanks to the following:

My agent Teresa Chris

The team at Accent Press

Clive Hopwood and Pauline Bennett from the Writers in Prison Network

Wendy Robertson, a former fellow writer in residence

Peter Bennett, 'my' former governor

Iain and David for their legal advice.

Kate Furnivall for her acute observations

Everyone involved with the Koestler Trust

Betty Schwartz who started me off

My husband who gives me space to write and for his support

IN

Chapter One

They were having a summer dinner party! Claire mouthed the words inside her head with a sing-song lightness that matched the warm evening sunshine outside. 'Simon and I are having a dinner party!' There had been one or two gatherings, of course, since they'd got married two years ago, but it still felt like a delicious novelty.

It was so lovely to do things – normal things – together as a couple! Even now, after being on her own with Ben, she had to pinch herself when Simon wrapped his arms around hers at night. 'This is my husband,' she would say to herself in wonder. It felt so good. So comforting.

On impulse, Claire had invited a woman whom she'd recently met at thhe meanse tennis club and had just moved here with her new husband. It would be nice, she told herself, to have someone else who *wasn't* planning a silver wedding!

Just to be sure everything ran smoothly, she'd asked Alex and Rosemarie too and for once, despite her work deadlines, she was reasonably organised, even down to polishing the old mahogany dining room table with lavender wax. She'd decided what to wear too: those new creamy crepe trousers with the clingy sea green top and the long dangly emerald earrings they'd bought on their honeymoon in Italy. How she loved putting together contrasting 'clashing' shades to accentuate what Simon called her pre-Raphaelite hair.

'What are you going to cook?' he now asked, nibbling her ear as she leafed through her Mary Berry winter recipes.

'Goats' cheese tartlets for starters and rack of lamb for the main course.' She leant her head back into his neck, breathing in his warm skin mixed with that citrus aftershave he always wore. 'Plus a quiche in case anyone is vegetarian. I was going

1

to do pavlova for pudding but I'm not sure now.'

Simon put his big warm arms around her and pulled her towards him, making her melt. She arched up her face to look at him. When they'd first met, she'd been struck by his brilliant blue eyes and brown skin that had seemed like a tan. It was only later that she found out his father was half-Indian; a heritage which he was both proud and wary of, depending on his mood. For her part, she found him incredibly sexy; a sort of younger Imran Khan.

Now he spun her round so she was facing him, sending shivers of desire right through her. 'Vegetarian?' he repeated. 'I don't get people who don't eat meat! Imagine never having a bacon sandwich again!' Then he began to move round in circles, slowly, rhythmically, her head against his chest. '*Dance with me*,' he hummed, '*dance with me.*'

How she wished they were in bed right now instead of having people round! There was a noise from upstairs, indicating Ben was on his way down. Her son didn't like it when he caught them showing affection; disloyally, she found herself thinking that it was easier when he was at his father's for the weekend. But then, when Ben returned on Sunday nights, she could never resist questioning him casually about how Dad was and whether there'd been yet another girlfriend there.

Ridiculous, really, to be so nosey about her first husband's private life, considering how good it was with Simon! Besides, as Rosemarie was always saying, didn't she deserve some happiness after everything? Wasn't it right that she now had a kind man like this who told her she was beautiful and danced impromptu round the kitchen? Charlie would never have done that! And certainly not when guests were coming.

'I'm really sorry but I just haven't got time,' she said, disentangling herself. 'I've still got so much to get ready.'

Reluctantly, Simon released her, getting out his tool box to sort out the bathroom sink which was blocked yet again. That was the trouble, he was always saying, with these old places, but she loved Beech Cottage which she had filled with her paintings and rugs with their lovely midnight blues and salmon pinks; a much-loved refuge after the divorce.

'Fair enough,' he shrugged. 'You do the cooking and I'll make sure we don't have a leak during dinner. What are these Goodman-Browns like, anyway?'

'*She's* lovely, but I haven't met him.' Claire felt a flutter of apprehension.

'Better make sure we've got enough booze to liven things up.'

Drink! She'd been so busy thinking about the food that she'd forgotten.

'No problem.' He laid a hand on her shoulder and she felt that warmth seeping into her. 'I'll get it after sorting the sink.'

'That would be great.' Not for the first time, Claire wondered if anything could ever unsettle her husband. 'He's very laid back,' Rosemarie had told her three years ago when she'd announced, rather meaningfully, that an old uni friend of Alex's was coming down that weekend.

She, for her part, had protested that it was too soon after her divorce but Rosemarie had insisted she popped in for a pre-Sunday lunch Pimm's. Somehow, she had found herself staying longer, entranced by this very tall, but not particularly slim, clever, handsome, warm, funny man who told amusing stories and yet also listened to what she had to say.

'Why has he never married?' she asked Rosemarie curiously afterwards. 'He must be, what, forty-five?'

'Thirty-nine.' Dear Rosemarie was keen to promote his case. 'He's had a few long-term girlfriends but never found the right person. Seemed pretty struck on you, though.'

Everyone said it was quick when they were married within the year but it seemed right. So why, Claire would demand of herself every now and then, could she never quite rid herself of that odd feeling when Charlie rang to speak to their son?

Now in the kitchen, seeking reassurance, she reached out for Simon's hands. 'Kiss me,' she demanded, leaning back. His mouth came down on hers. Hard and yet soft, suggesting possibilities after the dinner party tonight.

3

'Mum?' Ben stood at the doorway and they sprang apart. Dear God! His hair looked even more extreme than yesterday when he'd returned from a sleepover with the sides shaved off and the middle section standing up in blue and silver streaks.

His friends had done it, he'd said casually in a voice that challenged her to make a fuss. She'd freaked out, of course and then Simon had calmly told his stepson not to be rude to his mother. 'You're not my fucking father,' Ben had yelled back and then there'd been another argument, resulting in a cold standoff between her son and husband.

'Mum,' Ben now repeated, totally ignoring Simon, 'I'm going out. Can you lend me some money?'

Claire's heart sank and she felt Simon stiffen. Her husband, who had never had children, didn't see why she should constantly 'top up' her son. But Ben was in his GCSE year and an after-school job might interfere with his schoolwork.

'You promised last week that you were going to mend the bathroom sink with me to earn your pocket money,' said Simon tightly.

'I *am* going to.' Ben spat out the words without looking at his stepfather. 'But not now. I'm going out.'

'And I'm doing the sink this minute.'

'I said I'd do it later.'

Someone needed to sort this. 'Look, I'll lend you this and then you can pay me back.' Opening her purse, she slipped her son a five-pound note. He looked at it as though expecting more.

'What time will you be back?'

'Don't know. I'll text.'

'And where are you going?'

Too late. He'd already gone.

'I thought we agreed you weren't going to lend him any more unless he earned it,' said Simon quietly.

She shrugged. 'He *did* help me make the new pudding. And he half-laid the table.'

Simon put a hand on her shoulder and his touch made her want to both cuddle him and push him away at the same time.

4

'He won't learn this way, you know.'

But he's been hurt, she wanted to cry. Damaged by everything that's happened. If Simon had had children, he would understand all this. 'He wants to be a child one minute and an adult the next. Please try to see that.'

Simon turned his back. 'I'll just sort out the sink before hitting the shops. See you later.'

The scene cast a shadow over the rest of the pre-dinner party preparations. It wasn't that Simon sulked after he had come back with the drink. Quite the opposite. He had breezed in, planting a kiss on her neck, as though nothing had happened, although she was beginning to recognise this breeziness as a sign that he was shutting off.

Was it, Claire wondered as she laid out the pretty floral place mats, really possible to know someone as well as she had known Charlie? And how long did it take for a man who'd been a long-term bachelor to open up to a new wife or get on with a boy who wasn't his own?

A prickle of unease ran down her spine as she wiped one of the wine glasses. Had she been wrong to give Ben money? And why hadn't her son texted, as promised, to say where he was with his friends. The worry niggled her all evening, although she tried to disguise it by looking after her guests.

Hugh Goodman-Brown, who had arrived in a blue blazer and cream trousers contrasting with Simon's casual jeans, was hard work! Initially it wasn't too bad when they were talking about teenagers and course-work especially as it turned out that his daughter was at the same school as Ben *and* in the same year. But then, running out of conversation, she desperately turned to careers. 'What do you do?' she'd asked.

His face wrinkled like a pug dog's with steel-rimmed glasses. 'I'm an F.A.,' he announced, draining his glass noisily.

An F.A.?

'Financial adviser.' He topped himself up without passing the bottle around. Very naughtily, she couldn't help thinking that the term 'F.A.' could mean something much ruder. The thought made her giggle and she had to pretend her wine had gone down the wrong way. Now what to say?

'I illustrate children's books,' she volunteered.

He nodded, fantastically unaware of a piece of broccoli that had lodged itself between his front teeth. 'Pay you, do they, or is it just a hobby?'

'They pay me,' she answered tautly. She glanced across at Joanna who had made the right appreciative noises about their 'beautiful house' when she'd arrived, wondering how she could have married a boor like this. Her lovely guest was now laughing gaily at something Simon had said. Irrationally, she felt a pang of jealousy. 'I would never do what Charlie did,' he often said.

Even so, she didn't like the way that Joanna's long elegant fingers reached out every now and then, touching Simon's arm as though to make a point. Women liked her husband! She'd seen the admiring looks in the supermarket and on the school run. When Simon had first told her how many girlfriends he'd had, she had felt both flattered – because she was the one he'd chosen to marry – and also frightened, in case he went off her as Charlie had done.

'Mind if I open another bottle?' boomed Hugh.

'I thought we agreed that you were driving, darling!' Her new friend's voice tinkled across the table disapprovingly. She was truly beautiful, Claire observed, in an ethereal way, with almost translucent pale skin and long blonde hair arranged in an artful knot with the side bits falling over those slender collar bones.

'I'm afraid that I can't do it!' She flashed a brilliant smile around the table. 'Definitely over the limit.' Stretching out her arms like a cat, Joanna almost purred; seemingly unaware that every man's eyes were on her.

Rosemarie raised her eyebrows in disapproval. She'd always been a bit of a prude. Simon called her 'staid'. Yet she was one of those women who, without being particularly interesting or good-looking, acted in a way that suggested she *was*. Tonight, she was wearing a calf-length pleated navy skirt. Joanna, in contrast, was in an elegant knee-length black dress, showing off her glossy ten denier legs.

'We could give you a lift,' Rosemarie continued in that correct clipped voice of hers, 'but ...'

'Nonsense.' Simon's dark reassuring voice cut in. 'I've just had half a glass. I'll take you back. But only if my wife allows me to have one more helping of her delicious syllabub before I go. Home-made you know.' He looked round the table as though expecting a round of applause for his wife's culinary skills. So loyal yet also rather embarrassing!

'Divine,' Joanna laughed gaily. 'Absolutely melted in my mouth! You must give me the recipe sometime.'

How old was she? Claire wondered as she promised to email it over. From a distance, she looked like a twenty-something model but when you were closer, you could glimpse fine lines, cleverly masked by make-up.

'We could get a taxi,' growled Hugh. Exactly! But now, Simon in his eagerness to please – too eager for her liking – was already getting up for his car keys.

'Don't be long, darling,' she murmured as he bent down to kiss her goodbye.

'I won't,' he mouthed back. 'Love you.'

Chapter Two

Where *were* they? Simon didn't believe in sat nav. 'I prefer my own instinct,' he was proud of saying. He'd been certain that he knew the way to the village where Joanna and Hugh lived but this didn't seem right. That old farm building and its rickety barn didn't look familiar. Nor did that garage and its *Closed* sign.

No good asking Hugh. The man had had far too much to drink and was asleep now in the front seat, nodding into his pink and white striped shirt and occasionally waking up with a jerk, only to start snoring again. Too late, Simon regretted his invitation to drive them home – a gesture prompted less by generosity than the urge to prevent the evening from dragging on any longer.

If Claire was here, she'd have asked Joanna for directions by now. But a mixture of his own male pride and her incessant chatter prevented him.

'Lovely evening ... so kind of you to have us ... so sorry about Hugh not being his usual self ... been a bit stressed at work regularly ... I hear you moved down from London when you married Claire ... So romantic ...'

Trying to block out her voice, he slowed down and looked around. Not a soul in sight. Only the leaves which swayed from the trees on either side of them and an owl which suddenly swooped in front of them, causing him to swerve slightly.

'Hugh and I still wonder if we made the right decision leaving Richmond ... We've only been down here for six months but I still feel dreadfully homesick and so does Hugh's daughter ... did I tell you that she'd moved down to be with us?

Please be quiet, he wanted to say. I need to concentrate, especially when your drunken oaf of a husband is snoring like that. The road was bendy without the London street lights he was used to and the hedges were so high that it was like being stuck in the Hampton Court maze. That had happened to him once with a French girlfriend and he had felt inexplicably claustrophobic – almost unable to draw breath – both in the maze and the relationship.

'Oooh! Is that an Ella Fitzgerald CD I can see? Could we put it on? I just adore jazz?'

Anything for some peace. Reaching over, he slid the CD into the slot and the car filled with Ella's hauntingly beautiful voice. Claire loved jazz too.

His mind went back again to the evening he had met this lovely woman with a gentle smile and beautiful auburn hair curling softly on her shoulders like that model in the pre-Raphaelite paintings; the one who was married to one painter but in love with another. Fed up with girlfriends over the years who had been obsessed with their appearances, he had been entranced by this vision who walked and spoke and laughed in a way that suggested she simply didn't realise how lovely she was.

Later, when he learned more about her life, he wanted to beat up her ex and, at the same time, sink to his knees and thank him for having left this beautiful woman free for him.

Amazingly, it had been incredibly easy to transfer to the Exeter office which was keen to have a defence lawyer having his experience. And although he didn't really like moving into a house which Claire's ex-husband had bought her after the divorce, he could also see her argument that moving again, would disrupt the boy.

Beech Cottage was in one of those hamlets which, Simon, soon discovered, were common in this part of the country. The pub and shop had recently gone (something which it could have done with, in his view) and the main social hub was a tennis club a few miles down the road which you had to drive to.

Most of Claire's friends either came from there or from the neighbouring houses which were studded in clusters around them; each with their own sizeable garden and driveway with farm-style gates that were difficult to open. In London, they would have gone for a fortune, but the prices here perhaps reflected the fact that it took a good three hours to get to Paddington.

Still, the scenery was beautiful with those rolling hills – clearly visible from the back of Beech Cottage – and thick woods where Claire loved to walk. 'Come on,' she would say, laughingly taking him by the hand. 'Breathe in the fresh air.'

Simon had to admit that it did smell different from London air. It was fresher with a dampness that tickled his nose. He just couldn't work out if he actually preferred it or not.

There was, however, something rather nice about living just twenty minutes from the sea. On the other hand, it was taking him some time to adjust to the slower pace in Devon and the way people said 'good morning' when they passed even if they didn't know you. If you did that in London, they'd have you down as a nutter.

Talking of whom …

'Lovely car, by the way!' Joanna was twittering on again. 'Amazing how roomy it is in the back, even though it's a convertible. Have you had it long?'

At least two years. He used to change his car every year before he'd got married. Porsches. Audis. Jags. He'd had them all. But it didn't seem so important now he had Claire and of course, Ben.

'Think you take a sharp left here.' Joanna's voice took on a slightly tighter edge, 'although it might just be the next one. Hard to work it out in the dark, isn't it?'

'Work it out?' snorted Hugh, waking up suddenly. A spray of spit flew out and landed on Simon's arm. Disgusting. 'Stupid woman! Since when were you ever able to work anything out?'

How rude. Simon was about to intervene but she got there first.

'Darling,' said Joanna in a plaintive tone. 'That's not very nice. I think someone's had a teeny-weeny bit too much to drink.' Simon glanced in the mirror to see her undoing her safety belt so she could lean over the front seat, sliding her hand under her husband's shirt. 'Don't be cross, darling. I can't bear it when you get angry. Whoops. I think we should have taken a right there.'

'Left, you silly bitch!' roared Hugh. 'It's left.'

Simon began to sweat despite the cold. 'Joanna, please put your belt back on. And Hugo, if you don't mind me saying, it's deeply offensive to call your wife a bitch.'

'I'll call her what I bloody like!'

'Fuck! Hugo! Leave the steering wheel alone!'

Then everything happened fast. The mobile phone ringing from the flesh of his gear stick. *Ben*. Simon's reluctance to pick it up because he hadn't got his ear piece in and then that uneasy feeling when it stopped in case the boy had needed him.

'*He wants to be a child one minute and an adult the next*,' Claire had said. '*Please try to understand.*'

The grip on his left arm from the brute in the passenger seat who was leaning over him now with heavy beery fumes and shouting 'Take a left,' against Joanna's tinkly 'Take a right'.

The phone again. Ben once more. The car parked on the left of the lane. Only just time to swerve to the right and ...

Oh my God.

The first thing that struck Simon was the cold, dark eerie silence. He tried to turn round to see if Joanna was all right in the back but his safety belt was twisted in a way that meant he could only just glance sideways. Hugh wasn't there.

It was freezing as though there weren't any windows. He could feel the night air sinking down into his lungs.

'Joanna,' he tried to say. 'Hugh?'

His fingers began to shake. Slightly at first and then in huge juddering motions as though they belonged to someone else. It was a terrible effort to make them pick up the phone. Thank God. He could see a bit now by its faint light. Appalled, he took in the huge hole in the windscreen, stretched out like a glass cobweb.

Forcing his fingers to work, he tried dialling 999 but they hit Home instead.

'*Hi! Please leave a message for Claire, Simon or Ben ...*'

'Claire.' Her name spilled out of his mouth in a giant sob. 'For God's sake pick up. Something awful's happened. Something awful.'

And then he heard a scream. So loud that it almost drowned the noise of the siren. A scream that was coming out of his own mouth.

Chapter Three

As Claire cleared up the post-dinner party mess, she kept imagining Simon sitting next to Joanna. She was just the kind of person who would automatically assume rights in the passenger seat. Her husband's hand would brush her knee accidentally as he changed gear and Joanna – whose ethereal beauty had entranced every man at the table – would give a gay flirtatious laugh.

Simon, Claire told herself, dumping the pudding plates down by the dishwasher, might contrast this with her own tetchiness before the party when they'd quarrelled over Ben.

Talking of her son, why hadn't he texted to say he'd got to his party safely or that he needed picking up? Claire began to wipe down the dining room table with angry circular motions. How she hated it when his friends drove! It had all been so much simpler when he'd been little and she knew exactly where he was.

The phone! It would be Ben – at last – ringing to say he was safe. But someone had moved the handset! Claire's eyes skimmed the kitchen. Where *was* the wretched thing?

Ah. There it was, hiding under the parish magazine. Picking it up, she heard the two-tone ring, indicating a message.

'*Claire. For God's sake pick up. Something awful's happened.*'

Simon? What was wrong? Was he hurt? An electric shock of panic shot through her as she pressed the shortcut button to Simon's mobile. It went straight through to answerphone.

And then, wondering if she was over-reacting but not knowing what else to do, she dialled 999.

An hour later, Claire sat numbly on a metal-framed chair,

shivering in her thin green dressy evening top. Thoughts were flying round her head. Stupid irrelevant thoughts like whether she'd remembered to turn off the Aga fan. Glancing up at the wall in front of her, Claire saw a cartoon figure on a poster demanding to know whether she'd purchased a current television licence. Its normality seemed cruel.

All that mattered was Simon. And Ben too, of course. But it was Simon she needed to feel. Simon who would hold her close and tell her that it was all right.

Her mind went back to when she'd been put through to the police surprisingly quickly. She'd tried to talk but fear had blurred her words as though she was drunk or simple.

'Can you give me your husband's registration number?' a sympathetic voice had said. And then she was kept holding on until a different voice asked her to come down to the police station without giving a reason, even though she'd tried to explain she needed to be at home for her teenage son.

'Please!' she felt her eyes filling with tears as she stood at the counter. 'Have you had any reports of an accident? I just want to find out why my husband was so upset.'

'We're still making enquiries,' soothed the kindly grandfatherly police officer on the desk, glancing at her thin top. 'Take a seat, dear.'

His calm tone made her feel that maybe Simon had just had a puncture or a bit of a prang. His panicky answerphone message might merely have been an overreaction. Maybe …

Yes! Her mobile. Simon! Delving into her bag to find it – quickly before it rang off! – she felt a pang of acute disappointment at the name '*Ben*' flashing up.

'Where've you been, Mum? I tried to ring Simon but he didn't pick up either. I'm staying over at Jack's. OK?'

'Fine,' she managed to say.

'What's wrong, Mum?'

'Nothing.' She glanced up at the grandfatherly police officer whose face was now worryingly solemn. 'I'll pick you up in the morning, shall I? About 11?'

'My son', she started to explain but stopped at the sound of

14

voices. Raised voices. Arguing.

'You've got it all wrong!'

That was definitely Simon! A balloon of relief rose up in her chest.

'I've told you God knows how many times!'

The shouting grew louder. What was going on?

'It wasn't the phone.' Simon's voice was getting louder. Nearer. 'It was because Hugh grabbed my arm.'

Then he came into view; dishevelled with a torn shirt, sweaty hair and a face pinched with fear. 'Simon!' she called out, running up to him. 'What's going on?'

'Claire,' he called out as the officer steered him towards another door off the corridor. 'Ring Patrick, for God's sake.' And then the door slammed shut, with him on the other side.

Frantically, she raced back to the desk. The grandfatherly police officer had gone. In his place stood a pretty young woman whose blonde hair was tied back severely from her forehead. 'If someone doesn't tell me what's happened,' she gasped, 'I'm going to go mad.'

The young police officer eyed her as though she'd jumped a bank queue. 'Mrs Mills? I'm afraid I must ask you to sit down.'

'No. Please. You don't understand.' The words were pouring out of her mouth in desperation. 'I need to ring someone but I don't have any reception here.'

Reluctantly, or so it seemed, the woman passed over a handset. 'One call. That's all.'

Patrick was one of the partners in Simon's office, Claire reminded herself as she fumbled through the telephone directory to find the emergency out of hours number. He was younger than Simon and, as her husband had frequently commented, rather too competitive for comfort. He hadn't, in Simon's opinion, taken kindly to a new, more experienced lawyer coming on board. So Simon had gone to some pains to show that he wasn't a threat and that there was plenty of room for them all. But he would help. He had to! Both he and Simon specialised in 'getting people off the hook'.

Sometimes, she wondered about the ethics of it all. The

other month, her husband had come back from court, pleased that his client had escaped a driving ban on the grounds that it would have meant he couldn't have driven his wife to hospital for her dialysis treatment. It seemed to her that if someone had broken the law, they should be punished. But if Simon wanted her to call Patrick, that meant he needed defending himself. So what on earth had happened?

'I don't understand,' she repeated, wondering if she was just being obtuse or whether it was because it was now gone 5 a.m. and she was too tired to take anything in.

Patrick shuffled uncomfortably in front of her in the police interview room. His narrow hips barely held up his dark navy-blue suit trousers. Did her husband's future really rest on this gawky twenty-something with a prematurely receding hairline?

'I know this is traumatic for you,' repeated Patrick, in a glib tone that made her want to yell at him, even though she wasn't a yelling kind of person. 'Your husband has told me exactly what happened and I have no reason not to believe him.'

There was a slight pause which made Claire feel sick. Until he'd arrived, she'd expected Patrick to sort out this whole confusing business. But one look at his creased forehead indicated it was more serious than that. Her mouth was dry. 'And what *did* happen?'

'As you know, your husband was driving the Goodman-Browns home.' Patrick's voice was flat as though reciting lines in a school play. 'They got lost. Hugh Goodman-Brown was drunk and verbally abusive towards his wife which distracted Simon. Then the phone rang. It was your son, Ben, but your husband didn't pick it up the first time because he wasn't hands-free. When it rang again for the second time, however, he panicked, thinking it was an emergency. He chose to answer.'

'Go on,' she said urgently.

'At the same time, Hugh grabbed his arm telling him he had taken a wrong turning. The red car which had been parked on the left had broken down only an hour before. The driver had just abandoned it without reporting it which he shouldn't have

16

done. That might work in our favour. Then, because the lane was narrow, your husband had to swerve to overtake it. Unfortunately, he thought something was coming in the opposite direction.'

'Fuck'. She heard the word – one which she never used – fall out of her mouth and Patrick's mouth creased disapprovingly. 'Was ... was anyone ... killed?'

'No.'

Thank God!

Patrick was shaking his head, solemnly. 'But Mrs Goodman-Brown is in Intensive Care. For some reason, she wasn't wearing her safety belt. Her husband, who was in the passenger seat, has suffered fractures and cuts. He was knocked out for a short time so they're still doing tests. '

Claire's mind raced. Intensive care? Relief mixed with shock. At least Joanna wasn't dead. 'And the car coming in the opposite direction?'

Patrick's face was scarily impassive. 'There wasn't one. It was the wall.'

'But if Hugh grabbed his arm, surely Simon wasn't to blame?' She sensed a glimmer of hope.

'I'm afraid it's not as simple as that. Your husband broke the law in answering his mobile. He was also over the limit.'

'He'd had one glass of wine. That's all. That's why he suggested driving them back.'

Patrick tilted his head questioningly. 'Was there any possibility that someone could have laced his drink?'

The suggestion was almost laughable. 'I don't think so.'

'Simon said you did the cooking. What did you make?'

Goats cheese tartlets. Rack of lamb. Cheese and red onion quiche. I was going to make pavlova but it was too crisp so I did rum syllabub instead. *Rum syllabub.* A cold shaft of fear went through her.

'Oh my God,' she said, suddenly remembering how she'd handed the rum bottle to Ben earlier that afternoon in the kitchen with the instruction to 'add a slosh or two'.

'Oh my God.'

17

Chapter Four

Once, years ago, Simon had nearly been arrested. It had been in a Czechoslovakian jail during a boozy lads' holiday. They'd had too much to drink and there'd been a scuffle with the locals. Even though he hadn't actually aimed a punch, he'd been thrown into the town's fleapit of a cell and forced to spend the night there before being chucked out in the morning with a bucket of water thrown over their heads and a warning, made up of gestures and broken English, that they were lucky to get off so lightly.

Truth be told, this was one of the reasons why Simon, after law school, had chosen to be a defence lawyer. He'd rather enjoyed the thrill of arguing his way out in a language that wasn't his own. How much more satisfying to do it for other people too.

Since then, he'd built up quite a reputation for himself in the large London city firm, with practices throughout the country. Well-heeled clients who had been caught for speeding, and were now in danger of breaching their nine points, were tipped off by others in the know that Simon Mills was the man to go to.

It wasn't just driving, either. Last year, he'd had a case which had been featured heavily in several papers about a wealthy woman who insisted her nanny had stolen a necklace. The woman's ex-husband, who was said to 'take a paternal interest in the young girl', asked Simon to take her on. He'd conducted the case himself because it was in the magistrates' courts and they'd won the case. It had given him a buzz, both professionally and personally.

It was almost like acting. Simon was secretly proud of his reputation for 'treading the boards' in court; waving his hands around somewhat flamboyantly to make the point. He nearly always got his clients off.

If his clients had already been arrested, he usually saw them in the Visitors' Room at a police station. But he had never before been on the receiving end in a British cell. It was, observed Simon, looking around, pretty Spartan. A hard blue plastic mattress on the floor. A thin grey scratchy blanket. No window. And no mobile phone to contact Claire or Patrick or anyone else who might be able to get him out of this hell-hole at lunchtime on Sunday when everyone else was having a normal life.

Still, at least Joanna and Hugh were alive, thank God! They'd told him that much after arresting him at the scene for 'dangerous driving' and the relief had swept through him as though someone had pulled a plug out of his stomach and cleared his sinuses in so doing. He couldn't have coped if he'd killed someone. How could anyone?

Besides, Simon assured himself, last night hadn't been his fault. Not really. OK. So he'd got lost and he'd picked up the phone when he shouldn't have. But if it hadn't been for Hugh pulling his arm off the steering wheel like that or the car simply sitting there on a single track road, none of this would have happened. Surely the courts would see that?

'Not necessarily, I'm afraid,' Patrick had said earlier that morning when he'd arrived, smart and superior in his checked suit and narrow lips and thin black briefcase. 'You were over the limit as well.'

Rubbish, he had insisted, shocked. You can't be over the limit with one glass of Chardonnay and not very good Chardonnay at that (Hugh had brought it). There had to be something wrong with the machine. It happened. Remember that case in Kent last month?

Patrick had made soothing, patronising whipper-snapper noises and said something about talking to Claire 'to see if she could throw any light on the situation'.

Claire! What would she be thinking? Sometimes – although he'd never admit this to anyone – Simon wondered if he'd done

19

the right thing in marrying her. Unlike her predecessors, Claire had shown him that love could make you warm and safe. The downside was that it made you vulnerable because you were too dependent on someone else's affection.

But now he had no choice. Now he had to depend not just on his wife but also – God help him – on this sharp hostile kid from the office.

'We're applying for bail,' Patrick had said crisply. 'With any luck we'll get it.'

That had been at least three hours ago, surely, although it was difficult to tell without a clock. His watch, a present from his long-dead father for his twenty-first had been cracked during the accident and stopped working, He also had a very sore right wrist and bruised ribs, although nothing else. 'Lucky,' the police officer had remarked, as though it was another sign that Simon was guilty.

He was also pretty sure that he'd heard the word 'Paki' outside. That was another thing which took people by surprise when they met him. *Mills* after all, sounded such a British name. Simon took a certain pleasure in watching them when he began to speak and observe how their faces relaxed at his well-spoken, clearly educated voice. But at the same time, it annoyed him. If his grandparents hadn't valued education and if his father hadn't married a white woman, his life might have been very different.

Footsteps. Simon's heart now quickened. Claire maybe. Or Patrick. The door was flung open and a blonde police officer with tied-back hair stood there impassively. 'You've got bail,' she said shortly with a look that suggested he didn't deserve it. 'You're free to go.'

Claire was waiting outside in the main seating area. There was a drunk next to her, reeking of urine and shouting at no one in particular, plus an old man who was earnestly telling the duty officer that he was meant to be meeting his wife outside Woolworths in town but she wasn't there.

'Mr Walker, there isn't a Woolworths any more,' the police

20

officer was saying in a gentle tone. 'Don't worry. Someone from your care home will be along to collect you shortly.'

Simon's eyes met Claire's. Was it his imagination or was she looking at him in a different way? Simon Mills. So-called dangerous driver.

'Let's get out of here,' she said, tucking her arm in his. 'Come on.'

'Any news on Joanna?'

'Still in intensive care,' she said quietly. 'But Hugh's been discharged. It's miraculous, given that he went through the windscreen.' Her fingers tightened on his arm. 'His arm is broken but he's all right, thank God.'

God? Too many years of boring services in the school chapel had drummed that out of him. But there was no harm in silent gratitude. Just in case.

Home seemed inexplicably different after what had just happened. The hall with Claire's slightly worn blue and pink rug appeared bigger, even though he had always felt it was cramped compared with his old bachelor loft apartment in London. Simon looked around, half-expecting to see the blue plastic mattress from the cell. Already it seemed like a bad dream and he felt bolder for having left it all behind.

Some of the dinner party stuff was still on the left of the sink, unwashed. Simon could see a wine glass with a rim of pink lipstick. Claire had been wearing a coral shade and Rosemarie didn't do lipstick, which meant it had been Joanna's. The realisation brought last night back into sharp focus and he began to shake again.

'Sorry.'

A voice floated into his head and then he realised it was Ben who had come into the room, wearing shorts and a crumpled red and black T-shirt with the words *Keep Off*

'Sorry,' the boy repeated.

'What for?' Simon was genuinely confused.

'For ringing you.' The boy's ginger freckles seemed more obvious than usual. 'We needed a lift and I couldn't get hold of

Mum, so I tried you.'

Simon shrugged, thinking at the same time that this was one of the longest sentences the kid had ever addressed to him. 'It was my fault. I shouldn't have picked up.'

'And for swishing all that rum into the syllabub,' Ben continued, fiddling with the large plug earring in his ear. 'I wasn't thinking.'

'Rum?' Simon froze, remembering that over-sweet syllabub and the second helping he had requested, to please Claire. 'What do you mean?'

It wouldn't be a strong defence, warned Patrick. There had been too many local cases apparently featuring over-brandied Christmas cakes. It wouldn't help the mobile phone offence anyway. There'd been a similar death near Taunton last year and there'd been considerable flack because the driver got off with a suspended. Chances were that the next ruling wouldn't be so lenient. But none of this mattered when a woman – Joanna with her tinkly laugh and ethereal face – was still in Intensive Care on a life-support machine.

Every morning, when Simon woke, there was a brief second-splitting moment when everything seemed all right and then he would remember.

'Why can't they try you immediately?' asked Rosemarie directly when she and Alex popped round the following week. They would have come sooner, they had said but 'a few things had come up'. Privately, Simon had been hoping that Alex might have had some ideas himself on defence but then again, he was a conveyancing lawyer.

'There's a queue of us dangerous drivers,' he'd replied darkly to Rosemarie's question. 'They can't get us through fast enough.'

The fear and embarrassment had made him sarky. As if knowing this, Claire squeezed his arm as she walked past, placing a jug of coffee before their guests. Usually they drank tea. The last time they had had coffee was when Joanna and Hugh had been here. The memory made his right hand shake again and he had to sit on it to hide it.

'Anyone know how she's doing?' asked Rosemarie, twisting the straps of her shoulder bag nervously. No need, reflected Simon, awkwardly, to ask who *she* was.

'Still on a life-support machine apparently, although it's difficult to find out.' Claire's voice hid, he knew, her panic. He had to hand it to her. She was being much stronger than he'd thought she'd be. Stronger than him. In bed at night, it was her now who held him, begging him to talk about it; stroking his back until he moved away with irritation because *he* wanted to be the strong one in this relationship.

If he opened up, he might just crack.

'We can hardly ring and ask,' he added.

There was a brief silence of consensus. Alex had hardly said anything since he'd arrived. His face reminded him of Patrick's. Disapproving. It made Simon feel dirty. For the first time, he began to understand how his clients must feel.

'I went down to the tennis club at the weekend,' volunteered Rosemarie.

'Were they talking about it?' Claire's voice was sharp and urgent.

'Yes.'

'And they knew it was me, I suppose?' Simon heard his voice sound more sarcastic than he'd meant.

Rosemarie nodded. 'They'd seen the local paper.'

Too late, Simon saw the look that Claire shot at her friend. The look that said '*I've kept it from him.*'

'Show me,' he said simply and without saying anything, Claire rose from her seat and placed the paper in front of him.

Local driver arrested on bail for dangerous driving.

Without saying anything Simon got up, walked up the stairs, and shut the bedroom door behind him. Sitting on the bed, he could hear Claire seeing out their 'guests'. Phrases like *He's not himself* and *All we can do is hope*, came floating upwards. When he heard Claire's own footsteps coming up the stairs, he waited for the door handle to turn and for her to find it was locked.

23

'Simon?'

What was there to say? You should have shown me? I'm not a kid who needs protecting? I'd have found out sooner rather than later?

All of these were true. Yet all were also false.

Lying flat on his back, Simon stared up at the ceiling, fists clenched as they hammered silently on the mattress to release the fear inside his body. None of this was making sense. And he had a horrible feeling that it wasn't going to get any better.

The hate mail started the following day with a typed note posted through the letter box.

Go back to London.

It took Simon back to the time when he'd been caught 'borrowing' a fiver from his father's wallet as a child and then beaten for it. Only this was much worse. A five-pound note could be replaced. The only way he could cope was to hide them from Claire. Pretend they had never happened.

Then came the other notes. All typed. Some had typos, suggesting a poorly educated bully.

You shuldn't use the fone when your driving.

Very true.

He wanted to go round to Hugh and say sorry but Patrick had strongly advised against it. He and Claire both asked to visit Joanna but that too was out of the question, said Patrick scathingly. Ben said he felt sick and couldn't go to school but Claire suspected he was being bullied. They didn't like to go to the supermarket in case someone saw them so Rosemarie and Alex were doing their shopping instead.

At night, he felt too ashamed to take Claire in his arms so he simply rolled away from her, hoping to find oblivion but discovering that he could only dream about walls and vans and metal screams. The senior partner emailed to say it would be best if he didn't come into work at the moment although they would continue to pay his monthly drawings for the time being. 'Talk to me,' Claire would plead at night in the dark. 'Tell me how you're feeling.'

24

But he couldn't. Unlike her, he'd had a lifetime of hiding his emotions as a one-man band. Besides, how could he admit he had fucked up all their lives – not least the one in the hospital bed. If he did that, he'd break. A flash of his father shot into his head. Simon squeezed his eyes tightly shut until it went.

Then, one Tuesday morning at 6.30 a.m. after waking much earlier – something he'd been doing since the accident – there was a knock on the door. Claire, doubtless hearing the noise dimly in her sleep, rolled over. The knock came again.

Slipping on his blue-and-white striped dressing gown, he went down the stairs, grabbing a poker from the sitting room en route in case it was one of the hate-mail writers. He wouldn't hurt anyone of course but it might frighten them off.

'Mr Mills?'

A pair of police officers stood on the other side, eying the poker suspiciously. 'May we come in, sir?'

He waved his hand in a 'welcome' gesture as though they were guests at another bloody dinner party. The woman spoke first with a tremor in her voice. She was so young that he almost felt sorry for her. 'I'm afraid we have a warrant for your arrest, sir.'

What for? Holding a poker? 'But I've *been* arrested. I'm on bail.'

Her male colleague broke in. 'There is a different charge now.' He cleared his throat.

'Simon James Mills, you are arrested on suspicion of causing death by dangerous driving ...'

Chapter Five

Claire woke from a nightmare in which she had been running away from Charlie down a supermarket aisle. 'I can't trust you any more,' she had screamed. 'Don't you see? I can't trust you.'

Her own screams woke her up and when she pulled herself up to a sitting position in bed, her body wouldn't register the logic of her mind. It continued to shake as though she was still married to Charlie and not Simon. Kind, loving Simon who would never let her down but who could never be Ben's father. Simon who, because he didn't have children of his own, couldn't understand that teenagers left piles of dirty mugs in their bedroom. Or left their coursework by mistake at bus stops. Or didn't offer to clear away supper.

Forcing herself to take deep breaths, she tried to focus on the neon alarm clock next to the bed. 6.33 a.m. Half an hour before she needed to get up. Then she noticed that Simon's side next to her was empty even though the sheet was still warm. It was then that she heard the low urgent rumble of voices downstairs.

'Simon,' she called out, pulling on her dressing gown. There was a silence. Then Simon's voice floated up the stairs. 'Can you come down?' Another silence. 'Please,' he added almost as an afterthought.

Her husband never called up the stairs! 'Come down if you want to say something,' he was always saying to Ben.

Quickly, she slipped into her gym slippers and made her way down. What on earth? Simon was standing in the hall with a police officer on either side. One, she noticed, was a woman. Young. Very young. But it was the stricken look on her husband's face that caught her. He was looking at her in a way that Ben had looked when she'd said they were going to leave Daddy. Like a small boy who needed comforting but was trying to look brave.

'Joanna's dead,' he whispered. And then, as though to make it clear to himself, he repeated. 'Joanna died.'

They charged him at the local police station before taking him to the magistrates court, which then remanded him in custody. 'What does it all mean?' she kept asking Patrick.

'He'll have to spend tonight in the police cell and then be sent to a holding prison. It's like a remand prison. People stay there until their trials.'

'Simon has to go to prison? Before he's even sentenced?'

Patrick gave her a patronising look. 'Death by dangerous driving is more serious than simply dangerous driving, you know'

Claire's skin prickled. Did he think she was an idiot? She knew that. But it had been an accident. A horrible accident.

'He's going to a place called Holdfast in Essex.' Patrick spoke as though it was a hotel! 'They couldn't send him to a local one in case he knew other prisoners there.'

Of course! Simon had been responsible for sending heaven knows how many people down. It wouldn't do at all if he had to share a cell with someone he'd helped to convict. If it wasn't for poor, beautiful Joanna, it might be mildly comical.

'Our best argument, in my view,' said Patrick (she could almost hear him drumming his fingers on the file in front of him), 'is that your husband was under severe stress due to the difficult relationship with your son.'

A horrid cold feeling shot through her. 'He said that?'

'The stress,' he continued, ignoring her question, 'made him pick up the mobile when it rang. Unfortunately, Simon's claim that Mr Goodman-Brown tugged at his arm, causing him to lose control, can't be proved. As for the pudding being laced with alcohol, I've already explained it's been used too many times. The jury may not buy it.'

'But Ben tipped a quarter of a bottle into it. He's told me.'

'Did you have some yourself?'

'No but ...'

'Then again, we have no evidence that your husband's levels

27

were due to the syllabub or because he actually had more than the half glass of wine he said he had.'

Patrick's words were closing in on her like a verbal spider's web. She felt choked. Tight. Unable to draw breath. 'Then what do we do?'

'Sit tight, leave it to us, and hand any more hate mail directly to me.'

'May I visit him?'

'You should be able to. I suggest you ring the prison for information on that. But don't be surprised if he doesn't call you. He won't be able to keep his mobile.'

As she put the phone down, it rang again. A word hissed down the line. So fast. So vehement that she almost missed it. Then it came again. 'BITCH!'

Hugh? Claire began to shake. She might only have met him once but she knew that voice; could picture all too clearly the pug-dog creases in his face; the steel glasses; and that rude, arrogant expression at the dining room table when he'd asked if she got paid for her work or just did it as a 'hobby'. But now, right now, he had a right to be angry.

'Bitch! Your fucker of a husband has killed my wife.' The voice began to weep. 'My Joanna is dead.'

'I'm so sorry, Hugh.' Claire too began to cry. 'I'm so very sorry, but it was a terrible accident. You have to realise that.'

'Accident?' The voice stopped crying. Instead, it sounded more like a deep low growl. 'It was negligence. Dangerous driving. And now you're all going to pay for it.'

There was a click. He had gone. Claire sat there in her dressing gown staring at the phone. Her mouth was dry. Her tongue stuck to her mouth. She wanted – needed – Simon.

'Mum? You all right?'

She lifted her face to him, seeing only a blur through her tears. 'Joanna's dead. Simon's been taken to prison.'

Her son, already taller than her, knelt down on the quarry tiles next to her and put his arms around her. He smelt slightly of BO and lager, presumably from the night before when he'd been out with friends. This isn't right, she thought to herself. It should be me comforting him, especially when he finds out they're going to try and blame him.

For a minute she felt resentment towards her son. If he hadn't gone out that night or if he hadn't been late, Simon might not have picked up his mobile. If Ben hadn't been so difficult towards her new husband, none of this would have happened. She let go of him and stepped backwards.

'It'll be OK, Mum.' Ben's voice was gravelly, reminding her of his father. Charlie. The old Charlie, before his affair.

'We've got through stuff before, Mum.' He hugged her. 'I'll help you. Promise.'

Chapter Six

They put Simon in an unmarked van. For a minute, he had thought they were going to handcuff him but then the officer in a dark heavy serge jacket and trousers with a chain around his waist, seemed to change his mind as though he realised Simon wasn't the type to make a run for it.

''Ere we go again, ducks,' slurred the man sitting next to him. He had tattoos all up his arm which looked, at first sight, like a floral blouse. The orange lipstick resembled a clown's.

'Back again? Thought you'd have had enough of us, George,' remarked the other officer tersely who sat in the back of the van with them while the first one drove.

'You know my name is Georgie, ducks.' The man flicked back his hair which was done up in a sleek, black ponytail at the back. 'And being bi isn't against the law you know.'

Simon listened with distaste. It wasn't dissimilar to the banter he heard day in and day out from his own clients. But now he was part of it.

'I know it's not illegal, Georg*ie*.' The officer laid a heavy sarcastic emphasis on the last part of his name. 'But nicking your boyfriend's jewellery is.'

'Borrowing it, actually.'

There was a snort of laughter from another man on the other side of Simon whose breath stank of stale beer and tobacco. 'Want to know why *I'm* here, man?'

Not particularly, Simon wanted to say. I don't want to be part of this grubby, seedy little crew. He winced as the large man elbowed him just above his waist where his ribs were still bruised and sore from the seat belt. 'It's 'cos I was stupid, that's why.' His eyes glittered and he was laughing as though at himself. 'Didn't know when to stop, that's why.'

30

There was a pause during which Simon knew he was being invited to ask more. Eventually his good manners took over. 'Stop what?' he asked.

The man grinned, revealing very straight and perfectly white teeth. 'I got two grand, man, but thought I could get more.'

'From where?' Simon was becoming curious now. Besides there was nothing else to do than listen to this maniac; the windows in the van were blacked out so he couldn't see where he was going. But in the corner of one, someone had managed to scrape away a bit of the black, leaving a small gap through which you could, if you bent down, just about catch a glimpse of the outside world.

'From the building society.' He spoke as though that should have been obvious. 'People don't check their statements, see. So they don't miss small amounts.' He waved his hand around as though to make the point but really, Simon suspected, to draw attention to the chunky gold-linked bracelet that matched the heavy chain round his neck.

'But how do you get into their accounts, ducks?'

Even the prison officer was listening now, Simon noticed.

'Hacking!' The man was grinning. 'Easy when you know it. You give a fake ID and then turn up in the branch to get your winnings. Except that, unfortunately for me, this geezer had twigged and there were the police waiting for me.'

I don't belong in this set, Simon wanted to scream. I'm not a criminal; I simply made a mistake. How could it be that a woman who was walking, talking, playing tennis for God's sake only last week, was about to be buried? The only way he could cope was to imagine a heavy metal gate slicing through his head and separating him from the image of her tinkly laugh in the back of the car.

It was at least a couple of hours before they got there. By this time, Simon had had to pinch the skin on his left arm again and again, in order to keep himself from punching the side of the van. Through the small gap in the window, Simon could see the countryside changing from hilly, sheep-ridden fields to a flatter terrain. Bedfordshire perhaps, where he'd had a girlfriend once. Alex used to joke – with a slight edge of jealousy to his voice – that Simon had had a girl in every county. It wasn't something he was proud of now. Not now he had Claire.

'Been to Holdfast before, ducks?'

'No.'

'Then you're in for a surprise and not a very pleasant one if you don't mind me saying. But hang on in there and you'll be moved in a bit.' He chuckled. 'Mind you, given some of HMP hotels, you might wish you'd been allowed to put up at this one. What did you do then?'

For a minute, he thought he was being questioned about his job. Then he remembered. 'I killed someone.'

'Fucking hell, ducks.' The man visibly edged away.

'I didn't mean to. It was an accident.'

The officer snorted. 'That's what they all say. Get ready, lads. We're here.'

Simon's first impression, as the back doors were flung open, was that Holdfast was a cross between a public convenience and a run-down polytechnic from the sixties. The sunlight, after the almost windowless van, hit his eyes so that he had to shield them with the flat of his hand to look around.

'In here, you. This isn't an observation point.' The officer who spoke was roughly pushing him towards a flat-roofed building. Inside was a smaller room which had an opening halfway up the wall and an officer standing on the other.

'Name?'

'Simon James Mills.'

'Classy!' said the transvestite behind him admiringly.

'That's enough, you. Address?'

Simon felt a tremor of unease. He didn't want to give out that in front of the men behind. 'I'll write it down for you,' he said in a low urgent voice.

'I said "*address*".'

There was nothing for it but to quietly give the details out loud, hoping the building society fraudster wasn't memorising

32

it.

'Personal possessions in here.'

A grey tray was being pushed towards him. 'I haven't got anything.'

'Sure you haven't.'

'No. Honestly. I've come here straight from bed.'

'Wish I had, ducks!'

The officer gave a nod to another officer standing behind them and Simon felt himself being searched. 'Empty your pockets!' Strange hands ran roughly down his outstretched arms and legs. When he had finished, he felt like saying 'See? Nothing there', like a child.

'Stores,' barked the officer.

'I beg your pardon?'

There was a deep throaty chuckle from behind him. 'Posh, this one, isn't he, man?'

'He means stores, ducks.' The purple-bloused man touched him lightly on his arm. 'It's where you get your prison fancy dress. We don't wear regulation stuff 'cos we're not sentenced yet but you can get joggers here and trainers.' He glanced at Simon's hastily put-on cords and brogues. 'More suitable than your outfit in this place, if you don't want to attract attention. Just make sure it's clean before you accept it; they don't always bother to put them through laundry.'

'Thanks.'

'Don't mention it, ducks. There'll be something you can do for me, I 'spect, before we're both out of this place.'

Right through the door and down a long corridor. No point in running off even if he'd intended to because of the officer who was walking behind him.

Stores turned out to be another counter except this time it was lower down so the officer's eyes were on his level.

'Chest size?'

'Forty.'

'Forty-two's the nearest I can do. Waist?'

'Thirty-six.'

'Thirty-eight then.'

33

'Shoe size?'

'Eleven and a half.'

'Don't do half sizes and we're out of Twelves.'

Simon found himself the recipient of a navy tracksuit and tight trainers – he'd stick to his brogues, he decided – before being ordered to take a right and then left. On down another corridor where a huge man with a shiny bald pate did a high-five in the air with the building society fraudster.

'How are you, mate?'

'Great! You?'

'Leave it!' roared the officer.

'If you want my advice, ducks,' said a voice from behind, 'it's to do what they tell you. Keep your head down and toe the line.'

Simon glanced over his shoulder and nodded. It seemed impolite not to do so but the gesture now seemed to solicit more advice. 'You'll find your room looks bare but you'll soon pretty it up. When I was in Wandsworth, I found some carpet tiles that someone had chucked out when they was doing a refurbishment. We're allowed certain personal possessions if you can get a visitor to bring them in: you know, radio, stereo. But if you're caught with a mobile or speed or a bottle of the hard stuff, you'll be shipped out.'

'Shipped out?'

Simon's mind was buzzing with overload.

'You *are* new at this, aren't you ducks? Moved to another prison, mate. I can see you're going to need a bit of looking after. Just as well your friend Georgie is here.'

'That's enough.' The officer rounded a corner and came to a halt. Ahead of them was a line of cells – not the open-bar variety as Simon had seen them on television, but solid fronts and a door that had a grill in front with a sliding partition. 'In here, Mills.'

It had been a long time since someone had called him by his surname. Simon found himself being pushed into a room containing two beds. Each had identical grey scratchy blankets, pushed up hard against opposite walls. There was no more than

34

a man's width in between. Under each bed, he could see an empty cardboard box which had *Clothes* scrawled on the side. No sink. No window.

Before he could ask where the loo was, the door slammed behind him. There was no noise. Only a tinkly laughter in his head. And the overwhelming need to cry followed by an even stronger need to put a blank mask over his face so no one – least of all, himself – could know what he was thinking.

Chapter Seven

Joanna was in the Death Notices sections of both *The Times* and the *Daily Telegraph*. '*Beloved wife of Hugh Tarquin Goodman-Brown and stepmother to Poppy. Died after a tragic incident. Justice will be done. Funeral at ...*'

The now familiar knot in Claire's stomach, began to tighten. 'Justice will be done? What do you think he means by that?'

Rosemarie shook her head. They were sitting in her little sunny conservatory out the back, its red geraniums merrily spilling out of terracotta pots. It seemed unbelievable to Claire that life could go on as normal.

'Maybe he expects Simon to go to prison. Sorry – I didn't mean to say that. Don't look so upset. Besides, didn't his partner say that he might just get a suspended sentence?'

'Possibly.' Claire sipped her sweet tea. Since they'd taken Simon away, it had been all she'd been able to swallow. Already, her jeans hung loosely round her waist and she felt hazy and distant from everything, possibly due to the effects of the tranquillisers which the doctor had given her. She'd had to tell him why she needed the tablets and the glance which had crossed his eyes had made her feel like a criminal. Sordid. Shame through proxy.

'Any luck with the paperwork?' asked Rosemarie, referring to the security forms which Claire had had to fill in to apply for a prison visit.

'I'm still waiting.' She ran a hand through her hair which needed washing. Claire was usually fastidious about her hair but since Simon, it seemed self-indulgent to bother about her appearance. 'It's so frustrating.'

'We would drive you but it's miles away, isn't it? We looked it up on Google.'

Claire felt a flicker of resentment at the picture of her two closest friends checking out her husband's prison on the net. It felt ghoulish somehow. 'It's all right, thanks.'

'So you're not scared of driving yourself? That's good.' Rosemarie reached out and touched her arm lightly. 'If it were me, I think I'd be neurotic in case someone ran out in front of me or did something that made me crash. In fact, it's affected the way I'm driving right now. Do you know, I found myself doing 20 through the high street instead of 30. The car behind was getting quite impatient.'

Me! Me! Me! Suddenly Rosemarie's presence felt claustrophobic rather than comforting. Claire rose to her feet, scraping back her Lloyd Loom chair that she'd found at an auction years ago when Ben had been a baby, and paint-sprayed duck blue. 'Look, thanks for the shopping but I've got a deadline and ...'

'You're still working?' Rosemarie's voice was shocked as if she had no right to carry on normally.

'I have to.' She heard her voice rise almost aggressively. 'I've got a deadline and we need the money. The firm is going to pay Simon's salary for the time being but who knows how long that will go on for. Besides, it helps me to cut off.'

'Goodness!' Rosemarie looked aghast. 'I don't know where you get your discipline from.'

It isn't discipline, Claire wanted to say. It's a burning need to draw which, thank heavens, is still there despite everything. Drawing and painting had always been her safety valve. It had got her through that dark time with Charlie and now it would have to do the same with Simon.

Rosemarie wouldn't understand. She wasn't an artist. She was a part-time PA. They had so little in common that if it hadn't been for the fact that she and Alex were the first couple that she and Charlie had met when they came down to Devon all those years ago, they might not have been friends.

'Have you spoken to him yet?' Rosemarie was still talking on her way to the door.

She nodded. 'Only briefly. They allowed him to make a

37

quick 'compassionate call' as they call it.'

'How did he sound?'

Was she mistaken or was there a sort of inferred glee in the questions? 'How would you expect someone to sound, Rosemarie, if they were sitting in prison waiting to know if they were going to go down?'

'Go down? But I thought you said he might get a suspended sentence?'

Claire found herself snapping now. 'Why not look on the net as you're so good at it? Last week, there was someone in the news who got eight years.'

'Maybe they deserved it. Anyway, there's no need to be rude.' Rosemarie's light blue eyes looked milky with hurt. 'We're doing what we can: getting your shopping so you don't have to face the stares from everyone in the queue; fielding questions at the tennis club from nosy parkers; going to the funeral ...'

She stopped.

'You're going to the funeral?' Claire's mind darted back to the obit. in *The Times*, giving details of the service. It was on Monday week. She'd thought crazily of going herself and of telling Hugh how sorry they all were until realising it would only cause a scene and make things worse, if that was possible.

Rosemarie's hand tightened on her brown handbag's shoulder strap. 'We thought we owed it to Hugh.' She spoke defensively. 'After all, we were two of the last people to see her alive.'

The note of self-importance jarred. Since The Accident, her friend had become almost superior as though relishing her role. Or was it that she, Claire, had changed and was now paranoid about what people thought and said?

'Sorry.' She reached out and touched her hand lightly. 'I can't help feeling edgy.'

'It's understandable.' The look in Rosemarie's eyes softened but only slightly.

'I'd like to send flowers. What do you think?'

'Rubbing salt into the wound, I'd say, to be honest.'

38

Rosemarie glanced down to the entry in the paper. '*Justice will be done*. If I were you, I'd keep a low profile. Things will die down eventually.' She clasped her hand to her mouth. 'Die down? Dear me. Forgive my choice of words.'

The date for Claire's first visit finally came through in the post on the day that their weekly local paper ran a report on the funeral.

NEW DEVON RESIDENT LAID TO REST AFTER TRAGIC ROAD DEATH shouted the headline.

More than a hundred people turned up to pay their final respects to the tragic mother who was killed in a road accident, earlier this month.

She was a *step-mother*, thought Claire before reading on, not a mother. Then again, what did that matter? She was dead, wasn't she?

39-year-old Joanna Marie Goodman-Browne had recently moved down to Windsea from London to start a new life with her husband Hugh. She was killed when a car driven by Simon Mills, one of her new friends from the tennis club, crashed in a country lane.

Simon didn't even belong to the tennis club.

Mr Mills, a lawyer, is currently in custody on a charge of dangerous driving.

How unfair! Anyone reading this would assume he was guilty.

A spokesman for the tennis club said 'It is a terrible shock to us all. Although we only knew her briefly, Joanna was clearly a lovely woman'.

She *was* a lovely woman! And nice too! But so was – *is* – Simon, Claire told herself. Her husband was a good, decent man just as her friend Rosemarie had described him before their introduction. Besides, she had promised to stand by him for better or worse, hadn't she? Pushing the local paper under the cushions of the sofa, she set off for the prison with Rosemarie's words still ringing in her ears. '*You're not scared of driving then? That's good.*'

Actually she was. Every move which she now made seemed alien after an unblemished driving record of twenty years. Should she be in fourth gear or third? At one point when overtaking a lorry, Claire found herself wondering which pedal was the accelerator and which was the brake. The responsibility of driving a vehicle which could kill someone seemed overwhelming. Her mobile was off, locked in the boot. In the past, she had occasionally picked it up when she shouldn't have. But never again.

The sheer terror of driving with cold sweat trickling down her back as she negotiated strange countryside and made wrong turnings, was almost but not quite enough to take her mind off her visit to Simon. Silly things were now going round her mind like whether she was wearing the right thing. Claire had put on white jeans at first but then taken them off in case they might be misconstrued as showy. Ordinary denims would look as though she hadn't bothered. In the end, she'd settled for a knee-length green and white dotted Reiss skirt and matching jacket that she usually wore to her meetings with her agent.

'Can you bring a postal order for ten pounds?' Simon had asked on the phone. 'We're allowed ten pounds a week – but not in cash – and out of that I need to buy phone credit and snacks.'

'I'll get you a phone card,' she had said but apparently that wasn't permitted. You were given a pin number apparently to which credit was added. You asked for certain phone numbers to be put on it but they all had to be checked first.

'Shall I bring in some clothes?' she asked. But apparently that wasn't allowed either. They had to be ordered from approved prison catalogues and even then there was a limit. Only five pairs of underpants. Five pairs of socks. Five T-shirts, although no offending slogans. No all-black outfits. No sweat shirts with hoods.

Any other necessary items like disposable razors had to be bought through the canteen which was a shop and not a café. It all seemed so weird.

So many dos. So many don'ts. Her mind did a mental

checklist of the form she'd been sent and the instructions. Park at the Visitors' Car Park. Bring ID in the form of a passport or driving licence. Leave your mobile and other personal information in the car. Anyone found passing drugs or alcohol or anything which is forbidden, will be liable to prosecution. Do not bring in chewing gum; Sellotape; sugar; hair pins; etc., etc.

Why not sugar, she had asked on the phone.

'They can make hooch out of it. It's an alcoholic drink.'

'And Sellotape?'

'Gagging someone.'

She'd never have thought of that! The list sifted in and out of her head as she took a left down another country road, according to the directions on the net. Claire sounded the horn as she went round the bend and then another, unnecessarily. There it was! A stark black-and-white sign informing her that she had arrived at HMP Holdfast. A grey crop of buildings lay before her with narrow windows and dirty brick. In front was a barrier with a man standing by it in black uniform and silver chain round his waist, and a small black pouch on the belt.

'ID,' he said without a 'please'.

Shaking, feeling as though she had done something wrong, she handed over her passport. Checking it, his gaze flicked from her face to the picture, taken just before Charlie's infidelity had come to light. Her forehead looked smooth. Her eyes trusting. Her gaze straight. A different, younger Claire, unaware of what lay ahead. She wanted to warn her.

'Straight through.' He barked rather than spoke. 'Park on the right. Leave your valuables and mobile in the car but take your passport in with you.'

By now, the patter felt like a nursery rhyme. As she parked the car, another one was stopping next to hers. It was an old Capri which had several dents in the side. Four, no five, people spilled out of it. They seemed like a family going on an outing judging by their easy banter and the casual way in which the women hoisted up their handbags on their shoulders and puffed out their chests which left little to the imagination in those low cut T-shirts. One caught her eye and, embarrassed, she looked away. Then, not wanting to seem unfriendly, she heard herself asking if they knew where to go next even though there was a sign just behind her.

'The Visitors' Centre.' One of the women jerked her head towards a high wire fence on the other side of the car park. 'Get your hands off him, Sheryl.'

It took Claire a minute to realise the woman was addressing a younger girl in the group who was cuddling up to a boy who looked as though he should have been at school.

'Yer first time here, is it?' The woman turned her attention back to her. Claire nodded. 'Follow us then. Sheryl, I'm bleeding warning you! Any more hanky-panky and you won't be seeing your dad. 'Sides, these cameras will get you. Get an eyeful of that lot!'

Claire looked up at a corner of the fence and saw the CCTV cameras. They made her feel as though she had something to hide.

'Yer insurance up to date and yer MOT and bleeding tax?'

She nodded, puzzled.

'Good, 'cos those cameras will be checking you right now. Mark my words. This way.'

They made their way, the women clip-clopping across the gravel in their heels. Claire couldn't help wondering what Rosemarie would make of it. She was also glad that she had turned down Ben's offer to go with her. This wasn't the place for an impressionable teenager.

They stood at the wire gate, waiting to be let in. Ahead was a queue and she could see an older couple looking as confused as she felt, proffering their passport for another check. Her turn now! It felt as it did when she'd visited her sister in Vietnam and the immigration officer had been so abrupt. Then another queue in a smaller room which had notices on the walls warning her once more that anyone found carrying drugs would be prosecuted.

'Yer haven't got any, love, have yer?' whispered the car park woman behind her.

'No.'

'Good. 'Cos the dogs will get yer even if it's in yer mouth.'

'In your mouth?'

'When yer kiss yer man.' She spoke as though Claire was being dim. 'It's a way of getting the stuff over. Well, one of them. The other's a bit painful!'

She laughed; a loud raucous laugh revealing gold fillings that sent shivers down her arm. "You know – up your backside."

How horrible.

'Next,' snapped another officer. This one was a woman who had blonde hair like Claire's and the same length. She smiled, wanting to say 'I'm not with this group behind,' but already she was being gestured forwards.

'OK. You can move through to the next section now.'

Her heart was thumping. Another corridor. A right and then a left. Through a door and into a room that reminded her of a long-ago school gym on exam days, containing rows of desks, except that this one had prison officers lining the walls.

And there in the second row at the back, she saw a man, sitting upright on his chair, a haunted, hunted expression on his unshaved face.

Simon? *Simon?*

Chapter Eight

His first thought was 'Thank God she's here'. His second was that he shouldn't have asked her to come. Claire's stricken face told him that – the way she looked around her with that scared look, searching for him amongst the tables of huge men, sporting tattoos down their arms and shouting in rough voices.

'Claire,' he wanted to call out but they weren't meant to do that. It was one of the many rules that had been given to them in clipped official tones in pre-visit instructions.

Then her eyes fell on him. 'Simon!' She brushed his cheek and as he breathed in her fragrance, he wished he'd been able to shave but the canteen had run out of disposable razors. 'They wouldn't let me bring a razor in,' she said incredulously. 'I explained you wouldn't use it for anything else but they wouldn't believe me.'

Of course they wouldn't! 'Thanks for trying.' Already his speech sounded stilted. He wanted to say how much he missed her and how awful it was in this place, like a treacle nightmare that he couldn't step out of because everything – the rules, the voices, the craziness of it all – had wrapped itself round him like some kind of evil cocoon.

But if he did, she would worry even more.

'What's it like?' she asked softly.

He hesitated, wanting to tell her the truth about being locked up all day with Aaron, a West Indian youth who smoked even though he wasn't meant to and waved filthy pictures in front of him of women in poses and situations that made his stomach heave and who insisted on calling him *Si* to rhyme with *sigh*.

'I'm getting through,' he said laconically.

'Do you have a room of your own?'

He wanted to laugh; she made it sound like a hotel. 'I have

44

to share with someone.'

'And is he all right?'

He nodded, not trusting himself to say more.

'Do you have to share a loo?'

'With him and eight others,' he said with an edge of a laugh. 'Probably best not to ask too much about the sanitary side.' Then a thought came to him. 'Do I smell?'

She shook her head and he realised that he probably did. The canteen had been out of deodorant as well although that was expected in next week. 'Did you bring the flip-flops?'

'Yes. But I could only get pink.'

Pink? They'd crucify him. He could hear the jaunts now. *Gayboy. Nance. Ponce.* The bullying in this place made his old school look like a kindergarten.

Claire frowned slightly in that way she did when she didn't understand something. 'Why do you need them? It's not really the weather now, is it?'

She was so sweetly naive. Then again, he would have been puzzled before coming in here. 'They're to protect my feet in the shower. Sometimes people leave unpleasant things there like razor blades or ... or other stuff. You can get hepatitis if you're not careful.'

Her appalled face showed him he shouldn't have said that. He looked away, letting the chorus wave from the tables on either side fill in the silence of the gap.

'I keep hearing Joanna's laugh in my head,' he said suddenly. Shit. He hadn't meant that to come out. Now her eyes were filling with tears.

'It's so awful, isn't it?' Her warm hand pressed his. 'I still can't believe it. I sent Hugh a note but he didn't reply.'

'Is he still ringing you?'

'No.'

The noise around them grew. The couple at the table next to them were clearly having a disagreement and it was hard to hear what she was saying now.

'I'm sorry?'

She leaned forward and he could see the dip between her

breasts. Why hadn't she worn something more suitable? The thought of other men looking, made him clench his fists under the wobbly plastic table. 'Patrick says you might get a suspended sentence. Then we can get you out of this place.'

The kid was crazy. Simon knew enough about this to understand the score. 'Don't get too hopeful, Claire. I might have to go down for a bit.'

'Go down?'

He'd forgotten that unlike him, she wasn't yet versed in prison jargon. 'Stay inside. Maybe six months or with any luck, three.'

Her eyes filled with tears again. 'Don't talk like that. Be positive. You've got to be.'

That's all very well, he wanted to say, but you're not in here.

'What do you do all day?'

'We don't sew mail bags if that's what you mean.'

'There's no need to be sarcastic.' Her eyes looked hurt. 'I just want you to confide in me. Tell me how you're really feeling.'

'I have.' He couldn't help snapping slightly. 'It's bloody awful in here.'

'I know.' Her hand squeezed his again. 'I'm sorry.'

He tried again. 'I read a lot – there's a woman who comes round with books. And we're allowed out for an hour a day to walk around a yard.'

'What's the food like?'

'I can't eat meat any more.'

'Why?'

How could he tell her that his mental picture of Joanna on the mortuary slab had made him feel sick when they'd produced sloppy stew that lunchtime in the prison dining room.

'I don't know.'

'TIME!' roared one of the prison officers standing in the centre.

She leaned across to kiss him but the officer at their side stepped in. 'Sorry, madam. No physical contact.'

Claire stood up. One of the men at the side table glanced at her breasts in undisguised admiration and Simon wanted to tell him to fuck off. To bloody well mind his own business.

'I'll come again as soon as they let me. And I'll write. Be strong, darling. I love you.'

Then she was gone, disappearing in a group of women with tanned legs and harsh voices, leaving him in a room of disappointed men with plastic tables and chairs and stained virgin blue carpet tiles.

Simon smashed his fist on the table in anger. 'You should have told her,' he said out loud, furious with himself for having chickened out. 'You should have bloody told her.'

Bad news, said Patrick during one of his phone calls. (The prison allowed you to take 'Legal' calls as they were known, but not calls from family.) A minister's daughter had been caught using a mobile phone and caused a crash. No serious casualties but she'd been sent to prison for nine months. It could set a precedent.

He didn't tell Claire any of this. No point in making her feel worse beforehand. Not long to go now. He tried not to count the days but it was impossible not to. And then one day, he woke from a dream in which Joanna with her lovely translucent skin and blonde hair, coiled up in a loose knot, was shaking him by the shoulders. '*Wake up,*' she was singing. '*It's Trial Day!*'

Simon sat bolt upright. 'Did you hear that?' he tried to say to Aaron but nothing came out. He padded across the cold lino floor and put his hand out, hesitating. The only things he could see above the cover were Aaron's dreadlocks and he didn't want to touch them.

Suddenly the dreadlocks stirred. 'Wassup, Si? Can't yer see I'm trying to kip?'

Simon was kneeling by his side now. 'Did you hear something? Did you hear a woman's voice just now?'

There was a low throaty laugh. 'You've been dreaming, Si! Sounds like a good one if a woman was there. If I was you, I'd go back to it.' His right hand came out from under the thin grey blanket, waving something. 'Want a dirty magazine to help?'

Until now, Simon had thought the waiting was the worst. But that was nothing compared with getting into a white van with blacked out windows – without the illegal gap to see out of this time – and being chained to a police officer as if he might run off, given half the chance.

Then there were the photographers. He hadn't expected any of this. '*Thank you very much,*' tinkled Joanna. '*I told you. I used to be a dancer. People remember me and besides, I wouldn't be surprised if Hugh has alerted the press.*'

He tried to put his jacket over his head to shut out the cameras and block Joanna's voice. 'This way, please, *sir.*'

He was getting used to the sarcasm now. Simon glanced round the court room. It was like so many that he had been in before, its heavy oak panelling, bland grey walls, and benches resembled a low-key church.

Until they led him into the dock, he could almost kid himself that he was here to defend someone else instead of speaking out for himself. But now, here he was, behind this huge oak counter, surrounded on all four sides by a rim of wood that made him feel he was in an open coffin. Once, as a law student, he and Alex had stepped inside the dock to know how it felt. It hadn't been like this.

He hadn't expected so many people to be there either. Rosemarie and Alex were up in the gallery along with some people he recognised from the village. No one nodded.

Simon's knees weakened as he searched the court for Claire. There she was, smiling faintly at him. Her lips moved as though she was saying something. 'I love you.' At least, that's what he thought she was saying.

Suddenly, the whole thing seemed ridiculous. He had spent his life defending people who were, for the most part, probably guilty. But he had known the tricks to get them off. It had been a game that he had to win in order to prove he was good at his job.

He could have defended himself; used those same tricks to save his own skin. But Joanna's question during the dinner party kept coming back to him. How did he feel about defending people who had done something bad? He had given her some waffle about evidence being interpreted in different ways but now he could see how shallow that had been. He had been responsible for the death of a wife and a stepmother. He had to pay. It was only right.

'Simon James Mills. You are being tried on the charge of death by dangerous driving. Do you plead guilty or not guilty?'

He tried to speak but the words stuck in his mouth. Besides, he couldn't hear himself think. Joanna's voice in his head was too loud. *'Go on,'* it seemed to tinkle. *'Say you weren't guilty! Pretend you weren't responsible. Pretend you didn't have an extra helping of syllabub containing excess rum or that you didn't pick up the phone. Then try to live with yourself.'*

'Not Guilty.'

Joanna snorted. *'I'm disappointed in you, Simon. Thought you were made of stronger stuff.'*

He was. He was. But now it would have been too awkward to say anything because the jury were being sworn in.

The young woman barrister was fluffing. Her sentences were rushed and her manner flustered. Simon had told Patrick to engage a QC of whom he thought highly but the chap was already on another case. Patrick had sworn this woman was good but she wasn't. Just look at her!

Her defence, punctuated by ums and ers and constant referrals to papers which she clearly hadn't read properly, sounded like a school play accompanied by a tinkling laughter in his head which simply wouldn't go away so that he caught only snatches of what was going on.

'Mr Hugh Goodman-Brown, wife of the deceased, interfered with Mr Mills' driving ... hand on the wheel ... The defendant knows he should not have picked up his mobile phone but there are extenuating circumstances ... difficult relationship with his stepson ... argument before the dinner party ... concern that the boy was in trouble ... Good man of impeccable conduct ... clean driving licence to date ...

Simon couldn't stop himself glancing over the public gallery. Ben! He'd told Claire not to bring him but at the same time, been unable to explain that Patrick wanted to use the kid as part of the defence.

Then he noticed that one of the women jurors – a short plump woman in an electric blue suit and a severe fringe – was frowning at him. The man on her right had nodded off. The youth next to him was staring straight ahead as though he wasn't here.

Simon couldn't bring himself to look up at the gallery to see Ben's reaction. Instead, he concentrated on a knot in the wood of the dock. It looked like a face. Not dissimilar from Joanna's. And it was laughing at him.

Shaking he looked up – straight into the eyes of Hugh. Of course. That was why he wasn't in the audience gallery. He was a witness.

'And do you deny, Mr Goodman-Brown, that you tried to grab the steering wheel?'

'Absolutely.' The man's pug-like face with his steel-rimmed glasses was fixed on the jury. 'Why would I do anything so stupid? I will agree that I shouted at him a bit.' He took his glasses off for a second and a tear slid down his cheek. Then he put them back on. 'I had to. He was driving too fast round corners, ignoring my instructions. I was scared for the sake of my wife.' He clutched the edge of the dock and held up a piece of card. 'My beautiful, beautiful wife.'

Christ! It was a picture of Joanna. Joanna laughing, her neck back and her hair tied up in that chignon knot which showed the lovely lines of her shoulders. The woman juror with the severe haircut had got out her handkerchief. So much, Simon told the wooden knot, for the 'stupid bitch' comments which Hugh had aimed at his wife during her final journey.

'What will you do, Simon,' she seemed to say, *'if the prosecution drags up that stuff from school? They could do it, you know, unless you plead guilty. What would Claire think then?'*

'To sum up …'

'Stop!'

He heard his voice ring out as though it was someone else's. 'Stop. I want to change my plea.' He brought his fist down on the dock and one of the women jurors shuddered. 'I'm Guilty.'

A sea of faces turned towards him. He could see shock written all over Claire's face. Up in the gallery, Alex and Rosemarie were actually standing up to get a better view of him.

Patrick was staring as though he had gone mad. His barrister was looking at him, a nervous expression on her face as though unsure what to do next. 'My Lord. I request some time with my client.'

The judge looked at him. 'May I ask if the defendant is sure about his plea?'

'Yes.' Simon heard his voice ring out. 'Yes I am.'

'Then I do not see any need to delay proceedings any longer.'

Simon listened, staring straight ahead as his clearly fed-up barrister made her mitigation pleas. 'This is a man of previously good conduct,' he heard her say tight-lipped. 'If he is sent to prison, his wife and stepson will suffer.'

So what, he could just imagine the judge thinking. And then there was a short break while the judge re-read various reports and statements. After that, he would be sentenced. He deserved it. Not just because of Joanna. But because of the other thing which he couldn't mention.

They took him downstairs during the break. An armed police officer stood outside the cubicle as if he might leg it.

'Why did you change your plea?' Patrick snapped when he came out.

'Because I did it,' replied Simon shrugging, just as he used to in front of his father before a beating. Honesty, he recalled, used to make his father even more heavy-handed. 'I drove dangerously,' he added, to enforce the point.

Patrick's eyes narrowed. 'I have to say, Simon, that I think you did the wrong thing.'

Simon wanted to laugh. He almost felt on a high. The man

was clearly pissed off because he'd been deprived of the glory that came with winning a case. 'Yes, Patrick but you're not me, are you?'

Then it was back to the court. Staring at that knot of wood. Don't look at Claire. Or the boy. Or Hugh. In particular, don't look at that picture of Joanna.

'I determine that Simon James Mills should be imprisoned for two years,' said the judge. 'In view of the two months already served, this will be reduced to one year and ten months.' There was a gasp from the gallery; it sounded like Claire's. There was another shout too – a man's roar. 'Not enough! Not long enough for a life!'

Two years! Simon tried to take it in. It might not sound long to someone else but he knew, from his clients, that two years could feel more like ten years. Yes, he would probably only serve half of that if he behaved himself. But to think that he could be walking out scot-free right now if he'd kept his mouth shut.

'*You did the right thing!*' tinkled Joanna approvingly. '*After all, you owe me, darling!*'

Yes but what about Claire and Ben. Too late, Simon wondered if he'd done the right thing after all. Now they'd have to manage without him …

Chapter Nine

Eight months? Rigid with shock and disbelief, Claire gripped the rail in front of her, watching Simon disappear down a flight of stairs by the side of the dock. Surely someone had made a mistake. It had been an accident! And why did he look so impassive, as though none of this meant anything to him?

So many questions. Not enough answers. And what would happen now? At the cinema, you saw the accused shouting out goodbye at his family or declaring his innocence. Come back, she wanted to scream out. Come back!

'Claire.' It was Patrick, white-faced and serious, walking up towards her. 'You can come downstairs with me now to the courtroom cell to say goodbye, if you want.'

Relief washed through her. So she was allowed, at least to do that. But her legs wouldn't move. Each foot declined to go in front of the other. Instead they stuck, resolutely, to the ground like leaden jelly. Patrick put a hand under her elbow but she indicated she was all right on her own, thank you. Somehow, she didn't want this man – who had failed to save her husband – anywhere near her.

'What the hell was he playing at?' he asked her angrily as they were escorted down a flight of stairs at the back of the courtroom. 'We had agreed. His original plea was 'Not Guilty'. It's as though he wanted to mess it up.'

His anger made her prickle. It was all right for her to be doubt him but not anyone else. 'He must have had his reasons. Besides, he felt guilty about Joanna.'

Patrick made a noise as if to say that was beside the point. Then he stepped to one side and she was shown through a door and then another and into a room that led into another. And there was Simon; apprehension denting his face.

'I'm sorry,' he said.

She'd been going to tell him that it was all right; that she understood he'd been under pressure in the dock. But suddenly, all the anger that Patrick had shown, now came out of her own mouth. 'Why?' she asked harshly. 'Why did you change your plea?'

He stared up at her, his eyes bloodshot, sweat bursting out on his forehead. It was like looking at another man. 'I owed it to Joanna.'

'Owed it to Joanna?' she repeated. 'What about owing us? Ben and me? You're going to prison now. Where does that leave us?'

His voice was only just audible through his hands. 'I don't know. I'm sorry.'

Instantly, she felt a wave of contrition. She'd been wrong to have a go at him like that. 'No. *I'm* sorry.' She walked up to him and planted a kiss on top of his head. 'It'll be all right, Simon. We'll get through.'

A sudden thought struck her; something she should have considered before but had avoided, hoping against hope that he would be released. 'What happens now?' She looked at the security officer who was just behind her. 'Where will my husband go?'

The woman's eyes were cold. 'You will be informed.'

Claire wanted to grab this woman and shake her. 'But when? How can I find him? When can I visit him?' The words spilled out of her mouth in chunks, each one merging into the other in shock.

The eyes grew colder. 'As I said, you will be informed.'

She sounded like an uninterested shop assistant! If it wasn't on the shelf, it wasn't there. But this was her husband they were talking about! Her Simon! 'It's not good enough.' Claire, who hated confrontation, heard her voice rising. 'It's not …'

'Time's up.' A voice at the door interrupted her. 'We need to move. This way, *Mr* Mills.'

Claire's mind felt as though it was on a merry go-round she had once taken Ben on when he was little. She had sat side-saddle because she had three year old Ben on her knee. Too late, as the roundabout started, she felt him slipping and although she'd tried calling out to the woman who was parading around the middle, a money belt round her waist, no one heard.

'Hang on,' she'd said desperately to him but she could feel them both going. It didn't matter about her, she'd thought, seeing the ground spinning beneath them beyond the circle of the roundabout. Only her son whom she had to save. Then, just as they almost went, the woman saw them and marched steadily over, supporting her just in time. Dizzy with relief, she'd staggered off, mumbling her thanks and determined never to get on a roundabout ever again.

And now she was back to feeling as though she was slipping from the horse, except that there was no woman marching towards them to rescue her. No Simon. And no Ben.

My God! She'd been so busy worrying about Simon that she'd forgotten her own son! Her boy who'd been used in the evidence as an excuse for his stepfather's behaviour. How could Simon have allowed that?

'Two years isn't too bad you know,' said Patrick smoothly as he walked her to the car. 'It would have been far more if the judge hadn't taken the mitigating circumstances into account. When you take off his time in custody, it should probably go down to a year or maybe less if he behaves himself.' He seemed almost upbeat now, she noticed, in contrast with his previous outburst. Maybe, Claire thought, he was pleased at the prospect of not having Simon in the office any more.

'Have you seen Ben?' she said, still stunned by the sentence.

'Probably needs time to think.' Patrick laid a brief hand on her shoulder. 'I don't know if this is the right time to say it but if I were you, I'd contact the office when you're ready to discuss the financial implications.'

'Sorry?' She was still looking around for Ben.

'This isn't really my place to say it but they may not be able to continue paying Simon, given the situation.'

Not pay him? A shot of fear vibrated through her. Then how

would they manage?

'Don't worry about it right now. I expect they'll write to him.'

Claire drove home at 25 mph, disregarding the impatient driver behind her. If only Simon had done the same. As soon as she swung gently left into her driveway, she turned on the phone and pressed 'Ben', desperately hoping that he would pick up.

'*Hi. You know what to do. Leave a message and ...*'

Where was he? Turning the key in the lock, her heart leaped with relief. There were his trainers in the hall. So he was back! Racing up the stairs, she pounded on his door. No answer. Panic gripped her throat as she tried the handle.

'Fuck off and leave me alone.' His voice was furious. Livid. As though it didn't want to touch the air between them.

'Let me come in. Please!'

'You tried to blame me. You made out it was my fault.'

'Not me.' Desperate to make him understand, she continued to hammer on the door while she pleaded. 'Or Simon. It was the barrister. She said it might help to get him off.'

'But it didn't, did it? And now everyone thinks it's 'cos we had a crap relationship that caused the accident.'

'NO! It's just that ...'

Oh my God. What was that noise? For an awful moment she thought that Ben had thrown himself through the window but then, glancing downstairs, she saw the brick on the floor of the hall and behind it, a gaping hole in the sitting room window.

White-faced, Ben opened the door, staring at the brick At the same time, her mobile rang. 'Bitch,' said a man's voice that wasn't Hugh's. 'Bitch. Anyone using their phone should be shot.'

'Who is this?' she said, her voice shaking. 'How dare you talk to me like that.'

Ben whipped the phone out of her hand. 'Give it to me. They've been ringing the landline too.' His eyes locked with hers accusingly. 'Different people. All saying the same stuff.'

'Get your things,' she said. 'Quick.'

'Too late.' Her son gestured out of the window where a car had pulled up and a girl got out. Claire recognised her as the reporter from the local paper who had tried to grab her for a 'comment' on her way in and whom she'd managed to dodge on the way out, thanks to Patrick.

Already the doorbell was ringing! 'The back door,' said Ben, pulling her. 'We'll go out through the garden. Come on, Mum'.

Somehow they made their way through the spinney at the back and along the private road towards Rosemarie and Alex's house. 'Claire!' Alex appeared awkwardly at the door. 'We were going to call.' His voice had a definite edge to it; a sort of guarded greeting. 'I'm afraid Rosemarie had to go out but I'll tell her you came round.'

'We need help.' Claire couldn't stop shaking.

'Someone put a brick through our window.' Ben cut in. 'Can we come in?'

Alex's cheek twitched. 'To be honest, I'm rather concerned about the effect all this is having on Rosemarie. Isn't there someone you can ring?'

'Forget it.' The words clipped out of her mouth in bitter disappointment. 'We'll sort ourselves out.'

Chapter Ten

Claire, Claire, Simon kept saying over and over in his head in the back of the van as if the chant might bring her back to him. They were taking him back to his cell at Holdfast, they said. He'd be there overnight and then moved the next day to a Cat C prison where he'd spend 'some time', being 'risk-assessed'. As if he was likely to deliberately hurt someone else!

But all this meant nothing, compared with Claire's stricken face when the verdict had been announced.

'How did you get on at court, ducks?' asked Georgie, passing him in the corridor as the prison officer escorted him back to his cell.

'Two years,' he said tightly. 'Should be released in one if I don't do something stupid.'

Georgie, who was dressed in purple jogging bottoms as though on his way to the yard for his half-an-hour exercise, made a sympathetic face. 'Poor you, ducks.'

Joanna's voice tingled in his head. *'If it was up to me, Simon, you'd have got life. That's what you took from me.'*

Simon shook his head. 'I pleaded guilty. I might have got off if I hadn't.'

Georgie's eyebrows rose. 'You're crazy, ducks. You haven't done bird before. Don't know what you've let yourself in for.'

'Get on with it,' said the prison officer moving Simon along.

'See you around!' Georgie called out over his shoulder. 'And good luck!'

'You've never done bird before.' The words echoed in his head as the officer slammed the cell door behind him, giving the instruction to 'get your kit together'. He hadn't. And now he was going to find out what it really meant.

* * *

Later, when Simon looked back, he found himself unable to recall the exact details. Maybe his mind had blanked it out in protection. Only stark skeleton details stood out. Locked up in a cell with a man who wouldn't – or couldn't – talk. Never-ending physical and mental tests as well as questions on whether he felt suicidal. Sloppy pasta. Mattress like a rock. A phone call to Claire telling her she wasn't on any account to visit him in this place.

Then – much sooner than was usual apparently – Simon was informed he was eligible for a D cat prison. An open prison where he wouldn't be locked up all day. Relief was tempered by apprehension. 'Does my wife know?' was his first question.

Claire, Claire. It was beginning to feel like a prayer now; the type he had said as a child when he hadn't understood the words but which had made him feel good inside. If things had gone differently at the trial, he could be back home with his wife and Ben. Could be sitting right now at the kitchen table, having supper with them.

Maybe they would be talking about moving and making a fresh start because after all they couldn't continue living where they were after The Accident. They could go back to London and merge into suburbia where no one would know what he had done.

'*No way!*' sang Joanna. '*You did the right thing, Simon, trust me. You need to pay for what you did to me. It's the rules!*'

She was right. But at the same time, he felt furious with the legal system. How could the jury have ignored the contribution made by Hugh with his stupid fat, drunken hand on the wheel or by Ben and his slap-happy dowsing of the rum syllabub? And what about the driver of the car, parked without thought? How could he, Simon, have spent most of his working life supporting a system which had now let him down so badly? There were no answers to any of that let alone the question which meant more than the others put together.

The one which he couldn't even voice out loud.

Half an hour later, he had packed his few possessions in the large see-through polythene bag they gave him. Not much because there was a limit on what was allowed. His radio. A spare pair of jeans. A photograph of Claire laughing at their wedding, his hand on her waist. Longingly, he thought of the Ian McEwan novel which Claire had tried to bring in but had been confiscated by the prison officer in case drugs had been somehow hidden in the paper.

Then came the knock on the door. 'Mills? We're off.'

It was one of the women prison officers; a stout woman who had a substantial chest and hips to match. 'But I didn't think I was being moved until tomorrow.'

'It's changed. Come on.'

The prison officer gave him a sharp look. 'You're the one what killed someone when you were on the phone, weren't you? My niece was run over by a hit and run. Still not right, she isn't. Scum like you shouldn't be allowed to live.'

He bent his head in acknowledgement. 'You're right. Absolutely right.'

Her eyes flashed furiously. 'Don't take the piss out of me, Mills.'

'I'm not. Honestly. Look, I need to let my wife know what's happening. She'll be worried out of her mind. May I ring her, please, to tell her I'm being moved?'

'What do you think this is? The bleeding Intercontinental? She'll be informed, when the paperwork is ready.'

'But when ...?'

Too late, Simon found his arm being yanked by another officer and marched out of the cell yet again and along the corridor. Out into a yard and then another and into a large white van along with a dark youth whose face was marked by a long scar down the right-hand side.

'Hi, man!' The boy put up his hand in a high five. For some reason he couldn't explain, Simon did the same. The boy's palm felt hot and sweaty against his. Instantly he felt the urgent need to wash his hands.

'What did you get, man?'

'Two years.'

''Snothing, issit! I've only got nine more months to do,

60

meself!' He was grinning as though they were swapping exam grades. 'Great, innit?'

Simon felt like he'd stumbled into the wrong play. 'Where are we going?'

'Freetown, man,' said the boy. 'Didn't they tell you?' His face shone. 'It's an open prison. Cool man. Really cool.'

He knew about open prisons of course, but only from a lawyer's perspective. Spencer, the boy who had the scar, was determined to fill him in.

'You can't just wander in and out like. You have to prove yourself like.' He grinned, scratching himself in the groin region; an area which was disturbingly revealed by a hole in his jeans. 'My brothers say it's like a holiday camp.' His eyes grew wistful. 'I'd love to go to that kind of place one day with girls, discos, and as much scram as you can scoff. Can you imagine, man?'

He didn't want to. All he could think about was Claire. Someone had to tell her where he was. Still, Alex and Rosemarie would be looking after her, he reassured himself. They'd have asked her and Ben over for supper after the verdict. They'd be comforting her right now …

'Freetown is great, man, though you've got to do what the screws tell you. They don't take any crap. But the best thing is that you can walk around! Breathe fresh air. I tell yer. I've been waiting for my D cat. for years.'

'D cat.?'

Despite having helped to send people to prison (or not) for years, Simon realised to his shame that his knowledge of HMP categories wasn't particularly deep.

'Man, you a prison virgin or something? D cat. is the best you can get.' He puffed out his chest. 'Started off in a B cat., I did. Did eight years there and then spent four years in a shitty C cat. And now here!'

Simon mentally totted up the years in his head. That meant Spencer had been in prison for a total of nearly twelve years. He didn't look old enough. He must have done something pretty awful but it seemed rude to ask. Then it occurred to him that he might well be locked up in a van with a rapist or murderer. 'I'm not like him,' he wanted to tell the prison guard. 'I'm not a criminal.'

'*Really?*' tinkled Joanna. '*So what do you call murder then?*'

Initially Joanna's voice, which kept coming into his head, had seemed no more than his own guilty conscience but now it had taken on a distinct presence. '*You killed me just as surely as some of the other guys in this place have chopped up others, darling,*' sang Joanna. '*I'm not sure about your new friend either. Look at the way he's eyeing your bits and pieces – and I'm not just talking about your body.*'

The boy was indeed eyeing his watch keenly. It wasn't valuable in monetary terms – especially now it had been smashed from The Accident – but his father had given it to him all those years ago and now, too late, he was wishing he had left it at home.

'*Distract him, darling,*' prompted Joanna. '*It's what I used to do with Hugh when he got threatening. Make small talk. Good gracious, don't they teach you anything at law school?*'

'So tell me,' Simon began carefully, 'what's this place like?'

Spencer yawned, revealing the gap of teeth once more and a couple of gold ones glinting from the back. 'There are huts, mate. Not cells. You have to share for the first few months and that can be crap if you don't like the person you're with. Or you might learn a bit from him, if you know what I mean. The good bit is that you get to go in and out of the huts. No locked doors or that kind of stuff. You have to put yer name down for a work party.' He leaned forward. 'Want a tip from me? Get yourself onto farms and gardens. Then you get to do outside stuff round the prison like cleaning the drains. Don't go on to stores.'

Despite having been introduced to Stores in Holdfast, Simon had a mental picture of a London department store. He'd had a girlfriend once, who was a PR for Harvey Nicks, one of his favourites. The store that was; not the girl, who'd been another wanting too much, too soon in the days before he was ready for commitment. Before he'd met Claire.

'If you work in Stores, you have to hand out clean clothes to people. You're allowed noo joggers every week but everyone comes in and says they've lost their trainers so can they have some more but they're lying like. Then if you say no, you can get beaten up.'

Simon waited for Spencer to say he was only joking but he didn't. His skin began to crawl.

'There's Education mind but I don't want none of that meself.'

A possibility arose in Simon's mind of maybe doing another degree. Memories of Jeffrey Archer came to mind. He'd always fancied studying Chinese and it would keep his mind occupied. Would there be a library there? Then he pulled himself up. For Christ's sake, what was he thinking of? He'd just killed a woman and wrecked his own family and here he was, already planning his next year's reading programme. 'Why don't you want anything to do with education?' he asked, more out of politeness than anything else.

Spencer snorted. His nostrils were wide suggesting that of a wild horse. Was that genetic or was it related to sniffing something, Simon wondered. 'It's just not for me.'

'Didn't you go to school?'

Another snort. 'Me mam tried to get me to go so she could entertain her man friends when I was out but the teachers gave up on me 'cos I used to keep climbing the tree outside and staying up there.' He beamed with pride. 'Can't tell you how many times they had to call the cops out and the fire engines too.'

'To get you down?'

Spencer shot him a pitying look. 'Nah. When I tried to set the school kitchens on fire.' He gave another yawn and stretched out his legs to reveal part of a blue and pink flame tattoo above his sock.

'None of this shit would have happened if we'd grown up somewhere different like.'

'What do you mean?'

63

'It was the estates wot did it. We didn't expect to be teachers or nothing clever like that.' He gave a short laugh. 'It was like what are you going to do then? Credit cards? Nicking stuff from shops? Grab cars? Drive them as getaways for the older boys on the estate who did post offices? Pick up stash for the dealers? Take it to get weighed and then drop it off?'

He began to look pleased with himself. 'I was on the way up when I got done. But you know what the best job is?'

Simon waited, hooked despite himself.

'It's not handling your stash. Getting others to do it for you and then pocketing the money.' Spencer looked wistful. 'But you have to go a long way before you can get that far!'

There was no repentance, Simon saw with a shock. To Spencer and thousands like him, this was just a way of life. A career path. Just then the van began to slow down.

'Here we are mate.' Spencer laughed, revealing another flash of gold at the back of his mouth. 'Home at last.'

Curious and scared, Simon peered out of the tiny gap at the top of the window between the blacked-out bit and the frame. There was a high wire fence which had rolls of more barbed wire on top. It looked forbidding; impenetrable.

Spencer shuddered. 'That's the Dark Side next to our bit.'

'The Dark Side?'

'Blimey man, keep up. Grimville, it's called. It's a Cat. B that is, like the one I was in 'cept I'm not a psycho like half those nutters there. You don't want to go near that place. It even scares *me*.'

Simon looked across at the high barbed wire fence and the dark grey building behind and shivered. What kind of men were inside?

'*The same kind as you, darling!*' trilled Joanna. '*Murderers. Now are we going in or not?*'

64

Chapter Eleven

Claire had been waiting on tenterhooks for a phone call from Simon when the mobile rang. '*Patrick*' it said on the screen. She answered it with a mixture of crashing disappointment and also expectation. Her husband, it seemed, had been moved to some prison called Freetown which was in Essex, of all places – a seven-hour drive away.

'It's an open prison which is excellent news,' Patrick had told her in a tone that suggested she ought to be extremely grateful. 'It means that when the paperwork is sorted, you'll be allowed to visit twice a week. After a while, Simon will be allowed out on town visits provided he's escorted. You'll be able to take him out for a day every now and then. And the good news is that it's the softest kind of prison you can get so he won't just be mixing with hard criminals. Offences normally centre around drugs, fraud, drink, and of course driving. There'll be some men who are coming up for the end of their sentences from other prisons but on the whole, Simon should be in reasonable company.'

It was so much to take in, this world which she knew nothing about! Town visits. Fraudsters. Men coming up for the end of their sentences. Did that mean they had committed more serious crimes such as … She paused, unable to form the word 'murder' or 'rape' in her head. No, she reassured herself. They wouldn't put him in a place with people like that.

'How are you doing?' asked Patrick.

Claire almost laughed. She was an ordinary woman who, until not long ago, had led a fairly normal life, give or take a marriage break up. Now she had a new husband in prison, a rebellious teenage son who was due to start a new term at school and a house that wasn't safe to live in any more. How did he *think* she was doing?

'Not great.' She glanced down at the list of rental houses she'd picked up from an agency in town. 'I'm still wondering if we really have to go.'

As she spoke, Claire peered out through the pretty pink and blue chintz curtains of the drawing room which she'd had to keep shut since the brick incident two days ago. The local handyman had come in to board it up but he had done so silently, giving her dolorous looks as though she too was responsible for Joanna's death.

'I think it's wise to move out for a bit, for your own safety.' Patrick's tone was slow and steady rather like the doctor's when he'd given her a prescription for tranquillisers that morning.

She nodded silently, thinking of the call she'd made to the rental agency. 'But they want references so I'll have to give my real name and then they might recognise me which will defeat the whole purpose.'

Claire could almost hear Patrick considering this. 'You might have a point. It's a pity the trial was covered so extensively by the local press.'

'There's something else.' Her hand tightened on the list of flats. 'Do you know any more about Simon being paid?'

'Hasn't he received the letter?'

She shook her head, even though he couldn't see her.

'I'm sorry about this, Claire, but I gather he's been struck off. It often happens if someone is convicted. Simon won't be able to practise as a lawyer again.'

Never work as a lawyer again? Her mind whirled with the implications. Simon lived for his job! Once she'd been to see him handle a case in court and had sat, mesmerised, in the gallery, stunned by the way he had strutted across the floor like an actor. When one of the witnesses for the other side had insisted that he had seen the defendant on a certain night, Simon had produced a document from the file in front of him and waved it in the air. 'Are you absolutely certain?' he had demanded.

The inference had been that Simon's document proved

66

otherwise. Afterwards, Simon had told her that this was a trick he sometimes used. The 'document' had in fact been blank but the defendant, who couldn't see that from the distance between them, had been rattled enough to withdraw his 'evidence'.

Claire had been both impressed and unnerved by the scene. If her husband could be manipulative like that in his public life, who was to say he wasn't like that in private?

It was then that she heard the crash. 'Mum!' called out Ben from downstairs. She flew down, three steps at a time to find her son standing by the kitchen window, giant shards of glass around his feet and a scared expression on his white face.

Not again! 'You're cut,' she said appalled, glancing at the blood seeping out from under the shoulder of his t-shirt. 'No. Don't press that tea-towel against it – there might be glass inside.'

'I was just standing there and the brick came through, just like last time.' He was gabbling from shock. She was shaking too but with anger. 'Grab your things.'

'Why?'

'We're going.'

'Where?'

'Anywhere. But we need to go to Casualty on the way.'

It was then that her mobile rang showing a number that she didn't recognise. 'Yes?'

'Claire.' Her husband's voice sounded distant.

'Look, I'm sorry. I can't talk. Something's happened. I'll ring you back.'

'You can't. It's taken me ages to buy my pin number from Canteen and then queue up at the phone. You don't understand.'

'And you,' she said fiercely, bundling Ben towards the front door while cramming the mobile between her ear and shoulder, 'don't understand either.'

Chapter Twelve

What had happened? Why hadn't Claire want to talk to him? Had she given up on him already? Simon sat on the thin grey blanket covering his bed and covered his face with his hands. He could cope with any of this shit around him. But only if Claire was still there, waiting for him.

He'd waited days to ring her. Days. There were so many questions he needed to ask. How was she doing? Was she all right? Was Ben all right? He needed to tell her too about this place. What it had been like when he'd arrived. His mind went back ...

There had been so much to take in. Stumbling out of the van, Simon had had to screw up his eyes in the light and looked wildly around at the unfamiliar surroundings.

Spencer had been right. The huts did look a bit like a holiday camp although there were grey and cream Portakabins too, dotted around like faded holiday caravans. These were for admin, apparently. Men were everywhere in maroon sweat shirts and jogging bottoms and long necklace-like identity cards round their necks. Huge men with shaved heads and thick necks. Small ones who had frightened-mouse expressions. A chalk-skinned albino who had bright red hair and negro-like lips. An old man leaning on a stick. Some walking. Some striding. One was running and Simon had to step sideways to avoid him. They seemed to be on a mission, he thought. But where? Surely there was nowhere to go?

'This way, *Mr* Mills,' one of the officers had said sharply with a sarcastic emphasis on 'Mr'. He followed, desperately trying to familiarise himself. Behind one of the Portakabins, he could glimpse a high wire fence looming out of the ground and bending round in a semi-circle as though it wanted as little to do with the open prison as the latter did with *it*. There was a door in the middle and in the distance, he could just about make out someone in black going inside just as another, in identical uniform, came out.

Nutters, Spencer had said nervously. Really? And if so, what on earth were the authorities thinking of to put an open prison next to a place for (apparently) seriously disturbed criminals?

'In here, please *Mr* Mills.'

He was shepherded into one of the Portakabins.

'Bag, please.'

Reluctantly, Simon watched as the officer, a tall thin, dark-haired man who had a chain round his waist, went through his belongings. Some were put to one side – like his razor – and the rest were handed back in a plastic bag.

'Can't I take that in? He pointed to the razor in its smart black leather case.

'Not allowed. Your watch please.'

'My watch?' Dismayed, Simon undid the gold clasp and reluctantly handed it over. The officer gave it an admiring glance, despite the cracked face, and Simon wanted to knock his lights out. 'My father gave it to me,' he said quietly. 'For my twenty-first.'

The officer's face tightened. 'You'll get it back when you're released.'

It was all he could do not to leap up and grab it. 'Remember,' his father had said when he'd given it to him, 'always do the right thing. Don't just do the best you can. Do *better*. People like us have to prove ourselves. Never forget that.'

People like us. His father had come from a time when being half-Indian was a definite disadvantage. Hadn't he suffered the same at school when boys who had aristocratic accents had clicked their fingers and called him a 'coolie'? It wasn't until he went to Oxford and found that his coffee complexion was actually a magnet for women that he began to be grateful for his looks. But he was in prison now. And he had a nasty feeling that his colour wasn't going to be an advantage.

'This way, *Mr* Mills.'

Feeling naked without his watch, Simon followed the officer through the camp, past more Portakabins until finally stopping outside a squat looking bungalow-type building which had 'G block' scrawled on a homemade sign outside.

'This is your pad,' said the officer carelessly sweeping his arm in an extravagant gesture at the corridor inside with rooms leading off on either side. 'First on the right.'

Determined not to show his emotions – one of the first rules he'd learned at school – Simon took in the metal bed and its blue plastic mattress; the thin blanket; the grey lino on the floor which was ripped and stained; the thin black curtain at the window, hanging half off its rail. He could do this. He had to.

'Your pad mate's not in at the moment,' said the officer. 'You've got ten minutes here to sort out your stuff. Then there's induction at the centre. Don't be late.'

He almost was – it wasn't easy to find his way round this place. But he got there just in time to find himself in a room full of about fifteen other men, some looking as though they couldn't care less (like Spencer) and others who seemed like scared young boys. Simon listened carefully to the officer – a woman whose cheaply dyed blonde hair was tied back in a pony tail – as she barked out a list of do's and don'ts along with rules about lock up which was apparently at 9 p.m. He hadn't been to bed at that time since he'd been at prep school.

'If you leave the prison without permission, you'll be shipped out,' added the officer sharply.

'So why don't they have a gate at the end of the drive to stop you escaping,' he whispered to Spencer.

'That's the whole point, mate,' he hissed back. 'They want to teach us responsibility, like. 'Course, it's different for the Dark Side. They've got double doors and wire and Christ knows what ...'

'Quiet at the back,' roared the officer.

Then there was the information on Canteen, which wasn't an actual place like you might assume. Just a form that you filled

70

in on Wednesday, circling items that you wanted like razors, deodorant, newspapers, or most importantly, a pin number so you could use one of the phones. Orders arrived the following Monday. So if you arrived at prison after a Wednesday, you had to wait until the next one to fill in your order. That meant he couldn't ring Claire for ages. Simon wanted to hit his head against the wall of this sodding place. She'd be out of her mind by then. So would he.

Then the officer assigned each of them to what she called a 'work party'. Each prisoner had to belong to one. There was 'farms and gardens' which meant digging the garden beds (Simon had only done the lawn at home as Claire was the plants expert); or 'works' which was best suited for people who had electrical qualifications; or the kitchen, where you helped make meals for the rest of the prison; or 'full-time education' which you could only do when you'd been Inside for a certain number of weeks, depending on your sentence.

You didn't get a choice. His work party was 'Stores', the one Spencer had warned him about.

Then on to the dining room because it was roll-call and if they weren't there on time to be checked, they'd get a strike against their name and a loss of privileges. Back past the library Portakabin which had a 'Closed' sign; the laundry room which emitted a rather cosy washing smell; another Portakabin where he could see a row of computers (you could do various IT courses); the 'shrink' building where you could get counselling to get you off drinks and drugs; and the Centre where staff signed in and out and where inmates were 'strictly forbidden'. There was also a chapel, he'd heard, and a Multi-Faith Room. It was like a small village.

Dazed, Simon made his way back to G Hut, getting lost a few times along the way. Some huts, he noticed, had tubs of flowers by the entrance where someone had tried to make an effort. But not his. He went in cautiously, aware of a nasty smell from the communal bathroom where the door was wide open. There was the drone of a television from someone's room as he went by and another man's door was open, showing a line of shirts hanging from the curtain pole.

Bloody hell! His own pad door was open. His heart beating, Simon went in. A thin, wiry man was lying on his bed, listening to music so loud that Simon's ears hurt. He nodded at Simon.

'Wotcha! I'm Kevin. Like this stuff?'

'A bit loud, don't you think?' ventured Simon.

Kevin grinned. 'Tough.'

That night, Simon tossed and turned under the thin, grey blanket as Kevin played his music until 3 a.m. without anyone coming round to tell him to turn it down. For Christ's sake! He was a grown man. Not some teenager who stayed up all night. But the worst thing was not having Claire next to him. A cold feeling crawled through him. Supposing she had given up on him?

It was days until the pin number for the phone came through from his Canteen order. Then he had to queue up for twenty minutes because there was only one phone in the hut. That was when she blew him out as Spencer might have put it.

'*Look, I'm sorry. I can't talk. Something's happened. I'll ring you back.*'

Why didn't she want to talk? What had happened? Simon felt as though his body was going to explode. Unable to stop himself, Simon slammed the phone against the wall.

'Watch it, mate. I need to use that.' A big burly man distinguished by a shiny hairless head and a red and blue flame tattoo running down his right arm, now pushed past him to get into the booth. Then he shot him a slightly more sympathetic look. 'Your missus giving you a hard time then? Don't take it to heart, mate. They get like that sometimes. Listen. You couldn't do me a favour, could you, and read these numbers on the phone card? Me glasses have broken and I've got to get hold of the wife 'cos she hasn't been able to pay the bleeding rent.'

In the few days that Simon had been at HMP Freetown, he'd come across several pleas for reading help. The excuses were endless. Simon had read about prisoners and their literary failings but hadn't taken much notice to date. He'd also read something about family breakdown in prison but that hadn't meant much to him either. Until now.

Why hadn't Claire talked to him, wondered Simon as he walked back to his pad. What could possibly be so important that she hadn't stopped and spoken to her husband who was in prison; not some hotel where she could call back? It wasn't even as if Claire had written. Every morning, like everyone else, he waited in the queue by the window on the other side of which sat a prison officer who doled out letters in turn. And every morning he gave out his name and number – 121155A – only to be met with the same short word. 'Nothing.'

'*Who would want to stay married to a murderer*?' tinkled Joanna.

'All right! I get the point!'

'Get the point? What yer on about, your lordship?'

He hadn't known that he was talking about loud until his pad mate's voice hit him. Kevin, the thin wiry beady-eyed man who insisted on calling him 'Your lordship' on account of his 'posh' voice, was already back from the phone and tucking into his Pot Noodles. Out of the £9 a week that they were given for jobs round the prison, many of the men spent theirs on dried food which were a staple item on the canteen list.

It was also possible to order a daily newspaper but the cost of *The Times*, which he had never considered until now, would have eaten up his week's allowance.

'You was quick on the phone, then?' Kevin was talking with his mouth full, revealing small yellow bits of processed corn which had got stuck in his teeth.

Simon nodded curtly, not trusting himself to say anything. Already he could feel tears welling up in his eyes.

'No need to be fucking off, your lordship.' Kevin scowled at him. ''Snot my fault if you've got domestics.' He turned his back and proceeded to blast out Bob Marley from the huge ghetto blaster on his side of the pad.

'Isn't there some rule against playing music too late?' Simon had already asked one of the prison officers who patrolled each block of huts to check the men hadn't brought in one too many possessions. (They were each allowed a total of twenty, which didn't include clothes.)

'You can file a complaint if you want.' The officer, a young man sporting a gelled-back crest of a fringe, had sounded vaguely sympathetic. 'But you might not be very popular with your cell-mate.'

Simon soon wished he hadn't said anything because someone must had overheard him talking to the officer and told Kevin. ''Ear you don't like my taste in music, your lordship. Well too fucking bad.' After that, Bob Marley not only got louder but also later. He couldn't even rely on his neighbours complaining because their music was loud too.

Now Simon sat on the edge of his bed on the far wall to Kevin's, his head in his hands. There was a funny smell indicating that his pad mate was smoking something he shouldn't. He could report him for this but if he did, he knew what the consequences would be. The other day, someone had appeared in the breakfast queue with a bruised right eye claiming that he had fallen in the shower. The fact that he shared his pad with a renowned drugs dealer who had been shipped out after he'd split on him, was no coincidence.

'*By the way,*' trilled Joanna suddenly. '*Seen what your friend is reading?*'

He turned round. Kevin was sitting at the top of his bed in his black boxers, smoking his roll-up and leafing through a magazine which had a picture of a woman sitting, her legs splayed open. 'Want a deck?' he offered, catching Simon's eye.

'No thanks.'

'No thanks,' mimicked Kevin in what he considered to be a public school accent.

Simon stood up. The smell of the cigarette and the picture of that woman coupled with the disappointment of the phone call, made him need the loo. He tried not to go; it was easier than wading in through the pool of urine and faeces smeared on the seat. But sometimes you just had to.

He'd wanted to tell Claire some of this as well of course as finding out how she was. But maybe, he thought as he queued up for one of two lockable loos in a hut for twenty men, it was

74

just as well that he hadn't talked to her that night after all.

It wouldn't be fair on her to know what hell it was in here. He'd brought this on himself. And he'd have to sort it out himself.

Chapter Thirteen

When he queued up again to phone Claire, it went straight through to answerphone both on her mobile, the landline, and also Ben's mobile. What was happening, he asked himself during another restless night on a two-foot-six-wide bed and its pillow that could have doubled up as a slab of concrete.

He must have dozed off briefly because he woke as the morning tannoy voice blared through the loudspeaker in the corridor outside. Quick! The bathroom! Already, Simon knew that if you weren't head of the queue, you would be met with the usual pile of faeces.

Easing himself out of bed – the narrowness had done something to his back – he grabbed his regulation towel which was hanging by a tape from the back of the door and his wash bag. Too late. An enormous man pushed past him wearing nothing but a tight pair of Union Jack boxers, slamming one of two lockable loo doors behind him. The other door was jammed.

The man in the tight Union Jack boxers was taking his time. In fact, he seemed to be speaking to someone. Simon could hear the low hurried murmurs before realising that the man must somehow have got hold of a mobile phone which would be enough of a crime to get him shipped out immediately. Even worse, he, Simon might for all he knew, be held as an accessory if he didn't say something. Yet if he did, as Spencer had told him, he'd be in 'deep shit'.

The urge to pass a motion was getting stronger. Frantically, Simon knocked on the other locked door. Behind him, the rest of the pad occupants in G huts were trooping in. 'You won't get Gary out of there,' one of them said. 'He's having a wank.'

He was really beginning to panic now. If he didn't find a

proper loo, he was going to …

'Shit, mate,' said the voice of his pad mate. 'You're not meant to do that kind of stuff in the urinals.' He laughed. A nasty low throaty laugh. 'Maybe you're not so posh after all.'

Simon stared in horror at the brown mess that had slid down onto the floor from between his legs. He wanted to cry just as he had cried when he had 'had an accident' as matron had put it when he'd first gone away to school. The smell was appalling. 'I tried to hang on,' Simon said, feeling like a nine year old.

'Better clear it up, mate,' said someone else. 'It's not nice for the rest of us, is it?'

At that point, the tannoy started with its tinny, crackling high-pitched whine. 'Roll-call. Roll-call.'

There was a general groan and then en masse the bathroom evacuated. He had to get moving. Being late for roll-call at 7.45 a.m. on the dot meant one warning. Any more might mean that he wouldn't be allowed a visit from Claire – if she wanted to see him still. Frantically, Simon scooped up the mess with some loo paper and then washed his hands raw in the basin. Pulling on his regulation green trousers and T-shirt, he legged it towards the dining room. A woman officer was standing at the head by the cold toast and bowls of porridge. She shot him an impassive look. 'Number?'

121155A. He knew it off by heart now just like he had known his boot number at school.

'You're late.'

'I know. I'm sorry but …'

The officer made a note on the pad in front of him. 'You've got a strike.'

He felt sick; unable to eat anything.

'*Two more and you're in trouble!*' tinkled Joanna. '*Better not be late for work, had you?*'

On his first day in Stores, Simon had taken over from an inmate who was about to go out to work and could hardly hide his glee. Work, he told Simon, usually meant sorting out bags in a charity shop or cleaning up a park or doing something 'what

77

helps others, like'. It was 'fucking fantastic' because you got to leave the camp in the white van every morning and do your stuff before coming back at 4 p.m. You even got to go out at lunch time and you could get lucky if you played your cards right.

Simon thought of the times he had gone to the local charity shop to buy books and wondered if, without knowing, he'd been served by someone who was on day release from prison. It almost made him laugh and take his mind away from the job in front of him. He had, so his predecessor explained, to give out work uniform, depending on which work party the applicant was in. White for kitchens. Green for farms and gardens. And so on.

Stores also provided a dull maroon tracksuit for prisoners who hadn't brought in their own clothes or weren't able for financial reasons to get family to send stuff in. (This led, he noticed, to some resentment from those who weren't able to afford designer tracksuits.) There were also rules on what clothes you were and weren't allowed to wear when you weren't working. Overall black (top *and* bottoms) were forbidden although one or the other was acceptable. Hoodies were banned.

'Watch out for the ones who say they've lost stuff but want something else, man.' The departing inmate had grinned toothlessly at him. 'Trainers are really hot. If you work with them, they might be able to help you get something you want, like. But don't get caught or you won't be able to go out to work.'

The induction session had taught him that this was what he was working towards. A few months at Stores until he could get on to the lists for Education, which was currently full. Education was meant to be an option for everyone although it consisted mainly of classes building up towards levels one and two which were only GCSE. He had an MBA, for God's sake. Then work, provided he was considered 'eligible'. And then, maybe, Out.

He didn't want to think about that bit because if he did, he

78

wouldn't be able to cope with the months in between. 'Two years is nothing, mate,' someone had said to him in the dinner queue the other week. 'I've had three years in this place. Another three months and I'm away.'

The man in question was going to work on a building site, driving himself in his own car. Simon had been amazed when he'd first discovered this but it was apparently the way it worked. Depending on the length of your sentence and your behaviour, you were allowed to go out to work providing you returned by 5 p.m. when you were searched to make sure you hadn't brought back drugs with you. Not surprisingly, it wasn't easy to find a job. Many employers were reluctant to employ men still doing time. The best bets were building sites and bars.

How had it been that he had lived his life as a so-called defence lawyer without understanding what it was really like after sentence had been passed?

Now, he headed for the low hut near the dining room with the corrugated roof and the word 'Stores' scrawled in black paint on the door. With any luck, there would be time to call Claire after work and before roll-call at lunch. Meanwhile, there was a queue already forming and a short stout Liverpudlian whom he recognised from F hut which was next to his, gave him a sharp look. 'Where've you been, man? I've had to deal with this lot on my own. Get a move on, can you.'

Simon slid under the counter to face his first customer of the day: a tall thin white boy who didn't seem much older than Ben. He spoke in a quiet educated voice. That was another thing about this place. You got all sorts. There were a handful of other professionals like him; there were the sharp ones who had more savvy than educational skills. And there were some who had seemed to slip through the school net completely and could barely string a sentence together.

On the whole, the men went round camp on their own, although there were certain clusters who would hang together. This could be intimidating and Simon found himself feeling scared when he walked past, taking care not to make eye contact in case one of them took it as provocation.

Why was he so scared? Simon asked himself. It wasn't as though he wasn't used to being in the company of criminals. Yet there was something very different about being in a position of authority to being 'one of them'. Most of these men were perfectly capable of hurting him.

'*But you hurt* me,' protested Joanna indignantly in his head.

'Yes but that was unintentional.'

She sniffed. '*The result was the same as if you had taken a sledgehammer to me.*'

Simon began to shake. 'Don't.'

The boy in front of him was taking care not to look him. 'I've lost me trainers,' he mumbled.

'Poor diddums,' snorted someone behind him. Even though he was wearing a white T-shirt, a thick gold chain round his neck, and loose camouflage trousers, Simon recognised him as the man in the tight Union Jack boxers and the mobile phone.

'You're going to have to fill a form in,' he said, turning back to the tall, thin white-faced boy. 'It's got to be agreed by one of the officers before I can do anything. I suggest you come back tomorrow.'

'But I haven't got any trousers to wear until then. My others are dirty.'

The Union Jack man snorted. 'Come to the right place then. This geezer knows all about getting his pants dirty, don't you mate?' He jerked his head at Simon who flushed. Clearly the story of his accident had already started to do the rounds.

'I'm sorry.' The apology was meant to have been directed at the boy but somehow it sounded as though he was saying sorry for the bathroom. 'You'll need to fill in the form. It's the rules.'

The boy nodded and left the hut, his shoulders bowed.

'Next,' said Simon unnecessarily because the Union Jack man was already in front of him, sweat glistening on his chest where the top buttons were undone.

'I need another pair of trainers.' His eyes bored into Simon challengingly. 'Someone nicked mine.'

'May I have your name please?'

Someone in the queue behind let out a guffaw, repeating

what he had just said in an accent that was clearly intended to mimic Simon's voice.

'Macdonald.'

Simon found his name on the list. It looked as though Macdonald had been given a new pair of trainers two weeks ago and another pair the week before that. Spencer's words came back to him. 'Trainers are big here, mate. They're currency, like. We like to change them regular; they're a sort of status.'

He picked up his pen and put a cross by Macdonald's name. 'I'm sorry.' He was aware he was speaking in his lawyer's voice as he did when advising a client.

'Afraid you've already had your quota. We're not meant to make more than two replacements in one month.'

The man let out a low growl. 'Who says?'

'It's the rules; although you are welcome to fill in this complaints form.'

For a minute, Simon thought the man was going to grab the collar around his neck. Then the big hands fell back to his side. 'Listen to me, you little bit of shit. I used to be one of the most dangerous criminals in Britain. Used to know Ronnie Kray, I did. Get it? Now I'm going to come back tomorrow and this time you're going to give me those trainers. Got it?'

Simon was aware that the room had gone silent. If he gave in now, he would be seen as wet. If he didn't, he could be beaten up. 'Like I said, you will need to fill in the form first.'

There was a gasp from somewhere and then Macdonald slowly picked up the piece of paper which Simon had given him and ripped it into two halves before flinging them on the floor. 'You're going to be sorry for this,' he said quietly. 'You'll see.'

The hushed air in the hut continued after he left. Even his Liverpudlian co-worker seemed subdued. 'Better watch out for him. That one's got friends.'

For the rest of the morning, Simon continued serving over the counter, sticking religiously to the rules he had been taught. But when he left for lunch or dinner as the others called it, he had a nasty cold feeling in his chest. Looking round the dining room, he spotted Macdonald in the corner of the room. The man then said something to the others at his section of the table and several men stared at him. Simon took his sandwich and sat down, staring at the bits of grated cheese that fell out of the slices of bread.

'*Even I'm beginning to feel worried for you now,*' tinkled Joanna. '*Do be careful, won't you?*'

To his frustration, there wasn't time before lunch to ring Claire – he didn't dare risk a strike – so he had to wait until after tea. 'Please let her pick up,' he said over and over in his head. When she did, he was filled with such a relief that he found himself being angry with her.

'Why couldn't you talk to me, before? What happened? Do you know how difficult it is to make phone calls from this place?'

'Don't yell at me like that, Simon.'

Christ, it was so good to hear her voice. 'I'm not.'

'You are. Calm down and I'll explain. Ben and I had to move.'

'Why?'

'Someone threw a brick through the window. It wasn't safe.'

He hadn't even considered there might be repercussions from The Accident. Why hadn't he thought of that? He could see it now. There were some crazy people out there. He knew that from his work. His mind went back to a case ten years ago when a wife was murdered by a man in retaliation for her husband having run over his daughter. A bolt of terror shot through him. He couldn't let that happen to Claire. 'Are you all right?'

'Please. Don't worry.'

Then she told him about the seaside town she'd moved to. 'It's big enough for no one to know,' she assured him. 'And the rent is low. We're going to have to sell the house, you know. We can't afford the mortgage.'

'I've got my savings, remember,' he butted in. 'It's not enough to pay the mortgage but I've got to sort out how to get the money transferred into your name. Listen, I'm more worried about you. ' He tried to picture his wife and stepson living in a

82

place he'd never been to and failed.

'We're fine. I've also filled in the security forms for a visit. They said it could take as long as a month but then I'll drive over and see you.'

Drive? Suddenly, the idea of driving terrified him. It was such a long way. Supposing some crazy driver went into her? 'I'd rather you got the train.'

'I've got to drive. For both of us.'

He knew exactly what she meant. Just because he didn't feel able to get behind a wheel again, didn't mean he had to stop *her*. 'I love you,' he said.

Her voice was shakily calm. 'I love you too.'

Relief soared through him like a helium balloon. Claire still loved him. He could cope now.

'*Really?*' tinkled Joanna. '*Are you sure? Don't you think there's still something you need to tell her? About that thing at school?*'

Chapter Fourteen

On the first morning in Mrs Johnson's house, Claire woke, thinking for a split second that she was still in Beech Cottage. Then she saw the flimsy white curtains at the window instead of her blue and pink chintz and at the same time heard the screech of the gulls outside. It was then she remembered.

'Ben,' she called out softly. There was a shape at the other side of the bed. He had gone into his own room at first last night; a small box room, their landlady had said apologetically, but at some stage during the early hours, she had become aware of the door opening. Just as she had been about to yell out, she'd heard his voice. 'I can't sleep, Mum.' Even though he was far too old to come into her bed, she had let him in and he had instantly fallen asleep on the far side. It had taken her much longer to do so herself.

There hadn't been time on the phone last night to tell Simon how she had found this place. It had all happened so quickly. The bricks. The dash into the car and then, just as they were about to check into a bed and breakfast in town, the phone call from Alex who wanted to know how she was doing. 'We're worried about you,' he had said. 'You've got to make allowances for Rosemarie; it's difficult for her.'

There had been no need to elaborate. Her friend, who lived and breathed for her social life, wasn't able to cope with tennis club members who disapproved of her friendship with the wife of a dangerous driver. 'She'll come round in a bit,' Alex had said in a voice that showed he was embarrassed. 'In the meantime, if you need somewhere to live, I know someone who could do with the rent. We don't have to give your background. I could just say you're between homes at the present.'

Her hurt at Rosemarie's reaction was mollified by Alex's kindness. 'I'm doing it because you're the innocent party in all this, just like Joanna.' His voice took on a terse tone. 'Simon should never have picked up his mobile. Everyone knows you just don't do that sort of thing any more.'

Meanwhile, the '*someone who could do with the rent*', transpired to be a well-turned out widow in her late fifties who lived in one of those tall white Regency houses in a seaside town that was, as she'd assured Simon, big enough to blend into without attracting too much attention. It was about half an hour from Exeter where Ben was at school and there was a direct bus service.

He'd caught it only this morning even though she'd offered to take him in on his first day. 'If anyone gives you any bother, you must go to the school office.'

He had stared at the ground. 'Are you sure I've got to go? I want to stay here and look after you.'

He'd become so protective in the last few days! It wasn't right. Parents were meant to be strong. 'Don't you worry about me. I've got my book to finish.'

It was true. Her current project – a children's book for a small publisher – was almost due to be handed in. Yet the thought of doing something as normal as work seemed impossible.

Claire wanted to roll over in bed and howl. How could Joanna, who had been so alive one minute, be dead the next? How could her new life with Simon, which had saved her from the misery of her marriage with Charlie, be so cruelly shattered? How could she be living in two rooms at the top of someone else's house, in a place she didn't know, and without any of her things?

Holding her hand over her own mouth so her sobs didn't escape and wake her son, Claire stumbled out of the room and down the small flight of stairs to the bathroom which Mrs Johnson, her new landlady, had pointed out the evening before. Shutting the door behind her, she sat on the edge of the bath feeling the cold lino underneath her toes, and letting the tears roll down her cheeks. After a while, she heard a quiet knock at the door. It was Mrs Johnson, still in her dressing gown at 9 a.m.; a pale blue silk one which reinforced the air of elegance from yesterday.

'My dear, I don't want to interfere but it sounds as though you might need a morning cup of tea.' She held out a mug. 'I don't know if you take sugar or not.'

Claire managed to shake her head through her sobs.

'That's good, because I'm almost out! Now you're welcome to take this back to your room or else you could, if you like, come downstairs and have a chat. It's up to you, dear.'

Mrs Johnson's tidy house with its daily polished coffee table and china dogs on the mantelpiece in the front room reserved for guests, was clearly too big for her to cope with on her own. The kitchen, she told Claire, was the only room she used now apart from the small sitting room in the middle of the house where she occasionally watched television. It had been fine when her husband had been alive but now it was very quiet. That was why she took in the occasional lodger which was how she knew Alex. He had been her husband's accountant and still gave her financial advice.

'Did he say why I am here?' Claire asked, cupping her hands round the fine bone china mug which had a picture of a cat on it.

Mrs Johnson shook her head. 'You don't need to tell me if you don't want to.'

'I'd rather not. Sorry.'

There was a flicker of apprehension in the other woman's eyes. 'I haven't done anything wrong,' Claire added quickly. 'It's just that ... well, my life's changed in a way I didn't expect. We need a bolthole but I'm not sure for how long.'

Mrs Johnson nodded understandably. 'So many marriages break up nowadays.'

Claire was about to put her right but something stopped her. If Mrs Johnson knew the truth, she might well demand that they left.

'But what about your things?' probed Mrs Johnson gently. 'Couldn't you bring anything with you?'

With a pang, Claire thought of her mother's lovely writing desk, not to mention her paintings and her jewellery, all of which had been left just like that. Was that how refugees felt when they had to suddenly up sticks and go? 'Alex and Rosemarie are looking after them for me,' she said. That wasn't quite true although Alex had said he would try and keep an eye on the house. It would have to be sold, of course. They couldn't possibly meet the mortgage repayments, which was another thing she'd have to sort out.

'Sometimes, you know,' said Mrs Johnson patting her hand in a rather startlingly familiar way, 'it's best not to think about it all at once. I found that when my husband died. Now why don't you go and get dressed and I'll get some breakfast ready. If I'm not mistaken, I can hear the sound of someone else getting up upstairs.' She beamed. 'It will be nice to cook for a young person again!'

Claire spent the day doing practical stuff. Phoning the bank to ask for an overdraft. Ringing the estate agent to organise a valuation of the house. Ringing Patrick to see if he could chase the Visitor paperwork that had been sent to the prison. Apparently, her security details were still being checked, Patrick explained.

Aware that these calls had to be kept from Mrs Johnson, she'd made them from her bedroom which was on the third floor, hoping she couldn't be heard.

Then she set out her paints on the small dressing table – the only surface in the room – and tried to work. The illustrations she'd been commissioned to write were about a small rainbow fairy. It was part of a series which had proved successful in the past but somehow she couldn't get the shapes of the wings right.

Giving up, she threw down the paintbrush, put her head round Ben's door, and suggested a walk along the sea front. Her son responded with a shake of the head so she went alone, conscious of a huge empty space beside her that should have been Simon. God how she missed him!

Yet as she walked down the high street, Claire felt a tinge of expectation in the air that possibly, she told herself, came from a seaside town where the end-of-summer tourists were still dawdling.

And then she saw it. The sea, stretching out before her as far as the eye could see, ending in an almost perfectly straight horizontal line. Walking down the concrete slope to the beach, Claire made for a rock along the groyne and sat, legs cupped by her arms, watching the waves lap against the beach. Picking up a pebble, she felt the smoothness and traced the pattern with her index finger.

When she and Charlie had moved down to Devon before Ben had been born, they had chosen to live in Exeter for his work. But now she wondered how she could have passed by the magnificence of these waves that licked her ankles and made her feel there was something beyond all this pain, after all.

Claire wasn't sure how long she had sat there for but at some point, she was aware of her skin goose-pimpling. Picking herself up, she reproached herself for having left Ben for so long in a strange place. She also needed to buy something for tea. Now as she headed towards the local supermarket, she passed a building which had struck her earlier on. It was a rather lovely Victorian building possessing a large green door and, on it, was an advertisement.

ART TEACHER NEEDED. TEMPORARY POSITION. APPLY WITHIN.

Opening the door before thinking, she found herself in a large cool hall which had another door leading off it marked 'Office'. A woman sat behind a desk surrounded by piles of paperwork; she raised her face as though she was surprised to see anyone. 'I wondered if you could tell me about the job,' Claire heard herself say. And then, because the woman appeared to look blank, she added, 'The art teacher job'.

'Goodness! Is the notice still up?'

Claire's heart sank. The position had been filled.

'We'd found someone,' said the woman 'but it so happens that she rang today to say her husband was being sent abroad and she was going with him. Extremely inconvenient it is too at the start of a new term!'

'I could do it.' Claire's words tumbled out in desperation. 'I'm an artist. I illustrate children's books.'

The woman looked more interested. 'You do? Where did you teach last?'

'I haven't. But I could.'

'You *are* qualified, aren't you?'

Claire found herself nodding.

'Wonderful! Why don't you fill in this form and get it back to us tomorrow. Between you and me, it's probably a formality as we're a bit desperate. Can you start next week?'

She shouldn't have lied about the teaching qualification. Claire knew that. But by the time she reached Mrs Johnson's smart black door with its brass knocker, she had justified her behaviour. She needed a regular income. It wasn't much but it would pay the rent. Maybe, if her agent could get her more commissions, she and Ben could make do until …

Claire didn't want to think that far. Just 'until' would do. Opening the door with the key Mrs Johnson had given them, she placed her outdoor shoes neatly in the hall (a house rule that had already been explained) and went up to find Ben. He should be back from school but he wasn't in his room. A flush of panic gripped her. Then the noise of the loo indicated his whereabouts and immediately she felt another flush, this time of relief. It had been like this ever since the night of The Accident; always fearing the worst.

When Ben came out, he held his finger to his lips. 'What?' she said but he indicated that she should follow him. Their rooms were on the top part of the house but there was another door, beyond the bathroom, which Mrs Johnson had told them was not part of their accommodation. To her shock, Ben was now opening it.

'I don't think we should,' she began and then stopped. It was the room of a child. Not a young child but not a teenager like Ben either. There was a single bed in one corner, a blue candlewick bedspread on it. On the desk were several Lego models and in the bookcase lining one length of the wall, were rows of old classics like *The Famous Five*. There was a calendar on the wall too, showing a picture of a steam engine on the month of August. The year was 1979.

'I wondered how long it would be before you found this,' said Mrs Johnson's voice behind them.

Claire burned with embarrassment. 'I'm so sorry ...'

'It was my fault, not Mum's.' Ben's voice cut in. 'I found it this afternoon when I was bored and I wanted to show her. I'm sorry.'

Mrs Johnson was looking at the Lego models as though she had never seen them before. 'That's all right. Boys are curious. My Derek was the same.' She looked back at Claire with eyes that seemed shiny. 'I've kept this room exactly the same since he died. Twelve, he was. Two months off his thirteenth birthday. He was killed by a driver who was overtaking his school bus, just off the main road.'

She spoke impassively as though describing an event which had nothing to do with her.

'I'm so sorry,' breathed Claire. Ben's face, she noticed, had gone taut and white. Don't say anything about Simon, she breathed.

'Was the driver on his mobile phone?' asked Ben.

'Goodness me.' Mrs Johnson laughed shortly. 'They didn't have them in those days. Right. Now who's for tea? I know you said you'd bought something but I've made a lovely shepherd's pie and it's too big just for me.'

At school earlier, Ben had heard the whispers before he saw the faces. That's the kid whose dad killed someone ... Poppy's mum died 'cos of that boy's stepdad ... someone said they were in the car ...

Then came the outright hostility. You can't play in our team. You're scum. My dad says yours has got blood on his hands. You can't sit here. This place is taken.

90

The one good thing was that Poppy wasn't at school. Maybe she'd never come back. In some ways, that would be easier.

Tell the school secretary if you're bullied, Mum had said. She had no idea. No idea at all.

Chapter Fifteen

By now, Simon was beginning to understand the pattern of the day. Up at 6.50 a.m. to get into the shower room first. Roll-call at 7.45 a.m. Work at 8.30 a.m. Lunch at 11.45. So early! Back to work at 2 p.m. 'Dinner' at 4.45 p.m. when the rest of the world was still in the office. Evenings spent reading in his room or trying to phone Claire. When he couldn't get through – either because her answerphone was on or because the queue was too long before roll-call – he slammed his fist against the wall. When he did, their conversation was low and desperate with the same questions and the same answers.

'Are you all right?'

'Yes.'

He didn't believe her.

'Do you still love me?'

'Of course.'

He had to believe that one or he might as well give up.

Then he'd make his way reluctantly back to G Hut where men sat outside or in their rooms, the doors open, playing cards, listening to music, having a smoke and talking, sometimes loudly and sometimes in low hushed tones as though planning something.

Since the incident in the Stores with the man in the Union Jack boxers, Simon had been nervous of bumping into him again alone. Initially he even considered avoiding the dining room but the waistband round his regulation Robin Hood green tracksuit bottoms was beginning to slacken. He had to eat, didn't he? Besides, what could this thug do in a public area?

A few days later, Simon went into lunch to find Union Jack man sitting at one of the tables near the entrance. His eyes locked with Simon's. Forcing himself to look back, he made a

Don't mess with me either look. Then he proceeded to help himself to squishy potatoes in a pool of oil, hoping no one else noticed his hands were shaking.

'Heard you had a bit of a barney with that one,' said a thin chap at the table where he sat down. 'Best keep your distance. He was in Wandsworth with that bloke whatshisname, who did that big Bond Street raid in 2000. Only got another four months to go and he's been telling everyone that if they don't do what he wants, he'll be waiting for them when they're out.'

Simon felt a nasty shiver run down his spine.

'He'll be wanting those trainers when he comes back tomorrow,' added another man. 'If I were you, mate. I'd give them to him on the quiet. It's not worth the aggro.'

Simon carefully prodded some small peas with his fork. 'Someone needs to make a stand,' he said carefully. 'I heard him talking on a mobile in the loo this morning.'

'For God's sake,' hissed the man. 'Do you want to get us all shipped out? There's some stuff in the place which you don't talk about. Get it?'

'Posh darkie,' sniffed a thin, mean-looking man as he watched Simon dab his mouth with a paper napkin.

Simon found himself reddening, just as he had during his early days at school when he was still learning to harden himself towards racist comments which would never be tolerated nowadays. In prison, however, anything went. 'Bloody nigger,' was another comment he'd received the previous day when he'd spent too long in the shower. 'Need to get all the black stuff off, do you?'

It had been on the tip of his tongue to point out that actually, he was of Indian heritage. Then he remembered his father's advice when he'd gone back after his first term at school. 'Don't let them get to you. Rise above it.

Still, it wasn't easy, especially as he was far better educated than nearly everyone else around him. Simon began to shake as the horror mounted inside his head. What kind of place had he got himself into?

He spent the rest of the day finishing off at Stores and then taking his 'dinner' back into his cell with him. You could do that when it was a sandwich day like it was today. Afterwards, partly to get out of the pad which was already rocking with Bob Marley not to mention fumes from a cigarette which was definitely not allowed, he went for a walk round the camp.

Almost immediately, he passed the chapel, another Portakabin, but this time painted in white with amateurish sunflowers. The Portakabin next to that was the music room, from which came the sound of someone on a keyboard and a guitar. Simon was reminded of a critical article he'd once read in the *Telegraph* about prisoners being allowed to pursue interests like music and art. Only now could he see that this was surely beneficial. What would the public have them do? Sew mailbags?

If only the library was open but someone said the librarian was away at the moment and besides, it was only open part-time anyway. 'Cuts,' his informer had added, ominously. The man, a tall, youngish, dark-haired chap who had an intelligent air, was known round the camp as *Mr I Didn't Do It*. Apparently when the library was open, he spent all his time there going through the legal shelf to prove his innocence in case he was lucky enough to be granted an appeal.

After that was another Portakabin bearing a sign asking if he could be a Listener. He read it curiously.

Are you good at listening to other people's problems?

Could you help someone see something in a different way?

If so, you might be right for our Listening Team. See the centre for details.

The centre was where they had to queue up from the outside – only the staff were allowed inside – and then speak to someone through a window above. A Listener, he mused. Rather like the Samaritans perhaps. Simon, who had been a Nightliner at university, quite liked the idea of that. Maybe he would follow that one up.

'*I'd have thought you could have done with someone to listen to YOU,*' cackled Joanna unexpectedly.

'Fuck off,' he said out loud. 'Just fuck off and leave me

94

alone, can you?'

Her voice unnerved him as he headed back now towards his hut in G block. The only phone that was working had a long queue outside so maybe he'd come back when it had cleared. There was nothing worse than having everyone listen into your conversation. On the other hand, he didn't have long. At 9 o'clock, their doors were locked and that was it until the keys jangled outside the following morning at 7 a.m.

This was something else he was still getting his head round. If it wasn't for the fact that he was locked in all night with a Bob Marley maniac, he could almost kid himself that he could walk out of this place any time he wanted.

Instinctively, he glanced up at the tall wall and the barbed wire above it that separated the camp from the B cat. prison next door and shivered. It was then that he heard the tannoy shouting for him. 'Mills. Number A1112CB. To your pad immediately.'

At the same time, he could hear urgent voices rising from his cell. What was up? Moving past the other men who were congregating in the corridor and looking at him, he felt a surge of apprehension. Oh God. His mattress was on the floor. A magazine lay on his bed; revealing a picture of a woman smiling provocatively; her breasts exposed and legs parted. There was a staple through her red silk crutch. It was the porn magazine that his cell-mate had been pleasuring himself with last night.

'Mills,' repeated the officer, a look of disgust on her face. 'Is this yours?'

'Of course it's not.' He felt a shudder of revulsion. 'I don't look at that sort of thing.'

'Then why's it got your name on it?' demanded the officer.

Impossible.

'It's your handwriting.' The officer looked at him in a way that suggested he had something dirty on his face. 'We've checked.'

That was ridiculous. He picked it up, not wanting to touch it but needing to scrutinise the name on the front more carefully.

It was true. It looked exactly like his signature – the S shaped in that distinctive way and the M blending into the first name in a manner he had cultivated years ago when creating a unique signature had seemed so important.

'It looks like mine but it's not.' He went red as he said it, feeling guilty even though he wasn't.

There was a snort from his pad mate. 'That's what they all say.'

The prison officer was already filling in a form. 'You could get shipped out for this, you know.'

Simon felt a sickening lurch. Shipped out would mean being moved to a prison that wasn't open where he couldn't move around freely in the open air. 'But it wasn't me. I'm telling you. I've been set up.'

The officer had snapped his book shut. 'Let's see what the duty guv has to say to that, shall we?'

Forget the duty guv. What about Claire? Supposing she thought he'd been looking at that stuff. Simon wanted to be sick; wanted to go into the bathroom and throw up all over the floor but instead, he waited until the prison officer had left.

'What are you in for?' he asked his cell-mate in a dangerously low tone.

'What business is it of yours?' Kevin scowled back. It wasn't considered 'good form' in the prison to ask someone what they were in for.

Simon took hold of the man's collar and pulled it towards him, hardly knowing what he was doing. 'I said what are you in for?' He became aware that a silent group was gathering at the door but he didn't care. Let them call the officer if they wanted. It might bring out the truth.

'Fraud,' croaked the man.

He pulled his collar tighter. 'What kind of fraud?'

'I got money ... from someone's building society account. Stop. You're hurting me.'

Simon gave his collar another wrench. 'How did you do it?'

The man's face was getting redder and he was gasping now for air. 'I forged someone's signature.'

96

'Exactly! Just like you forged mine. Right?'

'Prove it!' The man's eyes were black and beady and he was screwing up his mouth. Then before Simon realised what was happening, he felt something wet fly into his eye. The man had spat at him. In horror, he released the collar.

'Prove it,' repeated the little man. 'If you hadn't made such a fuss about my music, I wouldn't have done it. But you're getting on my nerves, Mills, and now they'll have to move you. Just you wait and see. It's how this place works. 'Sides, a little bird told me that you'd killed someone. That's a lot worse than fraud in my book.'

'*He has a point, Simon,*' tinkled Joanna. '*Don't you think? Maybe you'd better not ring Claire tonight after all. I've got a funny feeling that she might not understand.*'

At roll-call the next morning, Simon was informed that he had to report to the duty governor on the Friday. That was two whole days away. Two days in which he needed to persuade that horrible little cell-mate of his to come clean about his forgery. In the meantime, the little piece of scum had played his music until 5 a.m. which meant he was almost comatose from lack of sleep.

'*Little piece of scum?*' repeated Joanna. '*Goodness. You are becoming one of them, aren't you?*'

Thank God he had the gym to help him shut out her voice. Most of the men lived for their twice-weekly half hour slots. They sweated and groaned over huge machines as though to prove how tough they were. But as he went in, thinking how different this place was from the smart gym that he and Claire belonged to at home, he spotted him.

Mr Union Jack Boxers. Sitting on the bench, about to lift up a pair of dumbbells on either side. For an instant, Simon considered simply walking back out but the man had seen him. His eyes fixed on him as he raised the dumbbells revealing a pair of shimmering biceps. 'Got my trainers ready, have you, Mills?

He spoke as though it was no effort at all even though he

97

was holding these massive weights in his hands. 'You'd better. Hear you're already in trouble over a magazine. Pity if it happened again, wouldn't it?'

Suddenly Simon realised what had happened. It wasn't the music which had made his cell-mate Kevin plant the porn under Simon's mattress. It was Union Jack who had somehow forced him to do it, probably through intimidation.

He moved towards him but before he could get there, there was a flash of black jogging bottoms and a gold chain. 'What about the money you owe me for that fucking phone, Macdonald,' shouted a voice.

Before he could take in what was happening, Simon heard a shout of pain. Appalled, he watched as the man in black joggers snatched the dumb-bells out of Union Jack's hands and brought them down on the man's face. Within seconds, it resembled a bloody pulp, red rivulets dripping down onto the floor. Someone else screamed and then there was the sound of a loud bell overhead. Within seconds, three officers came running in but by then the man in black joggers had melted away, leaving a crowd of them, including Simon, on the fringes.

'What happened?' yelled one of the officers as another knelt down next to Union Jack, whose head was rolling in a strange way at the side.

'Dunno,' mumbled the chap next to him.

'Someone must have seen something,' demanded the officer, glaring at Simon.

He tried to speak but his lie came out cracked and dry. 'I was at the other end of the gym. I don't know.'

'Out, all of you.'

They filed out sheepishly leaving the officers to deal with Macdonald.

'Do you think he's dead?' Simon whispered to the tall, pale youth he'd spotted earlier.

'If he isn't, he ain't going to look very pretty.'

Someone else laughed. It was then he felt the nudge in his ribs. 'Thanks.' It was the man in black joggers and a gold chain. 'I won't forget it.'

No, Simon wanted to shout. Do forget it. I shouldn't have lied. I should have told them the truth. But somehow he found himself nodding curtly and walking back to Bob Marley and G hut.

The following day, he was summoned by the tannoy voice to the Centre where he was crisply informed that he was no longer required to visit the duty governor. No explanation was given. However, when he returned to G hut to change for work at Stores, he found his cell-mate gone.

'Shipped out for collaboration,' said a voice at the door. It was the man in the black joggers and gold chain. 'Said I'd see you all right, didn't I?' He clapped Simon on the back. 'Got to look after each other in this place. It's one of the rules.'

Chapter Sixteen

Years ago, before she'd even met Charlie, let alone Simon, Claire had considered teaching after art school. But then she'd got a job in the illustration department of a children's book publishers and one thing had led to another. When Ben was born, it seemed right to turn freelance.

But now, faced with a classroom of young eager children, each one with their hands up and desperate to get their warm little squat hands on the palettes of poster paints, she felt an unexpected buzz!

'Mrs Mills, Mrs Mills! Can I go first? Can I go first?'

'Mrs Mills? Are we going to eat those carrot heads?'

Yes, the little girl with the Chinese eyes in the front row could go first and no they weren't going to eat those carrot heads! They were going to use them to print funny shapes all over the large piece of paper on the wall. It was going to be a wall hanging and maybe, later, they might make a shell painting using the shells she'd collected on the beach.

By the end of the forty-minute session, she realised she hadn't thought of Simon once. It almost felt as though she'd been unfaithful.

'Been to see your dad in prison?'

'What's it like in your old man's cell?'

The taunts at school were endless.

He's not my father, Ben wanted to shout but instead, he ignored them. Even his friends kept their distance, hanging back as though he was tainted.

But Poppy still wasn't there. Someone said she'd left. Someone else said she'd died along with her stepmother although he knew this bit wasn't true.

He simply wanted to talk to her. She was the only person

who might be able to stop her dad from upsetting Mum. Then Poppy's dad would stop putting bricks through their window. He and Mum could go back to being on their own again without Simon and maybe, just maybe, Dad would come back.

After afternoon register, he slipped out, walking down the drive and waiting for someone to stop him. But no one did. Even if they rang home, no one would answer because Mum was at work.

'Return to Exeter please,' he said to the bus driver and then took his seat right at the very back. The old woman next to him glanced suspiciously at his school uniform.

The bus lurched sending him sideways into the old woman and she glanced at him as though it was his fault. That's what Mum thought even though she didn't say so. If he hadn't called Simon to ask for a lift home, The Accident would never have happened and then they could all be at home still and he might have been able to have asked Poppy out. It was so unfair! Of all the girls in school, she was the only one he fancied. So why did Simon have to go and fucking kill her stepmother?

Poppy lived in a village that only had a bus twice a day. Ben hadn't realised this until he asked two different people at the bus station. The first person was more interested in answering travel questions from a woman behind him in the queue and the second gave him the information in a voice that sounded as though he should have known the answer for himself.

Then, just as he got on the bus and put his hand in his pocket for change, he realised he'd spent it all on the journey to Exeter. Better to walk instead.

It took one hour and twenty minutes. There weren't any pavements and one driver nearly shaved his side, except that Ben had the presence of mind to jump into the hedgerow just in time. Actually, he rather liked walking. It settled his mind somehow and by the time he walked past a sign that said this was Poppy's village and found the house, which had a thatched roof and a front garden full of roses just like she'd said, he knew exactly what he was going to say.

101

But then she opened the door and all the words just went right out of his head.

'Are you sure your father isn't in?' was all he could manage as he followed her into the kitchen.

Poppy shook her head and her pink fringe swayed from side to side. 'Even when he is in, he's not really here.'

She jerked her head towards the pile of empty wine bottles slumped at the bottom of the recycling basket by the back door.

'Is that because of the accident?' He stopped, wishing he could take those words back.

The pink fringe swayed from side to side. 'You've got to be kidding. He was like that before she met him. Thought she could change him like the others but I could have told her to save her breath.'

'The others?'

Poppy was putting a teaspoon of de-caff into a mug. 'The other women before her. They didn't last long either.'

He held his breath as she put the coffee in front of her, not wanting to say he didn't drink coffee in case he broke the spell.

'I'm sorry about what happened,' he began.

She looked up sharply. 'Why? It wasn't your fault.'

He flushed. So she didn't blame him!

'Why haven't you come back to school?'

Poppy seemed to consider the question. 'No one's made me.'

'What about your real mum?'

She passed him a packet of sugar which had a brown surface as though someone had dipped a wet spoon in instead of pouring it out into a sugar bowl. 'She lives in Greece.'

She spoke as though it was perfectly normal for a girl to live with her father and a series of stepmothers and a mother who lived in Greece. On the wall behind her hung a black and white photograph of Joanna, leaning into her husband's shoulder, and smiling down at him as though willing him to go on.

'Did you get on with her?'

There was a shrug. 'She was all right.'

Poppy was watching him closely now, sipping her own coffee. She'd got another nose stud, he noticed. It was very small and blue and sparkly. Quite pretty above the little diamond one below. 'What about you?' she was saying. 'Do you get on with your stepfather?'

He tried to think clearly. Even before The Accident, he was never really clear on this one. 'He's all right. He makes Mum happy. At least he used to. But he's always telling me to do stuff. Put my clothes away. Bring down mugs from my bedroom. Take my shoes off when I come in. Mum says it's 'cos he's set in his ways.'

Poppy's fringe got excited. The little upward curve at the end of her nose seemed to shine with approval. 'That's just how I felt with Joanna. She was better than some of the others but she was always having a go at me too and I told her it was because she didn't have kids of her own. Then she'd cry and Dad would get mad at me even though he was always making her cry too.'

She put down her mug. 'The night it happened, they had a filthy row before they went out and she said that if he didn't stop drinking so much, she'd leave him. That scared him. I could tell because he gets this nervous twitch in his right hand. Then he said he wouldn't drink so he could drive back and she could get pissed instead.'

Ben didn't want to think about that even though this was what he'd come about. Instead, he tried to focus on Poppy's legs which were rather short and dumpy under that dress she was wearing.

She was looking at him now in an odd way and he realised with a start that she thought he was eyeing her up. 'Why are you here, Ben?'

There was nothing for it. 'The bricks. I'm here because of the bricks.'

The pink fringe moved from side to side. 'I don't get it.'

So he told her about the first brick which had smashed the sitting room window and then the second that had cut him. And then he told her about how they'd had to move house and were living in some old woman's place and how barmy Mrs Johnson was nice to him because he looked like her dead son.

'How did he die?' asked Poppy softly.

'I'm not sure,' he lied. 'Do you miss Joanna?'

The second bit came out in a rush to hide the fib.

'I can't really believe she's gone, to be honest.' Poppy looked around the kitchen as though expecting her stepmother to come in. 'Nor can Dad. He says it's like she's gone to visit her brother in Dubai like she did last year.'

Her black eyes turned towards him. He hadn't realised how black they were until that moment. 'Do you think Dad is throwing the bricks then?'

Now she said it out loud, it seemed silly to think of a grown man doing that. But who else would? 'He's left horrible messages on our phone. Told us that he'd get Simon when he comes out of prison. Mum's really upset.' There was a short silence. 'She's had to go out to work 'cos Simon's lost his job.'

Poppy bit her lip. 'Dad's staying late in the office. I don't think he wants to come back at night because Joanna's not here.'

'Aren't you lonely?'

'I like being on my own.'

'Me too.'

They looked at each other in a flash of recognition and then the moment passed. Desperately searching for something to say, he stood up to give himself time. The kitchen looked out onto a largish garden. There was a basket by one of the borders with a trowel lying next to it as though someone had just got up from weeding and was about to go back.

'She loved the garden,' said Poppy, following his train of thought. 'She was nearly late for dinner with your mum because she was trying to finish something out there before they went.'

He nodded. His mum had been like that when they'd had a garden. Then he looked through the pair of French windows which led to a conservatory, like the one Mum had loved in Beech Cottage. Suddenly he saw something propped up against one of the wicker chairs. 'Is that her guitar?' he asked.

104

Poppy jumped up. 'It's mine! Great isn't it? Dad gave it to me for my last birthday.' She was back within minutes, cradling a huge maroon-coloured Fender. 'I've been having lessons but I'm still struggling with some of the chords.'

She played something to demonstrate and it made Ben want to reach out and take it from her so he could show her how it was done. 'Do you play?'

He nodded eagerly. 'My guitar's at home. My real home. Waiting for someone to get it along with my other stuff. It's not as good as yours but I love it.'

'I'm really sorry. Here.' She gave the magnificent maroon beast to him. 'Show me.'

It was amazing how comforting it felt to feel his fingers move across the strings. Part of him also felt thrilled that she was so clearly impressed. 'Wow! You're amazing. Can you teach me how to do that?'

She moved her kitchen stool so she was next to him. He could breathe her in and his body ached to kiss her. If it hadn't been for Simon, he might have done that but now it was unthinkable. 'Hold it like this. No. Like this.' Uncertainly, he cupped her hand round the strings to show her. 'Pluck it with the plectrum. Lighter than that. That's right!'

Somehow, she produced a sound that wasn't too dissimilar from the one that his ear told him was OK. 'Now try this …'

It wasn't until they heard the car in the drive outside that either of them realised how long they must have been, sitting like that. 'Dad!' Poppy sprang to her feet. 'Through the back.' Her voice was urgent. 'Wait till he's in the house and then go round the front.' She touched his arm and her warm hand on his bare skin sent his spine tingling. 'I'll ask him about the bricks. And I'll tell him some of the other stuff like your mum being upset and you having to move.'

His mouth went dry. 'Don't tell him where we are.'

The pink fringe bobbed from side to side. 'I won't. But listen. If I go back to school, can you give me some lessons at breaktime?'

He nodded. At another time, this would have sent his heart

105

soaring in excitement and disbelief. Poppy, the most amazing girl at school, wanted him to give her guitar lessons!

'See you.'

They both heard the key turning in the lock. 'See you,' he repeated back.

And then he began the long walk home except that Mrs Johnson's house wasn't home because that had gone along with everything else. Yet somehow, after seeing Poppy, everything felt a lot better.

When he got back, Mum still wasn't back from work.

'She rang to say she had a staff meeting dear,' said Mrs Johnson who opened the door to him. 'Fancy a slice of Victoria sponge? She laughed gaily. 'My Derek's favourite! He used to suck the jam out first, you know, and I'd tell him off.'

Ben shifted awkwardly from one foot to the other. Didn't she realise he was fifteen, not five? Mum said she was just lonely but he reckoned she was a control freak. 'I'm not really hungry, thanks.'

His stomach rumbled in disagreement. 'You sound hungry,' pointed out Mrs Johnson. She sang the sentence so the 'hungry' bit went up at the end. 'What did you have for lunch?'

Chips and a Mars bar, he was about to say but Mrs Johnson didn't seem to expect a reply. 'You know,' she said, 'in a funny way you remind me of my Derek. You even look a bit like him.' She pointed to the photograph of the small freckly boy standing on the hall table with a dog in his arms.

That was crazy! He looked nothing like the boy. He was bigger for a start and he didn't have freckles and he'd always been hopeless at doing anything with Lego. 'I like the dog,' he managed. 'I've always wanted one.'

Mrs Johnson beamed. 'My Derek adored Mungo. Went everywhere together they did. When my boy died, Mungo slept on his bed for months, waiting for him to come back.' Her eyes grew misty. 'I've sometimes thought of getting another.'

Now she was talking! Ben nodded. 'Dad was going to get me a dog but then my parents split up.' His memory flashed back to the time he'd heard his father tell his mother that thing about loving her but not being *in* love with her any more. He'd been outside their bedroom door at the time, unable to sleep because of the rows.

Mrs Johnson nodded sadly. 'It must be very difficult for you, dear. I'm so sorry. But perhaps they might get back together.'

It suddenly occurred to him that she was talking about Simon. 'Mrs Johnson thinks we've split up,' his mother had said. 'We're going to have to let her think that instead of telling her the truth. You do understand that, don't you, Ben?'

No. He didn't. 'Simon's not my real dad,' he heard himself telling Mrs Johnson. 'He's my mum's new husband.'

The woman's grip on the plate appeared to waver. 'New husband. Oh dear. And they've split up already? How sad.'

What had he said? 'Sorry. I've got to go.'

He scurried back up to his 'boxroom', as Mrs Johnson called it. It was smaller than his old room but he liked it. It made him feel warm and cosy even though it wasn't cold outside yet.

Then his phone vibrated. Someone had texted him.

'Cn't wait to strt plyng gitar!'

She'd left the 'u' out of 'guitar' but maybe that was just an abbreviation. Ben felt a thrill go through him. He just wished he hadn't said that stuff to Mrs Johnson.

Chapter Seventeen

Horrendous as the gym incident had been, Simon was aware of a quiet respect afterwards. A couple of stocky men nodded at him when they passed and a massive bloke who had tattoos on every inch of visible skin actually told him to go before him in the dinner queue.

'It's 'cos you kept your trap shut,' Spencer informed him that night. 'Everyone thought that 'cos you're a solicitor, man, you'd grass.' He grinned. 'Doesn't help that you're a white chocolate button either!'

A 'white chocolate button' was, he knew, a name for someone who had mixed blood. It put you in a difficult position because you had to prove yourself to both sides of the fence.

But it was the 'grass' comment that really upset him. Simon couldn't get rid of that nasty crawling sensation below his ribs. He should have told the prison officer what had happened instead of being relieved that the man in Union Jack boxers now wouldn't be able to come after him for new trainers.

But it was too late now. Even if he did come clean, he'd have been hard-pushed to have identified the attacker who was also his saviour. He'd been wearing a white t-shirt and black jogging bottoms for a start – the kind that most of them wore in the gym. He'd had a tattoo on one arm which wasn't unusual in here although he couldn't remember if it was the left or the right. And his head was shaved which, again, wasn't uncommon. The only thing he could have said for certain was that he was white. Maybe it would be safer if he kept all this to himself without even telling Claire.

As for Kevin, he could only be grateful that he and Bob Marley were no longer there although he felt apprehensive about who would come in next. In this place, he'd learned, you had to share a cell for the first six months at least and then you got a cell of your own. It was a stage which they all yearned for. Once he'd glimpsed a single cell through the window and had felt a huge wave of envy for the lucky chap who was lying there on his bed with the door shut, listening to the music he wanted to listen to or simply enjoying the silence away from everyone else.

How funny that a space which was no bigger than their utility room should seem now like a palace! Then he remembered that the utility room belonged to the old house and that Claire and Ben were having to rent rooms in a strange town and immediately he began to feel the tightening in his chest.

It was at that stage when the door of his cell opened and Spencer had sauntered in, a big grin on his impeccably white teeth. 'Yo there, man! Guess where I've been told to kip out.'

He slung a black backpack on the floor and then went back in the corridor outside to bring in several cardboard boxes. 'Couldn't believe it when they said I was sharing with you. Cool, innit?'

Simon managed a nod, wondering why Spencer was so enthusiastic. It wasn't as though they had anything in common apart from the fact that they had arrived in the same van. 'You should be glad I'm kipping with you,' he said, looking up from the floor where he was bringing out a rather expensive looking stereo unit. 'I can look after you. Make sure you don't get into any more trouble.'

'Why?' Simon found himself saying. 'What do you want in return?'

Spencer's face clouded and for a second, Simon felt he'd made a terrible mistake. This place had already infected him. He was suspicious of a boy who was genuinely trying to help him. Then Spencer grinned and his white teeth flashed. 'You're learning quick, mate!' Slapping him on the shoulders, he roared with laughter and Simon could smell something strange on his breath. 'All I ask is that you give us a bit of advice about my case. You're a solicitor, aren't you? You might be able to get me out earlier.'

Simon's heart sank. This wasn't the first time that someone had latched onto the fact he used to be a solicitor and had asked his advice. 'I can't,' he said to Spencer, fighting back the lump in his throat. 'I've been struck off.'

The boy stared at him. 'You've been hit? Who did it, mate and I'll belt them one.'

That made him smile. 'No one hit me, Spencer. When I say I've struck off, it's because the Law Society decided I wasn't fit enough to practise any more.' It didn't feel real saying the words.

'Practise?' Spencer's face was even more troubled. 'Wasn't you any good then?'

'It's an expression that means I can't work any more as a solicitor.'

Spencer waved his hand as though this was irrelevant. 'Yeah but they can't stop you giving advice, can they? Take this.' He pulled out a letter from the back pocket of his jeans and waved it in front of him. 'This is from my brief like and I don't understand a word of it.'

Simon scanned it quickly. It appeared that Spencer's wish to launch an appeal was unrealistic.

'I still don't get it.' Spencer was frowning over the letter. 'What does this say?' He jabbed a chubby index finger at the phrase 'reasonable doubt' and Simon suddenly realised something.

'Mind if I ask you something, Spencer?'

The boy's eyes hardened. 'Depends what you're going to say.'

'Did anyone teach you to read at school?'

A shadow of something – embarrassment – flitted across his face. 'I told yer in the van. I used to bunk off.'

'Up trees, as I remember!' Simon said teasingly.

'Yeah.' The boy's face relaxed and then he gave Simon another slap on the shoulder. 'Hey, if you can't be my solicitor, I've just thought of something else you could do for me. You could teach me to read and write.' His eyes were shining. 'Go on, man. '

110

'What about Education? Isn't there a class for that?'

'Yeah but it's going to make me feel stupid 'cos the others will laugh at me 'cos I don't know nuffing. But if you helped me, I could go into one of them classes and then they'd all be surprised 'cos I could do it. Go on, mate. If you do, I'll make sure no one dares to do anything to hurt you in this place. Let me know when I get back from my piss test.'

'Piss test?'

'If you're in for drugs, they have to check your piss to make sure you're not using any more. Blimey, man, you don't know nothing, do you?'

Sometimes, Simon thought he would go mad. He was so close to the outside real world but also so far. All he had to do was walk out of the gates, ring for a taxi, and make his way back to Claire.

But if he did that, he'd be moved to a 'closed' prison where you couldn't walk around and quite possibly get a longer sentence. If it wasn't for teaching Spencer in the evenings and becoming a Listener, he really would have flipped.

The Listener training was done, rather to his surprise, by a Samaritan who came in for two hours a month. As a university Nightliner, he'd done a 12-hour night stint once a month to help students with problems. He'd enjoyed it even though there were nights when no one called.

Here, the training was not dissimilar. You were meant to listen rather than talk but if the situation required it, you could add your own views providing they were guidelines rather than instructions. There were role plays too and advice on how the system worked. Basically, there was a list of Listeners' hut numbers up on the board and anyone could contact them to arrange an appointment.

The Samaritan was an earnest young man who had a small gold earring in his left ear. 'A Nightliner, you say,' he commented when Simon told him. 'You'll find the problems here very different from students at uni.'

Simon almost felt tempted to tell him about his own stuff but was worried that the earnest young Samaritan might not think he was suitable for a Listener role if he couldn't sort himself out.

'I had a bloke in here the other month who'd just found out he had a son he didn't know about. He was so thrilled that he went out and bought the kid a bike.'

Simon got a nasty feeling of premonition.

'The kid took it out on Boxing Day and rode it along the canal. Fell in and got drowned. Our bloke felt responsible.'

It was too much to take in. 'What did you say?'

The earnest young man gave him a searching look. 'What would *you* say?'

Simon thought for a minute. 'I think I'd tell him that kids have accidents sometimes and that it wasn't his fault. I might say that at least the two of them had known each other and that this would have meant a lot to his son.'

The Samaritan nodded. 'I think you'll do.'

The training also involved other men who'd already done their training, including one of the orderlies who was an albino with pale hair, white eyebrows, pink-framed glasses, and a negroid face. He was known as Bino – it rhymed with Beano – but didn't seem offended by this. Simon had learned on his first day that orderlies were prisoners who were considered suitable to help with certain departments in the prison such as the library or the Education office.

It was a privilege to become an orderly because you were treated with more respect by staff and some of the men, although others were jealous of your elevated status. You also earned an extra fiver a week. Bino was the library orderly – something Simon would have really loved even though the library was only open three days a week (when there was a librarian, that was) and had a limited number of books.

'Are you on for tomorrow night?' Bino was studying the rota in front of him. 'Only we've had someone shipped out at the last minute so we've got a gap.'

A Listener who had done something wrong and had therefore been moved to another prison? Simon wanted to ask what he'd done but stopped in time. 'Tomorrow?' He tried to think. At first, he'd counted every day as it passed and ticked them off in the chart he had made on a scrap piece of paper. But now the days were beginning to blend into one. 'That's fine.'

'Great.' The albino nodded energetically. 'Good luck.'

Evenings were a strange time in Freetown. Those who had not been there long enough to go out of the prison during the day, either on community work or on full-time jobs, often became stir crazy. They listened with longing to stories of mates who came back with tales of the outside. Someone in Simon's hut was working in a charity shop in Clacton-on-Sea and he'd managed to chat up one of the customers and take the girl out to lunch.

This was strictly against the rules. For a start, you were meant to work behind the shop bagging up items and not serving at the counter although, from what Simon could gather, charity shops were often so short of staff that this didn't always happen. Meeting women when you were out of prison for the day – especially on a Saturday if prisoners had earned the right to a day release in order to prepare themselves for eventual full-time release – was risky. Another chap in Simon's hut had told them how he had met this 'fantastic bird' in a pub and taken her number, promising to call her the following weekend. 'I had to make up some excuse not to give her my number,' he said ruefully. 'I could hardly give her the prison switchboard, could I?'

It was these kinds of stories, the pale man in glasses warned Simon, that he might hear as a Listener. He would also get men who were wracked with worry in case their wives went off with someone else while they were inside. Simon had silently winced at this. Was it possible that Claire might do that? No. Of course not. Yet there were two men on his hut whose wives had started divorce proceedings. Had their husbands trusted them too?

He'd feel better, he told himself as he headed for his first shift in the Listeners' Hut (a brightly coloured Portakabin which had daubing on the outside), when Claire was allowed a visit. Only another week now and then the paperwork should be through. If she hadn't made a mistake over one digit in her national insurance number, for the security check, she would have been here earlier. Part of him couldn't help feeling cross with her for getting it wrong. Supposing she had done it on purpose to delay her visit? No.

'*Why not?*' chirped Joanna. '*I might have done the same. It can't be easy for her to know she's now married to a murderer?*'

Why wouldn't she go away? Sometimes, for days, she was silent and he thought he'd got the nightmares out of his system but here she was again. Holding his hands over both ears to shut her out, Simon arrived at the Listeners' Hut. It was very small; about the size of his garden shed at home. Someone had put home-made posters on the walls depicting furrowed-browed men and balloons coming out of their heads, and the phrase *It's good to talk*.

Maybe, thought Simon, no one would come. In a way, it would be a relief. Who was he to think he could give advice to someone else? Hang on. There were footsteps. Someone opening the door. It was a young man – the one whom he'd noticed before, about Ben's age. He looked nervously at Simon. 'Have I come to the right place?'

Simon nodded nervously. 'Please. Take a seat.'

The boy perched on the edge. 'I've never done this before. Been to a counsellor, I mean.'

Then he put his head in his hands and began to weep. 'I shouldn't be here. It's not my fault.'

How many times had Simon heard that in the camp? 'Why don't you tell me about it,' he said gently. 'Start at the beginning.'

The boy's name was Will. He had been a politics student at a university in the Midlands. One evening, he'd gone out for a drink with his mates. They'd had about four pints each.

'We were about to go,' he said raising his eyes, red from the effort of talking, 'when this man barged up to me and said he was going to stab me with a knife. I didn't know him from Adam, honest. I thought he was crazy and I was scared he was going to hurt me or my girlfriend. He was a big bloke with tattoos and a vest and I didn't think I stood a chance.'

The boy was talking so fast that Simon had to concentrate hard. 'He was coming towards me so I pushed him as hard as I could.' His eyes implored Simon to understand. 'I didn't mean to hurt him – just defend myself. He fell backwards and there was this awful shattering sound of glass. I hadn't realised there was a window behind him and he'd fallen right through it. Someone called an ambulance and then some of this man's friends began telling the police that I had attacked their friend. I tried to explain but this policeman took me down to the station and I had to spend the night in a cell ...'

Simon wanted to put his arms around him but the pale man with glasses had said this wasn't a good idea. Sympathise, he had said, but don't touch in case you get accused of something. 'That happened to me,' he said quietly. 'Being put in a cell without expecting it. Awful, isn't it?'

The boy looked up. 'I couldn't believe it. But the worst thing was ringing Mum. She found me a solicitor who did Legal Aid through Yellow Pages because we didn't know where else to go and he got me out the next morning. It took another four months until I had to go to court but I wasn't that worried because my solicitor said I'd get off when the truth was told. But the judge was this old man who didn't seem to like the fact I was reading politics. And because this chap who got thrown through the window had to have 32 stitches, I was given a year's sentence.'

Simon silently groaned.

'I'm so sorry.' He searched for the right words. 'When are you likely to be released?'

The boy rubbed his eyes. 'Six months with any luck. My tutor at uni was really supportive and said he'd hold my place open for me but I'm scared my girlfriend won't wait for me. I mean, who wants a boyfriend with a record? Her parents are really shocked. And even if I get a degree, I'll have to put down my record when I apply for jobs. I'm ruined before I start.'

'Not necessarily,' said Simon trying to sound assuring.

But it was true. It was a story he'd already heard over and over again in his short time here. Men of previously good character were damned if they applied for most jobs with any standing because of their record. He'd also heard the phrase 'It wasn't my fault' or 'They made a mistake' so often that he no longer believed it himself. But this lad seemed different.

'Thanks,' said the boy getting up. 'It really helped to talk.'

Really? Simon felt he'd been useless. Maybe he wasn't any good at this listening stuff. But the following morning at breakfast, the boy made a place for him at the table and told someone else that the Listener service had really helped him which in turn, made Simon feel better about his next stint which was due to come up the following week. And then, when he queued up for his post the next day, he found a letter to say that Claire's visit had been approved and that she was coming the following Sunday.

It was different and yet the same as her visit at Holdfast. Different because the atmosphere was slightly more relaxed in the visiting room where the officers didn't stand by their tables but hovered at the main door in case anyone tried to make a dash for it.

Some hope! Someone from the hut next door had just walked out last Saturday by not coming back from a home visit. Then, rumour had it, he had turned himself in and got moved to a stricter prison for his trouble.

Yet this visit also felt the same as the last, because Claire looked terrified and he felt like a heel for putting her in this position.

When he first saw her, walking towards him in the visiting room, he almost didn't recognise her. She'd had her hair cut slightly shorter and was wearing a pale orange lipstick, instead of her usual pink which he preferred. He tried to brush her cheek and then hesitated in case he was told off like last time. By the time he realised the men around him were hugging their wives hello, it was too late.

She smoothed down her pale indigo cardigan as though it

116

was wrinkled. It was one he had never cared for particularly, partly because of a previous girlfriend who had only worn violet. Her voice was low as though she had a slightly sore throat. She smelt beautiful. God, she smelt beautiful. Every inch of him wanted to lean over and hold her. Instead, he was being forced to sit there stiffly like they'd had to at school during sixth form debates with local girls.

She leaned towards him and he wanted to kiss that sweet upturned nose. 'How are you, Simon?'

'OK.' He wanted to tell her so much but couldn't. The gym. The bloody pulp of a man. The threat from Union Jack shorts. It would only upset her. 'It's so good to see you,' he continued quickly. 'What about you? How's the new house?'

'Rooms,' she corrected him. 'They're OK.'

Was it his imagination or did her voice sound slightly brittle? 'And the job?' She'd told him about that in her last letter.

'I like it but it's tiring. Doesn't leave me much time to paint.'

He nodded. There was an art class here, he'd seen, but he had to wait to get to Education first. It didn't seem the right time to mention it.

'What about Ben?'

'He's gone back to school.'

'And has anyone said anything to him?'

'He won't talk about it when I ask but he's gone rather quiet.'

'So are you.'

He hadn't meant to say that but it came out.

'What do you expect, Simon? There were tears in her eyes. 'This place.' She looked around. 'It's awful. The other women are used to it. I heard them talking! Saying it was better than the other prisons their men had been in. We're stuck in two rooms and I can't even get back to Beech Cottage to get our stuff in case we're attacked. Everyone loved Joanna! We're the baddies in this.'

His throat suddenly developed a huge alien lump. 'I'm

sorry.'

There was a silence. 'Me too.' She reached out her hand. 'I shouldn't have said that stuff.'

'No. It's me who's got us into this mess.'

She didn't disagree so he proceeded to tell her about the Listening bit but left out the part about the gym dumbbells and the porn magazine. Then somehow, it was time to go. A crazy thought came into his head as he hugged his wife goodbye, breathing in her smell which reminded him of cinnamon instead of her usual Chanel. 'Do you ever hear her?'

'Who?' She was frowning.

'Joanna.' He felt really silly now. 'Talking in your head.'

'No.' She was eyeing him strangely now. 'Why? Do you?'

'Sometimes.'

She put out her hand to touch him. 'Maybe you ought to see someone, Simon. Is there a counsellor here?'

He wanted to laugh. 'Only me. I'm a Listener, remember?'

She gave him another hug but this time it seemed more like a hug that a mother would give a child. He didn't want to let her go.

'How's Hugh doing?' he said quietly.

Something flickered in her eyes. 'I don't know. But he's stopped phoning me, thank God.'

'Time,' roared the officer and then she was gone. Simon returned to his cell with a horrible feeling that the visit hadn't gone as well as he had hoped.

Chapter Eighteen

'I can't go back to visit him again,' thought Claire as she signed out along with the other visitors, including a couple in their mid sixties who had a bewildered look on their faces.

It had been horrible! Walking out of the Portakabin towards the Visitors' Car Park, you could almost imagine you were in an industrial estate containing those squat one-storey buildings and an automatic car barrier. But then you saw the black-trousered, white-shirted men and women bearing chains round their waists and stiff faces and you knew this was different.

Simon had been different too. He had looked quite rough – that stubble growth on his chin and those awful green track suit bottoms which the other men were wearing too. Even worse, he had smelt of perspiration when hugging her goodbye. Even if he'd been allowed to kiss her, she wouldn't have wanted him to.

Then there were the voices. If Simon really did think he was hearing Joanna, he needed a psychiatrist. Maybe she'd have a word with Patrick to see how she could go about getting that kind of help for him in prison.

At last she was back at the car. What a relief to get in and shut the door on this horrible place! Picking up her mobile which she'd hidden in the glove compartment, she found a missed call from Ben.

When she rang back, it went straight through to answerphone.

A picture of Simon came into her head. 'If you'd tried a bit harder with my son, this might not have happened,' she said out loud, banging the steering wheel in frustration. 'If you hadn't gone on about him taking his shoes off and spending his allowance, you might have forged some kind of relationship with him and then none of this would have happened.'

The elderly couple in the Hillman next to her were giving her strange looks, she now noticed. No wonder. Perhaps she was turning as crazy as her husband. She wound down the window to get some air.

'Excuse me.' The well-spoken woman getting out of the passenger seat was, at a guess, in her early sixties, wearing a navy blue woollen coat.

'I'm so sorry to bother you.' The woman's eyes searched hers. 'But I wondered if you could tell me what it is like in there?'

Was she one of those ghouls who went to prisons out of interest, Claire wondered? Or maybe – what a thought! – she was a victim?

'Our son's just been moved here, you see,' continued the woman. 'We were meant to be visiting him today but when we got here, he wouldn't see us.' Her eyes filled with tears. 'I think he's ashamed. But I want to know what it's like so I can imagine it.'

Poor things! Briefly, Claire described the Visitors' Room to her. 'I didn't see much else, to be honest. But the men all seemed fine.'

That wasn't strictly true.

'Do they give them enough to eat?'

'I'm sure they do.'

'He didn't hurt anyone you know.' The woman's voice rose. 'Someone at work asked him to do a favour so he did, not realising it was against the law.'

'I'm sorry.' She glanced at her watch. 'I have to go. My son is waiting ...'

As she said the words, she stopped, realising, too late, her insensitivity.

'Of course. Thank you, dear, for being so kind.'

Head bowed, the woman got back into her car. Without knowing it, the stranger had done her a favour. Of course she'd come back to see her husband again. How could she have thought otherwise?

* * *

120

'Why didn't you tell me?'

Her ex-husband's voice hit her as soon as she got out of the car at Mrs Johnson's. He was standing, next to his own car, arms folded; ready for her. 'Can you imagine how I felt when I went to the house and found it all boarded up? I thought something dreadful had happened.'

'It has.' She looked around, wondering where they could talk privately without having to take him into her bedroom inside.

'I know now.' Charlie's eyes softened for a minute and he ran his hand through his hair; a familiar gesture. It wasn't quite as thick and blond as it used to be but the realisation that she still found him attractive gave her a jolt. 'I got hold of Ben, thank God, and he told me. That's why I'm here.'

She felt a rush of relief. 'I've been trying to contact him since this morning. Where is he?'

'At a friend's. He said he'd be back by dinner.'

'Who?'

'Some girl called Peony or something. He's giving her a guitar lesson. Don't worry.'

Charlie never worried about something unless it was in Charlie world.

'What I want to know is why you didn't tell me that you'd left the house and moved into two rooms without so much as an email.'

He was getting cross now. That little tell-tale vein on his forehead was standing out the way it always used to. 'I thought you were in the States,' she began.

'We can get emails there, you know.'

'There's no need to be sarcastic.' To her horror, her eyes began to fill with tears. 'You were too far away to help and besides, why should I ask you to bail me out because my new husband had been put in prison for dangerous driving. It's up to me to sort out and ...'

'What did you say?'

He clutched at her arm and then, as though realising what he was doing, dropped it.

121

'I said it's up to me to sort out …'

'Before that.'

'Are you trying to punish me for leaving you?' She glared at him. 'OK. I'll say it again. My new husband has been jailed for death by dangerous driving. Ben must have told you.'

'No.' Charlie's face was very still. 'He didn't.'

'And he didn't mention the bricks?'

'What bricks?' Something dawned in his eyes. 'Is that why the windows were boarded up? Someone put a brick through your window?'

'Simon was driving some friends home.' Her voice was low. 'He picked up a call from Ben when he shouldn't have, and there was an accident. The woman in the car was killed.'

'My God.' Charlie's face was white. 'How awful.'

She could see he was horrified. Just as she would be if the positions were reversed. For a minute, she felt a wave of relief that she could share this nightmare with someone who knew her. For heaven's sake, they'd virtually grown up with each other. Bought their first house together. Had a baby together. Buried her mother together …

She stopped at the sound of a door opening. From the car, Claire could see Mrs Johnson coming out and waving from the porch. 'Who's that?' demanded Charlie ungraciously.

'My landlady. Sshh.' Briefly she nudged him. 'She doesn't know anything about it.'

Mrs Johnson was walking towards them now, a pleasant smile on her face and her apron flapping slightly in the breeze. 'I don't want to interfere, dear, but you're very welcome to bring your visitor in if you don't want to talk in the street.'

She beamed. 'My name is Jean. Jean Johnson.'

Charlie's innate good manners took over. 'Charlie Watson. Claire's first husband. Good to meet you.'

Mrs Johnson nodded as though she knew that already. 'Why don't you come in and talk in my sitting room. I need to go out anyway so you can have some privacy. I expect you've got quite a lot to talk about.'

* * *

'So your landlady really doesn't know?' asked Charlie. They were both sitting rather awkwardly opposite each other on matching maroon sofas and fluffy cushions to match. The mantelpiece was laden with china figures and the curtains were the thick, heavy kind that blocked out the sunlight as though it might be dangerous.

'No.' Claire looked away at a table which bore photographs of a small freckled boy, smiling at her. 'She thinks that Simon and I are temporarily separated.'

Charlie snorted. 'You could say that, I suppose. You won't go back to him after this, will you?'

'Why ever not?' His audacity shocked her.

'He's a murderer, Claire. How can you live with someone who killed someone else?'

Exactly what she had been asking herself since it happened. But now it all seemed clear. 'Because I love him. And because despite everything, he's a good, honest man who wouldn't look at another woman.'

He winced. Claire couldn't help taking pleasure from that. Despite everything, she still found it hard to accept that he could have been unfaithful. She would have lined up all the men in the world for that kind of thing and put Charlie at the end. Still might have if it hadn't been for his confession four years ago.

'He's restored my confidence,' she continued. 'And he tries to be a good stepfather to Ben ...'

'But they don't get on, do they?' He was bristling now. 'Ben's told me. Always criticising our son; telling him to do this and that.'

Claire felt a need to defend her husband. 'Being a step-parent isn't easy.'

'Nor is being an absent father.'

'Then you should have thought about that before you had an affair!'

As she spoke, Claire could hear her voice rising and, at the same time, the front door opening. If Mrs Johnson had had to go out, it hadn't been for long.

'Look.' Charlie's hands were reaching out towards her. 'I didn't come here for another argument. I was shocked, that's all, when I couldn't find you.'

'I'm sorry,' she heard herself saying. 'I should have said.'

'You had a lot to cope with. Moving house, feeling threatened, it couldn't have been easy.' She'd forgotten how his voice could make her feel it was all right even when it wasn't. 'I just want to tell you that I'm here if you need me. OK?' He looked around and his gaze settled on the china figures on the mantelpiece. 'I could find you somewhere else to live, if you like.'

'No.' It came out sharper than she had meant. 'Thank you. I've found a job to supplement our income.' She felt almost proud saying it. 'Teaching,' she added. 'I like it more than I thought possible.'

He nodded. 'Good for you, Claire.' Before she could realise what he was doing, he was moving towards her, brushing her cheek with his. It had been the first time they had touched for years! 'You know, I've always admired you, Claire, for your principles and although I don't think you're doing the right thing in standing by this man, I'm very moved. I only hope he realises how lucky he is.'

After Charlie left, Claire couldn't concentrate. Ignoring Mrs Johnson's 'you-can-tell-me-anything' smile, she simply thanked her landlady for allowing her to use the sitting room and went up to her room. Sitting down at the dressing table which acted as an impromptu desk, she tried to sketch the outline for the final page of the children's book she was working on but it wouldn't come.

Simon. Charlie. Charlie. Simon.

What, Claire mused, would her mother have made of Simon? She'd liked Charlie, although she often wondered what her mother might have said about Charlie's infidelity. Advised her to 'patch things up' perhaps? Her parents' generation had been good at that kind of thing. Indeed, she had never seen her own so much as hold hands. Was that the result of a past indiscretion or perhaps they didn't go in for showing affection either to each other or their daughter?

Certainly, they wouldn't have understood the all-engrossing passion that she and Simon had – something that had taken her by surprise from the moment that Simon's lips had first met hers.

Once, she had heard her father talk disparagingly about an older actor marrying a much younger actress. 'You can see what she gives him,' he had muttered. 'Why don't people realise that it's emotional compatibility that matters? Not physical.'

Was he right? Might she and Simon be weathering this storm more capably if their relationship had been founded on something more practical than pure and simple attraction? Quite possibly …

Nor, she suspected, would her parents have approved of what her father had often referred to as 'the cultural divide'. The irony was that Simon was almost more English than she was with his reverence towards the Royal Family and his correct public school manners.

No, the division came from the fact that he didn't have children. If anything, that was a far bigger chasm than a difference in nationality.

Maybe she'd be better off walking outside and clearing her head along the front. Amazing how the sea cleared her head and made her feel that everything else was insignificant compared with the waves that were lashing on the pebbly beach. It was high tide although that didn't stop holidaymakers sitting on the stones and pretending it was summer instead of autumn.

She'd just have to get on like the waves which came in, smashed their heads on the beach, and went out again before returning for more. Get on. That's all. And she would.

Ben couldn't concentrate on today's guitar lesson. Poppy wasn't a natural learner and it took every inch of his patience to go over the chords again and again. The effort was almost enough to distract him from being so close to her skin and smelling something that he couldn't identify but which was fresh and exciting.

People walking past in the park were beginning to stop by their bench and listen. He wished they would go away and leave them in peace but they couldn't go anywhere else. His room was too small and Mum or Mrs Johnson would only ask nosey questions. And they could hardly go to her house; not after what Simon had done.

'I talked to Dad about the bricks,' Poppy had said when they were arranging today's session. 'He said it wasn't him. But he went really red when I mentioned the phone calls. He seemed a bit surprised that you'd had to move too.'

'You didn't tell him where, did you?' Ben had asked, panicking.

'No, silly. I promised, didn't I?'

And then they'd met as agreed in the park and it had been great until his mobile had rung and it was Dad, wanting to know what the hell was going on because he'd come back from the States and turned up to take Ben out as a surprise and found the house boarded up.

So he'd told him to ring Mum and since then, all through this practice session in the park, he'd been waiting for her to call him for telling him off for putting Dad in touch. It was all such a mess.

But maybe, he thought as he gently put Poppy's fingers into position over the strings, this might be the break he'd been waiting for. Perhaps Dad and Mum might get back together now and then Simon could get out of their lives for ever.

Chapter Nineteen

Before marrying Claire, Simon would throw himself into work if something troubled him in his personal life. He had done the same when his parents had died.

Occasionally, there had been women who had hurt him. He had numbed the pain by arriving at the office at 6 a.m. and working steadily through the night if necessary. Such habits were not uncommon in London city practices so it did not attract a great deal of interest from his colleagues who frequently phoned home to get their wives to taxi over a clean shirt for the morning.

So Simon wasn't entirely surprised to find himself tidying up Stores long after his hours had finished in a bid to block out that strange taste of disappointment and unfulfillment after Claire's visit.

'What you doing here at this time, Mills?' demanded one of the officers making a regular security check.

'Tidying this lot up, sir.' Too late, he realised that the officer was a woman so to hide his embarrassment, he made a flamboyant gesture at the shelves behind him, track suits heaped on them in random sizes and trainers parted from their partners in odd sizes.

'Why?' Suspicion was written all over the officer's face. Simon often wondered what made a woman do this job. They weren't all butch as one might expect; this one was thin and scrawny and had a face like a small bird's.

'I like to get things in order. I'm not trying to steal anything if that's what you think.'

The face tightened.

'If you really want to know,' Simon continued, 'I'm trying to shut out other stuff in my mind. It helps me to do something simple and practical instead.'

Softening slightly, she nodded. 'OK. I won't report you then but you have to leave now. No one's allowed here after 4.30 p.m. and besides, it's nearly roll-call.'

Not for another fifteen minutes, he wanted to say but instead he nodded. 'Obey the rules, mate, and you'll be all right,' Spencer had told him. And he was right. Besides, after dinner, he had promised to give the boy another lesson which would kill another hour or two before bed.

'*Kill?*' tinkled Joanna. '*Rather poor choice of word, don't you think?*'

'Shut up,' muttered Simon as he marched back to his cell. 'Go away and leave me in peace, will you?'

Evenings, as Simon had already realised, were a strange, unreal time. The camp came to life when all the extra people streamed in at 5 p.m. off the white buses which had taken them to local community work in nearby towns. Some of the men were even permitted to use their own cars. However, they all had to be back by 5.30 pm for roll-call in the dining room.

Simon found this freedom extraordinary. 'Don't some of them just stay out and never come back?' he asked Spencer that evening when they were having a short break from discussing why 'their' meant something that belonged to a group of people and 'there' generally referred to a place.

Spencer threw him an 'are-you-stupid?' look. ''Course, man. But they always get picked up or else they hand themselves in like that geezer the other night and then they have to go to a closed prison. ''Snot worth it.'

Sometimes the brilliance of the prison system hit Simon with force. Making someone understand the importance of freedom like that was truly inspired. Indeed, he'd heard great things about governor number one even though he hadn't met him. That was another thing that Simon had learned. From the few prison dramas he had seen on television, he had always thought that there was only one governor. Now he had learned that there was a top governor or 'Guv' as the men referred to him and two others below him.

There was the sound of raucous laughter from the cell next door. The man who lived there – a weedy Mancunian, renowned for re-using other people's cigarette butts from outside the hut – had just started work as a driver so was probably regaling tales of his day to a jealous audience. Rumour had it that the Mancunian was in for throwing an electric fire in his girlfriend's bath some five years ago. He was now coming to the end of his sentence, most of which had been spent in Wandsworth.

'Do employers know that these men are in prison?' he asked Spencer.

''Course they do, mate. That's why we have Job Club.'

Simon had seen the sign but not realised what it meant.

'It's full of staff geezers who have contacts with places like charity shops and companies what need drivers,' sniffed Spencer. 'They get labour cheap and the geezers at this end get work. Then when they get out, they can say they've got experience like.'

Amazing. Why had he never stopped to think before what would happen to his client when he came out of prison?

'Can we do something else?' Spencer was still scratching his head over the 'theirs' and 'theres'. 'What I'd really like to do is write me own name.'

He couldn't even do that? Simon swallowed. 'Sure. If I write out a line of 'W's, you could copy them below. OK?

He glanced at his wall clock and its *Do Not Remove!* notice. If he was going to ring Claire, he ought to do so now before lock up but Spencer was now engrossed in his work. Besides, even if he did get through to Claire before curfew, what exactly would he say?

The letter came on the same day that he received the internal note from Education.

'*So you see,*' ended Claire's letter, '*it's almost impossible to drive up every week. It means leaving Ben for a full twelve hours and I think I need to be there for him, don't you? How about if I come up once a month instead? I was going to tell you this on the phone but you haven't called for ages. I expect there's a reason for it.'*

He put down the letter which succeeded in gently reproaching him for not calling, while allowing him a get-out.

'You don't want to talk,' tinkled Joanna, *'because you're ashamed of what you've done. Now how about opening that other letter: the one through internal post. You never know, they might be releasing you early. Only joking!'*

The letter was stamped Education at the top.

'Pleased to inform you ... space now available ... report to Education Admin ... need to inform your work party that you will be moving ...'

What did it mean about informing his work party?

'You have to get permission, mate, from Steve what runs Stores,' when he asked Spencer. 'Dunno why you want to go to Education. Haven't you had enough already?'

Yes, but you could always improve yourself. He'd also seen a poster advertising Spanish classes. Maybe he could do a degree. It would certainly help him when he got out. Spanish was considered a useful language in law.

The following morning he rose with a sense of something akin to excitement. He even found himself whistling in the shower. ''Sonly 6 o'clock, mate,' Spencer had grumbled when he'd got back. 'What's up? I was having this great dream about making out with two sisters and you've gone and ruined it, like.'

The image made Simon laugh out loud. He couldn't wait to get through breakfast even though someone had taken all the milk before him and there wasn't enough for his Rice Krispies (on his first day, he had requested muesli which had resulted in a scornful remark from the kitchen staff who were prisoners themselves).

By 8.00 am, he was standing outside the Education Portakabin before anyone else had arrived. Across the way, he could hear someone singing a hymn from the chapel and on the other side were the grunts and groans from men working out in the Gym.

Finally someone arrived to open up. Simon had seen the man before around camp but not realised until now, that he was in Education. Age-wise, he'd have put him at about 30 odd and he stood out by virtue of wearing a suit every day although the top button of his shirt was nearly always undone under a rather loud tie. Today it was peacock blue.

'Give me a minute, can you?' He nodded curtly at Simon as though he had no right to be early.

He went inside and Simon heard the door locking behind him. It was another ten minutes before he heard it being unlocked and by then, there was a queue of men behind him, jostling awkwardly from foot to foot and rustling little bits of paper, like his, declaring them, all eligible for full-time Education.

Someone behind him elbowed his way past. How rude. Irked, he followed. It took him a second to register his surroundings. There was a large table in the middle with chairs round it and, at the side, several small rooms with glass doors. The suit was already talking to the barger-in.

'*I wouldn't make a fuss if I were you,*' warned Joanna. '*That one's another lifer at the end of his sentence. Not someone to be messed with if you want my opinion.*'

For once, she had a point. Simon stood, waiting patiently for the door to open. Eventually, it was his turn. 'Yes?'

Simon gave him the suit his piece of paper. He almost felt as excited as he had done on the first day of his degree.

'Got permission from Stores?'

Simon nodded.

'You can start in two weeks.'

A wave of disappointment washed over him. 'Not until then?'

'No.'

He was writing something on another form. 'We've only got a vacancy on the numeracy class. Level Two.'

'But I've got a degree in law!' He tried to laugh. I was hoping to do one in Spanish.'

Now it was the turn of the open-necked man to laugh. 'Degree? You've been reading too many Jeffrey Archer books. Haven't you heard of cut-backs? We don't do degrees in prison any more – you're lucky if you can get an A-level class and, besides, the Spanish teacher isn't here any more.' He glanced at the timetable on the wall. 'You could do art, though if you want. It's part-time. Wednesday and Thursday mornings.'

Art? He'd always been hopeless at school but anything, anything, to relieve the monotony of handing out trainers.

'But you'll have to carry on at Stores or Kitchens for a bit. We'll let you know. OK?'

Simon sought out Spencer at lunch, aware he was becoming an unlikely confidante. 'Yeah. Heard the Spanish woman had a nervous breakdown after one of the geezers messed around in her class.'

'What kind of messing around?'

Spencer's eyes shifted from one side of the dining room to the other. 'Trust me, mate. You don't want to know.'

'But isn't there security if someone threatens the teachers?'

'Who said nothing about threatening? There are other ways of getting to them, you know. Still, you did get lucky with the art teacher.' Spencer gave a low whistle. 'That one's hot.'

'I've always wanted to draw,' Simon's voice came out more primly than he had meant.

'Yeah, well it ain't life-drawing, mate. Me brother tried to do that and got thrown out. He put himself up as a model.'

At that point, the man who had barged into the education office behind him took his seat at an adjoining table. '*Go on*,' hissed Joanna. '*Ask your friend what he's in for.*'

'What's that man over there in for?' enquired Simon.

Spencer barely lifted his head. 'You mean that chap with muscles who always pushes his way to the front of queues.' His voice was low. 'I don't even want to say his name, mate. But don't let your stepson near him during Visits. He's in for kiddy fiddling.'

*   *   *

132

The following Friday was his stint as a Listener. Already, word seemed to have got around that he was 'OK' and a couple of men had come up to him to say he'd helped 'sort their heads out'. It was a nice feeling.

'*Pity you can't do the same for yourself!*' tinkled Joanna but he ignored her. That really annoyed her. He could tell because she would sulk for a few hours before making another of her irritating comments.

That night, a new man came in, short and stocky with round glasses and a stomach that hung over his trousers. 'How can I help you?'

The man looked out of the window even though it was nearly dark. They often did this. It was as though looking somewhere else distanced them from what had really happened. 'I'm not a criminal,' the man began.

This was another common opening.

'But what would you do if you came home one day and found the missus in bed with another bloke?'

Simon stiffened. Every now and then a horrible image came into this head of Claire with Charlie. Even before he had gone into prison, he'd been unable to get rid of his jealousy. They had shared so many years together. Had a child.

'I'm not sure,' he answered truthfully.

'He was my best mate and he was fucking my wife behind my back so I belted him. Then the bloody geezer presses charges against me and I get GBH. Unfucking believable, isn't it?'

'Yes,' said Simon thoughtfully. 'It is.'

'So I've lost my home and I've lost my wife but do you know what I'm really upset about?'

'The children?' offered Simon. This again, was one of the common problems in the Listeners' Hut.

'The man made a gesture as though he was swatting a fly. 'Don't have any of those. It's my dog, I'm talking about. Slasher. He's a springer.' He grinned. 'I called him that 'cos it scares people but he's as soft as a baby really. The bitch doesn't want him so now they say he has to go into one of those refuge places.' The man's eyes moistened. 'Don't know how I can cope if they put him down 'cos that's what will happen if no one has him. I don't get out for another eighteen months. What am I going to do?'

Simon's mind drifted back to when Ben had first started asking for a dog. 'One day,' he and Claire had both said. One day.

'*It's not a bad idea, you know*,' said Joanna quietly without her usual tinkle. '*Might make the boy like you more when you get out, which would go down well with Claire.*'

'If you really get stuck,' he said quietly, 'I know someone who might have him on a temporary basis.'

'Really?'

'I'm not promising.' Simon tried to speak carefully. 'But I'll see what I can do. By the way, why is he called Slasher?'

The man's eyes shifted. 'It's a kind of joke. I used to do things with knives but I've changed now. Honest. All I want is to make sure that my dog has a good home.' His face tightened. 'You going to help me or not?'

134

Chapter Twenty

Claire was so cross that she could hardly think straight. What was Simon thinking of? It was all very well for him to be stuck in cloud cuckoo land in a place where he didn't worry about how to pay the rent or where Ben was (he'd *promised* to be back by now) but she had to live the real life. And now he was suggesting they had a dog!

Claire said as much – and more – to her husband when he rang that evening. He hadn't called before, he'd said (a slightly apologetic tone to his voice), because the queues were so long. Am I not worth queuing for, she wanted to ask, but then he had launched into this sorry tale about a springer who was about to go into a home unless someone could look after him 'just' for eighteen months.

'A dog?' asked Ben who had chosen that moment to come back and overheard her on the mobile. His entire face lit up in a way she hadn't seen for months. 'We're going to get a dog?'

'No!' She didn't mean to snap so sharply. 'We're not going to get a dog. Simon has met someone who needs someone to look after their springer. But it's not happening.'

Her son's face creased with disappointment. 'Why not?'

'Listen,' said Simon urgently over the terrible noise in the background. 'I've got to go. Someone's hassling me for the phone. Don't make up your mind right now. Think about it.'

He was gone. 'Don't look at me like that,' she said more softly to Ben who had put on his crestfallen look. 'You're not allowed to have dogs in rented accommodation. And, besides, who would look after it? I'm at work now four days a week.'

'I could walk it. And you could come back during your lunch-hour.'

This was all Simon's fault. A dog on top of these voices he

still heard. Maybe her husband really was losing his mind.

The following day – the last day of the summer holidays – Ben woke her up, a big grin on his face. 'I've spoken to Mrs Johnson and she's all right about it.'

Sleepily, she turned over, checking the alarm clock. 7.30! She should have been up by now to finish that outline for her publishers, not to mention ringing the estate agents about the house going on the market. Money was getting really tight now without Simon's salary.

'All right about what?' she mumbled, pulling on her dressing gown.

'The dog!' Ben's face was shining. 'She says she really misses her old Mungo and that it would be lovely to have the company again. She even said we could put his basket in the kitchen.'

Claire was fully awake now. 'Let's get this straight. You asked our landlady, without my permission, if you could get a dog?'

Ben nodded.

'And even if she agreed, how do you think we're going to pay for the food and the vet bills, and heaven knows what else?'

His face fell. 'I didn't know it cost anything.'

Why were teenagers so adult one minute and such kids the next? Simon was right! They had to choose between one or the other.

'I'm sorry, darling. But it's not on. I just can't take on any more responsibilities after what's happened. You do understand, don't you?'

He nodded. 'S'pose so.'

Claire managed to get hold of the estate agents on the way to work. Yes, they had got her paperwork now and it would go on the market today if she wanted it. Relief was mixed with agony at the thought of someone else living in Beech Cottage with its lovely beams and little paved garden.

'Would you like to go on our mailing list so you can find

136

somewhere else?' the girl had asked.

'Not yet, thanks.' She didn't want to say what she and Simon had already decided. Even when he was Out, they would have to rent because they might need the money from the house to live off until Simon found another job. She didn't even want to think about that stage yet or tackle the nagging question in her head about how Simon was going to work now he'd been struck off.

The phone call to the estate agent almost made her late for work. 'Work!' How odd it seemed to say that word. Claire hadn't been out of the house to work for years; not since the days before Ben had been born. Even during those few years on her own as a single mother, she had managed to keep going with her earnings as a freelance artist and also with the maintenance that Charlie religiously paid. He was very good. She couldn't fault him for that.

Now, however, she was having do her own stuff as well as her art teacher role. Yet in the short time she'd been at the school, she'd been surprised at how nice it was to talk to others and share coffee breaks.

Anything to block out the emptiness of not having Simon and the *supposing I had stayed married to Charlie* thoughts that wouldn't leave her mind. Murder versus infidelity. Charlie's crime now seemed the lesser of two evils.

'Morning!' Debbie, the cheery receptionist, beamed at her. 'Just in time for a coffee.'

'Great. Thanks.' Claire took the seat opposite her.

'How's it going then?'

'I love it here.' Automatically, Claire glanced across the corridor towards the Art Room which had her name on it. CLAIRE MILLS. It made her feel as though she was someone else, with a clean slate.

'Got everything you need?'

This was one of the great things about private schools. Claire had friends who taught in the state sector who were always moaning about lack of funding which meant they didn't have enough paints or canvasses. 'I think so but if I don't ...'

'Just ask!' Debbie finished the sentence for her. Putting the coffee in front of Claire, she stretched out on her own chair and yawned. 'Don't know about you but I'm knackered! My hubby and I had a late night with friends and we went to bed far too late.'

Claire thought of her own evening which had consisted of staying up until 2 a.m. to get on with the children's book deadline after an unsettling conversation with Simon. 'I'm on my own so it's a bit different.'

Debbie's face softened even more. 'Poor you. I hadn't realised.'

'My husband lives in Essex at the moment,' Claire said carefully.

Debbie's eyes flickered. 'That can't be easy for you or your son.'

'It's not easy. In fact, it's rather complicated.' She sipped the coffee to give her time to think of something – anything – that would change the subject.

'Tell you what!' Debbie's face was gleaming now. 'Some of the staff are going out for an Indian in a couple of weeks. Why don't you come with us?'

Claire was taken by surprise. 'I'm not sure. That is, I don't think I can.' Desperately she tried to think of a plausible excuse. 'I like to stay in to make sure my son is back. He's only 15. It's a tricky age.'

Debbie's face was disappointed. 'Pity. Let me know if you change your mind.'

Claire stood up. 'Thanks for the offer anyway. I'd better get on now.'

'You're so conscientious! We're all very excited about having you here, you know. We've had loads of teachers before but never a real artist who illustrates proper books! Some of the parents are really impressed!'

Claire found herself humming as she checked the handouts she'd prepared for their new topic this week. They were going to start with the colours of the rainbow and then she was going to show her class of eight year olds how to make a wash and let the colours soak into each other.

There had been a lot of work recently in the academic press about the power of colour as a healer and it was true. When she looked at the green arcs, she instantly felt calmer inside. And the red one made her feel energetic.

As she walked back to Mrs Johnson's, Claire was surprised to find she had a spring in her step. Maybe she was finally beginning to adjust to the situation. She had a job. She and Ben had a home. Simon would be out in a few months, provided he behaved himself. (How odd that a prison sentence could so easily be cut in two!) Meanwhile there was this all around them ...

Claire was continually surprised to find how refreshing it was to live so close to the sea. It almost seemed like a guilty luxury to be able to walk briskly down the high street and find that the shops ended suddenly with an expanse of water that went on and on for ever. It was almost like falling off the end of the earth which seemed fitting, given that her real world had disintegrated.

Yet at the same time, the sea gave her a strength that was much more effective than the tablets the doctor had given her to 'help you through this'. Just watching the waves (which could be furiously violent one day, hitting her with force as she walked down the esplanade and yet deceptively peaceful at others), made her feel that her own situation was more bearable than she had previously thought. If the sea could go in and out with regularity, despite its mood swings, then so could she.

Claire also loved the little seaside shops with their jaunty picture postcards and sculptures and art. The town was clearly a magnet for local artists and this seemed to brush off on people's natures. There was a generally more relaxed air and a general bonhomie which made her feel that maybe everything was going to be all right after all. Then a heavy feeling seemed to cloud over the rest of her body. Joanna was dead. Nothing would bring her back.

'Hello!' The front door was already being opened and Mrs

Johnson was welcoming her in, wearing a different pinny from the morning. 'How was your day at work, dear?' Without pausing for an answer, she added, 'Fancy a bite of quiche? Your Ben's back and he's tucking in already.'

Slightly taken aback, Claire followed Mrs Johnson into her kitchen to find her son working his way through a large plate of quiche and broccoli which he had always refused to eat at home. 'That was my Derek's favourite,' said Mrs Johnson fondly. 'I dug out the recipe again – haven't made it for years.'

''Slovely,' said Ben, his mouth half-full. Claire shot him a look to say, 'Don't eat with your mouth open.'

'Here you are, dear.' Mrs Johnson passed her an over-large portion. 'That should fatten you up a bit.' She passed her eye over Claire's slender frame. 'If you don't mind me saying, you need building up. Now, before you say anything, please hear me out.'

By this time, Claire already had a mouthful of quiche so was unable to say anything anyway but she had a feeling she knew what was coming.

'Ben's talked to me about this dog that your husband wants you to have. It's only for a year or so, I gather, while his friend works abroad.'

Ben's face turned away from hers.

'I love dogs! I must have told you about Mungo. Like I said to your boy, he can have a corner in the kitchen for his basket and we can all take turns in walking him. He'll be great company for all of us and, besides,' her eyes misted, 'I don't like to think of a poor little dog being put into a home. Do you?'

This wasn't fair. They were ganging up on her. 'We can't afford it,' she began.

'Yes we can!' Ben's eyes were shining. 'I emailed Dad and he said he'd pay you more every month for the jabs and the food and that sort of stuff.'

Mrs Johnson made a slight noise. 'Very generous of him, I'd say, considering the circumstances.'

If only she knew!

'I'm not sure.'

140

'Please,' said Mrs Johnson and Ben together.

Claire found herself nodding. 'All right.' She turned to her landlady. 'If you're really sure.'

'My dear, you'd be doing me the most enormous favour. I can't tell you what it's meant to me to have you both with me. I feel as though I'm a proper family again. By the way, dear, what is the dog called? Ben didn't seem to know.'

Claire felt a crazy urge to laugh out loud. 'Slasher,' she said. 'He's a springer. I believe they're rather lively.'

Mrs Johnson's face fell but only for a second. 'Never mind, dear. I'm sure he will be fine. Perhaps we could call him 'Sher' for short. It sounds a bit friendlier, don't you think?'

She'd tell Simon if he called tonight. Maybe she'd write him a letter as well. If only she could email! When Simon had first gone Inside, she had naively asked for his email address. 'Taking the mickey, are you?' the officer had demanded at the other end of the line.

Talking of emails, she ought to check her inbox in case her agent had left a message. Hugh? Her finger shook on the mouse. What did he want?

Nervously, she opened the message.

I know you will be surprised to hear from me but I would like to meet to discuss certain matters. May I suggest a week on Saturday at 11 a.m.? We could meet outside the cathedral.

Her first reaction was to politely decline. Yet didn't she owe him? After all, her husband had been responsible for his wife's death.

'Yes,' she typed simply. 'I will be there.'

Ben waited until his mother went to her room to check her emails before making the call.

It went through immediately to answerphone.

'Dad, it's me. I think she's going to email you to say yes about the dog. Thanks so much. There's something else. I heard her having a bit of a row with Simon on the phone last night. I think she misses you, Dad. But don't say I said so, will you?'

141

Chapter Twenty-one

Claire wasn't pleased about the dog! She told him so on the phone, but in the background he could hear Ben getting all excited and calling out that it was the best thing he had ever done and thank you. This made Simon feel good about the boy for the first time in ages. Besides, as Mick, the dog's owner, had said, it was important for a woman on her own to have a dog. 'Slasher's a good judge of character. He'll get at anyone who threatens your missus. Just make sure he gets lots of walks. Springers need exercise.'

Since when had he started taking advice from a criminal? Still, it was done now. Mick had arranged for a friend to drop the dog off at Claire's and apparently even the landlady was besotted. But Claire's frosty tone made him wonder if he really had done the right thing.

Slasher's owner, meanwhile, went round telling everyone what a 'star' Simon was. It didn't do him any favours. 'Getting all cosy with Mick, I hear,' said one of the men in the dining room and someone else sniggered. Like many men who had never been in prison before, Simon had initially been scared that someone would make a pass. Wasn't homosexuality meant to be rampant in prison? But apart from Georgie – who had arrived out of the blue last month from another prison and whose chumminess ('Hello again, ducks!)' had made Simon a target for gay jokes – he'd seen little evidence so far.

Then, two weeks later, came a letter in Internal Mail. His paperwork had been accepted and he could start art classes on Wednesday and Thursday mornings! The rest of the time he'd be working in Kitchens. That meant with luck he'd avoid direct contact with unsavoury characters like the thick-set child molester. But in another way, he balked at the idea of taking on a fresh job.

Was this, he wondered, how Ben had felt about doing something new at school? Maybe he should have been more supportive of the boy ...

There were two kinds of kitchen duties. One team cooked and washed up for the men in the prison dining room (not to be confused with canteen). And the other cooked for prison staff in the other kitchen.

Simon had been picked for the latter kitchen. He'd heard enough about it to know what it entailed. You had to be there immediately after roll-call and if anyone slacked, they risked the wrath of Jill, the outside cook in charge, who called them all 'boyo'. Before he'd gone into prison, Simon would have been amazed to find out that the staff food was cooked by convicts. Supposing they put something in the food? But, from day one, he discovered that as soon as they began to prepare the menu for lunch, you almost forgot you were in a prison environment because you were all under pressure to prepare heaven knows how many pounds of potatoes or carrots.

It reminded Simon of a summer job he'd had at about Ben's age when he had been employed in a local wine bar to chop up vegetables for salad. He'd been sacked after a few weeks, he recalled to his shame, because he hadn't been quick enough. No chance of that now under Jill's watchful eye.

'Not got those onions sliced yet, boyo?' she yelled out to Georgie who had been employed in Kitchens for the past month. 'You've got five minutes or I'll put you on to chicken.'

'C'mon Jill, you know the sight of meat makes me feel sick,' pouted Georgie whose glossy black hair was tied back in a purple scrunchie.

'Then you'd better get moving, hadn't you? And take that lipstick off.'

Georgie tutted. 'We've been through this one before, ducks! The guv's told you. It's in the Human Rights. If I was a woman in the full sense of the word, you wouldn't be able to stop me wearing make-up. And by the way, if you ever want a lesson in

143

make-up techniques, you know where to come to.'

'Cheek of you! Less of the back chat or I'll get you moved to Sanitary.'

Simon soon learned that Jill's bark was worse than her bite. 'Got a posh one here, haven't we? Better put you on the front to serve out at dinner time especially if the guv's got guests. We had a judge here the other year. Did you know that?'

She went on to name a member of the judiciary who had been given a short sentence for persistent speeding even though he hadn't actually had an accident. 'Really charming he was. Even arranged for one of the boys to look round the Lords with one of those visitor passes. Don't suppose you've got connections, have you?'

Joanna tinkled. *'Clearly she doesn't know you've been struck off.'*

Not again. He'd thought she'd gone for a bit.

'Cat got your tongue?' Jill clucked. 'Tell you what. I'll put you on slicing chicken fillets instead.'

'You should have seen me on the slab, Simon,' purred Joanna in his ear. *'That stuff reminds me of my old self.'*

There was a loud crash as Simon dropped the metal tray. 'What did you do that for?' Jill stared at the chicken bits on the floor incredulously. 'You just knocked it right off the surface.'

'Sorry.' Simon felt he was going to be sick. 'I didn't mean to.'

'Blimey, ducks,' said Georgie, 'you're as white as a sheet. You all right?'

Simon's face felt hot and he felt small beads of cold sweat trickling down his shoulder blades. *'Sorry,'* trilled Joanna. *'Did I upset you then?'*

'Shut up,' Simon yelled. 'Just shut up.'

'There's no need to be like that, duck.'

'I wasn't talking to you.'

Jill was giving him a strange look. 'Listen, boyo. If it wasn't for the fact that we're up against it, I'd send you back to Stores. But it's all hands on deck this morning so you'd better get cracking. Pick up that chicken now and give them a good rinse.'

144

Simon crouched down next to the scattered fillets with traces of blood round the flesh. 'I can't,' he whispered. 'They remind me of the accident.'

Suddenly there was someone next to him. Someone who began gingerly picking up the bits. 'It's all right, ducks,' said Georgie's voice reassuringly. 'I don't like it either but we need to help each other in this place.'

Somehow, Simon got through the rest of that morning. By the time 'dinner' came, he was exhausted. The heat of the ovens was overpowering There'd been the effort in getting together the menu, and now he'd been put onto the shift that served the staff.

It was a strange set-up. Jill perched on a stool behind a cash machine and the food was set up on a heated buffet bar. From 11.45 onwards, staff began to arrive. Simon was behind the buffet bar together with Georgie, charged with dishing out the orders.

Simon was amazed at how much some of the officers ate. They thought nothing of ordering sausages and mash and then a portion of chips on top. The chicken curry went down well that day but every time he served out a portion, he felt nauseous.

'*Mind you,*' confided Joanna, '*I've often dropped something on the floor and then given it to party guests.*'

He ignored her, determined not to make another mistake. 'Here comes the guv,' hissed Jill. 'Act snappy, will you? Looks like he's brought a guest. '

Simon looked curiously. This wasn't the number one Guv whom he'd once seen about the camp. This one must be one of the others. He was a tall man with a square-shaped head and bright inquisitive eyes that darted everywhere. His guest was a stout man in a pin-striped suit and steel-frame glasses. Shit. It was a solicitor whom he'd dealt with once in London. Bending down, he pretended to do something to the carrots in the tray.

'Two portions of veg, please,' said the governor eying the chicken. 'That looks good. Would you recommend it?'

Simon gave a non-committal grunt. The solicitor whom he'd recognised glanced sharply at him. He had recognised him.

145

Simon was sure of it. As the pair made their way into the dining room, Simon saw the solicitor say something to the governor who then looked back at him.

'Know him, do you, ducks?'

Simon nodded.

'It happens sometimes. I met an old girlfriend here once. Not nice, is it? But the good news is that it makes you stronger. Honest. Besides, you've got your art class to look forward to on Wednesday, haven't you?'

The deal was that you were allowed time off from your work party twice a week to do something that was educational. Art fell into this category. Last year, there had been someone who had run writing workshops, apparently, but her contract had expired and there wasn't a budget to replace her.

'Budget' was a word that came up frequently. You had to make do with the limited stocks in the kitchen because of the budget. It wasn't worth complaining about the smallish portions you got to eat yourself in the prison dining room because of the budget. Lots of the men complained they were losing weight although, to Simon's mind, they could do with it. There were exceptions, clearly, and he'd been particularly struck that week by an older prisoner from Sri Lanka who hobbled around on a stick. He too, he'd told Simon, was going on the art workshop. 'If we'd been illiterate, we could have gone on to full-time education but there isn't any point,' he said with a wry smile. 'I obtained my degree many years ago.'

If it hadn't been against prison custom, Simon would have liked to have asked what he was in for.

'I am looking forward to commencing my art lessons,' said the older man as they walked to the Portakabin where the lessons were being held.

'So am I.' Simon thought about telling him that his wife was an artist and then thought better of it. It was best to keep one's private life as separate as possible; Spencer had taught him that.

'I thought perhaps, they might be cancelled,' continued the older man. 'There has been a lot of trouble in the press recently

146

about prisoners enjoying themselves too much.' He chuckled. 'These people ought to be here themselves and then they would see it is not easy.'

'You seem to know a lot about it,' Simon couldn't help asking.

'I keep abreast of current affairs. I was a professional, you see.'

He said this with a degree of pride. 'Mind me asking what you did?'

'I was an architect.' The words came out clipped and distinct. 'Unfortunately, I made a mistake with something without realising, which is why I am here.'

The sentence came out as though it had been rehearsed.

'It is not easy.' The old man sighed. 'Someone of my age should be retired by now. I was just one year off. That is all. Still, I do not have long now. Ah. Here we are.' He chuckled. 'I believe the art teacher is very pleasing on the eye.'

Simon held open the door of the Portakabin. How extraordinary! All around him were canvasses of paintings which were surely good enough to have been entered into the Royal Academy's Summer Exhibition – which he always made a point of going to. There was a stunning picture in blue of a lake which had trees brushing the water. Next to it was an outline of a man whose hooked nose and penetrative eyes almost cut through the canvas. Below were the words 'Self-portrait'.

'I believe the class is through here,' said his new friend, pointing to another door. They went through. There was a large table in the centre with chairs around it but only four 'students'. The art teacher's back was facing towards him and Simon gasped with shock. It was her! The same small frame, the same pre-Raphaelite auburn tresses cut slightly shorter, the violet cardigan she had bought the week before The Accident.

'Claire!' he gasped. 'What are you doing here?'

He ran towards her about to take her in his arms and then stopped. The woman turned. She was like Claire but her nose was more aquiline and her eyes deep-set.

147

'I'm sorry.' He wanted the ground to open up and suck him in. 'I thought you were … I thought you were someone else.'

Flushed with acute embarrassment, he became aware of someone giggling at the table. It happened to me the other day, he wanted to say. I met someone I knew. The governor's guest was someone I used to work with. So it's not really that impossible.

'That's all right.' Her voice was deeper than Claire's and he realised that her face was fuller. Even so, there was a remarkable similarity. 'Coincidences do happen in life. Now why don't you take a seat and I'll tell you what we're going to be doing today. Ever used charcoal before?'

'How did it go, mate?' asked Spencer when he got back.

'What?' He pretended to be cool. It was a trait that had been instilled years ago by his father, and then by school. If you admit you really liked something, someone, somewhere, would take it away from you.

Hadn't that already happened with Claire? He could tell from her voice on the phone and the lack of visits that she was drawing away from him. The only way he could cope with the pain was to pretend that he was losing interest in her too.

'The art lesson, mate. How did the art lesson go?'

'Oh that.' He waved his hand dismissively. 'OK. At least it was a change. I don't think I'm going to be much good myself.'

'You never know. Might make your fortune one day. Didn't you say the missus was an artist?'

'Yes.'

He didn't want to talk. Instead he needed to sit and think on his own. Caroline-Jane, the art teacher, had unnerved him and not just for her similarities to Claire. What made a woman like her come to a place like this? She went to the Dark Side too; the one where the rapists and murderers were. He couldn't even think about that.

'Got your Listening stuff tonight, have you?'

Simon nodded. He'd almost forgotten.

'So you don't mind if I have a couple of mates back here

148

while you're out?'

Nice of him to ask, really. 'That's fine.'

Spencer nodded. 'Great. See you later, man.'

He could have done without the Listeners hut tonight but he was on duty. Maybe no one would turn up and then he might go to the library if the librarian was back from sick leave. The last one had thrown in the job because of stress. Blast. Someone was coming.

'*Oh my God,*' gasped Joanna. '*It's the paedo. Rather you than me, darling.*'

Simon stared in horror at the thickset man who lumbered towards him. 'You the Listening bloke?'

He nodded.

'I need to talk to someone.'

Simon felt his mouth go dry with revulsion.

'OK. Sit down.'

'They won't let me go to my son's wedding.'

'I see.'

'And I want to know what I can do about it.'

The man was glaring at him as though he could bend the rules.

'Have you been through the proper channels?'

'The proper channels? You sound like one of 'them', mate. I've filled in all the paperwork if that's what you mean but they still won't let me go. They say I still pose a risk to the community. What can I do about it?'

'I'm not sure I'm the right person to talk to about this.'

'But you're a Listener, aren't you? I want to tell you what I've done to prove I'm not a risk any more. It wasn't much. I just …'

'No.' Simon stood up, feeling bile rising up in his stomach. 'I'm sorry. I need to find someone else for you to talk to. Now if you don't mind, I have to go.'

Chapter Twenty-two

Claire was outside the cathedral early, not wanting Hugh to be first. This way, she could compose herself before his arrival.

She hadn't told Simon about Hugh's email. But she had, rather stupidly she felt now, told Rosemarie. In a way it gave her an excuse to ring her friend. Even though Claire knew she should be hurt by her friend's lack of support, she couldn't believe that a long friendship like theirs could end just like that.

'Hugh wants me to meet him,' she'd said on the phone after some rather cool preliminaries from Rosemarie's end.

'How awful.' Her friend was clearly shocked. 'I hope you said no.'

'Actually, I agreed.'

'Rather you than me. The poor man is almost unhinged apparently.'

'Poor man?' This was too much. 'If he hadn't grabbed the wheel, Simon wouldn't have crashed.'

'That theory was dismissed in court, I believe.' Rosemarie's voice cut through any possibility of a reunion. 'But it *was* proved that your husband picked up his mobile which in turn caused Joanna's death. No wonder Hugh is at the end of his tether. Goodbye, Claire. I think it's best if we don't speak again for a while.'

The conversation still rang round Claire's head as she waited for Hugh. If it had been Rosemarie in her situation, she would have rallied round. Even Alex hadn't been in touch for ages. And now, out of pity and obligation, she had agreed to meet a man whom, according to her old friend, was verging on the edge of insanity. Claire's fingers closed around her mobile in her pocket. If he tried to hurt her, she'd call the police.

'Claire.'

She'd been so lost in her thoughts, leaning against the wall like that, that she'd failed to notice him looming up.

'Thanks for coming.' If it wasn't for his distinctive deep voice, she might not have recognised him. He'd shrunk since The Accident and his large frame was now half the width it used to be as well as hunched slightly. His face looked gaunt and his eyes empty. 'I appreciate it. There's a tea room I know here, across the green. Shall we go there?'

She nodded, not sure what to say. The waitress seemed to know Hugh and led them both to a table by the window. Outside, yellow leaves blew across the green and a woman was struggling to do up her coat in the wind that had set in. 'Joanna and I used to come here every Friday,' he said, passing her a menu. 'She used to like looking out of the window just like you are doing now.'

Claire swallowed. 'I'm sorry.'

He inclined his head. 'You might be wondering why I've asked you here.'

Again she was unable to speak.

'Joanna and I had a very passionate relationship.' He stopped as the waitress arrived to take their latte orders and then continued when she had gone. 'But we also had our ups and our downs.'

Gratefully, she found her voice. 'That's quite normal in a marriage.'

Hugh's eyebrows shot up. 'Is it? My first marriage was extremely calm; almost boring, one might say.'

Maybe that's why it broke up, she wanted to say.

'That night,' Hugh continued, looking out at the cathedral which loomed up at them despite its distance on the other side of the green, 'we had had a disagreement.'

Claire held her breath. Was Hugh going to admit that he had indeed grabbed the steering wheel? If so, maybe Simon could appeal! Maybe …

'And that's why I feel so guilty now.'

Yes! Yes!

'Is that why you grabbed the steering wheel?'

Instantly his face turned thunderous. 'I did no such thing. In court, I swore on the Bible. Do you think I would lie?'

The table next to them turned round at his raised voice. It was like being with a completely different man from a few minutes ago. 'No. No. Of course I don't,' said Claire, forcing her voice to sound soothing. She needed to get the truth out of him; if she wasn't careful, he might just walk out. 'I just don't understand why you feel guilty.'

His eyes hardened. 'It's because we never made up after the argument. Don't you see? And now it's too late.'

'Would it help you to tell me what the disagreement was about?' she asked gently.

Hugh looked as though he was going to say something but then stopped. 'I can't. It wouldn't be fair.'

She nodded, biting back the disappointment. The 'disagreement' might have been new evidence to show that Hugh's mind could have been disturbed that night.

'I also asked you here for two more reasons.' His hand reached out and brushed her arm as though they were old friends. 'I gather that you have had to move house.'

She nodded tightly. 'Bricks were thrown through our windows. We weren't safe.'

'It wasn't me. I wanted you to know that.'

'Then who was it?' She heard her voice turning harsh.

Hugh shrugged. 'Someone in the village? Joanna was very popular, you know.' His eyes grew dreamy. 'Always laughing with that distinctive tinkle of hers. She was brilliant with Poppy, you know. When my daughter wanted to move down here after yet another row with her mother, Joanna didn't hesitate in welcoming her.'

Claire swallowed another mouthful of latte. It seemed all she could do in the circumstances apart from nodding inanely. 'What I really wanted to know,' added Hugh, 'was whether you and your son are all right.'

She hadn't expected this. 'What do you mean?'

'I believe you no longer have any income coming in.'

'That was true but now I have found a job; teaching art at a local school.'

'Good for you. But where are you living?'

'In rented rooms. Not far from here.'

'You don't want to tell me where.'

She hesitated. 'Please don't take this the wrong way but we are having to keep it quiet. The bricks, you know ...'

Her voice tailed off with embarrassment. 'Please.' His hand touched hers again. 'I'm not offended. I do understand. But there is something else I need to talk to you about.'

She'd wondered what the second reason was. 'Your son. Ben. He is at school with my daughter Poppy.'

'Yes.' Had he forgotten how they had talked about that on the evening of The Accident?

'Did you know that they are seeing each other?'

'What?'

'He's giving her guitar lessons apparently, in the park after school.'

So that explained what he was doing! And to think she was worried that he was hanging out with a bad crowd.

'That's nice.'

'No.' His voice rose again to the thunder of before and again, the table looked round in alarm. 'It's not. I am not having my daughter seeing the stepson of a murderer. Do you hear?'

Someone at the table scraped their chair back as though to leave. The young waitress was already scurrying across the floor towards them. Claire stood up, her cheeks burning. 'I'm leaving now, Hugh, but I am going to say one thing first. My husband Simon is the kindest, most generous, loyal man I know. He made a mistake. A terrible mistake. And now he is paying for it. But if you ever try to hurt or harass my son or me again, I will report you to the police. Do you hear?'

She was still shaking when she got back to Mrs Johnson's house. No one was in and for a minute she almost wished that her landlady would bustle out of the kitchen, proffering coffee and homemade Victoria sponge to divert her from the sight of Hugh, shouting at her across the table of the tea shop, that vein

153

standing out on his forehead.

Then she saw the note.

Gone for walk on the front with Slasher.

It was in Ben's handwriting. The front! Sea air was just what she needed right now to blow the morning out of her head. Going back out of the door again, she headed down towards the esplanade. When Simon had been at home, they had often said they would spend more time at the coast but somehow they never had.

As she marched purposefully past the shops with their clotted cream adverts and the ice cream parlours which were getting ready to close for the winter, she wished they had. There was truly something magical about living by the sea with the sound of the seagulls screeching with laughter overhead. Now it was October – in fact, nearly November – dogs were allowed back on the beach again and she could see, in the distance, a tall boy throwing a red ball for a black–and-white dog. Ben and Slasher! Behind them an older woman was trying to keep up. Mrs Johnson! Claire felt a sense of being left out and walked even faster down the concrete slope to the beach by the lifeboat station.

'Isn't this fun!' Her landlady's eyes gleamed with excitement. 'I'd forgotten how wonderful it is to walk a dog on the beach. Pity he won't respond to his new name – Sher is so much friendlier isn't it? – But there you are.'

'Look, Mum! He's a brilliant catch. A real natural!'

Claire watched as her son sent the ball high in the air while Slasher, his eyes never leaving it for a moment, raced along the stones to catch it in his mouth.

'Won't that hurt his teeth?'

Mrs Johnson shook her head excitedly. 'Not if it's soft rubber like that one. I hope you don't mind but I bought it as a little present for them.'

Claire's eyes stung either from the salt or her words. 'You're very kind.'

Mrs Johnson took her arm. 'No dear. It's you who are kind to share your lives with a lonely old woman.'

Claire watched Ben throw the ball again. For the first time that she could remember since The Accident, he seemed happy and if his guitar sessions with Poppy helped, that was all the better. There was no way she was going to tell him not to see Poppy again. Hugh had no right to say that.

The routine of going to work was definitely helping, Claire realised. How she loved teaching! 'Mrs Mills, Mrs Mills,' called out one of her children from Class 4. 'Can you show me how to make lime green again?'

It made her feel useful and also gave her a thrill when she spotted potential talent in a small child. Jasper, who worked steadily and quietly in the corner, had an astonishing gift for sketching outlines which went far beyond his years.

To her surprise, Claire found she enjoyed the company of the other staff. They usually brought sandwiches to the staff room at lunchtime and after a few awkward questions about her marital status, she managed to convey the idea that she was amicably separated from her husband. So when she mentioned without thinking that she was visiting him in a week's time, and someone said, 'You're still on good terms then?' She had been able to nod before deftly changing the subject.

The invitations to join their various social events had petered out now she had refused them so many times. Ironically, Simon was hurt because she 'didn't visit enough'.

'Ben's made friends with some boys from a local band. I don't want to leave him too long.'

'But you're still coming next week?'

'Yes. Charlie's having him.'

There was a pause. 'I see. So he knows about me being Inside.'

'I had to tell him.' She felt her skin getting hot. 'He heard through Ben and wanted to know if there was anything he could do.'

'Very nice of him.'

This was ridiculous! Simon had had goodness knows how many girlfriends whereas she'd just had the one long marriage.

155

There was no reason for him to be jealous.

'He's only trying to help out. I'm going to drop Ben off on the way.'

'So you'll see him then.'

'Only for a few minutes.'

There was the sound of someone shouting in the background. 'I've got to go.' Simon sounded fed-up. 'Someone's set the fire alarm off again and we've got an emergency roll-call. I'll try and ring you tomorrow.'

The phone went dead, leaving her standing there and looking at the receiver. His tone implied that setting the fire alarm off was not a one-off occurrence. And the roll-call bit made him sound as though he was in the army.

Me! Me! Me! He hadn't once asked how work was going or how she was managing in two rooms. As for Hugh, she'd tell him about that when she visited.

Your stepdad's a murderer!

Ben stared at the note in his locker before tearing it into pieces. It wasn't the first. Ever since the beginning of term, there had been the looks and not just from the other pupils but from the staff too.

'Another note?' Poppy was at his side.

He nodded.

'You did right to rip it up.' She started to walk with him towards the canteen just as she had done every day since returning to school. 'It's not fair.'

If it hadn't been for her support, Ben didn't know how he would have managed and clearly it surprised some of the others. 'Isn't your girlfriend the daughter of that woman your stepdad killed?' someone had asked.

Ben steeled himself. 'She's not my girlfriend. She's my friend. She wasn't the daughter. She was the stepdaughter. And my stepfather didn't kill her stepmother. It was an accident.'

Since then it had got a bit easier although he still hated it here. He couldn't wait for school to finish so he could get back to Mrs Johnson's and fool around with Slasher before seeing

Dan and some of the others. They didn't ask questions. They just wanted him to play in the band and hang out on the beach and other stuff. Ben still felt a bit worried about the 'other stuff'. He had told Mum he would stay at Dad's for the weekend when she visited Simon.

Ben only hoped no one would find out.

Chapter Twenty-three

''Snot good, man.' Spencer was sitting on the edge of his narrow bed and its thin regulation blanket, shaking his head which he'd shaved last week with a Bic razor from Canteen. It made him look older and harder.

''Snot good, man,' he repeated. 'That Rory's bad news. You should have heard him out. Know what I mean?'

Rory didn't seem like the kind of name you'd automatically associate with a child molester. But he'd learned in this place that personal attributes like names or ages, or even the way someone looked, didn't always fit the crime. There was a rosy-cheeked man in G block who looked for all the world like an average next-door neighbour. Turned out he'd been found guilty of arson. A child had died as a result.

'It wasn't me,' he kept telling anyone who would listen. It was hard to know if he was telling the truth.

Meanwhile, Rory was due to be released next year after twenty years. Frankly, Simon had always thought that 'Life' should mean 'Life'. Now he felt even more sure of it as he sat on the edge of his own bed, while Spencer went on telling him why he should have let the 'geezer' talk to him at Listeners. 'He's going to really take it out on you. Believe me, man.'

'But I couldn't just sit there while he told me ...' Simon's voice faltered. 'Told me what he had done.'

'Get real, man.' Spencer was thumping his own thighs in frustration. 'This is a prison you're in, not the Hilton. Most geezers are here 'cos they did what they're accused of, even if they say they didn't. ''Sides, *you* killed someone didn't you? Rory didn't murder that kid, he ...'

'*Stop it!*' shrieked Joanna. '*I don't want to hear.*'

'Leave it, Spencer,' said Simon sharply, putting on an

Eagles CD. One of the few pleasures he had since getting here was the arrival of a music system which Claire had sent in. Each of their personal items was counted during regular cell checks to make sure they didn't have more than the rules permitted. Spencer had a small tinny radio that crackled with Radio 1. They had agreed to take it in turns.

'Shit, man. You're not playing that stuff again, are you?'

'It's my turn,' said Simon rather petulantly.

'Well don't be long or you'll be late for fart.'

Simon looked up from the cover of Hotel California. He had bought it during the seventies with a girlfriend whose name he could no longer remember, although strangely he could remember the record shop in Oxford Street very clearly. 'Fart?' he repeated.

Spencer grinned, displaying those perfect white teeth. 'It's what the boys call 'art'. That woman what runs it, she's hot, isn't she?'

It was at times like this when Simon wondered what made him hang around with a boy whose morals and background were so violently different from his own. 'Don't be disrespectful.'

Respect, Simon had learned was a big word in prison. Men would kill if they felt they weren't getting the respect that they or their loved ones deserved. He was beginning to understand why.

'Disrespectful?' Spencer's teeth broke into an even bigger grin. 'Wow, man. Got it bad, haven't you? No hanky-panky with the staff or could get into big trouble. One of the officers went off with a geezer from A hut when he got out. Living together now, they are, with a kid of their own. 'Course she don't work for the prison no more. Wouldn't be allowed, I don't think.'

He had no intention of 'going off' with Caroline-Jane. She'd just struck a bit of a nerve, that's all; mainly because of her similarity to Claire.

'Have a good time at fart!' called out Spencer as he left. He could hear the boy chuckling at a joke which was already beginning to wear thin.

'*Better to laugh,*' tinkled Joanna, '*than sink into abject depression. To be honest, Simon, I've been a bit worried about you. I mean I know you're responsible for my situation but you're a good man at heart and I don't really want you going under. You need to chill out a bit. The art's a great idea if you ask me. Whoops! Have you seen who's walking towards you?*'

Simon's heart began to thud as Rory strode towards him. It was a cold morning but his huge arms, and their flabby bingo wings, were bare. 'You weren't there last night,' he said, coming up close.

Simon stepped backwards. 'You didn't book an appointment.'

'I need to talk, you know.' His small black beady eyes glistened. 'You can't turn me away just 'cos of what I've done.' He stepped even closer. 'When's the next time you're there?'

'I don't know. I need to ask the others.'

There was only one other Listener and he'd been in hospital having his gall stones removed but Rory wasn't to know that. With luck he'd be back soon and then Simon could explain the situation.

'Well, you'd better sort it or I'll go to the IMB.'

The IMB, Simon had learned, was the Independent Monitoring Board. It was a government body, made up of local volunteers to check that everything was being done as it should be in prison. If, for instance, the heating system was playing up again and wasn't fixed within the statutory time allowed, someone might ask for a visit by someone on the IMB. More often, however, they were asked to intervene if a prisoner's paperwork was delayed – which meant they couldn't get a day's leave when they were entitled to. Spencer had already warned him not to call them in too often or you got a bad reputation, man.

Now, Simon nodded. 'I'll let you know. Now if you don't mind, we're late.'

The man nodded. 'Going to fart, are you? Me too.'

No. Simon couldn't bear the idea of this floppy-bellied child

160

molester being in the same class as him, let alone within breathing distance of the art tutor. It wasn't right. How could her husband – she had been wearing a ring, he noticed – allow her to do such a job? It wasn't even as though there was a guard there to look after her. He felt himself bristling with indignation.

As for walking to art with Rory, there was no getting out of it. Uncomfortably, he strode ahead, trying to keep as much of a distance as possible, across the camp, past the laundry room where machines were whirring (as though this was a school and not a prison) and across the damp grass to the Portakabin where the art class was held.

'Morning!' Caroline-Jane gave them both a warm, welcoming smile as she ticked off their names in her register book. 'Come on in.' She was handing round a sheaf of A4-sized sugar paper sheets. 'That's right, do take one. I'm afraid I've only got one mirror between two.' She smiled. 'That's prison cuts for you.'

Mirrors?

'Self-portraits,' muttered Rory as he eased his large frame onto the chair next to Simon. 'We do them once a month.'

If he'd known he would have to sit next to this man, he wouldn't have come. Unable to stop himself, his eyes followed Caroline-Jane. She was even wearing the sort of clothes that Claire favoured. Slim-line black trousers with a tight-fitting jumper in turquoise. Too tight, he thought, for this kind of audience. He was aware of the others in the group nudging each other every time she turned her back on them towards the flip chart, to demonstrate how to get the outline of your own nose or judge the distance between eyes. It made him want to punch them.

'*Wondered if you had a violent streak hidden away,*' purred Joanna. '*I mean when you think about school and your father ...*'

'Shut up,' he snapped. To his embarrassment, Caroline-Jane glanced at him, surprised.

'Not you,' he mumbled. 'I was thinking of something else,

161

that's all.'

God, she'd think he was weird now. He'd put her off. But instead, she was moving in his direction. She smelt gorgeous – wasn't that Chanel? – and he had to press his finger-nails into his thigh to force himself to concentrate on her words as she leaned over him and Rory.

'That's good,' she said. 'But try making that eyebrow slightly higher.' He was horribly aware of her proximity as she directed his neighbour before turning to him. 'Yes. I can see what you're trying to do. But if you take another look in the mirror you might be able to judge the distance between your nose and ears a little better.'

Simon looked at himself in the tacky plastic hand mirror he'd been given. If he forced himself to concentrate on that, he might be able to stop thinking about Caroline-Jane who had now passed on to the group of kids giggling at the other end of the table.

'Need a hand?'

Rory was looking at Simon's so-called self-portrait. His egg-shaped head looked nothing like him and the eyes were almost cartoon-like. 'If you did this,' suggested Rory, his charcoal stick hovering over Simon's paper, 'you could ...'

Simon pulled his paper away. 'I don't need your help, thanks.'

Rory shrugged. 'Suit yourself.'

Caroline-Jane raised her eyebrows questioningly before going back to giving advice to a skinny youth who had a spider tattoo on his neck. How he wished he could go but there was still another hour left until the break. He spent it drawing and rubbing out charcoal lines again and again. How did Claire do it?

'Coffee, anyone?' The teacher's voice cut in on his thoughts. She glanced at Simon kindly. 'You just help yourself to a mug in the corridor outside. There's a kettle there too.'

He'd been told by Spencer that some classes were nicer than others. Not all offered drinks in a mid-class break and

162

presumably not all tutors were like Caroline-Jane. She was coming towards him now.

'How are you getting on?' She indicated that they should walk back to the classroom.

'Not great.' Simon tried to laugh off the ridiculous outline on his own piece of sugar paper. 'My wife's an artist but clearly it hasn't rubbed off.'

'Is she?' Caroline-Jane's face showed a keen interest. 'What kind of medium does she specialise in?'

'Watercolours, charcoal, that sort of thing.' He became horribly aware that he didn't really know. 'She does children's book illustrations. We haven't been married that long.'

He stopped, aware that the last two sentences didn't follow on.

'I see.' Caroline-Jane was nodding. 'And what caused that rumpus earlier on with Rory?'

He glanced towards the corridor to where Rory was drinking his coffee alone. 'I don't like him.' He dropped his voice. 'Do you know what he's done?'

'No.' Caroline-Jane's voice was sharp and she was moving away from him. 'I don't like to know what any of my men have done or else I wouldn't be able to do this job.'

'Why *do* you do it?' As soon as he said it, he knew he'd overstepped the mark.

Her cheeks suddenly revealed two red spots in the middle. 'Sorry, Simon, but I don't think that's any of your business. I try to keep a professional environment in my classes which is why I see you as students and not ... not anything else.'

He nodded, feeling justifiably reprimanded.

'By the way,' she added in a lighter tone. 'Have you looked at Rory's portrait? Rather good, isn't it? He's won several prizes over the years.'

Reluctantly, Simon obeyed. It was incredible. Rory might not have done his own features any favours but he had been truthful enough with that flabby jaw and piggy eyes and goatee beard. It looked almost professional.

'This place is full of surprises,' said Caroline-Jane quietly. 'I sometimes think any of us could have ended up in prison if circumstances had been different. Right!' She looked up at the others who were beginning to troop back in. 'Shall we get on?'

Simon didn't go to the next Listeners' evening. Instead he put up a notice saying *Cancelled temporarily due to staff shortages*. He felt bad about it but knew he simply couldn't cope with another confrontation with Rory. Instead, he'd wait until the other Listener was out of hospital.

'How does it work?' he asked Spencer in the dining hall one evening. 'Hospital, I mean. What stops someone just running away?'

'They have a guard next to them.' Spencer spoke with his mouth full, making Simon turn away. 'And they usually have a guard next to them.'

'But do they go in a special part of the hospital?'

'Depends, man.' There was a piece of sweetcorn stuck between Spencer's front teeth now. 'They might just be in a general ward if there's no room.'

Spencer leaned back and stretched, picking his teeth with his finger. Ugh! 'Think I'll get back to the hut. Something tells me we're due a search.'

'What have you got to hide?'

Spencer's eyes widened. 'Nothing, man. I just want to get my stuff tidied up.'

'*He's lying*!' tinkled Joanna. '*Bet he's got some stash under the mattress.*'

She could be right. Still, if there really was going to be a search – they happened regularly – it would be wise to get back to their room.

'Fucking hell!' exclaimed Spencer. 'Just take a look at this, man.'

It was the smell that hit him first. A horrible smell – just like the hole in the ground that had passed for a loo when he and a girlfriend had travelled through India years ago. And then he

164

saw the brown mess smeared on the walls.

'This is real shit. Someone's got it in for us, man.' Spencer shook his head. 'I said you should have listened to Rory. *Now* look what he's done.'

Chapter Twenty-four

Outside cleaning contractors had to be called in. Legally, apparently, no one else was allowed to do it – not even the Red Bands, the name for the group of prisoners who were selected to keep the huts clean. After they'd gone, both Simon and Spencer were physically sick in the loo. Then they took it in turns to use the shower. Even then, he still didn't feel clean.

'Do I still smell?'

Spencer sniffed. 'Can't tell. It's in my nostrils, man.'

'I'm going to find him.' Simon was putting on his clean pants. He'd given up by now when it came to privacy.

'Rory? You must be mad. You won't get nothing out of him. He'll just deny it. Anyone would.'

'I don't care. I'm not having it.'

Spencer laid a hand on his shoulder. 'Listen, man. This kind of stuff happens in prison. There was a geezer in my last prison what got shipped out for putting bird poo in the staff ice cream.' He snorted. 'They kept saying how tasty it was and had they got in a new flavour!'

Simon might have laughed if it hadn't been for what had just happened.

'If you make a fuss, it will come back at you. Understand?'

'I'm still going to find him.' Simon put on his shoes. Unlike most of the other men's trainers, his were casual brogues. 'I'm fed up with being a wimp.'

'*Ooooh!*' Joanna's voice tinkled. '*I do love a man who stands up for himself. About time, darling, if you don't mind me saying! I've a funny feeling you might just find him by the post window.*'

Every evening, a queue of men formed by a window behind which was the post room. You gave your name and then held your breath. If it was a lucky day, you got mail. If not, you suffered the ignominy of someone saying 'Nothing there' and then you were left wondering if anyone still cared.

Since moving down to the south-west, he'd lost contact with quite a few of his London friends and now, he didn't want them to know of his situation. Alex and Rosemarie were the exceptions but, so far, there'd been nothing from them, which hurt. He was also cross on Claire's behalf. Rosemarie was clearly more shallow than either of them had realised.

'*I could have told you that,*' tinkled Joanna. '*There you are. He's there!*'

Rory was mooching just outside the queue. Clearly he hadn't got any mail. 'Why did you do it?' demanded Simon urgently. He wanted to take the man by the collar of that grubby white T-shirt and shake him but there was no point in causing a scene. It would only get him into trouble.

'Wot?' Rory was looking at him in a manner that would have suggested surprise if he didn't know better.

'Mess up our cell like that.' He was growling now, fists clenched.

'Careful, ducks!' It was Georgie who had seemed to materialise from nowhere. 'Calm it or you're going to get one of the officers over. Now what's going on?'

'He,' muttered Simon fiercely, jabbing his forefinger at Rory, 'put … put poo all round my cell walls.'

Rory chuckled. 'Poo? Do you mean shit?'

'Don't you dare laugh!' Simon could feel himself shaking.

'Is that true?' Georgie was looking at Rory.

'No!'

'He's lying!'

'I'm not, mate. I've got one of those phobias about shit. Ask him!'

Now it was his turn to jerk his finger towards another man who'd just left the queue with a letter in his hands. 'I can't handle anything dirty. Not since I did my offence. This is my cell-mate. He'll tell you.'

The man nodded. 'He's right. Bloody nightmare he is to live

with. Has to wash his hands four times before he touches anything.'

'Then who did it?' Simon still found himself glaring at him.

'Don't ask me, mate.'

Georgie was guiding him towards the post window. 'Forget it, duck. It's not worth it. Trust me. Now why don't you see if you've got a letter from that gorgeous wife of yours?'

'How do you know she's gorgeous?' Simon could still feel the anger in his chest.

'I saw her, ducks, at Visiting.' He touched Simon's shoulder briefly. 'It's OK. You can let your anger out on me if it helps.'

There was a letter. But it wasn't Claire's writing. In fact, he didn't recognise the almost child-shaped capital letters on the envelope. Ben? No. Kids didn't write letters. Claire was always saying that. They emailed or texted.

Excitedly he opened it. Then stopped.

You killed the woman I loved. I'm going to get you for that.

Hugh. Despite the absence of a signature, the sender's identity was clear.

'Anything interesting?' enquired Georgie, politely.

Carefully, Simon tore up the letter into small strips and then tiny squares before stuffing them in his pocket to throw away in the hut. There weren't rubbish bins round the camp for fear of someone setting fire to them. 'It's nothing.' He laughed hoarsely. 'Nothing I can't deal with.'

Chapter Twenty-five

Somehow, Claire managed to deliver her illustrations on the day of the deadline. It had meant paying extra for the postage which she could ill afford – something she would have thought nothing of this time last year – but it meant her agent was happy.

'Is there any more work coming up?' she had asked, trying not to sound too desperate.

'Might be,' said her agent. 'Feeling bored, are you?'

Should she tell her agent what had happened to Simon? No. Something told her that being the wife of a prisoner might not be the best thing for her career. But his actions had now affected all of them and she had to be practical. It would take at least two or maybe three months to get paid for the work she'd just completed. It was the way freelance work went. Just as well she had the school job; even though the money wasn't great, it was something regular coming in at the end of every month until the house sold.

Meanwhile, there was the visit to Simon coming up and somehow she'd completely forgotten to organise the dog. 'Mrs Johnson, would you mind keeping an eye on Slasher for the day tomorrow?' she asked. It was a Friday and her school day had been particularly demanding – one of the children having thrown red paint at another in an argument.

'Tomorrow?' Mrs Johnson looked up from the Aga where she had baked a tray of cheese scones. 'Certainly, dear. Going anywhere nice?'

Claire had already prepared her answer which was between a white lie and the truth. 'I'm going to visit my husband, actually. He's taking me out to lunch so we can talk about things. Ben's going to his father's or else he'd look after the dog.'

'Don't you worry about it!' Her landlady looked down at Slasher who was sitting up, his ears pricked at the sound of his name. 'We'll have a good run along the beach.' She glanced at Claire. 'You look a bit washed-out, if you don't mind me saying. Fancy a cup of tea?'

Her landlady's tone indicated that an acceptance and the company was a fair exchange for dog-sitting the next day, even though all Claire wanted to do was to go upstairs and stretch out on the bed. 'That's very kind, but I ought to see where Ben is.'

Mrs Johnson beamed. 'Sitting next door in front of my telly with his cheese scone, he is. Shall we go in and join him?'

She ought to be grateful but somehow Claire felt as though she was being sucked in. 'Thank you,' she said quietly. 'May I carry that tray for you?'

Claire hadn't visited her first husband's apartment before. After breaking up they had occasionally met to discuss decisions about Ben in a coffee shop, rather than her coming back to his house or him to hers. It was as though, by mutual decision, they had agreed that it was part of moving on.

So when Charlie had casually suggested that she dropped Ben off on the way while driving to Essex, she had found herself agreeing. Now as they stood at the front door of a rather smart apartment in a prestigious part of Exeter, she felt deeply uncomfortable. Even now, after four or so years, it felt weird to think of the man she'd lived with for so long having another home.

'Hello,' said his voice when she pressed the security button.

'It's us,' she said, instantly regretting the informality. They might have been a mother and son returning from an ordinary shopping day. The possibility both shocked and reassured her. At least Charlie was still there. He wasn't dead. Or in prison. A welcome constant in her life which had seen too many changes in the last few months.

There was a click and the door opened. 'Up here,' said Ben, striding up the steps in front. How, she wondered as she followed her son, had it come to this? After all those years of living together as a family, her child knew where her former husband lived, while she hadn't even set foot in the place. It didn't feel right.

'Hi.' He stood at the door of his apartment waiting for them as they climbed the stairs. His tall body and blond curly hair seemed both strange and yet familiar, sending an odd sensation shooting through her – one that she couldn't name. 'Nice to see you. Want a cup of tea before you go?'

'No thanks.' She took a step inside and glanced round the sitting room which was a curious mixture of some of their old furniture and new things. There was the chair that she'd bought at an auction when she'd been pregnant with Ben. It hurt to look at it; to recall her blind faith at the time – that the future would be all right.

And there was a modern chrome coffee table in the middle which definitely wasn't her taste and which she hadn't thought would have been Charlie's either. Had she ever known him? Had she ever known Simon? 'I really ought to get cracking. Long drive ahead.'

He nodded but still she didn't move. Behind him, she could spot a silver-framed photograph of Ben as a toddler and next to that, another of her and Charlie on their wedding day. How weird that he should still want to display that!

'Thanks for having him,' she said, quietly. Ben had already gone into the back room with his stuff.

He looked surprised. 'He's my son, Claire, not a guest. I was going to have him anyway after being away. How are you doing?'

The last bit threw her, not so much the context of the sentence but the kind, gentle tone in which it was said. She bit her lip. 'It's not easy.'

If she craned her neck slightly, she could see Charlie's bedroom. There was a large double bed there and the sheets were rumpled as though unmade.

'Mind if I use the loo?' she asked suddenly.

'Of course not. It's through there.'

It was very neat. Very shiny and very clean with chrome

171

surfaces. On the wall was a bathroom cupboard. Her heart racing, she quietly opened it. Inside was a shaving brush and an unopened tube of toothpaste. Nothing to indicate a female presence. What had she been hoping for? A lipstick? And why was she looking anyway?

Coming out, she found Charlie was bending over his music system with Ben, showing him a CD. They both turned – same profiles, same enquiring expressions – and she felt instantly in the way.

'What will you do this evening?' she asked.

Charlie shrugged. 'The cinema, I thought. Maybe a takeaway.'

She felt another pang that she wasn't included. 'Have fun.'

'Thanks.' Charlie looked as though he was going to brush her cheek goodbye. Then he stepped back. To her shame, Claire felt disappointed.

'Bye, Ben.' She gave him a quick cuddle but he pulled away. With a pang, Claire realised that a display of affection would, in her son's eyes, be a betrayal of his father. This was what divorce did to kids. Instead, she kissed the top of his head. 'See you tomorrow.'

It was crazy. She and Charlie had been divorced for nearly four years. Two years on her own. One year of normal married life to Simon. Almost four months of her husband Inside.

Surely it was enough time for her to have moved on? So why did that scene of domesticity with her ex disturb her so much?

The thoughts kept whirling round and round her head as she listened to the voice on the sat nav telling her how to get to the prison. Halfway, she stopped to fill up and then again, she stopped for another break, mindful of the signs that told her that Tiredness Kills.

And then, just as she was beginning to think that she would never get there, the Visitors' Car Park sign loomed up before her.

The search didn't seem as obtrusive as before. Maybe,

thought Claire, as the woman officer's hands deftly frisked down her sides, she was getting used to it. There was another woman in the same group as her who seemed more like her than the others by virtue of not being covered in pancake make-up or wearing a short tight skirt. They both gave each other a wry smile as they queued up while a sweet-looking black Labrador was walked past them by a boy in uniform.

Would he smell Slasher on her? But he simply walked right past her and then sat neatly by the feet of someone behind, looking up at his handler. 'Please come with me, sir?' said the boy. Claire couldn't resist glancing behind to see a small, wiry man being led to another Portakabin, a worried expression on his face.

'Drugs,' someone else muttered in the queue. Really? She'd always thought that sniffer dogs would bark or do something dramatic if they found anything – not just sit at someone's feet.

Claire looked again at the woman who seemed a bit like her (even their long woollen navy coats with the shawl collar detail were similar) and she could see she thought the same thing.

She was tempted to say something but then they were being led across the yard that she remembered from before, and into the same room full of all those tables and there was Simon, looking up for her face in the sea of people pouring in. He spotted her after she had seen him and his face lit up. At the same time, she felt a surge of warmth pouring into her. Now she was here, it seemed impossible to her that she could ever have had the kind of doubts that had been niggling all the way down.

'Are you all right?' His hand on hers made her feel warm and good again.

She spoke simultaneously. 'How are you doing?'

This time, instead of being stuck for something to say or feeling awkward at the newness of it all, they couldn't get it out fast enough. Yes, he assured her, he was managing. He wasn't great in the Kitchens – they both laughed at that – but the woman in charge was all right really and at least it meant he got a bit more to eat. She'd thought he was thinner.

'I've become a Listener,' he added. 'It's a bit like being a

173

Samaritan.'

What kind of people did he see, she wanted to know but he simply said it was very confidential. There you go again, she thought disappointedly. Shutting me out. Then he asked her how she was. She wasn't going to tell him about Hugh in the tea shop but somehow it came out.

'He wants me to stop Ben seeing Poppy.'

'Maybe you should.' Simon was frowning. 'The man sounds unhinged. I don't want you doing anything that might upset him.'

Just what Charlie had said when she'd told him on the phone. It struck Claire that she might sound out different strategies in life on her ex and her current husband to see what was best.

'What are you smiling at?' he asked.

'The dog,' she replied quickly. 'He's really changed our lives. I know I didn't want him at first but you were right. He's a great distraction for Ben, not to mention our landlady.'

Then she filled him in on Mrs Johnson and the new friends Ben had made in town, not to mention their band. 'Just so long as it doesn't interfere with his exams,' commented Simon. His authority, as a non-parent, irritated her.

'I'm sorry I can't visit more often,' she said, expecting him to reassure her.

'Next month will be Christmas.' His voice was quiet compared with the loud chattering around them.

'I know.' Be positive. That's what Charlie had said to her. 'Not long then to go.'

His eyebrows rose. 'Every day seems like a life sentence.'

'It's not easy for me either.' Her words crackled with resentment.

He reached for her hand and then stopped, as if remembering the rule about no physical contact. 'I'm sorry. I'm particularly worried about Hugh. He's unstable. I don't want you meeting him again.'

A tinny bell sounded in the background and one of the officers roared, 'Two minutes left now.' Simon was reaching down under the table. 'I've brought you something.' It was a childish picture of a rainbow! The sort of thing her class might have done.

'I've started art classes. I know. It's not very good but it's my first proper attempt. Trust me, you'd agree if you saw my self-portrait.'

'It's ... it's very nice.'

'You'll need to check with security that you can take it out.'

Another bell was ringing now and they were being told to leave. Suddenly, he cupped his hands on either side of her face and drew her to him, kissing her properly with such passion that it took her breath away.

'Check that man!' roared an officer. Immediately, there were two men around her husband, prising his mouth open. 'Nothing,' said the other almost disappointedly. My God, Claire realised sharply. They thought she'd been passing on drugs!

'Out, you.' They were moving him away now towards another door. He shouted out something. It sounded like 'I love you.' And then he was gone, leaving her with so many mixed emotions that not one of them made sense.

The kiss both burned and comforted her all the way home. She'd intended to stay at a motorway lodge but the visit had left her on such a rollercoaster of emotions that she felt awake enough to drive back. Besides, she wanted to sleep in her own bed.

How odd, she thought, as she parked outside Mrs Johnson's and tried to let herself into the house as quietly as possible, that she should be thinking of it as 'her own bed'. Did that mean that ...

'Claire!'

Mrs Johnson was standing in the hall, her hair in little pinned-up curls and wearing a cream towelling dressing gown. Her first thought was that she usually called her Mrs Mills. Her second was that something awful had happened.

'Have you got Ben with you, Claire?'

A sickening feeling lurched through her body.

'He's with Charlie.'

'No, he's not.' There was almost a satisfied gloat to the words as though her landlady was pleased she knew something that Claire did not. 'He turned up here at ten. Just gone to bed, I had. Your poor husband – I mean your first one – was in a terrible state – said he only went out of his flat for ten minutes to get a takeaway and, when he got back, Ben had disappeared.'

Her mouth dry with fear, she tried to ring Charlie but then realised her mobile had gone dead and that her charger had disappeared. When she finally got through using Mrs Johnson's landline, she barely recognised his voice.

'He didn't say he was going out,' he kept saying over and over again tightly. 'You don't think Hugh has got him, do you?'

'I don't know.' Claire was trying to think straight but it was difficult with Mrs Johnson breathing down her neck.

'Did he say anything about Ben going out with friends?' prompted her landlady loudly behind her.

'Did he say anything about going out with friends?' Claire repeated.

'Only that he'd had to miss band practice tonight.'

Claire's heart leaped. 'That might be it. I'll call you back.'

'No. Wait for me. I'm driving over.'

She put down the phone, not wanting to waste time in arguing. Mrs Johnson ran with her to the front door with Slasher jumping up behind her and barking. 'I'll come with you.'

'No thanks.' Claire knew her landlady meant well but she was *so* pushy. 'I appreciate this but I've got to do it on my own. Besides, Slasher's all wound up. It would be really helpful if you could stay with him.'

'Very well.' She didn't hide her hurt. 'But if you want any clues, most of these boys practice on the front in the beach huts.'

'Aren't they closed up now?'

Mrs Johnson smiled ruefully. 'I see you still have a lot to learn about teenagers, Claire.'

176

He hadn't meant to leave Dad's. But Gary and the others had kept texting him to say that they really needed him for practice that night and that, if he missed it, they'd have to get Joe in instead. This other boy had been badgering them for ages to let him play instead of Ben.

So as soon as Dad went out to get the Indian, he slipped out and got a bus back to town. If he'd asked permission, Dad might have said no.

Band practice had been cool but he would have enjoyed it more if he hadn't had that nagging feeling that Dad would be worried. He'd left his mobile behind at the apartment in his rush to get out and when he asked if he could borrow someone's, he couldn't remember Dad's new number. So he tried to ring Mum but her phone was switched off.

It was then that Gary produced a bottle of whisky. After all that stuff about bringing Joe in if he didn't get to practice, he hadn't liked to turn it down and now he was feeling rather distant and less worried about his parents.

When the knock came on the beach hut door, he'd thought it was them but the two men who came in had uniforms on.

'OK, lads. Empty your pockets.'

They'd all had to give their names and addresses except that they all gave false ones and when it came to Ben's turn, his head was so muzzy that he gave Simon's surname instead. 'Aren't you the lad whose father got done for killing someone on the road?' asked one of the men.

'Stepdad,' he muttered.

And then one of the other boys looked at him in a weird way and Ben knew the game was up. 'F– off, all of you,' he yelled and pushing past, ran out of the beach towards the sea.

Chapter Twenty-six

'No family apart from the wife, then?' asked one of the officers, after Claire had left. Simon was queuing up with the others, waiting to be searched before leaving the Visitors' Hall. 'People like you usually have hordes of people wanting to visit, Uncle Tom Cobley and all.'

'People like me?' repeated Simon carefully. 'Are you referring to the colour of my skin?'

The officer shifted awkwardly from one foot to the other.

'Because if you are,' he continued, 'I believe there are rules against that sort of thing.'

The officer's eyes grew steely. 'Only trying to be friendly.'

Fuck off, Simon wanted to say, pushing past and heading for the library. He didn't want to go back to his cell and face questions from Spencer about how his visit had gone, man. Instead, he just wanted a bit of peace to work out what to do about Hugh. He also needed time to savour the taste of Claire in his mouth.

He hadn't meant to kiss her like that but just seeing her there, her beautiful eyes fixed on him, did something to his insides exactly the way it had done when he had first set eyes on her. It wasn't until his mouth had pressed down on hers that he had realised he was doing it. Even if he did get punished, it would be worth it. Christ, he must have been mad to have had the hots for Caroline-Jane. She was nothing compared with his wife.

'*Old habits die hard,*' sniffed Joanna disapprovingly. '*Just because you used to flit from one girl to another before you got married, doesn't mean you can do the same now.*'

She'd got it wrong. He'd only looked at Caroline-Jane because she reminded him of Claire. Now her visit had given

178

him hope. Claire loved him! He could see it in her face and it made him want to burst out into song.

'Hi.'

Simon looked up at the voice from the desk. Library staff were supplied by the council. It used to be run by a small woman in grey who had scurried around as if in constant fear of being attacked. But she'd been off sick for ages. Maybe this was the new one.

'I'm Mark.' The friendly-faced man had ginger hair and matching freckles. 'Nice to see you.'

Was this a trick? Simon looked at him suspiciously. Staff didn't say things like 'hi' or 'nice to see you', apart of course from Caroline-Jane and she was different.

'Hello,' he said slowly, conscious that his voice and pronunciation immediately made him stand out from the majority of the other men.

Mark held out his hand in greeting as though they were in an office. 'Are you a regular in here?'

'I would be if it was open more often.' Simon looked around the shelves which had a fine layer of dust. At one of the tables sat Mr I Didn't Do It, bent over a thick book and a notebook. He looked up briefly, nodded, and returned to his notebook.

'Hopefully, things are going to change now.' Mark's voice sounded sympathetic. 'What kind of books do you like?'

Simon smiled ruefully. 'I used to be a lawyer so there wasn't a spare hour for reading. But when I was younger I always had my nose in a novel.'

'Great!' Mark beamed. 'Then you can make up for it now you have more time. Take a look at these.' He waved his hand towards a shelf by his desk. 'I've got some new stuff in. I'm going to be starting a book club too on Tuesday nights. Fancy helping to run it with me?'

He was tempted. Then again, supposing he made a mess of it like the Listeners. 'Go on, mate.' It was the dog man. He slapped him on the shoulder. 'Simon here's a good bloke. He found a home for my dog after I got nicked for fraud. You can trust us. We're not murderers.'

179

'*Really?*' said Joanna sharply.

'Right,' said Mark excitedly, as if the dog man hadn't used the 'm' word. 'Thought we could start with something like *The Curious Incident of the Dog in the Night-Time.*

He had the same enthusiasm as Caroline-Jane. What was it that got them going about this place? 'I'll put up some posters but it would be great if you could spread the word.'

Simon wandered off to the Historicals shelf and Slasher's owner whom he privately thought of as 'Dog Man', followed him. 'How did your visit go, then? Saw you giving your missus a snog!'

Go away, Simon wanted to say.

'I was at the table next to yours. Couldn't help hearing some of that stuff about some bloke pestering you. Hugh, wasn't it?'

Simon glared at him. 'Conversations at visits are confidential.'

'Don't be like that, mate. Nothing's private in this place. I was just trying to help, that's all.'

'Help? How?'

The dog man lowered his voice. 'I've got friends. They can do stuff. Take this Hugh out if you want …'

'Stop.' Simon held a copy of the *Habsburgs' Thirty Years War* between him and dog man as though in defence. 'I don't want to hear any more or I'll have to report you.'

'Come off it.' The dog man looked as though he was going to snarl. 'You're not an officer. 'Sides, it's us who ought to report you. You're getting a bit of a reputation you know, always mumbling to yourself about some woman called Joanna and saying 'shut up' out loud. Does the missus know you've got someone else?'

Simon laughed bitterly. 'Believe me. She knows all about Joanna.'

The dog man's face changed to one of admiration. 'Bloody hell, mate. I don't know how you do it with a cracking bird like that and all. How's my Slasher, by the way?'

'Very well. My stepson dotes on him apparently.'

'Dotes?'

'Loves him.'

'Right.' Dog man took a few seconds to digest this. 'Hope he doesn't make him all soft. He can have a mind of his own, that dog.'

Simon wiped his hand over the fine dust on the Habsburg cover, relieved to have achieved some kind of balance in the conversation. 'Don't worry. So can my stepson.'

The following day was Sunday. Simon wrote two letters to Claire and tore both up. He was glad that art had been moved to Mondays now so he could lose himself in his paints.

Caroline-Jane wanted him to 'explore different colours' and 'play around' mixing them on the cracked tin plate she had given him for that purpose along with some cracked tubes of paints, a jam-jar of water, and a sheet of sugar. 'If you put this cobalt blue with this yellow ochre and add more water, you'll get something like this,' she said, leaning over him.

All his original intentions now flew out of his head. Christ, it was all he could do not to stroke her skin and smell it to make sure she really wasn't Claire.

'Got it bad, haven't you?' cackled Joanna. *'Pity that Rory insists on sitting next to you. Still, I suppose you can't choose your bedfellows in a place like this.'*

It was as though the man was following him. Wherever he went now, whether it was the dining room or the post room, Rory wasn't far behind. Now as they sat round the table in the art room, the man was sitting so close that, every now and then, his knees bumped into Simon's. How repulsive.

'The Listeners' Hut still not open then?'

Simon shook his head, trying to concentrate on the green hues in front of him.

'That other geezer still in hospital?'

Simon nodded.

For a few minutes, Rory fell silent although he kept sucking in his breath as he drew and then expelling it as though in concentration.

'Blue is a great healer,' said Caroline-Jane to the class in general. 'Not everyone realises that colours don't just give us

181

inspiration but also make us feel better. If we have a sore throat, for instance, we should imagine a blue band of colour around our necks or, even better, put on a blue scarf.'

'Kinky,' someone said and there was a wave of giggles.

'Wow.' She'd stopped next to him and for a moment Simon thought she was referring to his rainbow. Then he realised she was talking about Rory's. He glanced across. The man was meant to be doing his life portrait but instead there was a small boy standing next to an apple tree.

'Is that you as a child?' asked Caroline-Jane softly.

Rory nodded. Then, suddenly, he picked up a stick of charcoal and drew a black patch behind the tree.

'Is that someone waiting for you?' asked Caroline-Jane even more softly.

Another nod. Then he picked up the paper and ripped it from top to bottom before flinging it on the floor. The rest of the class fell silent.

'Did that man hurt you?' Simon's voice rang out.

Rory nodded. Then he grabbed Simon's own sheet of paper, turned it over and began sketching furiously. A small girl stood in front of the tree this time. The shadow behind the tree came seconds later.

'You hurt a child because you'd been hurt yourself,' said Caroline-Jane.

The class shifted awkwardly.

Rory nodded.

'I tried to tell him,' he said jerking his hand towards Simon. 'But he wouldn't listen.'

'Yes, but that's no excuse, is it?' said a kid at the end of the table who had blue and red tattooed flames down his neck. 'What you did was disgusting.'

'I've changed now.' Rory was painting madly again. 'I've learned stuff and when I get out, it's going to be different.'

The rainbow was growing before Simon's eyes.

'No one believes me.' He looked round the class. The look in his eyes might have been resigned or might have been desperate. 'But you'll see. You all will.'

'There was no need to put shit all over my cell,' said Simon. Caroline-Jane looked shocked but it had to be said.

'That wasn't me, mate.'

Simon was about to say he didn't believe him but then the door swung open. An officer stood there, scanning their faces.

'Mills,' he barked. 'To the centre. *If* you don't mind.'

'What you done, mate?' cackled someone further down the table. Simon felt himself flushing. It would be the kiss. He'd be punished now by maybe having to do extra jobs round camp or having a visit cancelled. But it had been worth it.

Following the officer, he ignored the curious looks. Shit. They were going to one of the governor's offices.

'Mr Mills.' The woman at the desk spoke quietly. 'I'm afraid we have some news to give you. Would you like to sit down?'

Ben had disappeared. Run away. He was meant to have been staying at Charlie's for the night but had slipped off for band practice with his new town friends and then got caught by the police for drinking. For some reason, he'd given them Simon's surname and they had recognised it. Ben had then rushed out of the beach hut they'd broken into and disappeared.

That was Saturday night. Today was Monday. Claire would be frantic.

They'd allowed him to ring her.

'Are you all right?

Her voice was tight with hysteria. 'What do you think?'

'Where's he gone?'

'How am I meant to know?' She was screaming at him now or was that the wind and the seagulls? 'I'm scared he might have drowned himself.'

There was a man's voice in the background, soothing her. 'Who's that?'

'Charlie. He's as frantic as I am.'

Charlie and Claire, looking for their son. An equation which had nothing to do with him.

'*You can't get it right all of the time.*' Joanna's voice

183

sounded sorry for him. '*Have they got Slasher with them?*'

Of course. The dog! 'Get him! Send him running along the beach.'

'Who?'

'Slasher. Maybe Ben will come out from wherever he's hiding if he sees Slasher.'

He could hear Claire repeating his suggestion to Charlie. 'Daft idea,' he heard the man say.

'I have to go. Keep searching.' She was weeping. 'I'll call the prison if there's any news.'

Chapter Twenty-seven

When they got to the beach huts, all they found were two whisky bottles and a couple of empty cigarette packets.

Charlie sniffed the air. 'No cannabis,' he said. 'At least that's something.'

He and Claire had then driven around, frantically looking for a black hooded teenager. By morning, any remaining energy had been sucked out of her eye sockets.

That had been two days ago. Two days of combing the beach and local towns while the police told her they were doing all that they could. Then came Simon's phone call. 'Slasher,' he had suggested. 'Get Slasher out there looking for him.'

It was a crazy idea! Years earlier, when she'd been a child, they'd lost a cat and her father had suggested walking the dog round the neighbourhood to find him. They never had.

Yet Mrs Johnson seemed to think it was worth it. When Claire had suggested the idea, she had slipped into her navy anorak, grabbed a torch, and disappeared into the foggy night.

'I think we ought to go back to the old house,' said Charlie again.

'Really?' It was odd the way they'd become a team again. 'You could be right; although I'd have thought he would have avoided it after the bricks.'

Charlie took her arm gently. 'I don't mean your old house. I mean "ours".'

The *ours* sent a bolt of excitement and fear through her. 'It's worth a try,' she said slowly.

Together they drove through the city and out on to the other side towards the Dorset boundary. Some women, she knew, would have put up with an unfaithful husband for the sake of the beautiful house they used to own, but at the time she had never wanted to see Charlie again.

Pulling up outside the white gates, they looked wistfully at the wisteria creeping up the honey stone face. 'I'll knock at the door and explain.'

Claire nodded. 'OK.'

It was almost as though they had gone back together in time, she thought, watching him go up to the door and pounding the heavy old door-knocker. Was that the same one, she wondered, that they'd found in an antique shop near Stroud all those years ago?

Someone appeared: a man about Charlie's age. She saw them talking urgently and then Charlie returned, marching down the drive past the lavender bed that she had once planted, disappointed determination written all over his face.

'No,' he said shortly. 'But at least he knows, just in case Ben turns up.'

The tears which she had kept back for so long flooded out now. 'It's been so difficult for him. The divorce. Me marrying again. You having all those girlfriends. Hiding out in rented rooms. It's more than many adults could put up with, let alone a teenage boy.'

Charlie squeezed her arm gently. 'But he's strong. He's got my genes and yours. You've coped with all this too, Claire, in a way I hadn't expected and I admire you for it.'

She sat, straight ahead, as he drove on, not trusting herself to speak. 'I made a mistake,' Charlie was saying. 'I admit it. But I've learned my lesson. God help me, I've learned.'

Still she couldn't talk.

'Simon.' He paused as though saying the name was an effort for him. 'Simon is a lucky man. But from what I gather, he doesn't understand Ben.'

She found her voice. 'It's difficult for him. He doesn't have children. But he's not unkind to him if that's what you're implying. He's just a bit strict.'

'Strict enough to make him run away?'

'I don't know.' Her voice came out as a cry. 'You can't jump to conclusions, Charlie.'

He had always tried, she remembered now, to twist the facts around so that his views seemed saner and more plausible than anyone else's. But Simon was no better; often shutting her out because he'd been used to doing things alone. Did she really want to live the rest of her life like that? Her split from Charlie had made her stronger; capable of moving on, instead of putting up with something that clearly wasn't right.

'Let's just try and find him, shall we?' she said, 'before we try to analyse why he went.'

It was cold on the beach and Ben had had enough. Why did all these people come down year after year to sit on pebbles and shiver behind windbreakers? If he ever got big with his music, he'd buy somewhere in Florida where it was warm and he'd never have to see anyone here ever again.

He'd miss Mum, though. And Slasher. A longing seeped into his bones. He should have brought him with him; they could have cuddled up together and kept warm.

Ben shivered as he crawled up against the back of the small dinghy. If he hadn't found the boat, on its side like a long-forgotten shell, a rip through its wooden middle, he didn't know what he would have done. Thank goodness for the old blue tarpaulin which someone had left inside the boat. It was damp yet it had given him just enough shelter to stick it out along with the cheese sandwich in his pocket and the half-eaten bar of chocolate that he and Poppy had shared the other week.

Poppy. He'd miss her too if he went to Florida.

His stomach rumbled. At first, he'd been so hungry after the cheese sandwich and the chocolate that he didn't know what to do but then it was as though the rumbles in his stomach belonged to someone else and he could observe them rather than feel anxious. He was beginning to feel quite lightheaded too. Maybe it was because he hadn't drunk enough. He'd found a bottle of water on the beach which someone had thrown away. At least, he hoped it was water. It tasted all right.

Ben's eyes began to close and the lifeboat around him seemed to shrink with the rest of the world. This would be his second night. Part of him had expected to be found by now and then the decision would be taken out of his hands. He'd tell Mum he was sorry and he'd give him a bit of a telling-off and then she'd go back to work because there wasn't any money and he'd have to return to school where everyone would look at him because he was the kid who had run away.

The alternative was to never go back and become one of those kids you saw in the streets in Bristol who slept in doorways with dogs that had spotted scarves round their necks. He didn't want that either.

'Ben,' called the wind. 'Ben!'

He couldn't feel his fingers now and his bones felt like the sticks that Mum used to put into those plastic ice lolly containers when he was little.

'Ben! Ben!'

This part of the beach was the quiet part. The bit where no one came because you had to climb down through a steep footpath that ordinary tourists didn't know about. That's why he and the band had liked it. They could smoke and drink without anyone knowing.

'Ben!

The wind's voice was getting louder and the mist was licking his face, making funny little moaning noises.

'Ben! Thank God. You're here.'

Now he was dreaming about Mrs Johnson. Ben felt an overwhelming longing for her warm kitchen and her soft Victoria sponges which had been like the ones Mum had made before Dad had gone.

'Put this around you, pet.'

Something warm was being draped around his shoulders and he could feel water on his lips as though someone was trying to give him a bottle.

'It's water, love. You're dehydrated. That's right, Slasher, give him a cuddle.'

Slasher? Ben sank his face into the dog's fur. It felt comforting and he breathed in and out, feeling his own breath coming back at him.

'My Derek used to come down here, you know.'

Mrs Johnson was sitting next to him now inside the upturned lifeboat. 'He said it was the only place he could get some peace.' Her voice dropped slightly. 'Of course, I knew he was really having a smoke and a drink with his friends.'

This wasn't right. Mrs Johnson's son had been a goody-goody.

'It was that that killed him, you know.'

'The car,' he managed to say. 'Knocked over by a car when he was twelve.'

'No, love.' Mrs Johnson's arm tightened around him. 'That's just a story I put out for people who don't know me. My boy took an overdose just after his fourteenth birthday. Not far from here as a matter of fact. He might have been all right if it hadn't been for the tide coming in.'

He could sense the waves now, getting closer and closer. Suddenly he wanted to get up and run back to Mum but his legs wouldn't move. 'Blame myself, I do.' Her arm was getting tighter as though she was keeping him there. They'd both drown together, he realised suddenly in a fit of lucidity. Mum had always said there wasn't something quite right about her.

'I changed his room back to what it looked like when he was younger and none of this nasty stuff had happened. It made it easier to pretend it hadn't happened.'

Ben could understand that.

'We used to argue, you see.' Mrs Johnson's voice was making him feel sleepy now. 'Only teenage arguments but his dad didn't understand that. He was too strict.'

'So's my stepdad,' he heard himself mumble.

'Really, dear?' She was giving him some more water now. Gratefully, he gulped it down. 'Maybe if he and your mum make up, he'll come back and you can sort it out.'

'He can't. Not for ages. He's in prison for killing someone in a car accident.'

There was a strange noise – the kind his mother used to make when they watched television together and she thought she knew who had done it. 'I see. That must be difficult for all of you.'

Her grip tightened again and he could feel the sea roaring towards them.

'Not long, now, dear. Not long.'

'No.' He staggered to his feet. 'I don't want to die!'

'Die?' She was standing up next to him, holding him tightly so he couldn't run off. He hadn't realised old people had such strength. 'You're not going to die, dear. Mum's on her way right now to get us. Didn't you hear me call her on my mobile?'

'Ben! Ben!'

Was that Mum or the wind?

And then she was there, holding him to her, rocking back and forth, her arms folded round him; smelling of roses from the old garden and the stuff that came from the white and gold bottle on her dressing table.

He was vaguely aware of his father standing just behind but it wasn't him, he wanted. 'Mum,' he cried, holding tight. 'Mum!'

Chapter Twenty-eight

Simon had run away once at Ben's age; thinking himself to be violently in love with a girl from home. There'd been one hell of a fuss. Her parents had called his parents and his father had marched him back to school where he'd been caned.

Only now did he realise that his father's fury had probably been relief. But it was worse in prison where you felt so bloody useless.

'Not knowing is the worst bit, man,' said Spencer sympathetically as he watched Simon pace up and down his side of the pad. It was lock-up time although, judging from the level of music from the other side of the cell, no one was going to be able to sleep for a while. 'Felt like that myself when my kid was being born.'

Simon stopped. 'You've got a child?' It seemed impossible. Spencer was no more than a boy himself. 'You never mentioned it before.'

His cell-mate made a wry expression. 'Yeah, well to be honest, my baby's mother wouldn't let me see it when I got out. Now they've moved somewhere and I don't know where. Didn't even want my money, she said, 'cos she didn't know where it came from.'

There was something in that, thought Simon as he started pacing again; thoughts whirling round his head. Supposing Ben had gone and got himself drowned?

'He could be anywhere.' Spencer was sitting on the edge of his bed, looking out of the window hopefully.

'I know,' muttered Simon grimly.

'Every time I get out, I look at kids on the street to see if one of them looks like me.'

To think he had thought Spencer was worrying about *him*.

The boy was so self-centred. Maybe that's what prison did for you.

Spencer was still staring outwards. 'Funny thing is that I know I'd be a good dad, know what I mean? I'd take it to football matches like and I'd teach it to defend itself without breaking the law.'

Simon had never particularly wanted children but, if they had happened, he liked to think he would have got married first. Most men here had a series of 'baby mothers' whom they'd impregnated before moving on.

He took a deep breath. 'You know, I thought twice about marrying my wife because she had a son.'

'Don't blame you, mate.'

'But there was something about her that I just couldn't give up.'

Why was he even trying to explain his feelings to a kid? Wait! The door was being unlocked and one of the prison officers stepped inside, an unreadable expression on her face. Simon's heart quickened. They'd found him alive or ...

'I've got some news for you.' The woman looked at Spencer. 'It's all right,' said Simon quickly. 'You can say it in front of him. I just need to know.'

The woman nodded. 'There's been a phone call from your wife. Your son has been found. He's fine.'

'Stepson,' Simon was about to say automatically but then stopped. Ben had been found. That was all that mattered. And he was OK. Relief flooded through him followed by anger. How could the little sod have put them all through this? 'Can you tell me more? Where did they find him? Can I use the phone?'

'Sorry.' The officer was already backing out. 'Not during lock-up. You'll have to wait until tomorrow.'

Tomorrow? Claire would think he hadn't bothered. She might not realise he wasn't allowed to call. Simon sank to the edge of his bed, face in hands.

'It's all right, man.' Spencer stood awkwardly over him. 'He's not dead, is he? To be honest, I was beginning to think

192

the worst.'

'But I can't ring home.'

Spencer nodded. 'Welcome to the world of prison.' He lowered his voice. 'There's a bloke on the other side of the hut what's got a mobile. I could put in a word for you if you like.'

'*Don't even think about it!*' screeched Joanna. '*If you're caught, we'll be shipped to a closed prison faster than you can dial 999.*'

She was right. 'It's OK.' Simon stood up and looked out of the window. It was dark now and you couldn't even see the Education hut. 'I'll wait.'

After roll-call the next day, it was straight on to kitchen duty. Simon was on carrots. Rounded slices instead of the long thin ones he liked to do at home; enough for 200 odd people.

At 12.30 sharp, it was lunch. He had a choice of either eating or using that time to get to the phone in G hut. The last option was best because everyone else would be eating but it also meant he'd have to go hungry.

'Claire?'

Bugger. She had her answerphone on.

'Claire. It's me. They told me about you finding Ben. I'm so relieved. In fact that doesn't begin to describe it. It made me think a lot about him and me.' He paused. 'If I was too hard on him, I'm sorry. It's just that my father ...'

He paused again. How could you explain your relationship with your parents in a few minutes on an answer phone? 'I'll tell you more when I see you. I would have rung earlier by the way but I wasn't able to get to a phone until now.'

Blast. The message time had run out. He'd ring again tonight. Meanwhile, his stomach was lurching on empty. Jogging across camp to the dining room, he arrived out of breath. 'Sorry, *Mr* Mills. Dinner's over.'

'Lunch,' he wanted to say. 'It's called lunch in the middle of the day and dinner at night.' But what was the point? With any luck, Spencer might have a spare Pot Noodle in return for another reading lesson.

By the end of the week, he still hadn't received a letter from Claire. Every time he called, her mobile was off. Clearly she was hacked off with him for not having rung as soon as he got the news about Ben. She thought he didn't care. Didn't he realise that he might not be a parent but he still had feelings for the kid? He tried writing her a letter but the words wouldn't come.

There was a limit to how many sliced carrots you could throw yourself into every day but at least there was art, thank God. He'd progressed from colour charts now to copying one of the many postcards that Caroline-Jane brought in. The other men fell on them with crows of delight and, not for the first time, Simon realised that small pleasures, on the Out, assumed massive significance on the In. Incredible how you could release all those pent-up emotions on to paper.

'That's coming on,' said Caroline-Jane, sitting next to him. He was copying a small boat that was setting sail from the beach. 'If you made the sail go that way instead ...' Deftly she made the scene come to life.

'I don't know how you do it,' he said admiringly.

She shrugged but he could tell she was pleased. 'We all do different things in life.'

'I used to be a lawyer in my old one,' he said quickly. He'd been wanting to get that in ever since they'd met to show he was different from the others. It was gratifying to see the fleeting look of surprise across her face. 'I haven't done anything violent,' he added quietly.

Joanna laughed nastily. '*Really?*'

'I was involved in an accident.'

Caroline-Jane stepped back and he became conscious that the others were listening. 'May I see you after the class, Mr Mills?'

He nodded, feeling even more of a fool than he had when his parents had taken him back to school after running away at fourteen.

*   *   *

She waited until the others had left before speaking. By then, Simon's sketch was almost complete. 'That's very good,' she said nodding at it. 'You can paint it next week.'

He nodded, waiting for her to tell him off about being too familiar earlier on.

'What does it mean to you?'

'What?'

'Your painting.'

He considered. 'Hope, I think. It's someone getting away; finding freedom again.' Stupidly his eyes began to fill with tears and he had to blink them back.

'You know,' said Caroline-Jane, beginning to clear the paints away, 'I don't want to know what my students have done. But most people are here for a reason. There's no graph which means one crime is worse than another.'

He nodded. 'I drew the boat because my stepson went missing by the coast but now they've found him. I was hard on him when I lived with him and his mother. Now I wish I hadn't been.'

Caroline-Jane nodded. 'Prison gives you time to reflect. I find that myself even though I go home at night. 'She put some of the charcoal into a box. 'Why don't you send him this painting and tell him why you did it?'

That night, he wrote two letters. The second was to Hugh. How do you write an apology letter to the man whose wife you had killed?

'*Keep it short,*' advised Joanna. '*He'll be so mad he might not get to the end of the first sentence.*'

So he did.

Dear Hugh,
I am sorry I killed Joanna. I should not have picked up the mobile. I ought to have looked at the map before taking you back so I knew the way. I do wish you hadn't grabbed the steering wheel, however. If you want to keep sending me more letters telling me how much you hate me, that's fine. But please

don't do the same to my wife.
Yours,
Simon.

P.S. Do you ever hear your wife in your head?

By the end of the following week, he received a letter back from Claire. Ben was all right but a bit subdued. It had been a shock for all of them. Meanwhile, her mobile had been cut off because she couldn't afford her contract any more and the house still hadn't sold. She was coming to visit the following month. It would be Christmas by then.

The week after that, he had finished his picture and reluctantly resumed Listening duties in the hut. Thank goodness the child molester had been steering a wide berth around everyone for some reason. With luck he wouldn't pitch up tonight.

'Wotcha.'

Simon nodded as a bulky man in a T-shirt, even though it was freezing outside, came in. '*Cool hair,*' whispered Joanna, referring to his bald pate with two side plaits hanging down from behind either ear. They seemed curiously at odds with the man's deep voice.

'Would you like to sit down?'

Some of the men, he'd found, preferred to stand up. Others wanted to look away while they talked. This man chose to sit down, face to face. 'I'm out of here in two weeks.

Lucky sod. 'That's wonderful.'

'No.' The man was looking down at his trainers. 'I don't want to leave.'

'Why not?' Simon was dumbfounded.

'I've spent more of my life in prison than out of it. Don't you see?' His eyes were boring into Simon's. 'At first when I got done, I nearly went nuts especially when Patrick died.'

'Patrick?'

'Me son.' He spoke as though Simon should know. 'Came off his motorbike by White City and you know what?' He looked as though he was going to grab Simon's shirt to drive the point home. 'This officer, when he came to tell me, said that my son had been killed. I said, 'Which one?''

Simon's blood was beginning to run cold. 'You had two?'

The plaits were nodding. 'Yes and he said he didn't know which boy it was. So for twenty-four hours I had to sweat it out until I knew whether it was Patrick or Chris.'

'I'm so sorry.' Simon would have taken the man's hand if it might not have been misconstrued.

The Plait Man nodded. 'After that, I had to get on with it. So I did. Twenty years it's taken me to get to this stage.'

Twenty years? Then he had to have been a murderer. Simon felt rather cold despite the fan heater which was blazing out.

'And now I don't want to leave 'cos it's all changed. Me wife's gone off with someone else. I'm nearly fifty and that's too old to get a proper job. 'Sides, who'd have me with my record?'

A Listener's job, Simon knew, was to listen to someone and not try to solve his problems. You could gently steer them in the right direction but you weren't meant to give them an emotional prescription.

'If you're not sure where to live, there's the St Giles Trust to talk to,' he ventured.

Plait Man made a dismissive gesture. 'I can live with me brother if I want but I won't know what to do. Here there's work stuff to take my mind off it. A routine.'

Simon felt himself struggling. 'You might find that when you get out, it's all right.'

Plait Man shrugged.

'I've always found that fearing something is actually worse than when that thing really happens.' That was better.

'Maybe.'

'If I were you, I'd try to live each day at a time when you get out. You've been away a long time. It's natural to be fearful.'

Plait man stood up. 'OK. Ta.'

'By the way,' added Simon. 'Are you still in touch with your other son, Chris?'

197

Plait man sniffed. 'Doesn't want anything to do with his old man now. He's an accountant, you know.' He grinned. 'I'd never tell him this but I'm real proud of him.'

Had he helped or had he been useless, wondered Simon as he watched his new client lurching out of the door.

'*Well, darling, put it this way*,' purred Joanna. '*That trite stuff wouldn't have made me feel any better*.'

Thanks.

Anyway, he was doing all right with Spencer who could now read the notices in G hut. Suddenly, Simon was being inundated with requests from others who needed help with writing all kinds of things from their names to tricky letters to the wife.

'Fucking hell, man. Open up!'

Simon woke to the sound of Spencer at the door, rattling the door handle. Everyone else on the corridor was doing the same. Overhead, a helicopter was buzzing and a siren was screaming.

Something had happened, thought Simon as he staggered out towards the window.

'Shit me.' Spencer was behind him now as they both watched someone being carried on a stretcher. 'That's a stiff.'

It was too. The blanket was over the entire body but he could just make out something dangling towards the ground.

It looked like a long plait.

Chapter Twenty-nine

Claire hadn't been able to believe it when Mrs Johnson had found Ben. He wasn't dead. He hadn't been taken in retribution for Joanna. He was alive. Shivering. Blue with cold. But alive.

'I'd say he's in pretty good shape considering,' said the doctor at the hospital. 'You can take him home if you like.'

Home? He clearly thought they were all still together. Claire felt like a fraud. 'We'll go back to my place,' Charlie had said. Mrs Johnson had slunk off before they'd even got to hospital. When Claire had thanked her, the woman had hugged her tightly back and said they needed time to themselves as a family now.

A family! She'd thought they'd stopped being that but Ben's disappearance had proved different. Now, here they were, back at Charlie's apartment, its Conran dining room table and steel chairs so different from the old mahogany furniture they had had when they were together.

It felt odd.

'Are Mum and I going back to Mrs Johnson's or what?' demanded Ben as he wolfed down the fish and chips they'd bought on the way back.

'I thought you two might want to stay the night,' suggested Charlie in that casual tone which she knew so well. It generally hid a deeper meaning. 'In the guest room. It's a double. I've got wireless too and there's a laptop.'

Ben didn't need inviting twice.

'Do you think he's emailing his friends?' asked Claire after he'd rushed off.

'I hope so. Either that or Facebook. The sooner he gets back to normality the better. He's going to feel embarrassed now but it will blow over.'

So true. For all his faults, Charlie understood how teenage boys ticked, unlike Simon. 'Where shall I put away the placemats?' she asked, helping him, to clear away. It felt so weird to be asking her first husband about his domestic details.

'In the third drawer down on the left.'

She opened it. Inside were the silver napkin rings they used to have, each one monogrammed with their initials. 'H', 'C' and 'C'. When they'd broken up, they had divided their possessions with a certain amount of tension. He must have had these.

'You've kept them,' she said, indicating the rings as she put them on the table.

'Of course.'

'When are we going to talk to him?' she said, changing the subject.

'Later, when he's had a chance to unwind. Don't you think?'

Yes. Simon would have had a blazing row with Ben by now. Charlie's approach – going in with a Coca Cola half an hour later – was far better. 'Your mother and I were worried sick, you know.'

Ben's face went stony. 'I said I was sorry.'

'We wanted to know why you did it.'

'Mum knows.' His voice was quiet.

She struggled to find her own. 'You mean it's because of Simon.'

It sounded weird to say his name out loud in front of Charlie. Ben nodded.

'You find it embarrassing that your mother's husband is in prison.'

Charlie almost sounded pleased.

Ben nodded.

'It's not really surprising.' Charlie reached out and patted his son's hand sympathetically. 'It can't be easy for either of you having to leave your home and live in a couple of rooms. That's why I've got a suggestion to make.'

Claire looked up in surprise. He hadn't mentioned this. 'I propose that Ben comes to live with me for a bit. No, hear me out. Just until you have sold the house and bought your own

200

place. I'm not going to be travelling so much any more so I'll be here. It will take the focus off you, Ben, just until all this blows over.'

How could she have trusted him? This was outrageous. It was making Ben choose between them. Yet at the same time, Charlie's words made sense. If he lived here, his father could protect him in a way that she might not be able to, simply because of her connection with Simon.

'What about Mum?' Ben was throwing her an agonised look. 'Can she live here too?'

She reached out for her son's hand. 'I can't, darling. That wouldn't be ...' Wouldn't be what?

'Appropriate,' suggested Charlie. 'Your mother is married to someone else now.'

'What about Slasher?'

'I'm sure we could sort something out. Tell you what. Why don't you have a shower and go to bed. It's getting late and you must be exhausted.'

It was true. His eyelids were drooping and he was almost lying on the dining room table. She waited while Charlie found him a towel and then after he had showered, went into kiss him goodnight. 'I'll always love you more, Mum,' he whispered as he clung to her.

'You mustn't talk like that, darling,' she said despite the rush of relief that flooded through her. 'It's not a contest.'

He nodded. 'If I did live here, I'd still see you every evening, wouldn't I?'

She bit her lip. 'Not every evening because I have to work. But definitely at weekends.'

His eyes were closing now and she could hear the steady pattern of his breathing. Her heart heavy, she went back out into the dining room.

'You didn't tell me you were going to do that,' she said angrily.

'It makes sense.' Charlie was calmly making coffee in a sparkling chrome percolator. 'I need to protect him from the repercussions.'

'Repercussions? Is that what you call it?'

She was beginning to remember now how he always deflected criticism with questions. 'All right then.' He put a cup in front of her. 'Death by dangerous driving. Let's call it by its real name.'

'It was an accident.'

'Claire, your husband broke the law.'

'So did you! You broke our wedding vows.'

He sighed, leading the way to his sofa; a black leather design that she had loathed on first sight. 'Don't go through all that again.'

She perched on the edge of a chair instead. 'Why not? That's what caused all this, isn't it? Some woman at work whose name you refused to give me.' She could feel the anger rising now as all the details came flooding back into her head; details which she had fought to obliterate for so long. 'If I hadn't found that lipstick in the car, I'd never have known.'

'I told you. It's over. It's been over for years.'

'But you shouldn't have done it in the first place!'

His face was getting red now. 'What drove me, Claire. Have you ever thought of that? I'll tell you. I had a wife who was more interested in her painting and her son than her own husband. What else was I meant to have done?'

She could hardly believe her ears. 'What else? You could have talked to me about your feelings first before you got into bed with someone else ...'

The door behind them opened and she stopped. Ben stood there, wearing an outsize T-shirt of his father's. He was staring at Charlie. 'I just heard what you said, Dad. You're bang out of order. Can we go home, now, Mum? I want to see Mrs Johnson and Slasher.'

The local paper ran a front page story with the headline *Teenage boy found safe after 48-hour search.*

Luckily, because they knew so few people in the town, there wasn't the big fuss she'd feared. She'd had to tell the school of course – both Ben's and her own – and again, they were very

202

sympathetic. 'The sooner he gets back into a routine, the better,' Ben's headmaster had said. 'We'll look after him. Don't worry.'

Meanwhile, now the emergency was over, she hadn't spoken to Charlie for days. 'It's all right to be angry with him,' said Jean Johnson after she'd told her everything. They were sitting in the kitchen with a cup of tea. Ben was upstairs doing his homework with the dog. 'I've always found in my experience that anger is very close to love.'

Claire flushed. 'I don't feel anything for him any more.'

Jean gave her an odd look. 'It's not easy to forget someone you were married to for a long time and had a child with. I should know that.'

This was getting too much! Too personal. She might owe Ben's discovery – possibly his life – to her landlady, but if she didn't set some boundaries, Claire had a feeling that Jean might try to take over their lives. 'You know,' said the older woman, her hand on the teapot with its pretty seagull design, 'I don't know whether I should mention this but there's something I ought to tell you. When Slasher found your son, Ben told me something.'

Claire's heartbeat quickened.

'He said your husband is in prison. Sugar, dear?'

Thrown by both sentences – the last almost seemed like a ruse to distract her – Claire nodded dumbly. 'He is. There was an accident.' Her voice began to squeak. 'Simon crashed the car. He was trying to ring Ben at the time. Someone ... someone died.'

Jean Johnson's face was rigid. Scarily emotionless. Claire's chest felt as though someone had pulled a plug out of it. 'I expect you want us to go now, in view of your son.'

Jean shook her head and reached up for her arm as though to pull her down. 'Not at all. I take it that Ben has kept my confidence too just like I kept his.'

What was she talking about?

'I told Ben how my son hadn't been run over at all. I just say that to people until I really know them well enough to tell them

203

the truth.' Her face softened. 'He took a tablet. A drug. It was the first time he did it, I was told by his friends, and the last. '

Wow! She hadn't expected that. 'I'm so sorry.' Claire's eyes filled with tears.

'Thank you, dear. To be honest, neither of us recovered. My husband died young of a heart attack and everyone around here thinks I'm a bit touched. Maybe I am.'

Claire hugged the woman briefly. 'If you are, so am I. But I'm so glad we found each other. Thank you.'

'No, my dear. It's me who needs to thank you. Now do you think Ben's ready for his dinner yet? Spag bol! Used to be my boy's favourite. Well one of them, anyway. And by the way, don't think I'm interfering, but I wouldn't be too hard on your husband. As you say, it was an accident and we all make mistakes, don't you think?'

Hugh's email popped up in her Inbox the following week. *Sorry to hear about Ben but glad he's OK.*

Claire's skin prickled with fury! *You said you were going to leave our family alone,* she typed back. *So why are you writing nasty letters to my husband in prison?*

The reply came back immediately. *I'm not. He must be mistaken.*

Did he think she was stupid? If he wasn't so irrational, she'd ring him up but emailing seemed safely distant. *I don't think so.*

There was a pause of ten minutes then which proved she was right. He was just trying to think of a good excuse. Then a message popped up. *I'm not going to demean myself by arguing but I will say one thing. My daughter was rather upset when I said I wasn't happy about her seeing Ben so I have agreed that he can continue to give her guitar lessons after all. They may come to the house if they wish.*

At least that would be something to tell Simon when he rang. Since Ben had been found, it had been harder and harder to talk to him. Part of her blamed him for not having rung immediately he'd got the news.

'They wouldn't let me,' he had said.

Rubbish! He'd surely have been allowed to talk on compassionate grounds. He didn't understand, that's what it was. Didn't realise what it was like for a parent to find a child again. Don't blame him too much, Jean had said. But it was tough. Not long now until she visited him again. And then it would be Christmas. Charlie wanted them to spend it with him. She'd declined at first. But the more she thought about it, the more attractive the idea seemed.

'Coming to the staff Christmas party, then?' asked Debbie one morning.

Claire had already worked out her excuse. 'I don't think so. I ought to stay at home with Ben.'

Debbie looked at her. 'You can't be with him every night, you know. It doesn't work that way with teenagers. If they want to do something daft, they will.'

It was true. Since the running away, Ben had rejoined the band somewhat surprisingly. One of the boys had just turned up at the door and said they needed him so he'd gone back to band practices on the understanding that he didn't drink or smoke.

She only hoped he was obeying the rules.

'So how about it?' Debbie handed her a pen and sheet. 'We're going to that new Chinese in the high street. Go on. Put your name down. You need a bit of fun.'

When Ben thought about how he'd run away, he felt really stupid. But then Gavin from the band had turned up and said they needed him or they'd have to find a new guitarist. 'Sides, his uncle had done time for a burglary so none of them was bothered about Ben having a stepdad doing bird.

Poppy had been really glad to see him and when a couple of kids started whispering at school, she'd told them to fuck off. 'Dad says it's OK for you to give me lessons now,' she said.

He still felt awkward. 'I don't get it. Why are you being so nice to me after Joanna?'

They were sitting in the common room and the others had all left for double maths. They were late but she didn't seem to care. 'Don't you get it, silly?' She leaned towards him and before he knew it, had put a very gentle kiss on his cheek. 'Because I fancy you. Always did. Before you-know-what.'

With that, she jumped up. 'Shit, is that the time? Mrs Rogers will kill us.'

And he had followed her speechlessly into double maths where he'd been unable to concentrate for a minute.

Then, the following week, a parcel had arrived for him. At first, he'd thought it was from Dad but, when he opened it, it was a picture of a small boat setting out from the shore.

'That's quite good,' said Claire. 'But who on earth sent it to you?'

Together, they read the note. *To Ben. I did this in Art and wanted to send it to you. The boat means hope. I'm sorry that my actions have put you in a difficult situation. Love Simon.*

Chapter Thirty

Plait Man had topped himself. That's what everyone was saying although it wasn't official yet. Had hung himself up by stringing together his bedsheets and fastening them somehow to the top of the shelf which they all had as routine fixtures in their pads. Some used them for clothes or music. Simon stored his books there. Plait Man had used his as an execution tool.

'It's my fault,' Simon said to Spencer as they stood in a huddle in the small narrow corridor that ran through G hut.

Spencer yawned. 'What you on, man?'

'Nothing.' How could he expect the boy to understand? Elbowing his way through the crowd, he made his way to the officer who was standing by the door of the hut, trying to get them into some kind of order. He was a tough-looking man in his fifties whose small eyes were dwarfed by his large, hooked nose. 'May I speak to you?' said Simon in a low, urgent voice.

The officer didn't even look at him. 'Later.'

'Please.' Simon raised his voice. 'You see, I think all this is my fault.'

They took him to a small room off the centre and invited him to sit down on a plastic chair. His right knee wouldn't stop shaking and he could see the officer noticing.

'You'd better tell me what this is all about, *Mr* Mills, before I decide if I need to get you before the guv.'

Simon closed his eyes. He found that he could think better that way in prison because it shut out the noise and the look in the officer's eyes. A look that said 'I've got to work here but it doesn't mean I have to like you.'

'I'm a Listener.'

There was no response.

207

'That means ...'

'I know what that means, Mr Mills.'

This time, Simon noticed, there was no accent on the 'Mr'. The man's voice sounded gentler. 'Please tell me what you have to. We've got a prison to run here.'

'The Plait Man ... I mean the man who died, came to see me last night in the Listeners' Hut. He said he was dreading his release date and that he didn't know how he'd cope when he was free. Apparently he'd been in prison for more years than he'd been out of it.'

'Many of them have.'

The prison officer's voice was definitely more sympathetic now. 'I told him that, when he got out, it would be all right and that the fear of something was actually often worse than doing that thing that scared you in the first place.'

'Like the line about the ant in Shakespeare.'

'Exactly!' Simon opened his eyes and was shocked to find that the officer's face looked completely different. Open. Understanding.

'Sounds like good advice to me.'

'No. Don't you see? It couldn't have been or he wouldn't have killed himself.'

The officer took a sharp intake of breath. 'That's not official yet. But even if it was, you can't blame yourself. You said what you felt what right at the time.'

Simon was so astounded he could hardly talk. He had expected some kind of retribution or maybe a sharp dismissal; not this. 'Thank you,' he said humbly.

The man's eyes smiled. 'We are human, you know. The problem is that you lot only see the uniform, not the person behind it. By the way, I don't know if it might help, but have you ever thought of going to one of the chapel services?'

'The God Squad?' sniffed Georgie. 'I tried that once when I had a happy-clappy boyfriend but it didn't do nothing for me.'

'My mum used to belong to the Gospel Choir in White City,' offered Spencer.

'Was that before or after she got into credit card fraud, duck?'

They both laughed out loud until Mark, the librarian, shot them a 'You're meant to be quiet here' look. 'Staying for book club?' he asked.

Simon nodded. They were already on the fourth chapter of *The Curious Incident* which had even got Spencer interested. 'That kid's a bit like me, man. He doesn't always say or do the right things.'

Privately, Simon had thought the hero was like him, too.

'There's an evening service on Wednesdays,' offered Mark, handing them each a leaflet. 'As well as Sunday mornings.'

'Thanks.' Simon didn't want to talk about it now. Besides, there was only one copy of *The Curious Incident* and they were each reading a page before passing it on. He needed to concentrate.

Sunday came and went but he gave chapel a miss. Anyway, the prison officer's words had helped. He had tried his best with Plait Man, hadn't he? But then the dreams started and he kept seeing one sole knot of hair dragging on the ground.

To distract himself, he tried to concentrate on his kitchen duties. Jill had discovered he could make pastry (another bachelor talent) so had elevated him to chief quiche-maker. Twice a week, he had Art. He'd never be any good but even so, the pictures he was producing – copies of postcards that Caroline-Jane brought in – were better than he had ever thought he might do.

Then there were his lessons with Spencer and letters for the men.

If he kept busy, he might cope with the prospect of Claire's imminent visit.

'*Feeling nervous?*' demanded Joanna one night. Her voice shocked him. She hadn't been around since Plait Man's death and he thought he might have got rid of her.

'*Not surprising, really, darling. It's not great for a marriage, being apart?*' Joanna sighed. '*Trust me. I should know.'*

He dressed with care for Claire's visit. He'd saved up his canteen money to buy a new disposable razor although unfortunately, he'd nicked himself on the chin.

Then he shrank his only Burberry jumper in the communal washing machine. It didn't look good. Nor did his trousers which, thanks to the prison food, were hanging loose at his waist. He'd put in for an application form for new ones to be brought in but that could take weeks.

By the time he was sitting at the table in the Visitors' Centre with all the other men (making lewd jokes) Simon was feeling as nervous as he had on the first visit. It would be the first time he had seen Claire since Ben had run off and been found again. He'd done it, she'd told him, because of 'the situation'. So it would be perfectly normal for her to blame him.

Here they came. Simon looked up, keeping his eyes fixed on the door as the women, some men and a few children streamed in. The noise grew louder, due to all the exclamations and greetings and, within minutes, a couple of arguments which the officers immediately homed in on. But where was Claire?

His mouth went dry and it reminded him of the one and only time he'd been stood up, back in his thirties. He'd arranged to meet a much younger girl he'd dated a couple of times outside the Royal Albert Hall but she had never shown up. He'd given away the tickets in the end rather than go in on his own and had felt cross for weeks because she hadn't got in touch. Only now it occurred to him that something might have happened to her just as it might have happened to …

No. Here she was. Walking quickly in, her hair slightly ruffled; mouthing, 'Sorry I'm late'. A young man was walking just behind her, looking around wide-eyed.

Bloody hell. It was Ben.

'I wanted to come and say thanks for the picture.' Ben's face kept flicking from his to the other tables in the centre. 'I hope that's OK.'

A few weeks ago, Simon would have been irritated by the boy's presence because it meant he couldn't have a private conversation with Claire. But now he was touched. It took guts to come to a place like this.

'It's really good of you to come.' As he said the words, Simon realised he could have been talking at a dinner party. 'Don't be nervous. No one's going to cause any trouble here; not with the officers around.'

Ben nodded tightly. He'd taken his plug earrings out now, Simon noticed.

'Are you all right now?' Simon wasn't sure if he was phrasing this right.

'Yes.' Ben nodded again. 'It was silly of me to run away.'

Simon felt Claire's hand reaching for his under the table. He squeezed it back. 'Not at all. In fact, it reminded me of something I'd forgotten. I ran away at your age too.'

'No way!' Ben's face was shining. Claire looked surprised too. It was a bit of a gamble telling them both the full story but what the hell. 'I was about your age and thought I was in love with a girl at home. I was at boarding school then. So I went back to see her and nearly got expelled.'

Claire was laughing now. 'You never told me that.'

He tried to make light of it. 'It was years ago. But, as I said, it reminded me of how I felt at that age.' His words were getting lost in the noise around them so he raised his voice slightly. 'I'm sorry if I haven't understood before, Ben. When I get out, it will be different. I promise.'

Claire was looking at him in the same way she used to before The Accident. 'Thank you,' she was mouthing and then, because she'd been late, the bell rang and visiting time was over already.

'I haven't asked you about your work,' he said urgently as they rose to go.

'Everything's fine,' she said. 'What about you?'

He had wanted to tell her about Plait Man but he couldn't, not with Ben there. 'Fine. I've made you a Christmas present. It's going through security at the moment.'

'We had to leave our gifts at the desk too.' She smiled. 'I expect they're being checked as well.'

'What are you doing on Christmas Day?' His chest quickened with fear in case she was spending it with Charlie.

'Probably having lunch with Mrs Johnson.'

The relief softened the blow that the Visit was over now. 'Everyone out now, please.' The officer, the one who had been kind to him over Plait Man, was standing by his table.

'Bye.' He wanted to kiss her on the cheek but it would get them into trouble. Instead, he held out his hand awkwardly to Ben and shook it. The boy's eyes were darting left and right at the men and their families as he did so. 'Happy Christmas,' said the boy. And then, rather awkwardly, 'Thanks for having us.'

Happy Christmas, thought Simon to himself as he walked back to G hut. Who did he think he was kidding? How could it be happy when he wasn't with Claire? Then he thought back to last year when Ben had gone to Charlie's and Claire had spent the whole day feeling wretched because her son wasn't there and he hadn't understood. Then, when Ben had come back for Boxing Day, he'd had a go at him for not getting up until lunchtime and having breakfast when they were eating a proper Boxing Day lunch. He'd been too fucking hard on the kid, he realised now too late. Just as his father had been with him.

The boy's voice just now came back to him, floating like an innocent cloud over this place. '*Thanks for having us,*' he had said. The other men would have roared with laughter if they'd heard but the courtesy showed the kid was trying. It would be different, he had promised Ben, when he got out. He intended to keep that promise.

'Feeling lonely? Trying to make a new start? Then come to our Christmas Service on ...'

Simon glanced up at the notice on the outside board. Why not?

Four days later, he found himself in the small white hut which someone had daubed on the outside with a variety of mixed paints, making it look more like a beach hut. Inside, however, was a ring of chairs which had proper wooden backs and red seats, unlike the plastic ones in the rest of the prison.

As he went in, one of the men who worked in the kitchens with him handed him a hymn book and a sheet. The vicar was a tall, thin older man who had a gentle manner. He shook his hand and told him he was welcome.

The service was short but full of Christmas hymns that Simon recognised from his school days. When he filed out afterwards, along with the others, the vicar shook his hand again and said he hoped he might come again.

He would have liked to have agreed but what was the point? Nothing could take away the fact that he was a murderer.

Not just of one person. But two.

Chapter Thirty-one

Everyone said Christmas would be horrible in prison. Even Spencer who was normally upbeat, warned the food would be 'shit' because it was always a skeleton staff, no pun intended. Georgie was moping because his brother's wife had just had a baby and he wasn't there for its first Christmas. 'Don't they mind you being gay?' asked Spencer curiously.

'No.' Georgie looked indignant. 'They take me as I am. Besides, I do their hair for them.'

Of course. Why hadn't he realised that Georgie was a hairdresser? It seemed obvious now having those lovely glowing locks.

In fact, Christmas wasn't too bad. The food wasn't shit at all – there were second helpings of roast potatoes which would have been nothing in Simon's old life but meant a great deal more now. There were organised card games in the dining room afterwards and then someone invited him to join in a game of Monopoly back in the hut.

All he really wanted to do was talk to Claire on the phone but it took ages to queue. As he stood waiting, he read a few more chapters of *Curious Incident* and then found that he'd bookmarked the page with an envelope containing a Christmas card that Caroline-Jane had given each one of them at the end of the term.

'Try painting your way out of your low spots,' she had written. 'I also hope that you will help me put together a joint art exhibition at Grimville in the New Year. I'll be giving you more details when we start again in January.'

Grimville? Simon's blood froze. He didn't like the sound of that.

'You going to use the phone or what?' demanded a voice

214

behind him.

Yes! She was picking up.

'Hello?' Claire's voice sang out. 'Simon! At last!'

Keen to explain the delay, he tried to tell her about the queue. 'It's all right.' She cut in. 'You've rung now. Are you all right?'

He'd thought he was but the sound of her voice now made him desperately homesick. 'I miss you.'

'Me too.' As she spoke, there was the sound of someone laughing and a dog barking.

'Are you with Mrs Johnston?'

There was a slight pause. 'Yes but ...'

That was a man's voice in the background. 'Charlie's there,' he stated numbly.

Claire began to babble. 'That's what I was going to tell you. He came in to give Ben his present.'

'And he's stayed for lunch?' He wanted her to deny it.

'That's right. You don't mind do you?'

'Get a move on, mate. We all want to talk to our missus, you know.'

'I've got to go.' Simon felt his fists tighten. 'I'll call tomorrow.'

'Simon ...'

Slamming the phone down, he walked briskly to his cell. As though on remote, he got out the paints that he'd 'borrowed' from the art room. He didn't have any paper but what the fuck. There were the walls, weren't there?

Chapter Thirty-two

Claire put down the phone from Simon filled with a sense of deep foreboding. She'd been hoping that he wouldn't ring when Charlie was there. It had been her first thought when her ex-husband had called unexpectedly with Ben's present and a large bottle of champagne. The plan had been for him to pick up their son during late afternoon but there he was, standing at Jean's doorbell, beaming as though he was a guest who had arrived bang on time.

'We're still having lunch,' she had said.

'Don't worry!' cooed Jean from the kitchen, whose hearing was sharp when she wanted it to be. 'There's plenty for one more.'

And then Ben had come out into the hall together with Slasher who began licking Charlie's fingers enthusiastically and she could tell from the look on her son's face that despite the tricky scene in Charlie's flat the other week, Ben wanted his father to come in.

That had been just before the phone call. Now Simon was going to get completely the wrong idea.

'That was delicious, Mrs J,' said Charlie stretching out on the sofa afterwards. Her landlady seemed to like it, rather than seeing it as over-familiar. It annoyed Claire, however, reminding her of her ex-husband's arrogance.

'Absolutely delicious!' Charlie repeated, rising to his feet. He hadn't had anything to drink, Claire noticed. Not even half a glass of wine which he used to allow himself before driving somewhere. Was that because of The Accident? 'But we really ought to get going. I've got a surprise planned for this evening.'

He glanced at Claire. 'I could try and get a third ticket.'

She hesitated for a moment. Ben wanted her to come – she

could see that. Yet at the same time, she could just imagine Simon's face if he called again and Jean told him she was out.

'It's all right, thanks. You two have some boy time.' She tried to make light of it. 'Sounds intriguing, though. I didn't think any of the theatres were open on Christmas Day.'

Charlie tapped the side of his nose knowledgeably. It was another habit, she suddenly remembered, that had driven her mad. 'I don't want to spoil it. Ready Ben? Don't forget to thank Mrs J.'

It was as though he was trying to take over, by acting the resident parent.

'No need for that, dear.' Jean was giving Ben a hug. 'He's always thanking me. Now off you go and have a good time. No, Slasher, you can't go too!'

To her surprise, Charlie bent down and gave her a kiss on the cheek, dangerously close to her mouth. The action didn't go unnoticed by Jean.

After they'd gone, Claire made to go up the stairs to hide the tears which had inexplicably started to smart in her eyes. 'I'll be down in a second,' she said in a strangled voice, 'to help with the washing up.'

'That can wait.' Jean was putting on her anorak. 'Why don't you come for a walk with me instead along the seafront. It's really blowy out there, perfect for blasting away all the hassles that come with this time of year.'

She was right. The fierce spray of the water soaked them as they walked briskly behind Slasher who was tearing up and down the pebbled beach. 'That's what I love about winter,' said her landlady. 'Dogs are still allowed on the beach. We used to bring Mungo here.'

Claire was still feeling too upset to talk. In her head, she could see her son and former husband having fun somewhere without her, while her real husband was in a cell, assuming that she was having a great time with Charlie. And what had that kiss been about?

Jean linked her arm through Claire's. 'It will get better, you know. Time is a great healer.' Her landlady looked out over the sea. 'My life has been a lot better since you both came along. I've had lodgers before but never a mother and son.'

Claire swallowed. 'We both have Alex to thank for that.'

'Ah yes, Alex.'

'He's your accountant, isn't he?'

Jean nodded. 'His father knew my husband. They're an old Devonian family as you might know. But the two men are very different.'

'Really? We – that is Charlie and I – have known Alex and Rosemarie ever since we moved down here from London.'

'How well do you really know them, though?' Jean's features looked sharp and pinched in the wind.

Claire hesitated. 'They both took my side after Charlie and, in fact, they introduced me to Simon. But Rosemarie dropped me after the accident.'

Jean made a sympathetic noise. 'I worry about you, dear.' There was a silence as they both looked out across the beach to where Slasher had diminished into a small black speck that was now making its way back to then. 'You have two men who care for you. Your husband and your ex. If you want my advice, don't rush into any decisions.'

That evening, Claire turned down Jean's invitation to watch television and logged on to her emails. Incredibly, her agent had sent one yesterday, on Christmas Eve.

I know you're probably busy with family stuff but I've just had a publisher who wants some ideas – illustrations and text if you can think of it – for a book that would appeal to the 9–12– year market. They're very keen to involve reluctant readers who come from troubled backgrounds.

Instantly, a picture of the girl and her brother at the table next to them at the prison came back to her. The girl had had bright red ribbons in her hair which clashed with its auburn colour and she was trying to talk to her father but being drowned by both her brother and a large angry woman wearing hooped earrings. The word 'maintenance' figured prominently in the conversation and 'site fees'. She had wondered at the time if they were travellers.

Claire switched off her laptop and picked up one of her charcoal sticks. Within minutes, she was back in her old world; the only one that she felt truly comfortable in.

As New Year approached, Claire couldn't help thinking about this time last year. She, Simon, Alex, and Rosemarie had all gone out to dinner together at a lovely Italian bistro just outside Exeter. Ben had been staying with friends whose mother knew Claire and who had rung just before midnight to assure her that all was well.

No worries then about staying out late with band friends and drinking too much.

'What are you doing for New Year?' asked Jean interrupting her thoughts. 'Only I thought I might get a DVD in and one of those nice meals for two from M & S.'

Claire knew she should feel grateful towards Mrs J and she did; she really did. But the idea of making polite conversation on the most emotional night of the year was too much. Ben was going out with the band. 'That's very kind but I think I might just catch up on my work and then have an early night.'

'Work?' Jean tutted. 'A young woman like you shouldn't be working on New Year. Another cuppa, dear?'

In vain Claire had tried, over the years, to explain to others that she didn't see her painting as work. It was what she did like breathing and she would need to do it even if someone didn't pay her.

It had been an issue with Charlie when they'd been married, although Simon had always given her space and respected her work.

'Mind you,' added Jean. 'I admire your paintings. Not that I was snooping but I had to go into your room to measure up the window – time for some new curtains, don't you think? – and I saw that picture of the little boy and the dog on your desk. I hadn't realised how good you are!'

Claire prickled. It was her room. She was paying money for

it out of her salary now the savings were running out. Jean had no right to snoop. Not for the first time, the woman's kindness and curiosity began to close in on her.

'Maybe you're right.' She stood up. 'Perhaps I shouldn't stay in. In fact, there's a staff party in one of the local pubs. I might go to that instead.'

'Sounds really exciting!' Jean's face beamed and for a moment, Claire wondered if she should ask her. The woman was going to be on her own. She had saved Ben. Yet she could also suffocate them if Claire wasn't careful.

'Maybe. Anyway, I must go back to my room now. I've got something to finish. Thanks for the tea.'

'You don't mind if I go, do you?' she asked Simon later on the phone.

'You must.'

His approval surprised her.

'I won't stay long.'

'Don't be silly. It's important for you to mix with your work colleagues. I can't expect you to sit at home just because I'm here.'

Was he being sarcastic? 'How's everything?'

'Fine. I'm doing quite a lot of painting.'

'What of?'

'Walls.' He laughed. 'There are a lot of them here. Look. I'd better go. There's a queue. Have a good time. All right?'

It had been years since Claire had gone into a pub on her own. How weird it felt without Simon beside her. 'We'll be in the back!' Debbie had chirruped on the phone. Trying not to breathe in the stench of beer, Claire made her way through the crowds, all intent on celebrating the New Year.

'There you are!' Debbie gave her an unexpected warm hug. Several faces smiled in greeting. There was Lizzie who taught media studies and Bob who did maths and over in the corner was Eileen, head of Spanish. 'What are you drinking?'

'Diet Coke, please.'

'You've got to have something stronger than that!' She turned to see a big bear of a man whom she hadn't seen before. 'Here. Have a slug of this.'

He thrust a glass of something sparkly into her hands. Claire hesitated. She hadn't had a drink since The Accident and, even before it, she'd only been a light drinker. But she needed something now to obliterate the picture of Simon inside. It tasted bubbly. Light. Innocuous.

Garth was a good listener. 'Let me get this right. If this man – Hugh, you say – could be convinced to admit that he grabbed the steering wheel, your husband could appeal.'

Claire's hand clutched the glass stem. Somehow one drink had become three. 'That's what the lawyer told us at the time.'

'And now this Hugh is harassing you.'

The drink made her words come out in a rush. 'He's sending Simon letters and I think he was behind the campaign to drive us out of the house.'

'What about your son? Is he all right now?'

Claire groaned. 'He comes in reeking of drink when he's out with his band but he hasn't run away again.'

Garth put a hand on her shoulder. 'Poor you. It must be very difficult. How are you managing financially?'

Was he expecting her to buy the next bottle? If so, she didn't have enough. 'It's difficult.' Claire could feel her own words getting distinctly blurry. 'I work a bit but we're also on benefits.'

Someone was tugging on her arm. 'Claire! ' The voice sounded as though it was coming from a long way off. 'We're going back now. Can we give you a lift?'

When Claire woke up the next morning, she had a terrible pain down the right hand side of her head. The pub. Too much to drink. Ben. Ben!

Leaping out of bed, she dashed into his room. Thank God. His head was under the duvet and she could see it rising and falling. Who had got in last – her or him? To her shame, she couldn't remember.

That was the last time she was ever going to have a drink, she told herself, knocking back a couple of paracetamol. She spent half the day finishing the dog in the painting but he still didn't look right. Giving up, she took Slasher along the front, hoping the wind would inspire her. She'd take Ben to see Simon again on the next visit, she also decided. It had done some good, she was sure, on both fronts.

The following day, she went downstairs into Jean's kitchen, feeling much brighter. Her landlady was sitting at the table with the local paper in front of her. Immediately Claire sensed something wasn't right.

'What is it?'

Silently, Jean pushed the paper towards her.

Stepson of death-by-driving murderer gets drunk. Mother lives on benefits. Is this how you want your tax to be spent?

There was a byline below it.

Garth Walker.

Chapter Thirty-three

'Why did you do it, Mills? You were about to get moved into a single cell and now you've blown it.'

A room of his own! For so long, Simon had been waiting for this: peace and quiet at last without Spencer's prattle. And now he had messed up. Of course, he'd known he was going to get into trouble for daubing the walls of his cell after his phone call to Claire. At the time, he hadn't cared. Not even when Spencer had come back from football practice in the yard and whistled in a low appreciative way, before declaring he'd 'really copped it, man'.

Now, face to face with governor number one, Simon began to feel a flicker of apprehension mixed with remorse. The man standing in front of him in his off-the-peg, not very well cut grey-striped polyester suit, would consequently categorise him along with all the other yobs in G Hut.

'Why did I do it?' Simon repeated the question. Repeating the other person's question was a legal trick he'd learned over the years. It gave you extra time and it often made the other person feel rather awkward just as it did when you used his or her full name. Simon didn't know what Governor Harris's full name was although his initial was 'R' on the door. Roger didn't really suit the unpolished accent or the slicked back black hair. Ron maybe, or perhaps Rod. How did one become a governor number one anyway?

'Come on, Mills. Stop wasting my time and yours. I want to know why you painted your cell wall.'

'Why do you care?' Simon felt a flash of anger. 'Why don't you just give me one of your detentions or whatever you call it and we can call it quits.'

'Because,' said Governor Harris, motioning that he should

sit down, 'I like to get to know my men. Especially when they've stepped over the line.'

He might have felt the same, thought Simon grudgingly, if he'd been in the other man's shoes. Ignoring the invitation to sit down, he crossed the governor's beige carpeted office to look out of the window.

It was a nice view for a prison. Outside was a lawn from the days when this place had once been a small stately home for a proper family. Although it was January, Simon could spot a couple of optimistic green shoots poking out of the large bed in front.

'I used to have an office that wasn't dissimilar to this,' said Simon, still looking across the lawn towards the Visitors' Car Park.

'Tell me about it.'

It seemed discourteous not to.

'I used to be a solicitor.'

'I know.'

'Then I killed someone.'

Governor Harris glanced down at the file in front of him. 'That's one way of putting it. Others might see it as a tragic lapse in an otherwise unblemished life.'

Joanna's shriek was so unexpected and high-pitched that it shook him. '*Tragic lapse? Whose side is he on?*'

Simon struggled to shut out her voice. 'I did something I shouldn't have done.'

'*Better,*' sniffed Joanna.

'What about the wall?' persisted Governor Harris. He glanced again down at the file. 'You've been exemplary since you got here. Joined the Listeners; polite to staff; an active member of the art group. So much so, it seems, that you ran out of canvas.'

Was that meant to be a joke? The governor's face wasn't smiling but there appeared to be a twinkle. 'A rainbow, I believe you were painting. Aren't they meant to be a symbol of hope?'

All Simon could remember was that he had felt the huge

224

urge to lash out. The paints, together with a bottle of tomato sauce that Spencer had nicked from the dining room, had made quite a picture.

'I'd just been on the phone to my wife. She was having Christmas lunch with her first husband and their son.'

The governor's face now took on a resigned look as though he had heard this before. 'That must have been difficult for you.'

'That's what I was taught to say in my Listening training,' said Simon urgently. 'It's called empathy. Well I don't need your fucking empathy. I need to get out of here before that bastard gets back with my wife. He treated her badly but she still feels something for him. I know it. And they've got a son, Goddamit, who didn't like me before I came Inside, let alone now. He ran away the other week because he's being bulled about having a murderer of a stepfather. They've had to move house because there isn't any money coming in to pay the mortgage. They're living in a two-bedroom bedsit because someone put a brick through the window of the old house. And you want to know why I painted a bloody wall.'

A cup of tea was being put in front of him. Was this a test to see if he would throw it at the governor?

'My wife always says that a cup of tea puts things in perspective.' The governor was sipping his. 'One of the things we try to do is help to keep families together when they're separated by a prison fence. I see from your notes that you're quite a long way from your wife.'

His right temple began to throb. 'She only comes here once a month.'

'And you feel she could come more often?'

The throbbing increased. 'Yes. She works and she's got the boy but if the positions were reversed, *I'd* see her more often.'

Governor Harris looked thoughtful. 'Teenage boys need keeping an eye on. Your experience here will probably have shown you that already.'

Simon considered Spencer.

'What does your wife do?'

He wanted to laugh. 'She's an artist. Illustrates children's books.'

A light lit up in the governor's eyes. 'Would I have heard of them?'

Simon named a few titles and the Governor looked even more intrigued. Good. He'd really know he was different from the other men now.

'Is that why you took up art? To compete with her?'

For Chrissake! 'Are you a psychologist?'

'It was part of my training,' answered the governor easily. 'Look, Simon. I'm just trying to work out how we can resolve things without getting you shipped out.'

'*Said you'd be in trouble*,' butted in Joanna snidely.

'You might not like it here,' continued the governor, picking up his pen. 'But if you were in a confined prison, you'd soon wish you were back in an open one.'

'Holdfast,' muttered Simon. 'I was at Holdfast before the trial.'

'Ah, yes.' The governor's words hung heavily in the air.

'I'm sorry.' The words came out desperately. 'I'm really sorry. It won't happen again, I promise.'

The governor's pen was moving across the page. 'I'd like to move you to a closer Open Prison nearer your wife but there aren't any spaces. You've got four months left of your sentence, right?'

Four months, one week, and two days.

'I'm going to recommend that you become a library orderly. A vacancy has just arisen. You'll have a month of that and then you can start your community work.'

Simon was just about to thank him but realised the man was still speaking. 'I'm also going to agree with your art teacher's request to include you in her team visit to Grimville next month.'

Simon's blood ran cold.

'Actually, sir, I'd rather not. Caroline-Jane – I mean the teacher – mentioned it before Christmas but I don't want to go over there.'

Automatically, he glanced across the lawn to the left where the high metal fence divided the two prisons.

'Why not?'

'Because it's full of murderers and rapists.' His mouth tightened. 'It's disgusting.'

The governor made a questioning face. 'Don't you believe that we should have a second chance in life? Your newly discovered talent – I believe that's how your art teacher described it to me – might inspire some of them to change their lives. I'm a great believer in the power of art and literature.'

Simon took another quick look at the books that lined the study.

'OK. I'll do it.'

'Good.' The governor stood up. 'Just one more thing, Mills. When you get back to your hut, you'll be given a bucket and brush to rub off your rainbow.'

'Thank you, sir.'

They were standing by the door now. 'But you can still keep rainbows in your heart, Mills. No one can rub them off there.'

'He's a nice bloke.' Mark the librarian was listening to Simon's story. It was a week later and it had passed faster than any of the previous weeks, thanks to his new job.

Carefully, Simon put another row of books back on the shelves. Already, he'd been surprised by the kind of people who came in. The Dog Man was a regular; always heading for military histories. Then there was the very quiet man on the other side of the corridor from him in the hut who got through a new comic book once a week.

Once, the paedophile came in and Simon felt sick when he took out a book called *How To Write For Children.*

'Can't you stop him?' demanded Simon after he'd gone.

Mark shrugged. 'Tricky one, that. Lots of people write here. They say they've got the time at last.'

'Do you know what he's in for?'

'No. I don't want to.'

Simon felt sweat running down his back. 'Maybe you ought

227

to. Trust me, a book on how to write kids' books isn't really suitable.'

'I'll look into it. Thanks.'

'Don't say I told you.' Simon felt nervous. 'I don't want any trouble.'

'I won't.' Mark produced a new book from behind the counter. 'Take a look at this. It's Sebastian Faulkes's latest. Thought we might give it a try at the book club. What do you think?'

It was at times like this, thought Simon, that you could almost – for a few minutes at least – forget you were in prison.

For the last month (since Christmas) Claire had been sounding distant when he rang. Often, he could only get through to her answerphone. When they did speak, she didn't seem to listen to what he was saying and when he asked her about her job in the school or how Ben was, her replies had been vague.

It was clear as day. She was seeing Charlie again. The thought made him physically throw up in the loo, with its brown stains in the bowl from previous users.

'You don't know that, man.' Spencer was lying on his back on the bed, working his way through a Quick Read that Simon had found for him in the prison library. It was a Sunday and some of the men were on a Visit.

Those lucky sods who had been there for long enough to qualify for privileges were either out for the day or back home providing it was close enough for them to get back by 5 o'clock roll-call. If they didn't, the punishment was no visits for three months and if it happened more than once, they could be shipped out.

'I wouldn't blame her.' Simon was pretending to sketch something on a piece of paper he had smuggled back from art. 'He's got money. He's Ben's father. And he's not in prison.'

Spencer wrinkled his face. 'Doesn't mean she loves him though. Listen, Si, what does this say?' He placed a thick stubby index finger on a word.

Simon got down from his own bed and looked over the

228

boy's shoulder. 'Opportunity,' he said out loud. 'Remember we had that the other day? It's got two "p"s in it because opportunity is such a great thing that it deserves more than one "p".'

'Cool, man. Know what? You oughta be a teacher when you get out. Not a solishitur.'

'Hah! Not with my record.'

Spencer looked disappointed. 'You could be a cleaner for London Transport then. That's what I want to do, like my cousins.' He grinned. 'Helped you do a good job on your wall, didn't I?'

That was true enough.

'You going to the Dark Side with that art teacher then?' Spencer jerked his finger at Simon's sketch pad. He'd learned, since sharing the cell with the boy, that the kid's mind bounced from one subject to another.

'I suppose so.'

They both looked out at Grimville, glowering at them from over the wall. 'Ain't you scared of it?'

'Sort of.'

'You wouldn't get me going in there, I can tell you. I've been in places like that.' Spencer shivered. 'Once ...'

He stopped as a low plaintive whine rose into the air, falling and rising in tone that set Simon's ears on edge.

'What's that? It sounds like an air raid.'

Spencer was pressing his nose against the glass like a child trying to make out what was going on. 'Fuck me. Sounds like the prison alarm from next door. Something's happened at Grimville ...'

Chapter Thirty-four

Claire felt disgusted with herself! How could she have been so stupid? What on earth had possessed her to drink too much cheap bubbly and then pour her heart out to a complete stranger in the pub?

Even Jean couldn't find her usual positive words. 'Maybe it might blow over, dear,' was all she could come up with. As for Ben, how could she begin to explain to a child that his own mother had snitched on him by telling a reporter about him drinking and then running away?

'Maybe you won't have to, dear,' said Jean as she sat there, shivering over the sweet cup of tea. 'Teenagers don't usually read national newspapers, let alone local ones.'

But everyone in their small town was an avid reader of the bi-weekly paper that Garth worked for and when Claire went to buy some fruit and veg from the greengrocer, she was served in silence instead of the usual jolly banter.

What would happen when she went back to school? Debbie had rung her on the day the paper had come out. 'I'm so sorry,' she said, with the emphasis on 'so'. 'I feel responsible.'

'Why?' she asked wretchedly.

'I brought Garth along. He's a neighbour and at a loose end. The trouble with journalists is that they're never off duty.'

Claire wanted to say it was all right but couldn't. True, she had spoon-fed him the lines but it was still so wicked of him.

'Mind you,' added Debbie. 'It was quite a shock to all of us. You did say you were separated; not that your husband was in prison.'

'I didn't lie.' Claire found herself stammering. 'I just didn't feel able to ...' She left the rest of the sentence hanging in the air, conscious that her excuses were making things worse. Then she thought of something. 'Have you got his email?'

Debbie sounded hesitant. 'Yes but …'

She could feel her voice being firm. 'Can you text it over, please.'

'What are you going to say to him?'

'I don't know yet.'

'There's something I ought to tell you, Claire.'

She knew it.

'The headmaster wants to see you. Before term starts.'

Maybe, Jean assured her, the head just wanted to reassure her; check she was all right. It was possible, wasn't it? But now, as she entered his study, Claire felt less certain.

'Ah, Mrs Mills.' The head usually referred to his staff by their first name. 'Please sit down.'

She did so, uncomfortably aware of the local newspaper neatly folded in front of him.

'Tricky business, this,' he said, glancing down at it.

Claire nodded.

'I have to say that I am disappointed you chose not to reveal your background when you applied for the job.'

He raised his eyebrows, waiting for her answer. Claire felt her throat thudding. 'I didn't feel it was strictly relevant.'

The eyebrows twitched. He had a bald head which made him look rather like an intelligent worm. 'On the contrary. It is extremely relevant. Parents pay a great deal of money to send their children here and I've already received several phone calls, complaining that one of the teachers is married to a man serving time.'

Claire felt her cheeks redden. 'My husband is a solicitor.'

The head nodded. 'That's as maybe but he still killed someone, albeit in an accident. It's the sort of publicity which is not good for the school.'

'But you can't punish me for something that my husband did.'

The headmaster looked at her sadly. 'I'm afraid there is something else, too, Claire. You weren't totally honest about your qualifications, were you? Even if it hadn't been for this unfortunate business, we would have had to have let you go.' He gestured towards a file lying in front of him. 'We should have checked before you started but, as you know, we were desperate for someone. It has only recently come to my attention that you aren't a qualified teacher at all.'

Now he'd think she was as bad as her husband. 'I'm sorry.' She spoke quietly. 'I needed the job so badly.'

He made a wry face. 'You're a natural teacher, Claire. That's the irony. But we have a duty to our parents and they expect people with the right paper qualifications.'

Of course they did. 'What do you want me to do about it?'

'I'm afraid I will have to ask you to withdraw, Mrs Mills. You are a very talented artist but you were given the job on the understanding that you were a proper teacher. I am sorry.'

'Mum. How could you?'

Ben met her in the hall as she came back from the interview, hot with fury even though it was cold and rainy outside.

She took one look at the paper in his hand and felt as though someone had punched her in the stomach. 'I'm sorry.'

His eyes glistened with tears. 'I can't go back to school ever again. Everyone will know.'

As soon as he said it, she realised it was the truth.

'I've lost my job.' She spoke quietly, both to Ben and to Jean who was standing at the kitchen door. 'I'm not sure what we're going to do.'

His eyes were fixed on her. Steady. Trusting. Convinced she could make it all right again. The heaviness of the responsibility made her scared.

'Dad will help us.'

'No.'

'He's already rung me. He says we can live with him.'

'Are you sure that's a good idea?' This was Jean. 'Sorry. I shouldn't have said that. It's not my place. But I do have a suggestion to make. My brother lives in London and he's looking for help. It wouldn't involve too much – just cleaning and cooking his meals. He's a writer; bit of a recluse really. Supposing I ring to see if he might take you in? Just until your house sells and you can find somewhere of your own.'

The more Claire thought about it, the more she realised that it wasn't a bad idea. London would be nearer Simon and it would buy them time and space away from this place. The downside was that Ben would have to go to another school at a critical point in his education. She felt terrible about that.

'What about my band?' Ben glared up at her from his bed where he'd taken to lying. 'You can't take me away from it.'

'You could come down here at weekends and stay with Dad. That way you won't miss the practices.'

'OK.' He looked slightly mollified but she still felt horrendously guilty. When was she ever going to be able to create a firm base for her family, or what was left of it, again?

Charlie was very good! Claire had to give him that. He'd thought the move was a sensible idea too and was enthusiastic about having Ben down every weekend. Too enthusiastic. It wasn't fair, she couldn't help thinking, that he had been away for months on end with work without seeing his son and now expected to pick up the pieces as though he'd been a conscientious father all along.

Just look at the way he was throwing himself into 'the next stage' as he called it, showing all the gusto of a project manager. 'I've drawn up a shortlist of schools in Islington,' he announced after driving Ben back from a cinema trip the following week. Islington was where Max Romer, Jean's brother, lived. 'We've been through them, haven't we, son, and came up with this one.'

Her ex-husband handed her a printed out Google page showing a picture of a group of teenagers in casual jeans and T-shirts in a computer room. It had always been her who had done homework on schools until now. 'Have you rung to see if they have a place before you get all excited about this one?'

'No, because I thought that, as it's state, we wouldn't need to.'

His naivety astounded her. 'Haven't you read about good state schools being oversubscribed?'

In the end, there wasn't a choice, particularly in view of the fact that term started next week for most schools. Indeed, there was only one which was willing to take Ben on.

Meanwhile, Claire had spoken to Jean's brother who had said, in a very quiet, slow voice at the other end of the phone that no, he didn't need to interview her because a reference from his sister was good enough. 'I have to tell you,' he went on to say in such a soft tone that she had to strain to hear him, 'that I was not very keen on taking a dog. However, my sister tells me that he is very well-behaved. If however, I find this is not the case, I will have to re-think the situation.'

Claire glanced at Slasher who was curled up in his basket by Jean's Aga. 'I promise you that he won't give you any trouble.'

There was a slight sound at the other end of the phone which might or might not have been a humph. 'My sister tells me that you are an artist.'

'Yes ...'

He continued in the same slow unhurried tone, overriding what she had been about to say. 'I believe you know that I am a writer. I need peace. Absolute peace. Can you guarantee that your son will give me that?'

Claire was beginning to feel warning signs flashing. 'He likes to play music but I will make sure it is not too loud.'

There was another silence. 'Very well. We will give it a go then. My sister will give you the address. I will see you on Sunday evening. Dinner will be at 8 p.m.'

Before packing up, Claire sent three emails and wrote one letter followed by a short note.

To Garth Walker. Your article betrayed my naive trust in you and has resulted in my son having to change schools and the loss of my job. I hope you can sleep easily after this.
Yours, Mrs Mills.

It might not do any good but it got it off her chest. Ditto for the next one.

Rosemarie. You might be relieved to know that Ben and I are moving away. We will no longer be an embarrassment to you. Please thank Alex for his kindness. Claire.

Then the third email.

Dear Hugh. We are leaving the south-west. I hope this will be of some comfort to you. Yours, Claire Mills.

The letter was purposefully practical.

Dear Simon,

This is just a quick letter because I haven't had a phone call from you. You probably haven't been able to get through. Things have happened at this end. We're not hurt physically but we have to move away from this place. My landlady has a brother in London whom I'm going to keep house for and Ben is going to school there. It will mean we are closer to you for visiting. The house has still not sold but when it has, we may have enough money to buy somewhere small or rent our own place. Please ring on my mobile as soon as you can. All my love as always, Claire.

But the note said it all.

Dear Jean,

Thank you. You saved us. We will never forget you.

Love from Claire, Ben, and Slasher.

Finally, an apology.

Dear Headmaster,

I deeply regret the embarrassment I have caused.

Kind regards,

Claire.

Chapter Thirty-five

We're not hurt physically but we have to move away from this place.

Simon read and re-read Claire's letter, trying to make sense of it. What did she mean about not being hurt physically? It implied that someone had been getting to her in another way. Simon clenched his fists. If it was that bastard Hugh, so help him, he'd kill him.

'*Dear me,*' tittered Joanna. '*That wouldn't look very good in court, would it?*'

'Shut up.' Simon knew he was talking out loud but Spencer wasn't in his cell. Recently, he had taken to hanging out with a new man who had been in prison with him before. Simon had noticed that there was a lot of hugging and backslapping between men if they recognised each other from previous jails. There was also bad feeling if they hadn't got on.

'*Back to the letter, darling. Your mind is wandering again.*'

'Whose fault is that?' he said out loud again. It was true. His mind did wander and he found it hard to concentrate on one thing at a time. It was this place that did it to him. An open prison was a contradiction in terms. You were given the illusion of being free but if you so much as walked out of those gates without permission, you were slammed up somewhere else. It was like standing outside a sweet shop and being told you were a potential customer but not quite yet.

'*The letter,*' prompted Joanna. '*I told you that you should have tried to ring her more often.*'

'I did! But it was always engaged. And you know why? It's because she was probably on the phone to bloody Charlie.'

'*Ooh dear, you are getting this jealousy-of-the-ex thing bad, aren't you?*' Joanna's voice sounded more sympathetic now. '*I felt the same about Hugh's wife at first but then when I got to know him more, I began to realise why she did a runner. Talking of runners, did they ever find out why the alarm went off over the road the other day?'*

Rumours had been running wild on that one. Simon could still remember how the hairs on the back of his neck had stood up when he'd heard that terrible cat-like sound on the other side of the wire fence that separated them from the murderers and the rapists.

Someone had said it was a false alarm. Someone else reckoned there'd been a break out. There was also a rumour that one prisoner had been hurt by another. None of them could be proved but whatever had happened, the alarm had stopped after about ten minutes and then it was as though nothing had happened. That was the thing about this place. No one told you anything.

Simon was still nervous about going to the Dark Side. But he also couldn't help feeling he owed it to Caroline-Jane. And to the governor.

'Ready?'

They had walked the short distance – too short – from Freetown to Grimville, across the camp road that divided them and were now waiting outside the huge metal door that led into the huge prison, wire walls screaming up around it.

There was him, Caroline-Jane, and also a man called Jack from her class who was, in Simon's view, a much more accomplished artist. Like him, however, he hadn't known he had it in him until coming into prison. He used to work in IT, he'd told Simon. Maybe he was in for fraud.

As they waited, a family group joined them. The woman, who had long straggly blonde hair with an artificial flower in it, was wearing bright red lipstick, high heels, and a black leather coat as though she were going to a cheap wedding. She was hanging on to the arm of a younger man complete with gelled-back hair in an ill-fitting suit who might or might not have been her son. Someone else was coming too. It was an older couple who were looking around them with sharp frightened looks.

'It's Family Day on C wing,' Caroline-Jane said quietly. 'The one next to ours.'

Family Day?

'Every few months, each wing invites family and close friends to visit the men.' She was whispering which meant her face was closer to his so he could breathe in her smell. 'They sit and chat in the community lounge. Have a cup of tea. Catch up.' She glanced up at the older couple who were speaking quietly to themselves. 'It's not a very natural situation but at least it allows them to try and maintain contact.'

She spoke as though she felt sorry for them. Yet these men had done the worst things imaginable. He'd probably, he realised with a sickening thud, read about their cases during the last twenty years. Thank God he'd never personally defended a murderer himself.

Joanna's voice tinkled. *'Ironic, don't you think, darling, given that you killed me. Now pay attention. We're going through the gates. Oooh, how exciting!'*

It wasn't. It was bloody terrifying. One of the officers was searching him now, frisking him down his body and then doing the same to Jack before flicking through his sketch pad and Jack's portfolios without saying a word.

Caroline-Jane had gone through another entrance, presumably because she was staff. He and Jack were then told to go through another door where they stood in line. Another officer accompanied by a rather handsome black Labrador walked down the line past them. The dog didn't stop. Simon didn't know if that was the right thing or not.

Then through another door where they had to wait until it clicked open and out into a yard where Caroline-Jane was waiting. 'All right?' She looked slightly worried. 'I know this takes a bit of getting used to.'

Jack laughed nervously. 'You can say that again. Do you really do this every afternoon after you finish our class?'

She nodded.

Simon didn't like that idea at all. She was too beautiful. Too

238

vulnerable. Nervously, he watched as she they approached another set of gates. She pressed a bell and within a couple of minutes they were in another courtyard, this time adorned by immaculate flower beds. On to another set of doors, outside which – rather incongruously – stood a rack of umbrellas.

'You're not allowed to take them in,' said Caroline-Jane, seeing their faces. 'They could be used for all kind of things.'

Deftly, she took one of the keys hanging from her belt and opened the door in front of them before putting the key back in her pouch. 'Aren't we going to have a prison officer with us as protection?' asked Jack, alarmed.

Caroline-Jane shrugged. 'There'll be officers on the wing.'

Surely this was even more reason for a woman not to do this kind of job. Simon could feel himself prickling with fear as they walked down a long corridor, resembling that of a hospital or airport. Two men sauntered past in black shorts and T-shirts as though they'd been to the gym. 'Hi, Caroline-Jane. How are you doing?' asked the one who had blue and red tattoos down his legs.

How dare they talk to her in such a familiar voice?

'Aren't you scared?' asked Jack quietly.

Caroline-Jane seemed to hesitate. 'When I first started, yes. But then you get used to it. Once you start talking to the men, you find that they're not as different as you might think.'

Different? Of course they were different. They had done terrible things, hadn't they? Things which he and Jack could never have done.

'The exhibition is on A wing,' said Caroline-Jane, reaching for a smaller pouch key. There were two gates in front of them now, each one made of heavy metal. It looked as though you could easily catch your fingers in them. Simon clutched his sketch pad with clammy hands. Even Joanna was silent.

They were truly Inside, now. Not like Freetown where you could walk around and breathe in fresh air. Here, the air smelt stale and the walls closed in. If he had to do his time in a place like this, he'd go stir-crazy.

In front of him stretched another corridor but narrower than the one outside. A young boy was leaning against the wall, examining his nails. He looked up as they came in and his eyes darted round first Jack and then Simon, taking in the sketchpad. He was wearing baggy tracksuit bottoms, a slightly grubby-looking white T-shirt, and a gold chain.

'Hiya, Caroline-Jane.' He was chewing gum.

'Hi.' Her voice sounded unnaturally bright and it struck Simon that, despite her earlier words, she was nervous too. 'Coming to the exhibition?'

'Didn't get approval.' The boy sniffed. 'Sorry.'

'What did he mean?' Jack whispered.

'The men have meetings with staff every week,' said Caroline-Jane quietly. 'They need permission from their peers as well as staff before they can go to any event. This way.'

She led them into a small office. On the other side of the desk sat a youngish officer whose spiky hair reminded him of a glossy hedgehog. 'Hi, Caroline-Jane.'

They all knew her. Suddenly Simon realised she had another life. Every day she would leave the safer environment at Freetown to come to this place. Christ! If he were her husband, he wouldn't allow it.

The officer was pushing a book towards them. 'Sign here please.' It was next to an old copy of *The Sun*, open at page three. 'You're in the community room. About sixteen takers from the list. Ready?'

'Sure.' Caroline-Jane's voice was now formal and crisp. They walked past a noticeboard on the wall bearing a list of names. 'That's our job schedule,' said a man wearing a round-neck jumper who vaguely resembled Simon's old squash club secretary. Only the prison ID chain gave him away. 'You know. Laundry. Cleaning. Positive Pull-ups. That's Neil's job. He has to praise us for stuff we get right to raise our self-esteem.'

What right did a rapist or murder have to self-esteem? They were going in to the dining room now where three men, huddled at a formica table, stared curiously and then looked away past a fish tank which was being cleaned out by a tall thin grinning bloke. 'Hello.'

Simon eyed the tank. 'You're allowed to keep pets?'

The man grinned again. 'They belong to all of us but I love fish. Always have done. So I volunteered to clean them out. The bloke next to me has got a budgie. Teaching him to talk, he is.'

'Crazy,' muttered Jack. 'There's a bloke in my hut what got seven weeks for microwaving his rabbit.'

Caroline-Jane's face darkened. 'You're in someone else's home. We observe the same courtesies that we would on the Outside.'

Even if she was wrong, they shouldn't annoy anyone. It might not be safe.

'Want a cuppa?' grinned one of the men at the table.

Was he joking? They might have done something to it. 'I've just had one thanks,' he replied casually.

The man laughed. ''Course you have.'

They were passing a sign now on a door.

Quiet please. Psychodrama in progress.

'The men have therapy every morning both from professionals and each other,' whispered Caroline-Jane. 'It's like positive peer pressure. You might get a rapist asking a bank robber why he had done it and vice versa.'

Jack snorted. 'That's rich.'

Yes – but part of him grudgingly admired such a daring approach. 'And does it work?

Caroline-Jane nodded enthusiastically. 'There's a much lower re-offending rate. Sometimes, men are moved directly from here to a D Cat., like Freetown.'

'Fucking hell. I don't want any of these weirdos sharing a pad with me.'

'You might want to think about that, Jack, when you meet them. That's one reason why Freetown is next to Grimville. It's to show people here that there is a next stage to aim for.'

At that moment, a grey-bearded man came out of the psychodrama room, greeting Caroline-Jane warmly. Then he turned to them. 'First time in the Dark Side, eh? Come on in and see what we get up to. It's OK. My men have agreed.'

It was a large room, rather like a community hall. A man

241

about his age displaying a drooping moustache was sitting opposite an empty chair; the others were lined round the walls. Everyone's trainers were spotless. It reminded him of what Spencer had said. Clean trainers were a sign of rarely going outside.

'The purpose of this psychodrama session is to address past issues,' the grey-bearded man was saying. 'Frank here is talking to his victim in the chair.'

But there was no one there.

'*Use your imagination*,' prompted Joanna. '*She's a bit like me, actually.*'

Frank shuffled awkwardly, hands in his pockets. 'I'm sorry. Honest.'

He glanced up at the grey-bearded man who nodded in encouragement. 'If I'd known your name before I did it, I might have stopped.'

Simon froze.

'I misread the signals. Thought you were giving me the come-on.'

Jack made a choking noise.

'If you hadn't been wearing that scarf, it would have been all right. But my mother had a scarf that colour. So when you said no, I wanted to punish you like she used to punish me and ...'

The man was weeping now in huge loud noisy sobs.

'I'm off!' Jack was making for the door. 'This is sick. Really sick.'

'No, man.' It was one of the two men sitting at the side. 'It's making us face up to what we did. Frank here would have apologised to his victim if she'd still been here but this is the best he can do. '

'What about her relatives?' Jack was getting really upset now. 'You can't make it up to her mum or her dad or her boyfriend or ...'

'There's the Forgiveness Trust,' the grey bearded man said quickly. 'It arranges for offenders and victims to meet up. Frank here is seeing his victim's relatives here next month.'

'Then I hope they'll smash him one.'

Privately, Simon agreed. 'Childhood abuse,' whispered Caroline-Jane as she took them along the corridor, 'is responsible for many crimes. Men repeat the pattern. It's very sad.'

'*Do your better,*' his father had said. '*Not your best. Your better.*' Had that been a form of childhood abuse? The constant need to be perfect. Was that why he had become slightly arrogant over his record of winning cases? Why he had gone on driving the Goodman-Browns home, even though he didn't know the way?

Why he'd ignored Alice when she'd said she wanted to stop?

'*You were seventeen, Simon.*' Joanna's voice was quiet. '*You were immature. So was she. Besides, she was the one who started it.*'

They were going into another large room now, with a seventies-type maroon carpet, mended in parts with wide black tape. At one side was a table football table with a giant television screen on the wall and on the other, was a row of framed pictures.

'The men did them in my classes,' explained Caroline-Jane with a hint of pride.

Simon stared at a large oil, showing a small bewildered boy next to a woman holding her head in her hands. There was a speech bubble above them; instead of words, there was a picture of a man's head and shoulders. The message was clear. It was a family, broken by the separation of prison.

'This is good.'

Caroline-Jane looked pleased. 'It won a prize in the Koestlers; a national arts award scheme. We got twenty-five last year.'

As she spoke, a bell rang. 'Freeflow's started.' She looked around. 'It's when men are allowed off other wings to go to events like Education or talks like ours.'

Simon's mouth went dry. He and Jack were meant to do about five minutes each. ('Just tell them about yourselves and how Art has helped.'). He'd given countless talks at law

243

conferences in the past but now he began to sweat as the men shuffled in.

They were of varying shapes and sizes. Large stomachs protruding over their waistbands. Academic types – thick-rimmed glasses and intense expressions. Shaved heads. Men who could have passed for office colleagues. Most wore baggy black track-suit bottoms but one or two had smart trousers and striped shirts.

They all looked curiously at Simon and Jack as though they had been flown in from Mars. *'Goodness,'* whispered Joanna. *'I didn't realise it was going to quite so intimidating. Rather you than me.'*

Caroline-Jane spoke first. It was a general introduction along the lines of how art could really help people in prison and that it wasn't just the pastime that the press made it out to be. It allowed inmates to come to terms with their crimes because they often found themselves painting something which made them re-evaluate their lives. It was, she added, a legal release from the turmoil in your head.

Several heads nodded at this. Then suddenly she turned to him. 'I'd like to introduce two of my students from the open prison next to us, here. Neither of them painted or drew before they came in so they are going to tell you what it has meant to them and how you too could feel similarly inspired. Simon, would you like to go first?'

Unsteadily, he rose to his feet. He'd prepared a speech but now the words felt inadequate and besides his mouth wouldn't open. There was a horrible pause and then someone began to shuffle.

'Show them your work,' hissed Joanna. *'Forget the speech. Just show them the pictures.'*

'Hi everyone.' There was another horrible pause. 'This is my sketch pad.' He held it in his hands, leafing through his pages.

'Until I got here, I never thought of drawing even though my wife is an artist.'

'Is she famous?' someone called out and Simon shook his head. Maybe he shouldn't have said that bit. What if someone tracked her down? He'd compromised her safety enough as it was.

'I used to be a solicitor.'

There were several hisses but most sounded friendly like the sort of hissing that you got at the pantomime when the bully appeared. 'Then I did something wrong without thinking.'

The man in the front row, whose enormous belly easily outdid everyone else's, was looking at him intently now and there was silence. 'I couldn't believe it when I got put into prison either.' He looked around with dark beady eyes. 'Do you know, when I was put Inside, people didn't have mobile phones?'

Someone snorted.

'Everything was so different in here from what I was used to.'

'You can say that again, mate.' This was from someone he couldn't see at the back.

'But one of the things that got me through was sketching.' He glanced at Caroline-Jane who was nodding reassuringly. 'I wasn't much good at watercolours but I really liked the feel of the charcoal.'

Someone tittered. 'I'm still a beginner but this is what I've done so far.' He held up his sketch pad. 'This is a picture of my hut that I sketched the other night, sitting outside.'

'We don't get outside, mate,' someone called out. ''Cept for half an hour a day.'

'But you will.' Caroline-Jane glanced at the officer who was sitting by the door. 'When you eventually get to a D cat.'

This was what it was all about, Simon realised. Encouraging men to keep going without breaking out. 'And this is what your place looks like, seen from my side of the fence.'

Several necks on the front row craned out towards him and there were general 'Can't see' murmurs. 'Would you like to pass it round?' asked Caroline-Jane. Rather reluctantly, he let his sketch pad go.

'It's all right for you,' shouted out one man in a Star Wars T-shirt. 'You've got a proper job to go back to. This art's just a hobby for you.'

Simon's mouth went dry. 'Actually, I won't be allowed to be a solicitor again.'

'What did you do then?'

It was a matter of honour, Spencer had always said, that people didn't ask this question until you got to know someone really well.

He gulped. 'Something that resulted in another person being killed.'

There was a hush. Jack edged slightly away and the big-bellied man from earlier stood up, scraped his chair on the lino and walked out.

'*Thank you,*' said Joanna stiffly, '*for telling the truth.*'

Caroline-Jane's face was rigid.

'It was a terrible mistake and I am paying for it now.' Simon spoke quietly, aware of the sea of eyes on him. 'I don't know who has got my pad but if you turn to the back, you will see something. Would you mind holding it up, whoever has it?'

'It's a hill,' called out a voice.

'I can just about see it from my hut on the Other Side. In my head, I imagine that I am still climbing that hill and when I get to the top, I know I have made it.'

'What about coming down?' someone yelled out.

Simon nodded. 'That's part of the image too. This time, I'm going to make sure that I come down much more carefully.'

Caroline-Jane's face looked less rigid now. 'Thank you,' she began. And then stopped at the loud ringing from the corridor. The officer leaped up, reaching for his walkie-talkie.

'What would you like us to do?' asked Caroline-Jane. There was a tremor in her voice.

'Sit where you are,' he yelled in a voice that chilled Simon's veins. 'No one is to move.'

Chapter Thirty-six

He'd let her down. Again. Simon had promised – absolutely promised – to call tonight but her mobile remained resolutely silent. She even switched it on and off to check it was still working.

'Sure you don't want me to help you move?' Charlie had asked but she had shaken her head.

'It's all right, thanks. We can cram most of our stuff into the car. Alex is coming round with the rest.'

'Alex?' Her ex-husband frowned. 'Thought you weren't in touch with those two after they dropped you.'

'Rosemarie dropped me,' she corrected him. 'Alex was the one who found me Mrs Johnson, remember?'

They'd been standing by her car which Charlie had helped to load. There was still Jean to go back and say goodbye to. 'Anyway,' she added crisply, 'we'd better be off. You'll meet Ben off the train at Exeter this Saturday then, when he comes down for the weekend?'

'Of course.' Charlie leant across and kissed her on her right cheek, close to her mouth. Embarrassed, she took a step backwards. 'I admire you, Claire.' His eyes shone; the way they'd done when they'd first met at uni and she'd known he was interested. 'You've grown into a much stronger person than you used to be. Not many women could cope with what you're going through.'

The kiss sat on her cheek all through the way to London. Not in a bad way – which it should have done – but not in a good way either. Meanwhile, Ben had fallen asleep on the back seat with Slasher on his lap. Claire stared straight ahead, concentrating on the road. Since The Accident, she'd driven ultra-carefully.

But the thoughts wouldn't stop.

Perhaps the kiss had merely been a mark of affection; she was, after all, the mother of his son. But had his remarks about being stronger, been a compliment or one of his superior comments? Of course she was stronger. She had to pretend to Ben it was all right.

She glanced again in the mirror at her son on the back seat. Why was it that teenagers looked so young when they were asleep? Slasher too was gently snoring, his nose in Ben's lap. Amazing really, how he had adjusted so easily to them even though he'd been living with someone else. Maybe adults were the same, deep-down, thought Claire. We like to think we mate for life but when things change, we move on, some faster than others. Just look at Charlie.

As for Simon, she always thought she'd be there for him when he came out but maybe he didn't want that now.

After all, he still hadn't rung.

By the time they got to the address that Max had given her, it was dark. Thank heavens for sat nav. If Simon had had it that evening, it might have all been so different. No. She mustn't think about that now. She had to concentrate on this part of her life; the new bit, so she could try to hold it all together.

'Are we here?' Ben sat up with a jerk as she pulled up outside the house. She'd need a parking permit, Max had told her. He would organise that although it would come out of her wages.

'I think so.' She gazed up at the dark grey building overlooking a park. She'd grown up in north London years ago and, to her mind, this was more Holloway than Islington. A couple of boys, Ben's age maybe, walked past. One kicked a can towards the car.

Slasher was beginning to whine. He'd been very good; they'd only had to stop once on the way so he could relieve himself at a motorway station. Now, however, it was clear he needed a pee.

'I'll take him somewhere.' Ben had his grown-up voice on;

she knew he wanted to help even though he was still cross with her about the article and having to leave his friends.

She glanced at the park opposite. 'You could go there but don't let him off the lead because he doesn't know it yet. I'll say hello.'

Nervously, she went up the small flight of steps. Some of these houses, she'd noticed as she'd driven along the street, were divided into flats. This one was on its own. Max must be a very successful author, she thought, as she rang the large white circular bell.

It seemed to be an age before she heard footsteps on the stairs. Several times, Claire glanced back at the park, wishing now that she hadn't let Ben take Slasher without her. Finally, the door opened and a man stood there, blinking behind owlish glasses as though surprised to see anyone.

'Yes?'

'I'm Claire.' Then, because it still didn't seem to register, she added. 'Your sister's former lodger.'

'Come in.'

She cast a desperate look at the park opposite. Where were they? 'I'm just waiting for my son.'

He stopped in the dim light of the hall, frowning. 'Coming later, is he?'

'No, he ...'

She stopped, almost overcome with relief as Ben and Slasher bounded up. 'Sorry. He took ages.'

Jean's brother blinked again. 'You must be the son and this,' he looked down, 'is your hound. I do not like dogs but my sister tells me this is a very well-behaved one. I do hope so.'

Slasher emitted a very low growl. 'He's never done that before,' said Claire quickly. 'It's all rather strange for him.'

'That's life for you.' Max moved towards a tall flight of stairs which loomed up at the far end of the dark hall. It was lined with books. 'This way. I shall show you to your room and then introduce you to the kitchen. I trust supper will still be ready on time?'

Supper? But he'd said it would be at 8. Too late, she realised

249

that had been a command rather than an invitation. 'I thought spaghetti bolognese would be easier to start with. You'll find the ingredients in the fridge. The boy can help you set the table, I expect, but I will show you your room first. I have a lot to get on with tonight and we've wasted enough time already.'

'He's treating you like a maid!' Ben's eyes shone with indignation. Clearly, his earlier anger towards her had gone and now it was Max he was furious with. 'Slasher doesn't like him either and you know what a good judge of character he is.'

Claire turned to draw the curtains and hide her face. She didn't want Ben to see the anger that she too felt. A few months earlier, she would have felt despondency but now she wanted to march straight downstairs and tell Max that she was here to be a part-time housekeeper and not a slave.

On the other hand, if she did that, he might just tell them to go immediately and then where would they be? Better, perhaps, to wait until tomorrow and see if he still behaved in the same way. What was it that Simon used to say? Everything felt better in the morning.

She glanced at her phone. A missed call! But it wasn't from the usual anonymous *Unknown*. It was Charlie. Against her better judgment, she rang him back.

'Hi. We're here. What's it like? Difficult to tell yet but …'

'Is that Dad?' Ben virtually snatched the phone off her. 'May I speak to him?'

She nodded. From the sound of the footsteps going back down the stairs, it sounded as though it was time for her to get down and cook that spaghetti bolognaise.

Half an hour later, she could honestly say that she had done her best, considering. The 'considering' included a kitchen which clearly hadn't been updated since the fifties – cracked, speckled formica tops and an oven that had an encrusted top that clearly hadn't been cleaned in weeks. Her heart ached at the thought of her old kitchen.

As for the fridge, well, all she could hope was that they didn't get food poisoning. The mince was only just within the

250

sell-by date but it had been placed on top of a packet of mouldy brie.

Instead of bothering Ben, who was unpacking his haversack in the box room next to hers, she had rooted through drawers and found tablemats bearing pictures of faded meadow flowers covered in brown stains. The cutlery, in one of the formica drawers, had needed a good wash – something she had to do with the sliver of soap in the sink since there didn't seem to be any washing-up liquid. If Jean hadn't said Max was her brother, Claire would never have thought they were related.

'Ah, supper is ready, I see.'

She turned round to see Max striding into the kitchen. It was much lighter than the hall – its fluorescent light bars higher so she could see him more clearly. In some ways, he looked a bit like a younger Alan Bennett. He was now wearing a black polo-neck jumper, jeans, and brown flip-flops. His face also appeared friendlier although maybe that was due to the whisky on his breath.

'I'm afraid this isn't as ship-shape as I would have liked it. My previous help left some months ago in a bit of a hurry.'

She was beginning to see why. 'We need to get a cleaner in.' Her words were more forceful than she had intended. 'The arrangement was that I would be your part-time housekeeper – not a domestic help.'

He nodded, as though taken aback. 'Quite so, quite so.'

'Can you arrange to find one or shall I go through Yellow Pages tomorrow?'

He blinked again, rapidly. 'I would be grateful if you could do that. I believe there are some telephone directories somewhere.'

'I also have my own work to do. Jean may have told you that I'm an illustrator.'

At that point, Ben came down, looking lost. Her heart went out to him.

'Which school is the boy going to?' asked Max, sitting down at the table expectantly. He spoke as though Ben wasn't there.

'The one on the corner of this road, sir,' said Ben.

251

Claire felt a shot of pride at her son's good manners. 'Are you now? Well, it's close. I'll say that for it, and it's not been in the news for a while.'

Ben looked at her with a panicky expression.

'Now, is dinner ready?' Max looked at his watch. 'I must say, it smells all right. Come on. I like to eat on time so I can write another chapter before bed.'

Later, after she'd washed up and done what she could with the kitchen surfaces, Claire went with Ben to take Slasher round the park one more time. There were a surprising number of people there, given how late it was. Several groups of youths walked past and one boy stopped to pat Slasher. Again he growled.

'I don't know what's come over him,' worried Claire.

'It's all very new to him.' Ben sounded more like a parent than a child. 'The noise doesn't help.'

As he spoke, there was the sound of another siren ripping the air. At home, there had hardly been any. It all seemed so frenetic here. So busy. Crowded. Dirty. Threatening. How she missed the sea! How she yearned for Simon's arms around her.

'Do I have to start school tomorrow?' he added. 'Couldn't I have just one day to adapt?'

Claire was torn. She could see why he needed some extra time but, then again, he'd already lost a week and during the crucial GCSE year, that wasn't good. 'I think it would be best if you went in.'

Ben said nothing. He was scared, she knew, and she understood that. Gently, she touched his arm. 'I'm sorry,' she said.

'Don't be.' His face looked angry in the light of the streetlamp above. 'It's not your fault. It's his.'

Was it? His words haunted her all evening. If she'd been a different kind of wife, would Charlie have left? Could she have hung on to Simon? Maybe it was time for her to change. Be stronger. Tougher. For Ben's sake as well as for her own.

That night, she couldn't sleep, tossing from side to side,

wondering why Simon hadn't called. There'd been messages from Charlie (again) and Alex as well as her sister from Vietnam and also Jean who had sent a text. *Do hope it's gng all right. Max can be a bit odd but he's all rt. Pls keep in touch.*

Who would have guessed, thought Claire, as she finally drifted off to sleep, that in less than a year, their lives could have changed so much. Was that what everyone thought when something happened to tip their world upside down. And if so, why didn't more people talk about it to warn others in advance?

During the night, at some point, she thought she heard the shattering of glass but it was far away, like a dream, so she turned over and went back to bed. The next thing she knew, as she woke to find light streaming in through the curtains, was that someone was coming into her room.

'Mum, Mum, wake up!'

A shaft of cold premonition shot through Claire as she took in Ben, standing over her. 'Slasher's gone. And someone's smashed into your car!'

Chapter Thirty-seven

Simon woke with a start after a disturbing dream involving Claire, Ben, and a dog. He was about to tell Spencer about it – they'd fallen into the habit of telling each other about weird dreams – but then he saw the curtainless window and the view of Freetown facing him. Then it came flooding back. He was on the Other Side. The side with rapists and murderers …

'Everyone stay put,' the officer had shouted last night and they had frozen, even the men. As the alarm continued, they heard footsteps running down the corridor.

'No one runs in this place,' muttered a thin wiry man next to him. 'Something must have happened.'

Caroline-Jane made her way to the officer standing, hands on belt, by the door. They spoke quietly before she came back to them. 'What's happened?' hissed Jack. He already had that kind of very pale white skin that looked like chalk, but he looked even whiter now.

'There's been an incident on the wing.' Caroline-Jane's voice was composed but Simon noticed her hands shaking. 'No one's allowed to leave at the moment.'

Simon felt a tightening sensation in his neck. They were trapped. He'd been terrified of that ever since he had gone through the gate and then through all those double doors with the locks. There was no way they could get out of this place. Anything could happen to them.

Jack began to whimper. 'Supposing one of them tries to kill us?'

The thin wiry man snorted. 'Don't be daft, man. It's probably just another alarm practice like the other week. 'Sides, you shouldn't worry about the murderers in this place. Most of

254

them have only done it the once and it's usually the wife.'

Caroline-Jane's mouth tightened. She'd hidden her hands, Simon noticed, under her notebook but he could still see that they were shaking. Claire's had done that when they'd arrived to arrest him. 'Don't worry,' he said quietly. 'We won't let anything happen to you.'

She started to say something but then stopped.

'I need to do a pee.' Jack was standing up.

'You can't yet, I'm afraid.' Caroline-Jane's voice was quiet.

'I've got to.' He walked towards the prison officer who must have told him the same thing because Jack then sat down on one of the chairs by the door, put his head in his hands, and began to cry.

Simon felt disgusted. They were all scared but if anyone deserved to weep, it was Caroline-Jane. She could, so easily, be Claire sitting here with that soft reddish-brown hair falling to her shoulders and her green eyes which were so like his wife's. He almost had to stop himself from putting his arm around her.

The men around him were getting restless; several had got up and were stomping round the room complaining it was time for dinner. One, who had steel-rimmed spectacles, announced to the room at large that 'all this is stuff is against our human rights'.

That's when Simon had his idea. 'How much paper do you have in your sketch pad?' he said, walking over to Jack. The boy was still crying but his pad was lying next to him. He flicked through. It was enough when added to his own empty pages.

'OK everyone,' he called out. 'Can you sit down please?'

Caroline-Jane looked up at him in surprise.

'We're going to do an exercise,' he continued.

'We're not kids,' muttered someone.

'This is an art exercise to see if you've got a hidden talent.' The word 'talent' seemed to do it and a few pulled up chairs. Simon turned to Caroline-Jane. 'May I borrow that box of charcoals you brought?'

Wordlessly, she passed them to him. Simon tried to

remember what he'd been taught. He'd been going to ask Caroline-Jane to do this but clearly she wasn't able to judging from her entire body which was now beginning to shake as the noises in the corridor outside grew louder.

'This is called charcoal.'

'You don't say,' grumbled someone in the back row.

Simon ignored him. 'You hold it like this. I'm going to pass some paper round and I'd like you to get into pairs.'

'We're not at fucking school, you know,' yelled out a burly chap sporting a goatee beard.

'One person from each pair takes it in turn to draw the other,' he continued, ignoring the outburst. 'Then after a while, you swap over. Caroline-Jane and I will walk round and give you some advice.'

'Can we sell them afterwards?' called out the thin wiry man in front.

'Maybe.'

'Blimey, we'll make our fucking fortunes.'

Simon glanced at Caroline-Jane. 'Please,' he whispered. 'I can't do this without you and it will keep everyone quiet until we know what's happening.'

She nodded. 'Right,' she called out, her voice wobbly. 'Now who would like some help?'

They managed to keep it up for over an hour. The footsteps had stopped now but still no one came in, apart from an officer carrying a stack of plastic glasses and jug of water. Clearly, thought Simon, this was no practice, otherwise they'd have been let out ages ago.

There were still a few complaints about being hungry – it was nearly six o'clock – but it was heart-warming to see how some of the men had really got into the 'exercise'. Simon almost forgot he was in the company of thieves and murderers as he walked from pair to pair. Even though he'd only been drawing for a short time, he could see what worked and what sometimes needed re-adjusting. 'Try making the face slightly narrower,' he told the man in steel-rimmed glasses. The other man, whom he'd been drawing, gave a belly-laugh. 'You've made me look like a fat bastard!' Caroline-Jane had been right, Simon thought, when she'd said that art was a great leveller. The concentration required stopped you thinking about the crimes behind the charcoal stick or paintbrush.

'*Come and look at this one!*' trilled Joanna as he walked towards another self-portrait, this time of a bald man who had a bluebird tattoo on his neck. '*It's really good!*'

Meanwhile, he could see, looking across the room, Jack was rocking himself back and forth on the chair, head in his knees. No one was paying any attention to him, least of all the officer, who was talking constantly in clipped tones into his walkie-talkie.

Then suddenly the door burst open and a sandy-haired man in his sixties, wearing a suit, walked in – an extremely serious expression on his face. His voice was bigger than his slight frame. 'Afternoon, everyone.'

'It's the bloody evening, mate,' someone called out. 'When are we going to eat? I'm fucking starving.'

'Please sit down and I will explain what is going on.'

Everyone did so apart from Jack who was still rocking backwards and forwards.

'You will no doubt have heard the noise outside.'

'Tell us something new, guv.'

'Unfortunately, we have had a tragic incident on the wing.'

A few of the men muttered. Simon felt his skin grow cold and he looked across at Caroline-Jane. She was staring straight at the governor.

'I have to tell you that it is a fatal incident.'

The governor was looking round the room as though gauging the reaction.

'Fucking hell.'

'Who is it?'

'Who did it? Was it an accident?'

'Is the pod closed now, then?'

The pod, Simon had already discovered, meant 'the kitchen'.

'As a result,' continued the governor, 'you will all need to be interviewed by the police.'

Now there was a stirring, men raising their voices in protest and some getting up off their chairs. 'Quiet,' roared the officer, touching his belt and gradually the room obeyed.

'I realise this is unpleasant but it is necessary. I want you all to remain in this room while we interview you one by one outside.'

The governor then looked straight at him and Simon felt horribly guilty. 'May we start with you, please, Mr Mills.'

Him? They wanted to talk to him? The last time he'd been interviewed by the police, they'd looked at him as though his very presence made them feel sick but this policeman was courteous and apologised for bothering him. It made Simon relieved to know that they realised he wasn't one of those men back in the room.

'*What's the difference?*' demanded Joanna. '*You are all guilty of ...*'

'Shut up,' said Simon fiercely and the policeman gave him a sharp look.

'Sorry.' He wanted to add that he was talking to someone else but that would have looked worse. 'I didn't mean you.'

The policeman's manner became cooler. 'I believe you were talking when one of the prisoners got up and left.'

A distant memory of a large man, distinguished by his protruding stomach and bald head, getting up and leaving, was coming back now.

'Do you recall what you were saying at the time?'

Simon's chest began to thump again. Panic attacks, Spencer had said when they'd first started. Breathe into a brown bag, man but there wasn't one to hand.

'I believe that I was being asked why I was in here and I explained that by accident, I had killed someone.'

The policeman nodded as though this was not news to him. 'Had you ever seen this man before?'

'No. Never.'

'You are certain?'

'Absolutely.'

'Very well then. Thank you. Just sign this piece of paper here, will you?'

He did as he was told. 'May I go now?'

'You will be found accommodation on the wing until we have finished questioning everyone.'

The beating in his throat tightened. 'I've got to stay here tonight?'

'No one is allowed to leave the prison at the moment. Governor's orders.'

When he got back to the community lounge, someone had switched the giant TV on and there was a trolley of sandwiches, most of which had already been eaten. Simon felt too sick to pick up the curled white crusts even though his stomach was rumbling. Caroline-Jane was in the interview room now and Jack was still rocking back and forth.

'It will be all right, mate,' said Simon, sitting next to him.

Jack's eyes were hollow. 'I want out of here. I don't belong here.'

'Nor me.'

'That's what I used to think.' A gentle voice interrupted them. 'But I've learned you can't say that now. Want to hear my story?'

Malik, a kind-looking man and a light brown skin not unlike Simon's, told them he had been married for two years. It had been an arranged marriage and he and his wife had been reasonably happy. They had a son and she was expecting another. He had just finished training as an accountant but money was tight – they needed a deposit for a mortgage – so he had borrowed from a client's account.

'I knew I could pay him back because an uncle had promised to repay a loan from India,' he said quietly, pulling up a chair next to them away from the television. 'But then he got ill and couldn't do it. I panicked so I borrowed some more from another client's account to repay the first. My wife didn't know any of this but kept asking me why I was so stressed. Then one of my cousins gave me some weed because he said it would help me relax. I'd never taken anything like that before and it made everything feel distant.'

He stopped.

'Go on,' said Jack, who had stopped rocking.

'This is the difficult bit.'

They waited.

'Money became everything to me. I was convinced that the more I could get, even if it was only a few pennies, the quicker I could get out of this. My wife was due to give birth the following week and I was desperate. One evening, as I was going home, I saw what looked like a pile of coins on the pavement. It was the drugs talking but I didn't know that then. They seemed to move and I knelt down and began to pick them up. Then they began screaming at me so I pushed them over. They rolled all over the pavement and I could feel jam running over my hand.'

'Blood,' said Jack faintly.

Malik nodded. 'The pile of coins had been an old man who was wearing a yellow raincoat. Without even realising it, I'd pushed him over and he'd hit his head on the pavement.' Malik's eyes took on a faraway look. 'He died that night and I was arrested for murder. I got life.'

Simon tried to find the words but couldn't. All he could think of was Ben drinking too much the other month; if he started taking drugs too, this could happen to him.

A couple of others had come up and were quietly listening. 'Everyone knows everyone else's stories,' said Malik. 'It's how this place works. We talk about our crimes in small groups and try and work out why we did it and how we can make sure it doesn't happen again when we get out. Some of the men get really angry with each other, especially if someone is a sex offender. I reckon that's what happened to Thomas.'

'Thomas?'

Malik nodded. 'The bloke who got up and walked out of your talk. He's been threatening to beat up one of the other blokes for weeks now 'cos he killed his mother. Thomas's own mother died last month and he wasn't allowed to go to the funeral.'

Guiltily, Simon recalled his own words at the time. 'My confession – about killing someone. Do you think that prompted him?'

Malik shrugged. 'Might have done. Who knows?'

'Can I tell you my story?' It was the thin wiry man in the front row who had steel glasses. 'You'll get out of this place faster than us so I want you tell the rest of the world summat. Most of us are here because of where we grew up. I was born on an estate. When I was a nipper, it wasn't so much what we were going to do but which branch of crime we was going to go into. You started off with nicking cars. Then you specialised. I did post offices. I'd go in with a toy gun and throw petrol over people. Then I'd threaten to set them alight. I never did, mind, but it usually scared them enough to hand over the money.'

Simon was too appalled to speak.

'How did you get caught?' This was Jack who had stopped rocking now.

'The geezer who was doing the job with me that day panicked and shot off so there wasn't a car outside to pick me up. I couldn't run with the cash 'cos it was too heavy and I wasn't going to leave it behind.'

'That's awful.'

The thin man frowned. 'I didn't murder anyone.'

'*Yes but you almost scared them to death*,' whispered Joanna.

'See that man over there?' They all looked. 'He raped his daughter.'

Could this really be true?

'And that one who looks like he wouldn't say boo to a goose? He murdered his wife when he found out she was having an affair and then called the police. Fat lot of good that did him. He got life too.'

'What will you do when you get out?'

Simon spun round. It was Caroline-Jane asking. The thin man shrugged. 'Who knows? Try not get into trouble again, I suppose.'

'I've been in prison for longer than I've been out of it,' said another man. He had an aquiline nose and had piercing blue eyes. 'Me parents split up and my mum put me in care. I ran away and nicked something and then got sent to a remand home. Got out of that and nicked something else and it just kind of went on from there. I haven't killed anyone although I did tie some people up for a few days.'

Simon stood up. 'May I talk to you?' He led Caroline-Jane to the other side of the room. 'I've got to get you out of this place,' he muttered.

She smiled. 'That's very sweet of you, Simon, but you mustn't worry. I know all these men; I've been here for two years, remember?'

'How can your husband let you do this job?' he demanded.

She flushed and then he realised. 'That ring you're wearing,' he said quietly. 'It's not a wedding ring, is it? It's one just for show.'

'I can't discuss my personal situation.' She flushed again, just like Claire did. 'It's not allowed.'

'You're a single mother, aren't you?' It was coming to him now. 'You have to do this to look after your children.'

'I told you, Simon. I won't be drawn. Now please.' She stood up. 'I need to know what is going to happen tonight. The police are unlikely to let us go until they found out who m–'

'Someone's been murdered?'

'Shhh.' Caroline-Jane looked shocked. 'I didn't say that.'

'*Yes, she did,*' cried Joanna.

'Yes, you did.'

Caroline-Jane stiffened. 'It looks as though the prison officer is going to say something.'

He and Jack had to go to two empty cells while Caroline-Jane went with one of the women police officers towards the main office at the end of the wing.

'I don't want to stay the night!' Jack was whimpering like a small child.

'Nor do I.' Simon felt a surge of strength coming from somewhere. 'But we have to do as we're told or we could be in trouble.'

The prison officer who was taking them along a corridor threw him a look. 'Pity you had to get caught up in this but rules are rules.' He went through another gate and flung open a door on the right. Inside was a smaller space than his half of a cell with Spencer. The bed was raised and had a rock-hard blue plastic mattress. The pillow was of the same consistency. There were no curtains. Outside, he could see 'his' prison.

'There's a bathroom at the end of the corridor but, if you want to go into the night, you have to push this bell. Only two are allowed outside at the same time.'

Then the door was slammed and there was a click. Next to him, he could hear Jack blubbering.

Simon sat on his bed, trying to get his head straight. Someone had been murdered on the wing. That much had been clear. It might or might not have something to do with the man who had walked out of his talk. Christ! Had he caused yet another death?

'*You've got to stop beating yourself up, darling,*' tinkled Joanna. '*Even I am beginning to feel you've paid your dues. By the way, weren't you meant to have phoned Claire tonight? She's just moved into her new place, hasn't she? Goodness me, she'll think you don't care, especially if she saw the way you've been looking at Caroline-Jane!*'

That night, Simon didn't sleep until the dawn light streaked the sky. Even then, it was fitful with that dream about Ben and Claire, and the dog. And that was when he woke up with the terrible realisation that he was on the Other Side.

Chapter Thirty-eight

They'd been searching for nearly five hours and still there was no sign of Slasher. This was unbearable. Ben couldn't cope without that dog. She had to find it.

'He doesn't know the area,' Ben kept saying over and over again as though this was going to make the dog appear. His tears had stopped now and he was walking next to Claire, in a determined march through the streets of Holloway calling out Slasher's name. If he'd been doing this at home, Claire thought, passers-by would have thought he was crazy but, here in London, several others (like the young woman with studded eyebrows they'd just passed), were also shouting at no one in particular or muttering to themselves. Maybe they were drunk or on drugs.

There was no question of Ben starting his new school today. When she'd gently suggested it, he had rounded on her with the words: 'If you think I'm doing that without finding Slasher, you know me even less than you think.'

The words had stung which was perhaps why she had also found the courage to tell Max that she was sorry but she couldn't start work until she had found their dog and that, in the meantime, he might care to call in that domestic service they'd discussed last night because there was no way she could start her duties as a housekeeper in a mess like this. She'd expected to be fired after that but Max had merely nodded and said that he would organise it, despite the fact that he too had work to do. Claire couldn't help thinking that, before Simon had gone to prison, she wouldn't have had the strength of mind to have stood up for herself like that.

But even strength of mind couldn't bring back Slasher. 'Is he chipped?' asked one of the many local vets they rang on her mobile while walking the streets, calling out his name. And she'd had to explain that no, he wasn't, because he didn't actually belong to her and that she was dog-sitting for a few months. The reproving voice made her feel like a bad guardian.

If they didn't find Slasher soon, she would have to ring the prison and leave a message – but saying what, exactly? That she had lost a dog belonging to a criminal? Claire shivered as she passed yet another man sitting in a doorway glugging back a bottle of whisky. What would Slasher's owner do? And how would Ben manage without him?

The only saving grace, as she told the disapproving vets' assistants, was that she had put her own mobile number on Slasher's collar when she first got him. 'How did you lose him, exactly?' asked one girl who sounded slightly more sympathetic than the others.

Claire watched Ben stride ahead through yet another street, calling out Slasher's name. 'We've just moved to London and it was our first night. He's been used to sleeping on my son's bed but the person we're staying with didn't want that and so we had to put his basket in the kitchen. Our landlord gets up in the night to work and somehow left the back door open when he went out for a walk.'

'In the night?' The girl's voice had an edge to it.

'He's rather eccentric.'

'Slasher, Slasher,' called Ben and Claire's heart felt as though it was squeezing itself into a ball of plain panic. It was like looking for a needle in a haystack.

'My car was broken into overnight as well and I'm worried that the person who did that might have taken him.' She kept her voice low when she said that in case Ben heard.

'Have you phoned the police?'

'Yes. They said they'd look into it.'

'Hmmm.' The girl didn't sound convinced. 'The best thing you can do is put up posters everywhere with a picture of your dog and your mobile number. But be prepared for some nutters who will just ring you anyway and demand a reward even if they haven't got him. We moved to London from Northumbria last year and we're still getting used to it.'

'Thank you.'

'I haven't been much use, I'm afraid.'

'You've been kind.'

'Slasher, Slasher,' rang Ben's voice as Claire put the phone down. They were going back onto a huge main road now, taxis and cars whizzing past them. 'Supposing he's got run over, Mum? It's so busy.'

Claire put her arm around her son's shoulders. 'The police will tell us.'

'But how will they know?'

She hesitated, not wanting to tell him what the police girl had explained: that if a dog was found dead, it would be taken to a special pound and then the owner would be contacted if there was sufficient ID.

'I wish we'd never come here.'

'Me too.' Claire suddenly recalled that newspaper article. 'I'm sorry but …'

Her right jeans pocket began to vibrate. 'Hello?'

'Is that Slasher?' A woman's shrill voice rang out in her ear.

Her heart began to beat. 'No. But have you got him?'

'Do you mean the dog?'

Claire's heart began to throb with hope in her ears and she had to shhh Ben who kept butting in, wanting to know what was happening. 'Yes, the dog.'

'I need to speak to Slasher first. That's what it says on the collar tag.'

'Slasher's the name of the dog!'

'Fucking hell. That's not 'cos he bites is it? 'Cos if so, I'm not having him in 'ere.'

Claire felt relief and panic seeping into her voice at the same time. 'He's really friendly. Please, just tell me where you are and I'll come and collect him.'

'Is there a reward?'

'Yes,' Claire heard herself say.

'How much, then?'

'Fifty pounds.'

266

'That all?'

Relief was now turning to desperation. 'Look, I'm a single mother and we've just moved here. I don't have any money.'

'You sound posh enough.' The voice turned sulky. 'OK. I suppose fifty will do. I'll meet you by Mandela Mansions.'

'Where?'

The voice was sounding fed up now. 'By Budgens off the Holloway Road. I'll be there in ten. Don't be late.'

The old Claire would have panicked but she couldn't do that now. She had just ten minutes to find Slasher and she wasn't going to mess up.

'What are you doing?' yelled Ben as she stepped into the road.

'Getting a taxi,' she yelled back.

Thank heaven. One had just turned the corner, its yellow light on. 'Budgens,' she said, half laughing and half crying. 'The Holloway Road.'

It wasn't a long ride but it came to nearly £8 and Claire had to scrabble around at the bottom of her bag to make up the amount. 'Sorry I don't have enough for a tip,' she said as she and Ben stood on the pavement outside but the taxi driver just shot off. Only then did she realise she didn't have any money on her to pay the dog woman if indeed she was there.

'I can't see him!' Ben's voice rose in panic as Claire looked around. There was Budgens all right but there wasn't anyone outside with a dog; only an old man bent over a shopping trolley as though it was a zimmer frame and a woman wearing a bright pink scarf over her head, a black hoodie and red jogging bottoms. She was leaning against the window, lighting up a cigarette. 'Excuse me,' ventured Claire. 'Did you just call me?'

The woman narrowed her eyes. 'I might. I might not. What's it to you?'

Ben tugged her by the sleeve. 'You've got my dog. I know you have.'

'Ben!' she started to say, appalled.

'She has! Look. That's his collar poking out of her pocket.'

The woman threw her cigarette on the pavement without bothering to stub it out. 'Sharp one, aren't you? I like that.' She turned her thin pinched face towards Claire. 'Got the money, have you?'

'Only if you tell me where Slasher is first.' Claire heard her voice sounding much firmer than she felt. 'And if you promise me he is all right.'

Ben gave a sob and made to grab her arm again. 'All right, sonny, all right. Your dog's safe.' She waved a grimy hand towards the cash point. 'Your mum can get her money out there and then I'll get someone to bring him down.'

Claire pressed one note into the woman's hand and pocketed the rest. 'You can have them when we have Slasher,' she said. 'And by the way, forget what I told you about him being docile. If I tell him to attack, he'll do exactly that. Now if you want your money, I suggest you take us straight to him.'

Mandela Mansions was a huge dirty white block of flats down a side road. Someone had crossed out the word 'mansions' and put 'shithole'. The woman walked straight past. 'You don't live there?' asked Ben.

The woman was already rolling up another cigarette as she walked on. 'Mandela is much posher than our place.' She grinned, revealing yellowy teeth. 'Used to live there, we did, when my old man got out but then they moved us on.'

Claire caught her breath. 'Got out?'

'Got out of prison.' The woman was lighting her cigarette now. 'Something you wouldn't know about.'

Claire glanced at Ben who shook his head. No, he said with his eyes. Don't tell her. They followed her up a flight of concrete stairs and then another before making their way gingerly along an outside landing which had a barred balcony which ran the length of the building. The woman proceeded to unlock the door with a key at the end of the string round her neck.

Slasher hurled himself towards them. 'You're safe. You're safe!' Never had she seen him look so happy.

'I fed him,' said the woman, putting her hand out for the rest of the money. 'Gave him some of my cornflakes.'

Claire just wanted to get out now but weirdly, the woman seemed to need to talk. 'Nice little thing, isn't he? I used to have one when I was married.' She looked around the room and Claire followed her gaze. There were photographs of children; school photos showing bright faced children in royal blue uniforms. 'Grown up now,' said the woman. 'Don't see much of them. Prison can do that to you.'

The realisation suddenly dawned. 'You were in prison too?' she asked gently. The woman nodded. 'After me old man got out, we were skint so we sold some stuff.'

Claire lowered her voice. 'Drugs?'

The woman nodded. 'I wouldn't have thought you'd know about that sort of thing.'

'My husband is Inside,' said Claire quietly. 'He killed someone in a car crash.'

The eyes narrowed. 'Fucking hell.' She lit another cigarette. 'What did he get?'

'Two years. Should be out in one'

The woman gave her a sharp look. 'You OK?'

Claire wanted to laugh. 'We haven't got any money; we had to leave our house because we were being bricked; and now we've come here to get away.'

'Take a deck at this.' The woman was pressing a piece of paper into her hands. 'It's a place wot helps families of prisoners. Helped me a bit, they did.'

Slasher was beginning to whine now, pawing at the door. 'He needs to go,' said Ben urgently.

'Don't let him shit in here.' The woman's tone changed. 'I've had enough crap to deal with this week. Off you go.'

She held out her hand. Claire took it. 'Thank you,' she said.

The woman looked embarrassed. 'I didn't do nothing.'

'Yes you did. I don't know what my son would do without that dog.'

'See you around, maybe.' The woman looked as though she was going to say something else and then slammed the door on them.

269

'She was all right, really,' said Ben happily as Slasher pulled him along the street, back towards the writer's house almost as though he knew the way.

Claire nodded. 'We've learned a lot in the last year, haven't we?'

Ben squeezed her arm and she realised it was one of the first adult conversations they'd had. 'What's that in your sleeve?' he asked.

She'd thought it was a tissue but as she pulled it out, something else fluttered to the ground. It was a dog-eared £10 note; the woman must have tucked it in when holding out her hand.

When they got back to the house, she barely recognised it. During the time they'd been searching for Slasher, the house had been cleaned from top to toe.

'Cost me a pretty penny,' said Max as he met them in the hall. 'But I must admit, it does look a bit better. Do you feel able to start your housekeeper duties now? By the way, I'm glad you found the dog. I'm sorry about leaving the door open last night.'

All this came out in a rush, in great contrast to the slow deliberate speech of yesterday and Claire instinctively felt that he was embarrassed. She also suspected that Jean might have told him off on the phone.

'Of course.' She moved towards the kitchen. 'Do you like steak and kidney pie?'

He nodded. 'Don't feel you need to start immediately. Get yourself sorted upstairs if you want.'

Their talk yesterday about her not being a maid had worked, she thought as she made her way up to the bedroom to wash and check her emails. She was definitely changing; becoming more assured. The thought occurred to her that Simon might find her changed when he came out. He'd be different too …

Now her hands closed around the piece of paper bearing the telephone number which the woman had given her. A charity, she'd said, that helped families of people imprisoned. She'd call them tomorrow. First she needed to check this email from her

270

agent.

Like your idea but need text to go with it ... Unusual ... Original twist ...

A pleasant tingle ran down her spine. The idea for a book, aimed at teenagers on how to cope if a parent went Inside, had come from watching Ben in the prison. Surely there had to be a market ...

Just as she was about to reply, her mobile rang. 'Mrs Mills?' said a clinical voice. Instantly every muscle in her body tightened.

'Yes ?'

She knew from the tone that something had happened and now she needed to know what, before the sudden tightening in her chest threatened to choke her.

'This is HMP Freetown. I regret you to inform you that there has been an incident.'

Next door in his bedroom, Ben put his face in Slasher's fur, nuzzling him. The smell reassured him; he could handle anything now, even a new school, especially now he had got Poppy's message.

Not long now. He could hardly wait.

Chapter Thirty-nine

'I don't see why they had to lock us up like common criminals,' complained Jack as they shuffled along to the shower and loo at the end of the corridor.

'Some people would see *us* as that,' pointed out Simon. 'You're here for fraud and I'm here for something far worse.'

'Don't be too hard on yourself,' tinkled Joanna. *'There were mitigating factors you know, like Hugh grabbing the wheel.'*

'There is nothing,' continued Simon firmly, 'which can excuse either of us. In fact, we could both be here.'

Jack shivered – either from revulsion or because it was so freezing in the bathroom. 'Speak for yourself. I borrowed money from a client's account. I'm not responsible for a loss of life. This place is a 'B cat.' For a reason. Before I came here, I didn't realise that there were different grades of prison according to the severity of your crime – and risk to the public, plus your means to escape – or that you had to work your way down them to get out. Did you?'

Simon nodded. 'You forget I was a solicitor once.' It still gave him a funny feeling to say that and for an instant, he recalled his father's look of pride when he qualified all those years ago. Just as well his father wasn't here to see him now.

'How the mighty have fallen.' Jack grinned, and in that instant, Simon decided that he didn't like the man. He could almost understand how, in a confined environment like this, a bloke could really get on your nerves.

Jack was in the loo now and came out, a disgusted expression on his face. 'Wouldn't go in there if I were you. Worse than ours has ever been.' He cast a look at the shower which had a cigarette end on the tray below. Don't fancy that either. Just have to make do, I will, until they let us out. You do

272

think it will be today, don't you?'

Simon had been hoping the same. He could hear noises outside but, unlike their hut, this corridor had an electronic door at the end; they couldn't get out until the bell went and it was time for breakfast. 'I don't know.'

Jack's eyes grew blacker and smaller. 'Why not? You're the solicitor, aren't you? What about our rights?'

He grabbed Simon by his shirt collar. 'If I don't get out of this place, I'm going to go mad,' he whimpered.

Simon thought of the men they had been talking to yesterday: Malik and some of the others. The funny thing is that they hadn't seemed threatening at all; in fact, some of them could have been a next-door neighbour.

'Calm down.' Gently he lifted Jack's hands off his shirt. 'It will be all right.'

'I haven't rung my girlfriend.' Jack was still whimpering although his hands were by his side now. 'She'll be panicking.'

Simon thought about how he'd promised to ring Claire. No doubt, she'd be cross rather than panicking; assuming he'd let her down again. 'I'm sure we'll be allowed to call this morning. Listen!' He held up a hand.

It was a prison officer; a small, lean grey man who officiously announced that they were to follow him to the dining room where they'd been given a sandwich the night before. Simon recognised Malik working in the pod and nodded. The man nodded back, grinning.

'*Doesn't look like a man who assaulted someone with a Samurai sword, does he?*' chirruped Joanna. '*And if you don't believe me, ask someone.*'

A plate of cold toast was on the table which, rather surprisingly, was laid with a plastic red gingham cloth. There were also packets of butter and jam. 'No marmalade?' enquired Jack.

One of the other men at their table, who had closely cropped orange hair, laughed. 'You kidding? If I were you, I'd make the most of what you've got. Mind you, there might be a bit extra now Thomas isn't here.'

Jack looked as though he was going to vomit.

'Is he all right?' asked Simon.

Orange man grinned. He still had food in his mouth. 'As all right as you can be, laid out on a mortuary slab. Had it going for him, mind. If it hadn't been for the bloke who did it, someone else would have done him in. You should have heard him going on and on about what he did to those kiddies.'

'How did he die?' Simon couldn't help asking.

'Sugar.'

'Sugar?'

'Sugar and boiling water, mate. It sticks. Don't try it.' He stretched over for some toast, without asking Simon to pass it. 'Food here's crap. It's sarnies today for dinner and then tea at 5 p.m. 'cos it's early lock-up.'

'Sugar and boiling water? So they …'

'That's right. You chuck it in their face and then beat them up.' Orange man chewed his toast thoughtfully. 'We told them. 5 p.m. is too early for the last meal of the day but it's the new rules 'cos of staff shortages. There aren't enough of them so they lock us up early. Means they have to feed us earlier. It's why we're so bloody hungry in the morning.'

This was horrible! Really horrible. It was another world which had somehow existed without him knowing until now. To think that he had been responsible, as a lawyer, for sending some people to places like this …

'Morning everyone!' Caroline-Jane's voice rang out brightly as she came into the dining room.

Simon jumped up. 'Are you all right?' He wanted to touch her arm; to tell her that he'd been worried about her all night and that he hoped her bed had been a darn sight more comfortable than his.

'I'm fine, thanks.'

'Where did you sleep?' Jack's question took Simon's out of his mouth.

'On some chairs in the office.' Caroline-Jane's voice was light but he could tell she looked tired.

'When are they going to let us out of here?' Jack sounded

panicky again.

'I'm not sure.' Something in her tone made Simon think she knew more than she was allowed to say.

'The police have finished interviewing us so presumably we can go soon,' he ventured.

'I hope so, but at the moment, it's lockdown on the wing. No one's allowed to go in or out until the police and the governor give the say-so.'

She was sitting down at their table now, nibbling cold toast. Did she realise, wondered Simon, what a contrast she made with her fresh smile and womanly figure sitting amidst a room of criminals?.

'Caroline-Jane!' One of the young officers came striding up. 'We've just had a call. You and your men can go now.'

Jack breathed out a sigh of relief. 'Thank you.' Caroline-Jane beamed back as though he was a hotel receptionist. She glanced down at her keys that were hanging round her belt. 'We'll just sign out, shall we?'

While they were waiting, Simon saw the orange-haired man coming out of the kitchen and stopping by the fish tank. 'Mind if I ask you something?' he said.

'Depends, doesn't it?'

'Malik. The man in the pod. He seems ... he seems quite a nice man. Should he really be here?'

Orange-haired man laughed so hard that the tub of fish food shook in his hand, threatening to spill its contents. 'Malik's one of the worst. Don't know what he told you but the truth is that he sliced his brother's head off with a Samurai sword.'

They walked, the three of them, up the main corridor towards the main entrance and through several sets of doors, each of which Caroline-Jane carefully unlocked and locked in turn, rattling each one afterwards to make sure it was secure. It felt good to walk beside her. To feel they were an equal team instead of her being the teacher and him the prisoner.

'We heard the man got scalded and beaten up,' ventured Jack.

Caroline-Jane unlocked another door to let them through before locking it again. 'Can't say I'm afraid.'

'Is it true that it was the bloke who walked out when Simon was talking? Was he the one who died?'

'I really can't comment, Jack.'

'Doesn't it make you scared to work here?' pushed Simon.

Caroline-Jane didn't miss a beat. 'If you thought like that, you wouldn't do it.'

She gave him a cool look before opening yet another door. A flood of warm spring sunlight filtered down on them. 'Yes!' Jack gave a little skip as they made their way across to the Other Side. 'I can breathe again.'

After signing in at the Centre, they were called into the number three governor's office.

'*Those earrings*,' commented Joanna enviously, '*are to die for.*'

Gov. Corry was indeed a most unlikely-looking prison governor, although Simon was beginning to realise that nothing was predictable in this place.

'I believe that you both had quite an adventure on the Other Side,' she began. Jack was staring at her skirt even though it was a good inch below her knee. 'You could say that,' he mumbled. 'Are we going to get compensation?'

Gov. Corry arched an over-plucked eyebrow. 'Complaint forms are in the main centre if you wish to fill one in. I was actually going to suggest that you both had the day off your work parties to recuperate.'

'Recuperate!' Jack was looking at her face now, instead of her skirt. 'Do you know what kind of an ordeal you've put us through? We had to sleep on a bed that was like concrete with a matching pillow and on a wing where someone had been murdered ...'

'Please stop right there.' Gov. Corry's face was steely. 'No news has as yet been released. I must ask both of you to refrain from mentioning the incident to any of your families until it has.'

Simon began to sweat. 'I need to ring my wife.'

'She has already been informed there has been an incident. She has also been told that you cannot call her until tomorrow. By then we hope that an announcement will have been made and the matter will be in the public domain.'

She was looking at each one in turn now. 'I must also point out that if either of you choose to inform the press either through a personal phone call or through giving details to your families, there will be severe repercussions.'

Simon nodded. 'Of course.'

'One more thing, Mills. You will be allowed to go out to work during the day, as from next week. You may also apply for a town visit in two weeks' time.'

A town visit? The very thought of going outside, with Claire at his side for a whole day, made him giddy with expectation, fear and excitement. As for going out to work – that was much earlier than he had thought. What kind of job would he be given? Only then did it hit him. If he was going out to work, he would have to give up the role of library orderly. Nor would he be able to go to Caroline-Jane's art classes any more.

Chapter Forty

What kind of an incident, Claire had demanded when she'd received the phone call from the prison. The voice at the other end had been sympathetic but in an officious manner. 'I'm afraid we are not at liberty to reveal details yet.'

Her chest closed in on her. 'But is my husband hurt?'

'No, but he will not be able to contact you for at least another twenty-four hours. This is why we are ringing. He has asked us to inform you of this.'

The voice was so clipped and sure! Claire's mind flitted back to the prison officers she had met during Visits. There was one older man in uniform who had learned to recognise her and always asked how she was as though she was a guest. There were others whose expressions suggested she was no better than the men Inside. Somehow she suspected this person was one of the latter type.

That was twenty-four hours ago. Since then, she still hadn't heard anything from her husband. Claire's fear had now turned to anger. It was clear that he'd got himself into trouble somehow by arguing with someone – probably a prison officer. She could just see it now! Her clever, arrogant husband, telling an officer that he had certain rights or maybe advising a prisoner, like that boy Spencer whom he kept talking about, to buck up and get a qualification.

Claire gripped her pencil and began furiously sketching. She'd complete the outline the agent had asked for and try thinking about a story to go with it even though stories weren't her thing. There would just be time to sort lunch for Max and then supper for Ben when he got back after his first day at school.

As she worked, her eye fell on the scrap of paper the dog

woman had given her. A charity for families of prisoners. That was all very well but frankly she didn't have time for that kind of thing at the moment and besides, she could manage on her own until Simon came out. She'd already proved that to herself.

It was nearly midday when Claire realised what the time was. Her art had proved a lifesaver since Simon had gone Inside, by blocking out all the thoughts that kept whirling around her head. But now, she told herself, as she hastily got up from her desk, she had another job to do as well if she was going to earn her keep.

Hastily, Claire made her way down the stairs to the kitchen. She had already put a quiche in the oven before starting work but should have checked it by now. Blast. It was slightly burned around the edges but if she cut out the dark bits and grated some cheddar on top, he might not notice.

'Ah Claire.' Just as she'd finished laying the table, Max came in, carrying a copy of a tabloid that she wouldn't have put him down as reading. Somehow he seemed like a *Times* or *Telegraph* man.

'This looks very good.' He nodded at the disguised quiche in the centre of the table with a bowl of salad that she'd also prepared earlier. 'Please sit down and join me.' She had wondered how this would work and had mentally prepared herself for the fact that she might have to make small conversation or none at all.

He helped himself to a slice of quiche; there was a slight tussle with the knife as Max tried to ease the slice off the dish. 'May I?' she offered nervously.

'Thank you.'

They both ate in silence for a few minutes before speaking at once.

'I'm sorry the quiche is a little ...'

'Crisp?' He frowned. 'It has an unusual texture, I agree.'

'I just need to get used to the oven, that's all.'

He frowned again. 'Is it different from yours?'

'When I had my own ...' She'd been about to say 'home'

279

but stopped because the memory was too raw. 'Before, I used to have an Aga. It's a different way of cooking.'

The frown relaxed. 'Ah yes. Our mother used to have an Aga. Wonderful invention, she used to say. Even dried our clothes and the odd Wellington boot.'

She nodded, trying not to let the tears which were welling up behind her eyes come out. Of course it was Joanna's death that was really dreadful. But talking about the Aga made her feel desperately homesick for her kitchen and the pretty views over the lawn.

'My sister tells me that you are having to sell your home,' said Max, matter-of-factly.

She nodded. 'Someone's coming back to see it for the second time this week.'

'When you sell it, you will presumably wish to buy your own place.'

Claire wondered how much Jean had told him. The truth was that they needed the money from the house to live on until or if Simon could find a job. Not many employers wanted someone who had a criminal record. 'I will rent for a while,' she said briefly.

Max seemed to digest this information. 'I am only asking because I would appreciate some notice before you leave.'

'Of course,' she said stiffly.

There was a silence during which he began to read his paper while eating. Claire toyed with the overdone quiche, wishing she had brought a book to the table if he was going to be so rude.

'Here.' Suddenly he stood up, pushing the paper towards her. 'I have had sufficient, thank you. This afternoon I have a meeting with my agent so I do not know what time I will be back. I would appreciate it if dinner was flexible.'

There he went again, treating her like a maid! Claire sat up straight. 'In that case, may I suggest a cold ham salad which I can leave in the fridge for you?'

'A cold salad?' Max seemed to be considering the idea as though it was entirely new. 'In spring? Very well. In the meantime, I have some shirts to be ironed in my dressing room.' He stopped as though remembering something. 'Providing, that is, that ironing is within your job description.'

She nodded, unsure of what to say.

Max stood at the door, a slight smile seeming to affect only one side of his mouth. 'I trust that my collars will not end up with the same brown tinge as the quiche!' Then he touched his head as though expecting to find a hat, and disappeared into the long hall which no longer seemed so gloomy now she had opened the window and put out fresh flowers.

'Honestly!' thought Claire as she idly reached over for the tabloid. It wasn't the kind of paper she normally read but she needed something to distract her. How could a brother and sister be so different? Then she caught sight of the headline on the front page and froze.

EXCLUSIVE! MURDER AT HMP GRIMVILLE. INMATE CHARGED.

Almost unable to breathe, Claire tried to make sense of the words which were blurred in her panic.

A 45-year-old man, who had been convicted of rape on five counts last year, was found murdered in his cell on Monday. The authorities have tried to keep the terrible news secret during investigations but an inside source has told us that another prisoner has been charged with his murder. It is said that the man was scalded with a mixture of boiling water and sugar which sticks to the skin and then beaten to death.

Was this the incident the prison had referred to in the phone call? No. Claire could feel the bile rising into her mouth. No. It couldn't be. Simon's prison was next door to this one. The two never mixed. He told her so. But then she recalled something he had said during his last phone call; about being involved with an art exhibition on The Other Side.

Dear God. Please, please don't let him be involved. Her husband wasn't a murderer. She had repeated that to herself over and over again after Joanna's death as though to assure herself. That had been an accident. But supposing Simon, who had always been on the side of the vulnerable, had taken it into his head to argue with some rapist or killer?

Shaking, she picked up the phone and dialled the main number. 'Press one if you know the extension; two for visiting hours; and three for the operator.'

Numbly, she pressed three.

He was working, said a clinical voice at the other end. Personal calls could only be taken in cases of extreme emergency.

'I saw the newspaper this morning,' she began, naming the tabloid. 'I believe my husband Simon Mills was involved in an art exhibition on the other side.'

'Please wait,' said the voice immediately.

She did so, for ages, wishing she hadn't taken the liberty of using Max's phone instead of her mobile. Finally, after what seemed like ages, she could hear voices in the background.

'Claire?'

It was Simon. She wanted to weep and scream at him at the same time. 'What's happened? Were you involved? What did you do?'

'Claire. Claire. Listen to me. Please don't cry. Don't shout either. I'm all right. I can't say much because I'm not allowed to. I'm not hurt and I didn't have anything to do with it. We all had to stay in the prison overnight until we'd been questioned. That's all.'

She was gasping with relief. 'You didn't get hurt by anyone? And you're back at Freetown?'

'Yes. And I've got some good news. I've been rottled. That means being released on temporary licence so I can go out to work during the day. I can also have a town visit next month. I don't even have to be accompanied, which is unusual. So you'll be able to collect me and we can have a whole day together. Isn't that wonderful? All right, I'm going.'

It took her a second to realise that the last sentence was directed at someone other than her.

'I'll call you tonight, Claire. I love you.'

Then there was the dull click as the phone cut her off.

* * *

282

She'd tried to continue with the outline upstairs but the right shapes wouldn't come. Usually they appeared as though someone was moving her hand but Simon's words kept resonating in her head. Giving up, she threw her brush on the desk along with the encouraging email from her agent, asking for more, and went downstairs to walk Slasher. The park opposite seemed like a good place to start but as she picked her way through the can tops and broken glass, she wondered if this was such a good idea. Slasher was straining on the lead but she didn't want to let him go. Supposing he just shot off?

'Who's taking who for a walk?' laughed a man as he strode past, throwing a ball for his own Labrador which looked like a curly teddy bear. 'You ought to let him go. That one's got some energy.'

Claire's arm was hurting from the pull. 'I lost him the other day and it was awful.'

'Likes the look of our ball, doesn't he? Tell you what, just let him play with my Bramble. If he makes a bolt for it, I'll help you catch him.'

By now, Claire's arm was almost out of its socket. 'OK.' Instantly Slasher shot off towards the other dog, nosing his ball and picking it up before running round in circles.

It was good for him, Claire thought, suddenly realising how much he'd been cooped up during the last few days. 'We used to live by the sea. He could run on the beach then.'

'The sea.' The man whistled with appreciation. 'I've always wanted to do that. What brought you here, then?'

'Lots of things.' Claire had said enough already. 'I've got to go now.'

The man was handing her something. 'Give him this to get him back. That's right.'

It was a treat which left a meaty stain on her hand.

'See. Good as gold now, isn't he? See you again, sometime maybe. What's your dog called, by the way?'

'Slasher,' she answered, giving up. 'It's a long story.'

Ben still wasn't back when she returned. His mobile went into answerphone every time.

'Shall we go and find him?' she asked Slasher.

Funny. Slasher seemed to know his way along the streets, sitting when they got to the main road that dissected theirs and occasionally making for the grass verge to do a wee. But there was still no sign of Ben.

And then she saw him, walking towards her, jeans covered in mud and his shirt torn. 'What happened?'

'Get off, Mum. I'm OK.'

He bent down to stroke Slasher who sniffed interestedly at his arm which, Claire could see now, had blood on it.

'Ben! Tell me!

'Someone tried to steal my mobile so I gave him one.'

'You what?'

'I punched him. Kieran told me to.'

'Kieran?'

'One of my new friends. He said that if you don't stand up for yourself on the first day, you'll get beaten up. So I threw the first punch and, as it turned out, the last.'

He grinned, looking pleased with himself.

'But the blood?'

'It's where I fell on the ground. Chill out, Mum. This is a different place from home. We've all got to change. What's for dinner? I'm starving.'

Max came home earlier than he'd implied, in a filthy mood. She could tell that from the way he slammed the front door and walked straight into the kitchen. Without even washing his hands, he went to the fridge and took his salad out.

'I shall eat this on a tray in the sitting room,' he said. 'What's for pudding?'

How rude! 'Apple pie. Shall I leave it out?'

He nodded curtly. 'If you will.'

'There's some left-over shepherd's pie if you want that instead of the salad.'

He grunted. 'Left-overs. That's all there is for people of my age nowadays.'

Something in his tone made Claire's heart soften. 'I take it that your meeting didn't go so well then.'

'What's it got to do with you?' The eyebrows knitted even deeper into his forehead. 'I pay you to housekeep for me; not be some kind of namby-pamby counsellor.'

Claire felt herself growing hot. 'I was only trying to help.'

'Well don't.'

Fine. She wouldn't. Instead, she'd just go back to her desk and have another go at her drawings. Ben was doing his homework upstairs. 'Are you OK?' she asked, putting her head round his door. The room was empty although the narrow bed was covered in books and magazines and CDs. At the other end, the window was open. Aghast, she looked out. There was a wide ledge below which wouldn't be difficult for a tall boy to jump onto and then onto the pavement. Leaning out of the window, she could see him walking down the pavement towards the crossroads. Where was he going?

Then she saw a small, slim pink-haired girl. They were hugging! They were quite a long way off but, unless Claire was mistaken, she knew exactly who the girl was.

Chapter Forty-one

Simon had seen the white vans leaving in the morning ever since he'd arrived. Everyone wanted to be on one.

'You lucky bastard, man,' said Spencer when he told him his news. The kid was hunched up on his bed with a mug of tea, skimming the Quick Read which he'd got from the library. 'When I get out there, I'm going to get myself some honey.'

That was something else everyone aspired to. 'Did you get some?' was one of the first questions that the men got when they returned from work or a town visit. It had taken Simon a while before he realised they were referring to sex.

'You forget I'm a married man,' he said, standing in front of their cracked mirror to view the one pair of cord trousers he owned here. 'Besides, look at Steve.'

The man, who'd been on G Hut, had had a job delivering parcels for a local courier as part of his community service. During his lunch hour he would nip off for a 'sandwich with extras' with his wife who lived locally. When he'd boasted about this to someone else on the hut, he'd was shopped and then shipped out.

'Not,' added Simon, 'that I know anyone round here.'

Just as well. There was no way he wanted to bump into someone when he was out but not fully released.

'When I went out to work last time I was In,' mused Spencer, abandoning his book, 'I met this cute girl at a fast food place. She asked for my phone number but I couldn't give her the prison's, could I? So I took hers but said I could only see her at weekends. She didn't like that and accused me of being married.' Simon made a sympathetic face, he'd similar stories before.

Spencer grinned. 'Then I admitted I was banged up during

the week so she said that was all right by her and she'd wait for me. We arranged to meet the next Saturday but she didn't show up.' There was a rueful shrug. 'That's what happens, I suppose.'

Would Claire still be waiting when he got out? Somehow, he couldn't blame her if she wasn't. Not after what he had done. If he was prepared for rejection, it wouldn't hurt so much. Hadn't life already taught him that, even *before* Joanna? 'I'm off now. See you later.'

Spencer had a look of envy in his eyes. 'See if you find some bargains. Them charity shops have all kinds of stuff in them. Me mam is always going in to hers. Found a tenner at the bottom of a box of old books once, she did. So keep your eyes peeled, you hear me?'

It felt unreal as he climbed onto the white prison van, taking a seat near the driver in case there was any trouble. Some of the rowdier younger men had nabbed places at the back of the bus just like the naughty ones on a school trip. What kind of jobs were they going to? It was usually bars or fast food chains, according to Spencer.

When Simon had first been told he was working in a charity shop, his spirits had soared. At last. He was going to be out in the real world. Yet now as the van wove its way through the villages into town, Simon found his fingers gripping the seat in front. The van's speedometer was only doing 30mph but it felt fast. Someone overtook them and, even though it was a clear road, his knuckles went white. The driver had the radio on but it was obliterated by the boys at the back who were singing 'Off to work we go'. Suddenly he wanted to be back in the safety of the prison.

'*Get a grip,*' scolded Joanna. '*It's only because you've been out of it for so long. You've been cosseted in prison, darling. It's time to start re-adjusting to the real world.*'

'Mills!' barked the prison officer up front. 'This is you.'

Wasn't anyone going to go with him? Simon walked awkwardly into the shop, clutching his identity tag round his neck and holding on to the forms he'd been issued with. He could just do a runner if he wanted.

'*Don't think about it!*' Joanna's voice rang out in alarm. '*Remember Tommy?*'

Tommy had been on A hut and had not returned one day after his day job. He was picked up the following month and was now in Wandsworth.

Inside the shop, he could see an oldish woman folding a cardigan on the counter and a younger one hanging up a skirt on a rail. It was like being at school on the first day, all over again. Maybe if he closed his eyes, he could pretend he was just talking to matron …

'Hello.' The older woman looked up. She had very cool green eyes which bore right into him. 'Bang on time as usual. Those buses usually are. Got your paperwork?'

He could tell from her manner that she had done this before. The other woman was giving him quick, sharp, nervous glances.

'Seems to be in order.' The older woman handed him back his letter. 'I'm Sarah and this is Jilly.'

Jilly nodded nervously.

'Please call me Simon,' he said. Then, wanting to reassure her, he added, 'I used to be a solicitor.'

The older woman smiled. 'We don't ask questions in this place, as you'll find out, Simon. Nor do we judge. Everyone has a past.'

She waved a hand around the shop. There were piles of clothes of all shapes, colours, and sizes as well as boxes of knick-knacks containing cutlery and chipped vases and glass ash trays. It reminded Simon of how he had been lukewarm about Claire's treasured old possessions, so different from his own modern taste. Had he been too judgmental?

'You're not allowed to serve the public,' said Jilly quickly. 'You do know that, don't you?'

Simon bristled. What did she think he was? A common murderer? He felt like replying that he had no intention of bashing them over the head. But instead, he clenched his fists by his side and merely nodded.

'It would be extremely helpful if you could go through all the bags in the back,' said Sarah quickly. 'There's a bin out there for rubbish and then other boxes marked 'china' and so on for items which are saleable. Does that sound all right? Jilly and I take it in turns to have lunch so I suggest you have your break when I have mine.'

Clearly Jilly didn't want to be left alone in the shop with a man who was doing time.

'That's fine by me.' He tried to forget the fact that he was a qualified solicitor and not a charity refuse sorter but the thought of Alex in a suit and tie, doing complicated deals, kept running through his head. 'Where do I start?'

By lunchtime, Simon realised how much hard work went into charity shops. His back was killing him but at the same time he had an amazing sense of satisfaction. By the time he got back into camp, it was time for supper.

'Going to check my homework then?' demanded Spencer afterwards and it was all Simon could do to summon up the strength to check his spellings.

'*You promised,*' Joanna reminded him tartly.

'I know I did.'

Spencer gave him a funny look. 'You talking funny again? What are you on? Ought to get some help for that, mate, like I do.'

It was no secret that Spencer went to the IDU unit twice a week for drug counselling where he saw a woman called Alison. When Simon had asked what she talked to him about, he mumbled something about rainbows and being strong enough to say no. Every now and then, in the evening, he took out a polythene bag which appeared to have white grains in it and tipped it into his tea. Simon only hoped it was sugar.

The rest of the week flew by. It was amazing what people threw away. Old moth-eaten cardigans that were fit only for the recycling dump; piles of discarded A-level notes; and sometimes a 'find' like a Clarice Cliff tea cup which he instantly recognised. 'My wife collects it,' he said and Jilly had looked surprised as though he had no right to recognise a name.

Thankfully, Caroline-Jane had started running an art class in the evening. It was only once a week but at least it was something. He was currently working on a copy of another postcard she'd brought in – it was of Venice where he and Claire had gone on their honeymoon.

He told Caroline-Jane as much and she nodded sympathetically. 'You must be due for your first town visit soon?' she asked.

He nodded. 'To be honest, I have mixed feelings. I want to see my wife but I'm also nervous.' He stopped. 'So much has changed.'

Caroline-Jane gave him a sympathetic look. The incident on the Other Side had definitely brought them closer; he could tell that. He was pretty sure that his presence had comforted her during the crisis. Claire on the other hand, seemed to be managing perfectly well without him. New house. New job.

'*Don't forget the old husband sniffing around*,' pointed out Joanna tartly.

Simon could fight for his wife, of course. But what if he failed? Might it not be easier to pretend he didn't care any more?

His town visit was set for a Sunday. As soon as he woke, he got dressed in the cords. They'd got dirty from the charity shop but there hadn't been time to wash them.

Spencer whistled as he got himself ready for chapel. 'Where's your wife taking you?'

Suddenly Simon didn't want to talk about it. 'I'm not sure. See you later.'

Anyone going on a town visit had to sign out and collect forms that identified the prisoner as being an inmate at HMP Prison Freetown. These had to be carried at all times. As Simon waited at the visitors' car park, he kept looking over his shoulder as though someone was going to tap him on the back and accuse him of leaving without permission.

By the time Claire's car swung in, his mouth was dry. She drew up next to him and smiled. Christ, she was lovely. He'd forgotten how gorgeous she smelt and how she endearingly tilted her head to one side when she saw someone. Even the new hairstyle seemed to suit her now. Instantly, all his resolutions about not caring too much evaporated into the spring air.

He got in and leaned towards her.' Thanks for coming.'

She was nervous too, he realised. It almost felt like a first date.

'Where are we going?' he asked excitedly.

'I thought we might have lunch.' Her eyes were steadily on the road. 'There's a hotel near here which does good food.'

A hotel? Did that mean she'd booked a room? He'd thought about sex, of course, so many times at prison that it had become almost routine now to pleasure himself before dropping off. They all did it. But he and Claire hadn't even kissed yet. Maybe, he thought, with a sickening thud, she didn't want him any more.

'*Can you blame her?*' interrupted Joanna.

'No,' he replied out loud.

'Are you OK?' Claire's voice bore a hint of alarm. She was driving much slower than usual. No need to ask why.

'Fine,' he said. 'Just fine.'

In the event, it was fine. Better than he'd thought. The food was amazing and he polished off the fish pie so fast that Claire had hardly started hers. It felt like premature ejaculation. He must have sex on his mind.

'Sorry. We don't get this sort of food in there.'

'I would have thought you'd have gone for the steak?'

Didn't she read his letters? 'I told you. I haven't been able to eat meat since …'

She nodded. 'Of course.'

'*Don't worry on my account,*' chirped Joanna. '*I used to love a good piece of steak myself. Besides, when a body is done, it's done.*'

'Shut up,' he said out loud. Claire looked at him startled.

291

'Sorry.' He gave an embarrassed laugh. 'Still hearing Joanna's voice, I'm afraid.'

She looked even more worried. 'Then shouldn't you get …'

'Tell me about Ben's new school,' he cut in, desperate to change the conversation. That got her talking and while she spoke, Simon looked around the dining room taking in the pretty lily wallpaper and the well-dressed people all having lunch together. What would they think if they knew where he'd come from and where he was going back to tonight?

There was so much to catch up on! She wanted to know about his 'terrible ordeal in the other prison' and he wanted to know how she and Ben were settling in in London. He also advised her to accept the latest offer on the house. It was a relief that she hadn't heard any more from Hugh.

When the bill came, he was appalled at the amount. 'It's all right,' said Claire, handing over her credit card. 'I've just been paid.'

He felt his muscles tense. 'I don't like the idea of you being a housekeeper. You're an artist.'

'I can do both.' Claire spoke evenly. 'Besides, we need the money.' She touched his arm. The warmth burned him. 'I was wondering, have you thought about what you might do when you get out of prison?'

Someone at the neighbouring table glanced over and Claire flushed. 'Sorry,' she said in a lower voice.

'I'm still working on it.' His voice was tense. Why did she have to go and spoil it all? 'At the moment, I'm rather enjoying working in the charity shop.'

The woman at the table next to them was definitely listening now. Irrationally, he wanted to shock her. 'It's the first time they've had a prisoner apparently.'

Claire scraped back her chair. 'Let's go.' She stood up, leaving Simon to follow her.

'Why,' she hissed in the car park, 'did you have to embarrass me like that?'

Simon slid sulkily into the passenger seat. 'Because I wanted to feel what it's going to be like in the future.'

'I can tell you one thing.' She put on her sunglasses even though the April sun wasn't that low. 'If you're going to do that again on the next town visit, I don't want to be part of it.'

It was on the tip of his tongue to say 'Fine' but then he saw the tear. Just one at first and then another, falling under her sunglasses.

'I'm sorry,' he said softly. 'I don't know what came over me. It's just that it's all so different.'

'I know.' She sniffed and buried her head in his neck. Then, at the same time, they both lifted their heads and kissed. It was so wonderful that they did it again in the Visitors' Car Park even though some of the men were watching. When she drove off, he felt agonisingly empty and yet also more alive than he'd felt for months.

The following morning, he was told at breakfast that, instead of going out to work, he was to report to Governor Corry.

'Why?' he had asked but no one would tell him. Upset at missing the bus – what would they think at the shop? – he made his way to her office. When he got there, he found not just Gov. Corry but also the head of security.

On the desk was a tabloid newspaper showing a picture of a tough looking man on the front and the words *INSIDE STORY*.

'Mills,' said Governor Corry without any preamble. 'I don't know if you've been following the reports in this paper about the murder in Grimville. But it is clear that information had been leaked to the press about the incident. I need to know if you are responsible.'

Chapter Forty-two

Claire drove back after the town visit, utterly confused. In a way it had been good to have had that argument with Simon because it had released the anger. Someone had needed to point out that he had it easy in prison. That he didn't have to worry about how to pay the bills and that it was her who was suffering on the Outside because she had to sort out the practicalities of being a single parent all over again.

Then when she'd seen his face, she'd felt awful. Thank God he had bent down and kissed her like that. It transported her right back to that very first evening when his lips had met hers and she'd known instinctively that he was the one for her; far more than Charlie had ever been.

And now he was gone! She'd had to leave him in the Visitors' Car Park even though every bone in her body wanted to suggest that they just ran away – with Ben – and hide where no one would find them.

Of course that would have been crazy. Only another four months and he'd be out. She couldn't wait although at the same time she was still scared because they had both changed.

The old her, for a start, would have told him about Poppy.

Claire had hardly believed her eyes when she'd looked out of the window and seen her son embracing the girl on the street corner. Her immediate reaction – to reach for her mobile – was automatic. 'What's Poppy doing here?' she'd demanded and then watched, from the window, as her son shoved his phone back in his pocket, said something to the girl, and walked her slowly back to the house.

She'd thought of so many things to say to them but when they arrived on the doorstep – Poppy's hair wet from the rain and a scared look in her eyes – she was reminded so forcefully of her own first love at that age, that she simply gave the girl a hug. 'Please don't tell me you've run away,' she said.

Poppy nodded. 'I missed Ben, and Dad's acting really weird.'

'What kind of weird?'

Poppy made the kind of face that indicated she felt bad about telling tales. 'He's drinking again for a start and then he goes round ripping down Joanna's pictures and saying terrible things about her.'

'But he adored her!'

There was a sort of snorting noise. 'That's what he wanted people to think but they had some really bad rows.' Poppy looked up at Ben. 'That night – you know – I overheard her saying that she'd had enough.'

Claire felt awkward. 'People say that sometimes without meaning it.'

'She did. I know she did. They were always rowing.'

The girl's voice rose just as one of the doors opened and then shut upstairs. It was Max's way of saying they were making too much noise.

'Tell you what,' said Claire quickly. 'You can stay the night on my floor providing you ring your dad and tell him you're here. OK?'

So Poppy had done that although from the loud barking sounds at the other end, Claire suspected that Hugh was not happy. He probably blamed her. 'I don't want to go back,' Poppy had said that night, but somehow Claire had persuaded her that she had to return to school but that Ben would be down for the weekend to stay with his dad so they could see each other then.

That had been four days ago and now Ben was staying with his father in Exeter while she was up here, driving back to a strange house in London after visiting Simon. 'We're a fractured family,' she thought with a wrench. This time last year, the three of us had been under one roof and even though there had been tension between Simon and Ben, it was better than this.

But what would it be like when he got out? She'd been looking forward to it for so long but now it was on the horizon, the idea scared her. She had changed. Almost more than him. What if he couldn't cope with that? What if she couldn't cope with him?

The house was dark when she got in which suggested Max was out. Claire went into the kitchen and opened the fridge. She was peckish after the drive and yet at the same, it didn't seem worth making a meal just for one. The thought of Jean, with her pinny and constant offer of tea and toast, made her feel nostalgic for what she'd just left. How different she was from her brother.

Then she heard it. Just a small noise which was more like a creak, really, right above her head. Grabbing the kitchen scissors, she wished she hadn't agreed to Charlie picking up Slasher along with Ben to drive them back home.

Carefully she tiptoed up the stairs, feeling her throat throbbing with fear. Just as she'd thought! Someone was in her room.

'What do you think you're doing?'

'Max!' He was standing there with the printed out email from her agent about her work.

'How dare you sneak around my room?' she began.

Max didn't look in the slightest bit embarrassed. 'I think you will find that it is my room but yes, before you say anything, I know you pay rent and that you're entitled to your privacy. The truth is that when the rain started, I noticed you'd left your window open so I thought I'd come in and shut it for you. Then I'm afraid, my eyes fell on the email on your desk and I couldn't help thinking that I might be able to help you.'

Was he telling the truth? It was difficult to tell from the way he was folding his arm as though it was her trespassing instead of him.

'Your agent,' he continued, 'wants a story to go with your idea about a boy whose father goes to prison. I could write that for you. Matter of fact, I am finding myself at a bit of a loose end at the moment. My own agent is being rather pessimistic about the state of the publishing world but children's books might just be a way of getting back in. What do you say? If it works and we get a deal, we'll split it fifty/fifty.'

Claire and Max spent the rest of the weekend tossing around ideas. She had to admit that he had some good ones. Instead of just having one small boy whose father had been sentenced, he suggested a brother and an older sister. 'Base the girl on that pretty overnight guest you had the other day. Niece, was it?'

'A friend of Ben's from home.'

'Perfect. Can you draw a smaller version?'

'Yes but …'

'Right.' Max gathered his notes. 'I need some time to myself to write although here are some outline scenes I've thought of. Why don't you do some of your clever pictures to go with them?'

She was so engrossed in her work that she hardly heard Ben coming back until Slasher's nose was in her face. 'Where's Dad?' she asked.

Ben shrugged. He seemed taller than when he had left for the weekend and he was wearing new jeans. 'He had to collect a friend.'

A girlfriend? 'Did you have a nice time?'

'It was all right.'

'What did you do?'

Ben was already logging on to Facebook. 'Hung out with Poppy when Dad went out.'

Her voice came out like a squeak. 'Dad left you alone?'

'We're nearly sixteen, Mum. Give us a break.'

But she didn't like it. She didn't like it at all.

Over the next few weeks, their life fell into some sort of discordant rhythm. Ben went down to his father's at the weekend, usually on the train, leaving Slasher with her. She preferred this as it gave her an excuse to get out and walk. She was on first name terms with Labrador man now and she'd also got to know some of the local parks.

297

It had been so long since she'd lived in London that she'd forgotten how much there was to do. Every weekend she visited the art galleries of her youth. The V & A; the RA; the Tate.

It was wonderful and it also gave her something to talk about when she visited Simon although sometimes she detected resentment in his voice. 'It's not my fault you're in here,' she had to stop herself from saying. 'It doesn't mean I can't enjoy myself.'

The rest of the time she spent doing the art work for the children's book which was really coming along. It wouldn't be long now, said Max excitedly, until they could send it to his agent. She pointed out that she would need to send it to hers as well and he had sniffed dismissively.

It also looked as though the house sale was finally going through. A few weeks ago, the thought of losing her home had made her feel sad. Now she saw it as the next stage. It would release money that they could then save and live off when Simon was out. In two months' time, they agreed, she would start to look for somewhere to rent.

It would need to be near Ben's new school which, thank heavens, he seemed to like. Maybe, just maybe, they could be turning the corner after all.

Ben hated coming back on Sundays. It wasn't because he didn't want to leave Dad because, after all, he hardly saw him anyway, thanks to Diana. Dad was always out which meant that Poppy could come round without anyone asking any awkward questions. It wasn't as though her dad was sober enough to care.

'I'm not ready yet, Ben,' she'd said last weekend when they had been lying on the bed next to each other, stark naked.

He'd buried his head into her soft flesh. 'I'm not going to push you,' he said. Ben had heard those words on television recently and thought they sounded right. 'But maybe in a few weeks,' he added, 'you might feel different.'

The boy on television had used that line too and the girl on the screen had kissed him in return which had led to things happening rather fast after that. But Poppy had edged away.

'I'm not sure. I need to wait.'

That's when he'd seen the bruises.

'They're nothing,' she'd said quickly. But he knew.

'Why did he hit you?' His fingers were clenched in fists.

Poppy shrugged. 'Because he drinks too much and gets out of control. That's what Joanna used to say.'

'Did he hit Joanna?'

'Sometimes.'

'Why don't you email your mother?'

'She's moved on to Morocco. Didn't I tell you? She's not online yet.'

It was almost enough to make Ben want to go back to Mum and put his arms around her to tell her how much he appreciated her. Instead, he put his arms round Poppy and said he'd always be there for her and that he'd be back the following weekend.

Then Dad had come back and asked if he'd done his homework which was a joke and put him on a train back to London where he'd get his bag ready for school the next day.

Except that there wouldn't be a next day. Not at school anyway. Because the real reason that Ben dreaded coming home on Sunday night was that he hadn't been back to school since that first week when someone had threatened him with a knife, just because he'd tried to hang on to his mobile phone.

Chapter Forty-three

''Snot fair, is it, man?' Spencer sat on the edge of his bed, which he'd draped in a Spiderman duvet bought from the Stores catalogue. 'They stop you doing your community work 'cos they think you've grassed to the press but they ain't got no evidence.'

Simon was sitting on his own bed trying to write a letter to Claire, explaining what had happened. He felt it might state his case better than a phone call in a noisy corridor where everyone else could hear you talk.

Spencer was leaning towards him now. 'How come they're pointing the finger at *you* man, and not this Jack?'

Simon was trying to make exactly the same point in his letter to Claire. 'They're not. They're holding us equally responsible until it can be proved who did it.'

'But those newspaper geezers aren't going to say, are they?' Spencer slapped his thighs in frustration. 'Me mate got into the papers last year and the bloke what writ the article wouldn't say how he got the story so he had to go and see these people somewhere and try and sort it out.'

Simon looked up from the letter. 'Do you mean the Press Complaints Commission?' He'd written to them as well.

'Dunno.' Spencer looked worried like a small boy who'd forgotten his homework. 'I just don't like to see you in this mess, man. Not when you've been so good to me.'

Simon wished he could put Spencer's voice in his letter; it might make Claire realise that he wasn't responsible. If only he hadn't had that conversation with her during the last visit when he'd said something along the lines of 'the rest of the world ought to know what happens in this place'.

Just his luck that an officer had happened to hear.

300

Apparently that was one of the reasons for the suspicion to fall on him.

'How long you going to be off work then?'

If only he'd leave him in peace. 'I told you. Until they can prove it wasn't me.'

'But what if they don't? They can't keep you in here any longer than your sentence, can they?'

That was another thing. 'To be honest, I don't know. I hope not.'

Caroline-Jane seemed surprised when he turned up for art class the following day. Perhaps she'd been told about the trouble he was in. He spent the first half of the session waiting for an opportunity to talk.

'They stopped me doing community work,' he said quietly just as they were going back into the art room.

She wasn't looking at him. 'I heard.'

'They say it was because I told the newspaper about what happened on the Other Side.'

She nodded as though she'd heard that too. 'It wasn't me,' he said urgently.

Her reply was so low that he wasn't certain he had caught it. But it sounded something like 'I didn't think it was.' The relief filled him like a balloon so that he scarcely knew what he was drawing for the rest of the session. If Caroline-Jane believed in him, he could cope.

Simon told the team that he couldn't be a Listener any more. 'I've got some personal problems,' he explained. 'I don't feel I can give it my best at the moment.'

Touchingly, one or two of the men he'd helped came up to him in the dining room and said they hoped he'd be all right. The Coin Man even offered to lend him his lucky 10p piece so he could make any big decisions. 'If it's heads, it's yes,' he explained. 'Tails is 'no' providing it's not a Tuesday ...'

No one had said his release date would be delayed because of that newspaper article but Simon himself felt dirty, as though a cloud had been cast on the good things that he had done in prison.

'*Life isn't fair,*' pointed out Joanna, who had been rather quiet of late. '*Just look at me!*'

Claire had written to say that she understood how he must be feeling but she couldn't come up this weekend because she had a meeting with her agent about a new project.

On a Saturday? Surely she could have made the time to support him. There was one person he could ask; someone who had contacts. Simon didn't like the idea but it could be his only chance. Luckily, he had just enough money left on his card to make the call.

'Alex? It's me. Simon. Yes, they do let you use the phone in prison. Listen, I need you to do me a favour. It's about that article in the paper. Your brother-in-law works for it, doesn't he? Can you find out any more?'

It took another five days for the letter to arrive and when it did, it wasn't from the man whom Alex had promised to contact. This one was written in a flowery loopy feminine scroll.

'Your wife writ back then, did she?' remarked Spencer who was behind him in the queue.

'It's not her handwriting.' Simon turned the letter over; there was an address at the back in Clapham, London.

'Got a sweetheart on the side then?' Spencer's eyes shone in admiration.

'No,' remarked Simon curtly before walking off in the direction of the football field where, until the tightening of security, they had been allowed to play on Sundays.

It was a warm day and he sat on the grass, aware that he was in danger of missing Art which would result in a late entry in the register. But he had to know who the letter was from.

By the time Art had finished, Simon was still sitting in the field, reading and re-reading the letter until he got to the final line.

With love from Lydia.

Lydia? *Lydia?*

The letter dominated his every waking moment for some days until one Monday when his name was called out after roll-call. 'Mills? To the governor.'

He knew it. They'd decided against parole because of the newspaper leak. He'd be stuck here for God knows how long and ...

Simon stopped as he was taken through the governor's door. Jack was there, a frightened expression on his face like a rabbit.

'Thank you for coming here, Mr Mills. I believe Mr Wood here would like to say something.'

Jack spoke to the floor. 'It was me. I leaked. I rang the paper about what had happened over at Grimville. They paid me. Quite a lot of money.'

Simon's heart leaped. 'So I'm in the clear?'

The governor gave a curt nod.

'And I can go back to community work?'

'If you wish. However, your ERD is coming up in May.'

ERD stood for 'Early Release Date' although it was a bone of contention amongst prisoners that the actual release date could be much later than that. It all depended on their 'risk' to the community. If they were still seen as possible trouble makers, they could be kept in longer.

'It is of the opinion of the board,' continued the governor as Simon's heart began to race, 'that you should be free to go then.'

When Simon got back to his cell, numbed by the news, Spencer was sitting at the end of his bed, dipping his fist into a bowl of cold water. 'Saw the guv, did you?' he grinned. 'I can tell from your face it was good news, you lucky geezer!'

Yes. It was. He slid his hand into his pocket to feel the letter was still there. But now something else had happened. Something even bigger. Something that he couldn't tell Claire about. Not yet, anyway.

'*If you ask me, it might finish her off,*' warned Joanna.

Chapter Forty-four

Simon was coming out soon! Claire had to say it over and over again in her head to convince herself. She had done the same, she recalled, when he had been sentenced. Only then she'd repeated the phrase 'He's going to prison' again and again.

Neither felt right. Yet hadn't this been what she'd been waiting for ever since the judge had given his sentence?

So much had changed since then. They didn't have a home of their own. She was stronger and more independent. And she and Ben were getting on just fine. Supposing he and Simon began scrapping again?

A small part of her began to wonder if, in fact, she and Ben might be better off on their own. No. That was selfish. She had to give them a chance.

Talk about everything coming at once! The day after Simon's phone call, she saw Ben off to school as usual with his packed lunch (apparently the canteen food was 'rife') and went upstairs to knock on Max's study door. Surprisingly, he invited her in with a flourishing welcoming hand gesture.

Claire looked around curiously. Every spare inch of wall was covered by books. His desk was a mass of papers and pencils – not pens – and there was a pile of books bearing foreign titles on the floor by his chair.

'My books in translation,' he said dismissively. 'Sit down, my dear. Sit down. I was going to call you up anyway so it's fortuitous that you are here. My agent loves my script. He quite liked your drawings too although he did suggest that he brought in another artist as well … no, don't worry. I told him this was your idea and that it wouldn't be fair. So he's spoken to a couple of his publisher chums and one of them has come up with a deal. Take a look at this!'

With another flourish, he handed Claire an email print out. Stunned, she read the offer. The publisher –an up-and-coming indie – was offering them both a substantial amount of money for the rights to print the book. 'I'll need to run it past my agent too,' she said, feeling stunned.

'Really?' Max raised his eyebrows. 'Why not just use mine?'

'I can't. It's not done like that.'

Max made a reluctant face. 'My goodness, you do play by the rules, don't you. Still, I understand that after your husband's experience.'

Her lips tightened. This was one subject which she and Max had never discussed, although she knew that Jean had informed her brother of their background. 'Talking of which,' said Claire tightly. 'My husband is being released next month so we will be handing in our notice.'

Max's eyebrows fell. 'So soon! That's extremely inconvenient, I must say. When I first took you on, it was on the understanding that it would be more long-term. We've only just got this place shipshape.'

'We?' Claire thought of the time she'd spent sorting out the kitchen and the rest of the house, making sure that there were regular meals, and still do her own work as well as keeping an eye on Ben. The man was so selfish!

'I had thought that you would be pleased for us,' she said stiffly.

'My dear girl, of course I am.' Despite the fact that there wasn't a vast age difference between them, Max always called her 'girl'. 'It's merely that it's a surprise that is all. I would offer to have your husband here as a tenant too but to be honest, since he has a record ...'

His voice tailed away. 'Thank you.' Immediately Claire wished she hadn't said that. 'I'm going to look for somewhere else to rent.'

'Nearby?'

'Probably, because of Ben's school. Now he's settled in, I

don't want to move him again.'

The eyebrows raised. 'Settled in? Is that what you call sitting in the park all day with his laptop?'

'*What* did you say?'

'Oh dear, now I've probably dropped the young lad in it.' Max didn't look sorry. He was grinning. 'I think you'll find, my dear girl, that your boy hasn't been going to class for a very long time.'

Why hadn't school told her? 'We wrote to you, twice,' said the receptionist sharply. So she'd asked them to check the address and it turned out that it had gone to another family. Same surname but a different street.

'In fact, we were about to send someone round to visit you,' added the receptionist. 'Has your son told you why he absconded?'

The same term that Simon had used when talking about one of the men in his hut who went out for a town visit and didn't come back. 'No,' said Claire grimly. 'But he will.'

She waited until he came back as usual. 4.30 on the dot. 'How was school?' she asked.

Ben nodded. 'It was cool. We had double science and I got 70 per cent in my English so …'

'Sit down.' She gestured towards the bottom of the stairs. Slasher was furiously licking him at the same time as though in protection. 'You haven't been for weeks. No, don't deny it. What have you been doing?'

Ben looked away. 'Sitting in the park.'

So Max had been right.

'Why?'

Ben turned furiously towards her. 'Because if I hadn't defended myself on that first day, I'd have got beaten up. After that, all these other kids kept coming up to me and saying I'd be for it now because I'd hit some boy who had a lot of friends and I was scared.' His face crumpled. ''Sides, I hate it here. It's too big and noisy and everyone goes around in groups apart from me.'

He flung himself against her and Claire wrapped her arms protectively around him. Slasher began to lick them both furiously. Just as well that Max was out or the noise would have disturbed him. That was one thing, thought Claire, that they wouldn't have to worry about when they had a home of their own.

'It's all right,' she said soothingly. 'We're going to move anyway. We'll find somewhere else to live.' She paused, wondering whether to tell him. 'Simon's coming out next month.'

Ben lifted his face. 'Really?'

She couldn't tell if he was pleased or not.

'Is that OK?'

He nodded. 'If it makes you happy, I suppose.'

Her heart caved. He was getting so grown up.

'I'll have to find you some work to do at home,' she said. 'Your exams are so close now ...'

'It's OK.' Ben cut in. 'What do you think I've been doing on my computer all day in the park? Poring over practice papers online that's what. Poppy's been emailing me some of her notes from school as well as doing some revision with me at the weekends at Dad's.' His face shone. 'I'll probably do better than I would have done here!'

Of course she had to speak to Charlie. 'Why didn't you know Ben was skipping school?' he'd demanded on the phone.

Exactly what she'd been asking herself. 'He went off to school every day with his bag. At that age, you don't take them to the school gates.'

You would have known that, she'd wanted to add, if you'd been at home when he'd moved to secondary school.

'I can't believe the school sent letters to a wrong address!'

'It's a big place,' she replied defensively. Didn't he believe her?

'And now you're going to find somewhere else to run to now that your husband is being released?'

Your husband was said in a slightly mocking way.

'Yes.' Claire forced herself to sound positive.

'You know,' he added in a softer voice, 'I've really enjoyed my weekends with Ben. I'm beginning to realise how much I missed out when I was abroad.'

'Yes, you did.' An alarm fluttered in Claire's chest. What was he leading up to?

'I made a mistake, Claire, all those years ago with that woman.' He said *that woman* in a voice that suggested it was all her fault and not his. 'I've changed now and so have you. I'm impressed, Claire, at how strong you've been through this difficult time.'

'Charlie, what are you trying to say?'

'It's not too late, Claire.' He spoke with an urgent softness. 'It's not too late for us to start again.'

It would never work! She'd told him so immediately, pointing out that she was married and that he had a girlfriend (something he didn't deny) and that it was impossible to go back. She'd also promised that if Ben was happy to do so, he could continue to see him at weekends and then, after that, she'd forced herself to get out a map of outer London and work out where they should rent.

The suburbs would be better, she'd decided. It would be more anonymous than Devon even though she longed to go back. There were times when she woke up in the morning, dreaming she could hear seagulls. Maybe one day, when all this had become the past. But not now.

The following week passed in a blur of activity. The task of finding a rented house inevitably fell to her since Simon wasn't in a position to do anything in prison. In the end, the solution came when walking Slasher in the park and bumping into Labrador man. 'Haven't seen you for a while,' he said. So she explained that she and her son were moving again, now her husband was coming home.

'Been working away, has he?'

She nodded.

You ought to look at that new city they've just built, if you want to rent somewhere cheap. My brother moved out last year. Loves it, he does, and there are plenty of spaces for the dog to run around if you pick the right spot.'

She'd heard of it of course but only in terms of it being a vast concrete sprawl. Now, as she thought about it, that seemed a perfect place to hide away and start all over again.

'Sounds good to me,' said Alex when he'd rung during one of his regular phone calls to make sure she was all right. She'd give him that. He'd kept up with her, unlike Rosemarie. 'Has Simon any idea what he's going to do?'

'No. There's something called Job Club apparently at the prison which tries to help people get jobs when they get out.'

'I don't envy them.'

The implication that employers wouldn't want to take on criminals irked her. 'They're not all murderers, you know.'

'I didn't mean that, Claire. I'm sorry. It can't be easy. Let me have a bit of a sniff around and I'll see if I can find something for him. The new city, you say. I know a lawyer there, funnily enough. Simon isn't allowed to practise of course but there might just be something he could do.'

It was almost sorted. She'd driven out to MK, as everyone seemed to call it, and drawn up a shortlist of UPVC-windowed houses which they could afford to rent within a short walking distance of the centre. She and Ben had also found a sixth form college which had offered him a place if he got the right GCSE grades.

Simon had been ringing every night sounding chirpier by the minute. He was sorting his paperwork out, he said, in the same kind of rushed voice he had used when working.

And then her agent rang. 'This deal, which your landlord has got for you,' he began. 'I suggest you think very carefully about it.'

'Why?'

'The advance money is a reasonable amount but if you read the small print, you'll see your landlord has the right to all the royalties. This book was your idea, Claire. Not his. I reckon he's taking you for a ride.'

She marched up to Max's office immediately, flinging his door open without even knocking. He glanced up startled from his computer.

'You were going to cut me out of the royalties,' she hissed.

Max's face immediately turned from irritation at being disturbed to conciliation. 'My dear girl, the words are mine so it's only fair ...'

'No.' She stood there waving her part of the contract in front of him. 'It was my idea in the first place so I want seventy-five per cent and you can have twenty-five. Otherwise, I'm not signing.'

She made to rip up the paper but Max stood up. He wasn't wearing any shoes and seemed much smaller than usual in his striped socks. 'How about fifty per cent?'

'Thirty.'

'Very well then, you drive a hard bargain but I will concur. Now if you don't mind, Claire, I'm in the middle of writing something and I don't care to be interrupted. By the way, I have a new tenant moving in next week so I would appreciate it if you could leave everything in the way in which you found it.'

'Mould and all then?'

Max smiled weakly. 'Touché.'

Truth be told, she'd mentally prepared herself to go for fifty per cent but now she had done even better. Her agent had wanted to negotiate for her but she'd been determined to sort this one out. Now she had won. It was a good feeling. It made her feel powerful. In charge. That way, no one was going to hurt her again.

'We're moving again,' Ben said into Poppy's naked shoulder. She stirred sleepily. They'd been just lying there all evening while Dad was out again and he'd been waiting for the right time to tell her.

'To that new city they've just built outside London.'

Poppy snuggled into his shoulder. 'I've heard of that. It's won all these awards for weird architecture.'

'I'll be going to a sixth form college.' Saying the words didn't make it feel any more real.

'Wish I could. Ouch.'

'Sorry.' He'd touched by mistake a new bruise on her arm. 'If I tell Mum about your father, she might be able to do something.'

'No.' Poppy sat up straight, the duvet covering her naked breasts. 'I told you. I can't. He can't help it. He just loses his temper. If I tell on him, I don't know how he'd cope.'

'OK, if you say so.'

Poppy took his hand and moved it to a place he hadn't been to before. 'What time did you say your dad was going to be back?'

Ben could hardly speak. 'He didn't.'

Chapter Forty-five

It was all happening at once. The letter from Lydia. Claire's news that she'd found somewhere for them to rent where no one would know them and where there was a decent sixth-form college for Ben. Not to mention the small matter of him being released.

'*I'd have thought you'd have been glad,*' chided Joanna. '*Speaking personally, I can't wait to be out of this place.*'

Of course he was glad. Yet at the same time, he felt scared, just as he used to at the end of term at school when they'd heaved the trunks out of the basement and begun hunting for rugby boots and lost pullovers so matron could tick them off against the list. (He'd once tried to explain this to Claire but she'd gone to a day school in London and been unable to fully understand.)

'It's amazing, man!' enthused Spencer, his voice laden with envy. 'Me, I got another one month, three weeks, two days.'

'It will go faster than you think,' said Simon, silently reproaching himself for the lie.

'Yeah, man but who's gonna help me with my reading like?'

He'd already sorted that out, he hoped, partly out of fear that without someone to keep this new interest alive, Spencer might fall into the company of some of the new boys who hung around in groups muttering sullenly. Friendship groups, he'd learned, could make the difference between staying out of this place and coming back in again. 'Jason's going to help you.'

'That geezer with the big head?'

Simon had to laugh. Jason, who had come in last month, did indeed have a head which was shaped like a rugby ball. He also had an inextinguishable air of optimism even though he'd just been sentenced to three years for fraud. Jason made no secret of the fact that before that he had been a keen player in a financial institution covering Hong Kong and the States.

He had, however, been happy to take on reading duty for Spencer and Mark at the library was also going to keep a watchful eye on him. Somehow, Simon couldn't help feeling responsible for the boy.

'*I know what you mean,*' tinkled Joanna. '*There but for the grace of and all that ...*'

'Are you going to stop when I get out?' he demanded.

'You talking out loud again?' Spencer shook his head. 'Better cut that out when you get back, man or your missus will get you locked up again.' He got up off the bed from where he'd been watching Simon pack up his stuff. 'Come on, you've got to get goin' with your paperchase. I'll help you.' He grinned, exposing drug stains on his teeth. 'Done it enough times myself, I have.'

Simon already knew that the 'paperchase' was something that everyone did the week before they were released. It involved rushing round from 'department' to 'department' getting signed off. In his case, this meant going to the library where he had been an orderly; the Job Club where they had organised work in the charity shop (something he rather missed actually); to the kitchens and the stores where he'd also worked, and so on.

It sounded easy but in practice it was a nightmare because the right person was never there. 'That's wot it's like in prison, man,' shrugged Spencer. 'Communication's shit, like. People say they'll be there or do something and they don't. It would be a lot easier if they let us have mobiles in here.'

The very word sent tremors down Simon's spine. When he got out, he'd already decided, he wouldn't have one. He wouldn't drive again either after his ban was up.

'*No mobiles and no driving?*' tittered Joanna. '*Goodness me, life's going to be different for us, isn't it?*'

The Job Club was next. When he'd first come across it, Simon had thought the title seemed at odds with the environment but since being in here, he'd been deeply impressed at how the three women and one man inside worked like beavers to persuade employers on the outside to give a temporary or permanent position to men who had a record. Most of the jobs on offer involved driving or working in bars or hotels. All of these had been suggested to him.

'Got something lined up yet?' now asked one of the girls who clearly had a bit of a soft spot for him.

He shook his head. 'Not much call for bent solicitors.' He tried to make light of it, as though it didn't matter but the girl wasn't fooled. 'Don't rule out the hospitality business,' she said, signing off the relevant document in his paperchase. 'Might be a start, don't you think?'

The chapel was the last but one on his list. It was housed, slightly incongruously, at the back of the IDU building where the drug counsellors worked. When he'd first found it, all those months ago, he'd been astounded to find the staircase leading up into a room containing a beautiful stained glass window and about five rows of chairs before an altar.

'*Told you we should have come here more regularly,*' chided Joanna.

But he'd been responsible for the death of a beautiful woman in the prime of her life. How could he possibly atone for that by going to chapel?

'*Thanks for the compliment,*' gushed Joanna '*but I still think you're wrong. Oooh look. Here comes the Vic. I have to say that for a man of the cloth, he's incredibly sexy. Wouldn't mind having my time again with that one!*'

The Vic, as he was known round the camp, was indeed striding up the stairs. He was a youngish man in his mid thirties, a wedding band on his left hand and a slight Scottish lilt to his voice. 'I hear you're off, Simon,' he said outstretching his hand. 'Good of you to make time to say goodbye.'

That was another thing about prison. Although communication could be hopeless when you were trying to find something out, everyone else seemed to know if something had happened to you. He wouldn't be surprised if the Vic was aware of the letter from Lydia which he carried everywhere but still hadn't replied to.

'Sorry I haven't been here, much,' Simon ventured.

The Vic motioned to one of the wooden seats at the back of the chapel. 'Want a chat now you're here?'

Reluctantly, Simon sat down. 'I used to have some sort of belief before.' He stopped, recalling the services at school which he'd attended, unquestioningly. 'But after ... after killing someone, I don't feel anyone can help me.'

The Vic looked solemn. 'You didn't do it on purpose, Simon. You told me about the mobile but there were mitigating factors. The car which was parked where it shouldn't have been; the possibility that your passenger might have touched the wheel...'

'I'm wondering now if that might have been in my head,' said Simon quickly. 'I hear things, you see. Often, I hear Joanna – she was the passenger who died – doing a sort of running commentary in my brain.'

'Really?' The slight note of alarm in the Vic's voice instantly made Simon wish he hadn't mentioned this. 'Have you spoken to the medical centre about this?'

Simon stood up. 'No. Please don't say anything or they might stop me getting out of here.'

As the Vic stood up, his body obliterated some of the light from the stained glass window behind him, framing him in red and blue streaks. 'Everything you say in here, Simon, is confidential. However, it would be a good idea to see someone when you're Out. Don't you think?'

He nodded. 'Actually, there's something else. Well, two things actually.'

Even as he said the words, he regretted them. It was too long ago now. Nothing anyone said could put it right. Alice was part of his past. A nightmare that could never be unravelled. As for Lydia, he couldn't explain that, until he knew more himself.

'Yes?'

The Vic's face was open. Ready. Waiting.

'It's OK.' Simon made a dismissive gesture. 'It's nothing

really.'

It seemed only fair to pay his respects to the Multi-Faith Room too. This was much starker – just a white-walled room although Simon noticed that there was a copy here, as there had been in the chapel of a slim book called The Book of Uncommon Prayer: a collection apparently of prayers which a writer in residence had asked inmates to write several years earlier.

There was a group of young boys here now, not much older than Ben, who glared at the interruption. They were chanting something that sounded vaguely familiar and, making his apologies, Simon went straight out back again.

On, past the gym where he needed to stop off to collect his sweat shirt which he'd left behind last week. Right now, there were only a couple of men running on the treadmill. One was the Coin Man! 'See you for dinner if it's heads,' he called out.

Simon did a thumbs-up but failed to find his shirt.

'*No surprises there,*' trilled Joanna. '*It will be stashed in someone else's cell by now.*'

There was only one more place to visit.

Sam, as they called the Samaritan who was their new team leader, had arranged to meet him in the Listeners' Hut. To give the man his due, he hadn't been surprised when Simon had said he needed to talk about a personal matter.

The inside of the Listeners' Hut was far more Spartan than the chapel, with its unpainted concrete walls and floorboards, but somehow Simon felt much more relaxed. 'Want to sit down and talk about it?' suggested Sam.

'Actually,' said Simon, looking out of the window and onto the education hut where he had optimistically thought he could do another degree when he first arrived. 'I'd rather stand.'

He stopped for a minute, wondering what Claire would say if she was in the room right now. Even Joanna was being uncharacteristically silent as though she understood the enormity of the situation. 'I'd like to tell you about someone called Lydia,' he said quietly. And then he began.

Simon woke up the following morning, knowing something was different. It took a few seconds for it to register. And then it did. In precisely one hour and forty minutes, he was going to pick up the black holdall containing his few possessions and bid goodbye to Spencer and Jason with whom he'd already exchanged contact details.

And then he was going to be Out.

'My watch.' Simon was going through the contents of the see-through plastic bag that the officer had given him. 'Where is it?'

The officer handed him a form. Everything he had taken into the prison was listed here: his wallet, his driving licence, his credit cards. Everything except his father's watch and his mobile phone. He wasn't too upset about the phone, which was easily replaceable. But the watch had sentimental value.

The officer gave him the sort of look that he'd seen staff give men who were trying it on. 'Then you couldn't have brought it with you, sir.'

Don't *sir* me, Simon wanted to scream. But if he did, they might stop him from leaving. He'd heard of men who behaved badly on the last day and got an extra month for their pains.

'It was my father's,' he said softly. Something in the officer's eyes flickered.

'You can fill in this form and I'll see what I can do.'

Shaking with anger and frustration, he did so. Then, picking up his bag, he marched out of the Portakabin where he had signed in nine months ago.

'I'll be waiting outside the Visitors' Car Park,' he had told Claire on the pay phone.

As he made his way there, walking past hedges and roses which were coming out in full bloom, he could see a couple of men from G Hut, getting into a newish Volvo to go to work. What an extraordinary place. How could you have murderers going to work from prison every day, promising to be back by curfew?

It was a tribute to the system, surely, that it worked. Well, more or less.

'Good luck, Mills!' one of them called out.

He waved his hand in greeting and looked down the drive. All those months in prison had taught him to know exactly what the time was, without a watch. Claire was late.

A hard knot of fear formed in his stomach.

Maybe she wasn't coming.

OUT

Chapter Forty-six

She was late. After a year of waiting for this day, she was late. Claire could scarcely believe her own stupidity. It wasn't as though she had overslept. Anyone lying next to her would have known that she'd hardly got a wink of sleep tossing and turning in a drowsy sea of apprehension and excitement.

'Please be on time,' he had said on the pay phone yesterday.

'Want me to come too?' Ben was standing at the doorway of his bedroom, his tall, lanky lean frame every inch his father's.

'No thanks.' She tried to find the right words to express gratitude for the offer, while, at the same time, explaining it would be better if she went alone.

'But what should I say?' Her son frowned anxiously. 'You know, when he comes home?'

'Just be yourself,' she said, giving him a quick hug.

If only, thought Claire, picking up her car keys, she could take her own advice. It wasn't a long drive to the prison from the new house. An hour and a half if she went slowly, which is what she always did now; out through the city fringes and then weaving her way through the villages with their brick and flint stone. Through flat farm land and then a sharp right into what looked like a council estate but which was apparently where the prison officers lived.

The other month she had seen a child coming out of one of the houses in school uniform. It seemed incongruous that normal life went on here.

He'd be in the Visitors' Car Park, he'd said. Waiting. She'd seen men hovering there before with their regulation see-through bag of possessions but now she could hardly imagine her own husband doing the same.

She rounded the corner. Her heart lurched. He was there.

321

Erect. Standing almost as though to attention. He'd had a haircut since her last visit. It was too short. The new brown cords she'd sent in were hanging off his waist, showing how much weight he had lost. And when he approached the car, there was something empty in his startlingly blue eyes that suggested he'd come from another world. She steeled herself, as he got in, waiting for his mouth to brush her cheek, but it didn't happen.

Claire felt a mixture of relief and hurt.

'You're late,' he said. Then he added. 'Get me out of this place. Now. Please.'

Simon looked out of the window, observing the hedges rush past in a blur. How he wished he hadn't said that bit about being late. But it had been so horrible, waiting in the car park, attempting to look nonchalant while panicking that Claire had bailed out on him.

It had happened to yet another bloke from B hut last month; the poor geezer had had to borrow money for his fare home. God knows what kind of welcome he'd had when he got there.

Bloody hell, she was going fast. Simon gripped the handle of the car door as Claire took a corner. The speedometer had to be wrong. It couldn't possibly be just 30. Mind you, everything seemed faster; especially the last week of getting everything together.

And now here he was, on his way 'home'. Not Beech Cottage but a two–bedroom house which he had never seen before, near a place where he had once done a case. (Ironically, he'd got off a drunk driver, claiming the other driver was more at fault.)

Everything was different, including Claire. Why hadn't she asked him before cutting her beautiful long auburn hair? Yet somehow that elfin style suited her; accentuating her amazing cheekbones and those wonderful green eyes which had greeted him with pity. Anger he could deal with. But not the 'p' word.

'Are you all right?' Claire glanced at him quickly.

'Don't,' he wanted to say because it meant taking her eyes

off the road. Only a few seconds was enough to change a life. He should know. Simon nodded, not wanting to speak because if he did, he might just cry. Spencer had warmed him about that. 'Getting out is a big thing, man,' he had warned. 'Don't be surprised if you get choked, like.'

He almost wished Spencer was here now so he could ask if it was right for his chest to be pounding with apprehension rather than happiness or why the car radio, which Claire had just switched on, sounded so loud. To explain what ex-cons did when they got home. Put on the kettle? Head for the shops, which was what they used to do on a Saturday morning?

'What do you want to do when we get home?' Claire asked, looking straight ahead now.

It was as though she'd read his mind. Or maybe she was as nervous as he was. Simon shrugged, aware that he hadn't so much as kissed her yet; not even a brush on the cheek. He couldn't even begin to think about what would happen when they went to bed that night. 'I don't know.'

'I've got chicken casserole in the oven.'

Hadn't she listened, during Visits? 'I don't eat meat any more. Remember?'

'Sorry.' Her voice was low. Repentant. 'How stupid of me.'

There was a silence. He tried again. 'Is Ben at school now?'

'It's half-term.'

If he'd been a real dad, he'd have known that. Would the boy be all right with him, like he was on the last visit? Or would he be back to his usual unfriendly self, shooting him hostile looks. Simon couldn't blame him if he did. The kid had a reason to do so now.

'It will be fine, you know.' Claire's hand reached out and touched his arm briefly. He could smell her scent. It was still the same. That was something.

'It's not,' she added soothingly as though comforting a small child, 'as though you haven't been out before.'

Simon wanted to say that it was different during the 'town visits' when you had to go back. He wanted to say too, that Claire was wrong. Nothing would ever be all right again. He might be a free man in the eyes of the law but he could never forget the night of the dinner party.

'I wish we could turn the clock back,' he began.

Claire nodded tightly. 'Me too.'

Suddenly, there was a ringing in his head. A tinkling that he'd hoped, desperately, had been left behind along with his green joggers and identity tag. *'What about me?'* laughed Joanna gaily. *'Don't I have a say in this conversation?'*

Simon froze. 'Did you hear something?'

Claire was fiddling with the tuner. 'It's just the radio. Do try to relax. We'll be back soon.'

Chapter Forty-seven

Claire watched her husband's eyes dart around like a frightened animal, as she pulled up outside the row of modern plastic-windowed terraces and parked in the bay marked 16A in faded yellow paint. A small child, racing down the pavement on her bike without an adult in sight, nearly scraped the car's bonnet. A woman sat on a doorstep opposite, smoking. Her next-door neighbour was weeding his garden. She'd taken care not to talk too much to any of them.

'It was all I could afford,' she said, defiantly, unlocking the boot and heaving out his black holdall.

'*I?*' he questioned, taking the holdall from her. 'Don't you mean 'we'?'

Of course she did, just like she hadn't meant to get the case out instead of leaving it to him. But she was used to doing things for herself and that included working out how much money they had – or didn't have.

'The rent was much lower than London which means I've been able to put the rest from Beech House into a savings account.' She turned the key in the lock, not wanting to meet Simon's eyes. 'At least living here means that no one knows us.'

Simon gave a dry laugh although she wasn't sure if that was because of what she'd just said or because he was horrified by the way the front door led into a hall so narrow that if he stood in the middle and stretched out his arms, he could touch both walls. 'There is that, I suppose.'

Claire saw him taking in the glass door that led to the sitting room or as the estate agents' blurb had described it, 'the lounge'. His hand rested on the plastic doorknob, so different from the antique-style round knobs on their old Victorian pine doors in Beech Cottage. 'What happened to my desk?'

'There wasn't room for it.'

It had been impossible to squeeze everything in. Ben's piano had had to go too. 'My father gave it to me,' he said quietly, running his hand along the back of the chesterfield as if getting re-acquainted.

'I would have asked if you'd been there.' Too late, she realised that had come out as a criticism instead of a statement.

'Where did it go?' he asked, moving back out past her and into the kitchen.

'I sold it.' Regretfully, she thought of the elegant oak desk and its inlaid leather writing pad. 'Sorry. I should have mentioned it but there was so much to sort out.'

He was standing now, looking out through the kitchen window and on to the small patio, weeds sprouting up through the cracks. She'd meant to have done a spot of gardening before Simon got home but what with college, the book, Ben, and the dog, there just hadn't been time.

Wordlessly, he went upstairs but Claire found herself unable to follow. Instead, she put on the kettle and wondered if he'd notice that her own dressing table, which she'd had since her twenties, was missing because there hadn't been room for that either.

Meanwhile, Slasher's empty basket, which just about fitted in the gap under the stairs, suggested that Ben had taken him out for a walk. Good. She needed this time alone with Simon although it would have been nice if he'd asked where Ben was.

Overhead, she could hear footsteps starting and stopping followed by the flush of the only loo in the house. By the time her husband came down, she had made a pot of tea and pulled out the two bar stools by the breakfast bar which she'd found in a charity shop. 'I'll get you a new dressing table when we can buy a place of our own,' he said, looking out at the pale wooden fence that separated their narrow garden from next door. 'I'll sort out those weeds too.'

She felt his arm reaching out for her and pulling her to him. A great gush of relief washed through her as she leaned against his sweatshirt, trying not to breathe in the whiff of BO. The old Simon would never have worn a sweatshirt or smelt like that.

'You're right. It *is* going to be OK,' he said, his lips brushing her forehead lightly. 'I promise.'

They spent the day covering practicalities, with Claire sitting next to Simon on the sofa. There was the financial side for a start although something prevented Claire from telling Simon about the book deal just in case it didn't come off. When it was signed, she would surprise him with the cheque.

Simon had told her about 'Job Club', which had put out feelers for him with local legal firms. He couldn't work as a lawyer of course but he had hoped he might be able to do something. 'No luck so far,' he had said in an offhand way, 'but it's early days.' She wondered about telling him that Rosemarie's husband had offered to do the same but decided against it. Nothing had come of that, so far, either.

They'd talked of her new teaching post at the same sixth-form college that Ben had got into. 'They're training me on the job,' she explained. 'I'm doing a City and Guilds on Tuesday nights but, in the meantime, they've let me loose. Apparently the fact that I am a published artist makes a difference.'

Then Simon, with a tremor in his voice, asked if she'd heard from Hugh and she was able to assure him truthfully that she hadn't. 'But Poppy and Ben are seeing each other,' she said lightly.

'What?' Simon's face looked as though someone had pricked him with a needle.

So then she'd had to tell him that the 'children' as she couldn't help referring them to, were quite possibly more than just good friends. 'At first, it was just Ben teaching Poppy the guitar but now they seem really fond of each other.'

Simon's forehead broke out into a mass of small beads of sweat. 'Hugh will go mad.'

'He knows. He's all right about it.'

'I thought you said you weren't in touch with him.'

'Only every now and then.'

'And what about Charlie?' His voice suddenly rose in an accusatory way which she had never heard before. 'You say Ben goes to him every weekend. Do you see a lot of him now?'

Claire moved away from Simon, positioning herself at the far end of the sofa. Suddenly, she didn't want to hold his hand any more. 'We talk every now and then about Ben. What are you implying, Simon?'

'Nothing.' He bore a sulky look which reminded her of a child. Slowly, she edged back towards him, taking his hands. 'Simon, I don't care for Charlie any more but he is the father of my child. We have to talk every now and then. Besides, he has a girlfriend.'

Simon's face lifted. 'How long has he been seeing her for?'

'I don't know. I'm not even sure of her name, but does it matter? We're here now together under one roof. It's our new start.'

He nodded. 'What about Alex and Rosemarie? Have you heard from them?'

'Alex has been very kind; more so than her.'

He nodded. 'She always was a ghastly snob.'

There was no denying that but just as she was going to agree, there was the sound of a key in the lock and a black and white shape rushed in, hurling itself at Claire.

'Slasher!' she said, looking round for his dog blanket to dry him. 'You haven't been in the reservoir again, have you? Ben? We're in here.'

The information was almost needless, so small was the house, but she wanted to warn him by the *we* that Simon had indeed come back. A tall gangly shape appeared through the glass doors. 'Hi.' Ben stretched a hand awkwardly out to Simon. 'Good to have you back.'

Something weird was happening – almost as weird as that feeling when she'd walked Simon down the front path. He was smiling. Correction. Both were smiling. Thank you! Thank you!

But then she heard another noise: a low guttural noise like a blockage in a sink-disposal unit. 'Slasher,' she said horrified as the dog bared his teeth at Simon. 'What *are* you doing?'

He was jealous, Claire tried to explain. Slasher had been used to being with just her and Ben. Yet the more she tried to justify Slasher's hostility, the worse it sounded. The dog, she pointed out, had had to move around too much.

'I know how he feels,' said Simon who had just come into the bedroom, a towel around his waist and nothing else. She'd already had her bath and was sitting up in bed wearing a nightdress. Before the accident, she'd never worn anything in bed.

This was a new Simon, she observed, a catch in her throat. A tense Simon who seemed to analyse every word of hers as though testing it for the first time. Who was edgy every time the phone rang or someone walked past. It felt more comfortable to wear something in front of this man whom she didn't know any more.

'Ben is genuinely pleased to see you,' said Claire trying again, watching him lie on top of the duvet. Didn't he want to get under the sheet and feel her? She'd been so scared of this moment when they finally went to bed. It had been so long! Would he be like some desperate teenager or would he be unable to do it? Maybe after all this time, he didn't want to. Frankly, *she* wasn't sure if she did.

'He was very welcoming.'

Simon spoke as though he was only half there. Outside, she could hear the hum of the distant motorway and the sound of some kids laughing loudly as they walked past.

'Tomorrow,' he said, sliding down now between the sheets, 'I'll go down to the Employment Exchange or whatever they call it nowadays.'

She felt a gasp escaping her as his legs encircled hers. Taking her gasp for one of pleasure instead of surprise, he turned towards her, tracing the outline of her breast with his hands. It was the same slow rhythmical movement that had first caught her when they'd met; so different from Charlie's hurried urgency.

'Simon,' she began, but his mouth was already on hers; hard

and meaningful yet soft at the same time. Her lower body turned to water without her permission and she gasped again as his fingers searched her body, preparing it the way he always used to even though it wasn't necessary.

When he entered her, there was a slight resistance and for a minute, she thought he might stop but no, there it was almost like a click. 'Oh God, 'he breathed. 'I've missed you.'

'So have I,' she tried to speak, aware that her body was separating now as though there was a giant pendulum swinging back and forth below her waist. Someone called out; too late she realised it was her and then he made a low grunting noise. 'I'm sorry,' he said, 'I came too soon.'

'No.' She held him, rocking him back and forth like a giant baby. 'I came just before you.'

'Really?' He framed her head with his hands.

She nodded.

'What's that knocking on the wall?'

'The neighbours! They do that if I have the radio on too loud.'

They both laughed out loud like a pair of teenagers. 'Do you think Ben heard?'

'I hope not.' She'd forgotten that possibility. 'Still, he's got to get used to it just like you and I have to get used to each other all over again.'

He nodded. 'You're right. But this is a good beginning, don't you think?'

'Yes.' She drew him closer again, squeezing her muscles and not wanting to release him. 'Yes I do.'

He fell asleep almost immediately, leaving Claire to toss and turn in the shaft of moonlight that fell through the thin curtains. How ironic that she'd spent the last year getting used to sleeping alone. Now another body felt like an intrusion.

Maybe they shouldn't have had sex after all. Supposing Ben had heard? It would have been, on reflection, better to have waited until he went down to Charlie's that weekend.

Then Simon, as though sensing her inability to sleep, began

to toss and turn. He was saying something; having an argument in his dreams. There was one sound which he appeared to be saying over and over again.

Claire strained to hear. '*Joanna.*' That was it. Her blood froze. She was the one subject that neither had been able to mention that day. It was too big. Too huge to put right.

'Joanna,' she said out loud. 'Please, Joanna. I'm sorry. Simon's sorry. Just leave us alone now. Let me make this work.'

On the other side of the far wall, Ben was unable to sleep. Had Mum and Simon really just made out? It had sounded like it. It was disgusting to think of older people doing that sort of thing.

In the streetlight streaming through his curtain, Ben checked his phone. *Cn't wait for the wkend*, Poppy had texted.

Ben reached over the side of the bed, quietly so as not to wake Slasher who was sleeping on his legs. He opened his rucksack and felt, past the folders from college, for the small square shape in the brown bag at the bottom. It was there. It had taken some nerve to buy it from the machine in the Gents but it was there all right.

I can't wait either, he texted back. *Lov u.*

Chapter Forty-eight

Simon woke with a start at 6.30 a.m., bracing himself for the stern footsteps down the corridor of G hut and the click of the door as the officer unlocked it.

Instinctively, he knew something wasn't right. Spencer wasn't snoring for a start. Then there was the light which, instead of streaming through the shoddily made curtains, was more muted. He stretched out, amazed to find that his feet weren't hanging over the edge. And then he remembered.

He was back. Not home because 16A wasn't home in the way Beech House had been, or indeed his own place in London. But Out. And he was with Claire except that, hang on, she wasn't next to him.

A huge gulp of panic gripped his throat so that he couldn't breathe. It was a re-run of yesterday when she'd been late and he'd thought she wasn't coming. Where the fuck was she now? Simon sat bolt upright, looking around for signs that his wife had indeed been next to him all night and that he hadn't been hallucinating. Her side of the bed was still slightly dented and there was a pale blue nightdress on the floor. Leaning over, Simon picked it up and pressed it to his face. It smelt of Chanel and that other post-sex whiff which he'd never been able to adequately describe. They'd made love. It was coming back to him now. It had been quick, he recalled with a twinge of embarrassment. Too quick. But amazing – at least for him. Clearly it hadn't been any good for her or else she'd still be here, in his arms, the way they used to snuggle up in the morning.

'You're up!' Her sing-song voice filled him with relief as she appeared round the door, holding a tray bearing two mugs of tea. So she was still here. He took in the tea. Before, he remembered, it used to be *him* who would bring in a mug for *her* before leaving early for the office.

'You're treating me like an invalid,' he wanted to say. 'Please don't.' But instead he took the mug, thanking her almost too politely in his awkwardness and hoping that she would get into bed next to him. Instead Claire hovered as though she too was thrown by this new scenario. She was also, he noticed now, fully dressed in jeans and a T-shirt.

He took a gulp and grimaced. 'No sugar?' It came out, without him meaning it to, like an accusation.

She frowned. 'But you don't take it.'

Simon made a wry face, recalling the prison tea which was only drinkable if you tipped two sachets in. 'I do now. Let me get it.'

She looked away, he couldn't help noticing, as he got out of bed, still naked. 'Ben's up. Here, take this.' She tossed him the pink dressing gown which was hanging on the back of the door. It was hers, not his.

'I'm not sure where yours is,' she added apologetically. 'There's still a lot of stuff I haven't got round to unpacking yet.'

He tried to make a joke of it. 'Does the colour suit me?'

She laughed nervously.

'There was a chap I used to know, Inside, who was a transsexual. Georgia, he was called. Nice man, actually.'

The nervous smile froze.

'Don't worry. Being inside didn't turn me the other way.'

Claire flushed. 'I didn't think it had.' She was coming towards him now, putting her arms round his waist. 'Last night showed that.'

He pulled her towards him, feeling himself hardening again. 'Not now,' she whispered urgently. 'I told you, Ben's up. Besides, I need to get going. He and I are both due to be in college today. We'll drop you off at the Job Centre if you like.'

Simon started to say that it was all right, he'd drive down himself but then he remembered. He couldn't drive for a year and then he'd have to take a course to prove he was capable. He also had to see his probation officer in town today. And,

333

although this was a small thing, he had to find the sugar jar. How ironic that this was his home yet he didn't know where anything lived, least of all himself.

Then there was the letter from Lydia which he should have answered by now. Or should he just carry on, keeping it in his pocket, so that all the different options were still there?

Ben was quiet in the car. Simon tried to make small talk but gave up after a bit. College was OK. Yes this place was different but it was OK too. Yes he was going down to Dad's at the weekend. Yes he was still in his band except that some of them had gone to uni now so they weren't sure how long it was going to continue.

'What's that on your ankle, Simon?' was Ben's only question and he had saved that until the last minute, just before Claire had dropped him off in this sprawling concrete town of glass buildings winking in the sunlight, and wide roads calling themselves 'boulevards'.

Simon glanced down at the plastic strip around his ankle. 'It's known as a Peckham Rolex,' he said lightly.

He could see Claire next to him, frowning. Don't tease him, she seemed to say.

'Sorry, I'm being facetious. It's a tag, Ben. A strip that records what time I leave the house and when I get back. '

Ben frowned. 'Isn't that a breach of your human rights?'

'I'm impressed! Some people might say so but I probably deserve it. They – that is the authorities – just want to make sure that I'm not going to run off.'

Claire had pulled up now outside a modern red building and turned the engine off. 'I still don't see why it's necessary,' she said quietly. 'It's not as though you're going to do it again, is it?'

Joanna laughed delightedly. '*Great sense of humour, your wife.*'

'No,' groaned Simon. 'Not again.'

Claire squeezed his hand. 'Sorry. What I meant was that I thought tagging was more for burglars or people who were

334

likely to re-offend.'

Simon, still thrown by Joanna's outburst, shrugged. 'Thanks for the lift. I'll get the bus back later.'

'Sure? I could pick you up but I don't know when I'm going to finish.'

'It's fine.' Then Simon suddenly remembered something. 'I haven't got any cash. And my card's expired.' Feeling like a kid about to receive his pocket money, he waited while Claire rifled through her purse and produced a crisp twenty-pound note.

'I'll go to the bank too and sort out my account.'

She nodded. 'See you later.'

Suddenly he felt that overwhelming panic overcoming him again. Supposing she drove off and never came back. He might turn up at the house and she wouldn't be there and …

'Simon. Are you all right?'

He forced himself to smile. 'Sure. Could you just write down our address again? I'm a bit worried I might forget it.'

'Really?' Claire looked anxious.

Simon looked away. 'I don't know what's happened to my memory.'

'Stress,' she said quietly. 'It's normal.' Then she patted his arm. 'But it will be all right. I promise.'

Despite his earlier resolutions, it was now clear to Simon that he wouldn't survive in this new world without a mobile phone. Otherwise, how would he get hold of Claire?

Bewildered, he stood in this vast shopping centre as all these people walked past him; some urgently and some dawdling. You could spend all day here and never leave. It struck him that it was like one of the estates that Spencer had described.

The noise was getting to him now and a child was screaming because it didn't want to get into its push chair. The mother – so young – was yelling at it.

'*Calm down*,' said Joanna kindly. '*Take a deep breath and go up to that information centre there to ask about a mobile phone shop.*'

The girl at the desk had a flawless complexion which looked

as though her foundation had been applied with the flat side of a knife. Georgie would have approved, thought Simon, slightly wistfully. 'A phone shop?' she asked as though he had asked for a sex shop. 'We've got loads of them. Which one do you want?'

He tried to explain that any would do but the words stuttered out of his mouth. 'There's one just behind you,' said the girl. 'Look.'

'Really?'

'They started up a year ago,' said the girl as though he should have known that. 'Really big they are.'

'*Lots of things will have happened while we were Inside,*' pointed out Joanna. '*It's like being away on holiday and then coming back to find that someone famous has died. Heavens, look at that queue!*'

It was crazy. Only 10 a.m. and already there was a long line of people waiting. Didn't anyone go to work any more? By the time Simon got to the front, his head was ringing from the music and Joanna was moaning that all she wanted was a nice cup of coffee and that there was bound to be a Starbucks round here.

'Be quiet,' he said. The kid salesman stared at him. 'Sorry. I didn't mean you.'

The youth gave him an odd look rather like the girl at the information centre. Simon glanced down at himself, half expecting to see a badge on his chest, saying 'JUST OUT OF PRISON.'

'I need a new phone.'

The boy's face cleared as he whipped out a stack of brochures and led Simon to a shelf loaded with an impossible array of blue, white, silver, and black handsets. At the same time he kept an ongoing commentary running with the words tariff and contract and texts and Blackberry and iPhones and goodness knows what else.

'Stop, please!' He put up his hand to push back the tide of words. 'I just want an ordinary phone!'

Somehow, he selected one which had some kind of contract

336

which seemed to make sense but then the boy pushed a form towards him. So many questions. How long had he been at his current address? One day. What was his previous address? He could hardly put the prison so he put Beech House. When did he live there?

The boy picked it up immediately. 'There seems to be a gap in the dates. We need to know where you were living between this address and your current one.'

Why?

The boy shrugged. 'Dunno. We just do. New rules.'

'I was abroad.'

'*Liar, liar!*' sang Joanna.

'I might have been!' he snapped back.

The boy stepped away. 'Excuse me one minute.' He was gone for ages. If he hadn't decided that he would, after all, talk to Lydia, Simon would have left it at that but here he was, coming back again. 'I'm sorry sir but your application has been turned down.'

'*I knew it,*' groaned Joanna. '*Bit mean, if you ask me.*'

Simon felt his fists clench. It wasn't fair. You could even get phones Inside if you knew who to speak to. 'It's because I've been in prison, isn't it?'

The boy's eyes glanced away. 'I don't know. The credit people just say you've been turned down.'

'I've done my time.' Simon was aware he was shouting now but he didn't care. 'I've done my time and now all I want is a bloody mobile phone.'

He felt an arm at his elbow. If the shiny plastic label on his upper pocket was to be believed, it was the manager. 'Let me escort you to the door, sir, or else I will need to call security.'

Security. Simon's heart began to pound again. He had to check in at probation in an hour. If there was trouble, he'd be back Inside again. They'd made that quite clear. 'Sorry,' he mumbled. 'I'm not feeling very well this morning.'

'If I were you, sir,' said the man wearing the manager label, 'I'd think about going to see your doctor.'

* * *

337

The confusion in the phone shop almost made him late for his probation appointment. It didn't help that he got the wrong boulevard. How many were there in this place and who was the piss artist that dreamed up these names for a concrete jungle?

'Tut, tut. You never used to use four letter words beginning with "p" before you went in.'

Joanna seemed much more talkative now they were Out. Eventually, after asking the way several times, he found the right place. It was another red-bricked building just like all the others around it, a small sign saying 'Probation' on the outside. Was it small on purpose so it might be missed easily and lead to the ex-offender getting into more trouble? Or was it to make it less embarrassing for the person going inside?

Furtively, Simon looked around him feeling as he had done at Ben's age when he'd first gone into a sex magazine shop. The door was heavy so he pushed it rather too much and it swung against the wall, making him look as though he was being aggressive.

'Sorry.'

The middle-aged woman behind the desk was staring at him in exactly the same way as the information girl and the phone manager. 'Take a seat,' she squeaked.

Idly, Simon picked up a magazine which was dated around six months ago. There was a profile of a famous actor who had just got divorced. When he'd gone In, the actor was about to get married to his now ex.

'Simon Mills?'

A skinny boy who had a slicked-back black fringe emerged from a door. He reminded him of one of the more youthful prison officers.

'Sign here, can you?'

Simon's hand wobbled as he wrote his name in the register thrust before him. Too late, he realised he'd failed to read the small print at the top.

'Call yourself a solicitor?' chided Joanna.

'I'm not any more.'

'Sorry?'

Simon gathered himself. 'I was just saying that I'm not a solicitor any more but I need a job.'

The kid was rustling through his papers. 'We can help you sharpen your CV and put you in touch with some training courses. There's nothing to stop you trying the Job Centre over the road, either, although you'll need to tell them about your record. You won't be able to take a job unless we've liaised with your employers.' He looked sombre. 'Otherwise there might be a risk of a former prisoner working alongside a member of the victim's family.'

He got the point. Still, it was worth trying. The Job Centre door was heavy. The last year had been made up of doors, he reflected. Mostly locked; even those that seemed open. A girl told Simon to take a raffle ticket from the machine on the wall. The only thing he might win was an interview, provided his number came up on the light before it was closing time. *If* he was lucky.

'Simon Mills!'

It was the same girl who'd directed him to the ticket machine. She led him to a desk surrounded by others, without privacy. Then she glanced at the forms in front of her.

'You're a solicitor?'

'Yes.'

'But you can't work as one any more?'

'No.' He lowered his voice. 'I've been in prison.'

She edged away.

'Nothing violent,' he added hastily. 'It was a driving offence.'

'*NOTHING VIOLENT?*' roared Joanna.

Simon gripped the edge of his chair tightly to drive her voice out of his head.

'Would you say you have people skills?'

He nodded, watching hopefully as she ticked a box.

'Admin skills?'

'Up to a point.'

'IT skills?'

Thank heavens for the computer workshop in the prison.

'Not bad.'

Spotty girl raised her chin disdainfully. 'Do you have any qualifications?'

'Sure. A degree. My legal qualifications …'

She broke in. 'I mean in IT?'

'No.' Too late Simon wished he'd taken the certificate which the computer workshop had offered.

'Driving licence?'

Joanna snorted in his ear.

'I can't drive for a year,' he ventured.

A cross.

'We'll let you know if something comes up.'

Fine. Just fucking fine.

Simon used part of the £20 that Claire had given him to buy a phone card. None of the phone booths were private. The huge woman next to him had rolls of bulk above her waistline that almost protruded into his booth. She couldn't have been very old, but she already had two small children in a double buggy and one in a sling.

Lydia's mobile was engaged. He waited a few seconds and then tried again. Still engaged. There was someone behind him now, waiting. Just one more time. Engaged.

After dithering for so long, he was desperate to speak to her. Simon felt like kicking the phone like the one on the left had been, judging from the buckled metal.

'Finished, mate?' The boy who was waiting said it in a friendly way.

'Sure.'

Now what? Claire wasn't due to pick him up for another three hours. He could get the bus back but then she'd worry if he wasn't at their agreed meeting place. Without a mobile, there was no way of contacting her.

It was then that he saw Ben walking past and going into a Costa Coffee. The boy was absconding again!

Swiftly, he followed. 'Ben?'

'Simon!'

'What are you doing here?'

'It's a free period.' Ben was looking at him in exactly the same way as the information centre girl, the mobile phone manager, and the spotty girl in the job centre. 'You thought I'd copped off, didn't you?'

'No.'

It didn't come out strong enough.

'I told you, Simon, I *like* college.' He and Ben were already at the queue. 'They treat you like adults. And my courses are cool.' He looked around him. 'I'm meeting some of the others here in a minute.'

Simon felt a flash of compassion, remembering how his own father used to embarrass him at times in front of friends. 'I won't hang around and cramp your style, then.'

'No. It's OK. Want a latte?'

He found himself allowing his stepson to buy him a coffee and together they sat at a table overlooking the centre. We should have done this before, Simon thought suddenly. Before the accident. They might have got to know each other better instead of reserving contact to heated discussions about bed times and allowance and DIY jobs.

'I'm sorry,' said Ben suddenly.

Simon hadn't been expecting that. 'What for?'

'Ringing you. You know. On that night. If I hadn't, you wouldn't have answered and then ...'

Simon wanted to reach out and touch Ben's hand but didn't feel able to. 'It's OK. It was my fault, not yours. If ...'

He stopped as a crowd of teenagers swarmed in. One of them – a girl in an impossibly short red skirt and black jeans underneath, called out a greeting as they queued up for baguettes. 'Got to be quick,' she called out. 'French starts soon.'

Immediately, Simon felt ashamed at having doubted his stepson. 'I'll leave you to it.' He got up.

'You can stay if you like.'

He shook his head. 'Thanks for the offer but I think I'm too old.'

Ben grinned. Then his face grew serious again. 'I know we

haven't always been good friends but I've been talking to someone and she … well this friend said that it's never easy for anyone when one of your parents gets married again.'

Simon really wanted to hug him this time. 'It's not. Maybe I should have tried a bit harder. I'm sorry.'

And then he left, not trusting himself to say any more in case he burst into tears.

The phone booth was empty now. There was no one else around. Perversely, now there was nothing to stop him, Simon wasn't sure if he wanted to go ahead.

'*If you don't make the call, you'll regret it*!' sang Joanna.

So he got out the letter and carefully dialled the number. It rang out and Simon's heart flipped. He'd been hoping it might be engaged again.

'Hi,' said a voice brightly. 'Lydia speaking.'

'Hello.' His voice came out cracked and just as he spoke, there was a burst of loud music behind him, forcing him to speak louder. 'This is Simon.' There was a pause. 'Simon Mills,' he added.

There was another pause during which Simon considered slamming the phone down and running.

Then she spoke. 'You rang,' she said, a distinct joyous catch in her voice. 'You finally rang.'

342

Chapter Forty-nine

Simon had been home for over a week now. How are you doing, Alex had asked when he'd rung unexpectedly during one of her college breaks. Luckily there was no one else around in the staff room. Personal calls were discouraged. Personal calls about husbands who'd just been let out from prison were on an even more elusive level.

'We're managing, thanks.' As soon as she said it, she realised she wasn't fooling anyone. Least of all herself. And certainly not Alex.

'It can't be easy,' he said, his voice laden with sympathy.

It wasn't! In fact, Claire blurted out, it was like being married to a completely different man. Instead of the strong, confident, clever hero she'd married, he had become nervous, always looking over his shoulder. He didn't seem to like going out of the house, either, preferring to stay inside and 'tidy up' as he put it.

'It's almost becoming an obsession,' she told Alex, feeling horribly disloyal. 'Simon's even taking over the kitchen, telling me what I should and shouldn't do. It's driving me nuts. He's happy to talk about domestic stuff yet he won't tell me how he's feeling inside himself.'

Alex's voice was sombre. 'Has he got a job yet?'

She laughed hoarsely. 'He's signed on at the Centre but apart from going down once a week to see them and the probation officer, he just mooches around the house. Keeps closing the curtains because he says he doesn't want anyone to know he is here.'

'Weird.'

'Exactly. He gets me to buy all the tabloid papers and every morning, he goes through them pointing out some criminal

343

who's just been released or a crime that's referred to. The other day, he claimed to know one man who'd just been released after spending all his time in the prison library to launch his own appeal. When he's not doing that, he paints all over the kitchen table.'

'Paints?'

'There were art classes Inside and apparently the art teacher told him he had talent. '

'Do you think he has?'

She snorted. 'He's awful! Really, Alex, you should see some of his stuff. It's like a child's painting – in fact it's like having another teenager around the house.'

'I'm sorry.' Just the acknowledgment made her feel better. 'Have you suggested he sees the doctor?'

'He won't.' Claire looked up as someone came into the staff room. 'Look, I've got to go now. I've a class to teach in ten minutes.'

Alex seemed reluctant. 'I've got to come up to London in a couple of weeks. Shall we meet?'

'That would be good. Thanks.'

Quickly, she put the mobile away and tried to concentrate on her notes for the next class. Alex's voice had been reassuring; Charlie too, had become quite a rock. Every now and then she couldn't help wondering what might have happened if she'd turned a blind eye to his affair …

'Still using the photocopier?'

The question came from the tall thin woman who had just come in.

'Not now.' She smiled, trying to show that she was open to a friendship. So far she hadn't really bonded with the rest of the staff. 'I've finished thanks.'

'Then make sure you turn it off.' The other woman made a point of striding over and pressing the orange button.

Claire nodded an acknowledgment that she had broken one of the 'rules'. The college was all right but it didn't have the same relaxed atmosphere that she'd had in the school back in Devon. Perhaps it was because she was the only art teacher; the others seemed to see her as an invader in a world of IT and maths and more traditional subjects.

Still the kids were great! Ben too was happy. She could only hope his grades would be all right.

'Morning, Claire!'

A sea of faces met hers, grinning. Teaching gave her such a buzz! Sometimes she was almost grateful for the terrible circumstances which had led her down this path. But the best thing was that it took her mind away from Simon doing his crazy child-like paintings on sugar paper in the kitchen, with Slasher growling suspiciously from the corner of the room.

When she got back that night, there was a pile of unopened post. Simon had washed up breakfast but neglected to make their bed. That was another thing! He was fanatical about being tidy in some areas and incredibly untidy in others. Plastic bags could sit on the kitchen surface for weeks unless she removed them. But if she tried to do the washing up herself, he would move in and insist on doing it himself.

He hadn't been like that before. Was it, as she'd been reading on the net, an attempt to be in control of certain areas of his life because he couldn't be in control of others?

No! She stared at the official letter on top of the pile. 'We're not covered for home insurance.'

Simon neatly re-folded the tea towel and glanced over her shoulder. 'It's because I've been Inside,' he said calmly, handing it back to her.

She stared at him incredulously. 'You knew about this?'

'Someone told me. Spencer I think.'

He kept talking about that man!

'Why didn't you say?'

He folded the tea towel again. 'I forgot. Sorry.'

'But that means that all this,' she waved her hand around 'isn't covered. So if someone burgles us, we can't get it back.'

'Sorry.'

'Anything else I ought to know about?' She hadn't meant it to come out in a sarcastic voice but it did.

'Probably.' He laughed. 'I expect other things will come up. They usually do, don't they? What's for supper, by the way?'

He was the one who had been at home all day. Did he expect a meal to appear on the table as it had in the prison? 'Tell you what,' she said through gritted teeth. 'Why don't I give you some money and you can go to the shop round the corner and buy something.'

Instantly a look of terror took over his face. 'I can't.'

'Why not?'

'I don't like going out.' He sat on the chair. 'I'm sorry but I don't. I want to stay in and be safe.'

His face began to crumple and instantly she felt sorry for him.

'It's all right,' she whispered. 'You're safe here with me.'

'No,' he whispered. 'You don't understand. Please. Just leave me alone.'

He pushed her away and ran upstairs, locking himself in the bathroom.

Stunned she sat there for a moment and then opened a kitchen drawer for the piece of paper she'd been keeping for emergencies. To her surprise, a woman answered instead of an answerphone.

'Hello?' Claire heard her own voice trembling. 'Is that the charity that deals with families of ex-offenders?'

It was a non-profit–making organisation, apparently, which gave advice to women whose husbands were in prison and had also left it. The woman on the other end of the phone listened patiently while Claire told her in hushed tones about Simon's behaviour.

There were things she might be able to do, to cope, said the woman when she'd finally finished. The charity ran mentoring groups all over the country and there was one nearby. Would she like to meet up with the leader?

When Claire got off the phone, she still felt better even though the bathroom door was still locked and Simon, from the sound of it, was having a very long shower.

That was something else he kept doing. 'Constant washing can denote a need to clear up past regressions,' said the site on the net.

Claire leaned against the wall, closing her eyes, wondering just how much more she could take.

The following day when she got back from work, the post was lying there neatly on the table, the envelopes ripped into tiny squares and the contents sitting next to them.

There was also the smell of baked beans.

'You've made a snack,' she said slightly irritated. 'I bought soya mince on the way back – now you'll spoil your appetite.'

Ben was stirring something in the saucepan. 'Simon and I have cooked dinner as a treat for you.'

She raised her eyebrows. 'Baked beans?'

Simon had his back to her. He was chopping something on the sideboard without using a mat but she stopped herself from criticising him. 'Save it for the big things,' she told herself.

'Not just baked beans,' he added. 'It's got tomatoes and garlic and peppers in it too. Spencer taught me how to make it.'

That man again. A common thief from what Simon had said. Yet he seemed to revere him.

'Besides,' he added, 'I told you. I don't eat meat any more.'

Simon had always loved his steaks! 'I thought that now you were out, you might change your mind.'

'Why?' He turned round and looked at her as though he hadn't seen her before. 'Joanna is still dead isn't she?'

There was a silence during which she realised, too late, she'd punctured the jolly atmosphere she'd come in on when her son and husband were actually working together instead of against each other. 'I'm sorry.'

Simon turned his back again on her to continue his chopping. 'I didn't know you'd got another book deal.'

'What?'

The question, hard on the heels of the meat issue, threw her.

'Another book deal,' he repeated. 'It's in the post. I wouldn't have opened it but you asked me to.'

Not *my* post, she wanted to say. Only joint post.

'Yes,' she began hesitantly. 'It was my idea but I had to find someone to do the text so Mrs Johnson's brother did it. The writer. You know, the one Ben and I stayed with in London.'

He nodded, still keeping his back to her. 'Interesting title on the contract.'

Blast. She should have told him before but had been waiting for the right time. Instinctively, she knew this wasn't it.

'*WHEN DAD GOES TO PRISON*' He turned round again, carefully putting the knife down. 'What's it about?'

Claire stuck her chin out defiantly. 'It's aimed at children whose fathers or stepfathers go to prison, actually.'

Ben cut in. 'That's really cool, Mum. But won't people think it's 'cos of Simon?'

Her husband's eyes were still coolly fixed on hers, waiting for a reply.

The words, pent-up for so long, flew out of her mouth. 'I got the idea because of what you put us through, Simon, and if you don't like it, frankly I don't care. You didn't have to worry about where the next pennies were coming for the next meal or how you'd have to pay the electricity bill. Look at this!'

She waved the gas bill that had also arrived in the post. 'Thanks to the advance I'm getting on the book, we can pay this now. What's more, the publishers think this could have hit a gap in the market and might do something. So if you don't like it, get yourself a job instead of slouching around here all day. And forget about your bean casserole because I'm not hungry.'

Slamming the door, she ran up the stairs and locked herself in the tiny bathroom. Her face and throat were hot and red but instead of crying, she was angry. It felt good.

'Mum.'

Ben was hammering on the door.

'Please, Mum. Simon wants to talk to you.'

'Well I don't.'

'Please.' Ben's voice was begging.

Why was Ben on Simon's side, instead of hers? Heavier footsteps were coming up now. She opened the door slightly.

'What do you want?'

'May I come in?'

Simon perched on the edge of the bath next to her. 'I'm sorry. You were right. It's just that I don't want the whole world to know about what happened and it will probably come out in the publicity for the book.'

Naively she realised she hadn't thought about that. 'Then again,' he added, 'if it does, maybe that's part of my penance.'

Claire put a hand on his knee. He didn't take it off.

'There's something else I want to tell you. Two things actually.'

'Are they good things or do I need to prepare myself?'

He took her hand. 'Good, I think. The first is that I've got a job.'

'Really!'

'It's not much. It's in a charity shop again and they're not paying me but it will build up my experience. My probation officer found it for me.'

'It was impossible to find anything else,' he said quietly, noticing her expression. 'You've no idea how hard it is to get employment when you have a record.'

She bit back her dismay. 'What's the second thing?'

He took a letter out of his pocket. 'I'd like you to read this.'

She made for the door. 'Simon, I've had enough surprises for one day. Just tell me who it's from and whether I should laugh or cry.'

His eyes were steady on her. 'It's from my daughter. Her name is Lydia – remember me telling you that was my mother's name? – and she's in her second year at uni in London. She wrote to me in prison because she'd seen something in the paper about the accident and, before you ask, I didn't know she even existed. Nor have I met her. I want us both to do that. Together. What do you think?'

Ben, Poppy, and Ben's dad were sitting together on the sofa watching a stupid quiz programme on television. Ben kept trying to hold Poppy's hand quietly but she just gave it a quick squeeze and then moved it away.

He knew what she was thinking. 'Wait until he goes out.'

But Dad didn't show any signs of going. Instead, he kept asking him questions which had nothing to do with the programme and everything to do with Mum. It had started when he'd let slip this stuff about Simon and this daughter of his.

'So how did this girl Lydia know that Simon was her father?'

Ben reached for Poppy's hand again. No luck. 'I told you, Dad. Her mum's a singer and Simon was her lawyer ages ago when he was just qualified. He had to help her with royalties or something and they kind of had a …'

He stopped. It was disgusting to think of adults having sex. Poppy giggled. 'They had an affair and the singer had a daughter 'cept she didn't want to tell Simon 'cos then she thought he'd have to marry her and by then they'd split up.'

Charlie nodded. 'But she must have told the daughter otherwise she wouldn't have recognised him from the piece in the paper.'

'Probably.'

'Why didn't she contact him earlier?'

'Said she needed to think about it, Simon said.'

'What does your mum think of it all?'

Ben hated it when each of his parents pumped each other for information.

'She's cool. They're going to meet her next week.'

Only the second part of that sentence was really true but he wasn't going to tell Dad about the funny look Mum had had on her face since the night of the baked bean casserole.

'Are you going out tonight, Dad?'

Poppy made a funny noise as though she was trying to hide a laugh.

'No. Why? Do you kids want some time alone?' Charlie got up. 'I've got some stuff to do in my study anyway.'

Ben and Poppy waited until he shut the door. 'We can't do anything,' said Poppy warningly. 'Not with him next door.'

He groaned, thinking of the packet that was left in his pocket

350

from last time. 'OK.'

'Tell you what!' Poppy leaped up, heading towards Charlie's extensive CD collection. 'Let's take a look at these.'

Ben hesitated. Dad was very careful about his stuff and didn't like it touched; a bit like Simon really.

'Take a look at this!'

Poppy was waving a CD at him and he glanced at the name – who was Ella Fitzgerald? – and the writing underneath. 'Jazz is for old people.'

Poppy turned it over. 'Certainly looks like your dad's kind of music, though. And someone else's apparently. Look.'

She handed it to him. *To my darling Charlie with all my love.*

The date was ancient. Five years after he was born. But it wasn't that which struck him. It was the name that came afterwards.

From your Rosemarie.

Chapter Fifty

Lydia had wanted to meet them in Covent Garden but he'd had to explain that he wasn't allowed out of the area. He hadn't mentioned the Peckham Rolex although he had a feeling that she might have found that vaguely amusing. Something told him from the tone of her letter that his daughter had a sense of humour.

'*Think you know her already*?' scoffed Joanna. '*Trust me, we never know our kids. Much as I love my stepdaughter, she's highly unpredictable.*'

Simon tuned Joanna's voice out of his head while he and Claire waited in the John Lewis café for Lydia to arrive. 'How do you know she is yours?' asked Claire, fidgeting nervously. This wasn't the first time she had asked this question; clearly his explanation before had failed to persuade her.

'I told you.' He craned his neck as a tall, confident young woman breezed in, looked around and then headed for an older woman sitting at another table. 'Her letter told me all about her mother. The date made sense and she also sent me a photograph of Francoise and me.'

Claire winced. 'How do you know she wasn't sleeping with someone else at the same time?'

Simon thought back briefly to the pretty young girl who had come to him all those years ago in such distress because someone had copied one of her lyrics. He'd managed to settle out of court before suggesting dinner. They'd had fun, he remembered There had been a photographer there who had taken silly pictures of the diners for a fee. And afterwards, it seemed quite natural for him to go back to her place. Just the once, they agreed. Neither had wanted commitment.

'It's possible,' he admitted. 'But she did call our … the baby by my mother's name.'

'You men are so naive sometimes!' Claire reached for the teapot. 'Maybe she was trying to frame you.'

'I don't think so,' he began. And then froze. A girl, close behind an elderly couple was looking around the café and now heading uncertainly towards them. 'Look,' he said quietly.

Lydia – it just had to be – was the spitting image of himself, but in a more feminine way. She had his light coffee-coloured skin. The same dark hair; although hers was curlier, and almost identical bright blue dancing eyes. Like him, she was very tall and skinny. When she opened her mouth to speak, he noticed that she shared the family dimple on her right cheek.

Wow.

'Simon?'

She held out her hand before turning to Claire. 'I'm so glad you're here too. It must be really awkward for you.'

Simon held his breath. 'Not at all,' said his wife. 'We're so glad to meet you. Aren't we, darling?'

They talked about everything. Simon wanted to know all about her childhood and Lydia described how her grandparents had played a large part in bringing her up in Buckinghamshire so her mother could continue her career.

At one point, Simon couldn't help butting in. 'I would have done my bit if I had known.' Claire had nodded as though in supportive agreement but Lydia had just shrugged. 'Don't take this the wrong way, Simon, but Mum wasn't sure about you.' She flushed. 'She was happy to have me but I think she felt rather embarrassed about sleeping with her lawyer.'

He had winced at that but then Claire asked another question (something about where she went to school) as though to divert the conversation onto safer territory while he waited on the edge of the chair to ask the really important bits.

'Are you musical too?'

She shook her head. 'Wish I was. I'm more science based. In fact I'm reading psychology at London University. I want to be a counsellor.'

So his daughter had her career plan all mapped out. Simon couldn't help shooting Claire a slightly smug look. 'Your mother must be very proud of you.'

Lydia's face stopped smiling. 'That's the thing, Simon. I didn't like to tell you in my letter but Mum died last May.' She looked away. 'It was cancer. Ovarian cancer.'

She was dead? Francoise – her joyous laugh and zest for living – was dead? Claire's face looked as shocked as he felt. 'I'm so sorry.'

'Thanks.'

'I don't get it.' Simon's mind was reeling. 'So how did you know it was me when you read about me in the paper? I thought your mother had showed you the article.'

Lydia shook her head. 'It was Gran. Mum had given her the photograph but she also told me about you from a really young age. When Mum was alive, I didn't want to trace you in case it upset her. Then after she went ...' Her voice tailed away.

'The woman who died when I was driving,' he said slowly. 'She had a stepdaughter who's a bit younger than you are.'

Lydia nodded. 'I know. It said in the paper.'

'So don't you think badly of me?'

Lydia shrugged. 'We all make mistakes. Mum was always saying that. The important thing is to learn from them.'

Had he been a mistake in her mother's life? Clearly. Yet, if so, why had his daughter been so keen to find him?

'I was wondering,' he began, 'I mean *we* were wondering if you were just curious to meet or whether you'd like to carry on seeing us every now and then.'

'Every now and then?' Lydia's eyebrows arched right up into her fringe. 'I was hoping we could see each other as much as possible. I know you said you hadn't got any kids yourself but you've got a stepson, haven't you? Can I meet him one day?'

Claire glanced at him encouragingly. 'Of course. You must come over to dinner sometime as well.'

Lydia's eyes glowed. 'That would be fantastic; although I'm really busy with uni work.'

How responsible! Just as he was about to say so, a waitress bustled up and explained politely that she was sorry but they were about to close the café. Only then did they realise they were the last ones there.

'My curfew!' Simon gazed in horror at Claire.

'Your what?'

He cringed as Claire explained. 'Simon has to be back home by a certain time every night. It's part of the conditions of his release, otherwise he gets into trouble. If we go now, we might just make it.'

She made him sound like a child but Lydia was giggling. Her own mother had done quite a lot of that, he now recalled. 'Sorry but that's quite funny really, isn't it? A bit like Cinderella.'

'You're not shocked?'

'No, Dad. You don't mind if I call you that, do you? Just tell me when we can meet up again.' Her eyes grew misty. 'I can't tell you how important your letters were to me. You're the only family I've got now apart from Gran and she's gone back to Barbados.' She looked at him uncertainly. 'Family is so important, don't you think?'

A flash of his father's coffin went through his head, alongside his mother, eyeing him accusingly. 'Yes, it is.'

Somehow they got back with four minutes to spare. Even if they hadn't, Simon knew it would have been worth it, despite Claire's hostility.

'If you ask me, she sounds too good to be true.'

'You're just jealous because she knows where she's going. Unlike Ben.'

'That's not fair.' She pulled up outside the house with a screech of the handbrake. 'You know what, Simon? I'm beginning to wonder if I know you at all. It's not just this.' She waved her hand at the plastic circlet round his ankle. 'It's all the other stuff. The obsession with making everything clean and tidy. Your crazy belief that you're some kind of hidden artist. Your constant talk about weirdos called Coin Man or Plait Man.

355

The way you call out Joanna's name in your sleep as well as some other woman called Caroline-Jane. And now this.'

Her eyes flashed. 'Don't start thinking that just because you've suddenly got an instant-made daughter, you know all about parenthood. Because you don't. Being a real parent is being there from the start. And you weren't.'

Simon undid his eighth black plastic bag of the day. He worked slowly and methodically, the charity shop woman said approvingly. The previous volunteer had been too hasty and missed stuff.

Her praise made Simon suspicious. Was she trying to boost his confidence or did she mean it? He was tempted to say that his thoroughness was due to OCD, according to his wife, but that would have been petty. Part of him felt she had been right when she had slung all those accusations at him the previous week; in fact, he could forgive her for most of that stuff apart from the last one.

It wasn't his fault he hadn't been there at the beginning for Lydia. How could he have raised a daughter if he hadn't known she was there?

'*I think we might have something here*,' chirped Joanna suddenly as he pulled out a small brightly coloured vase. '*A piece of Limoges, I do believe.*'

'Limoges, I do believe,' he said, echoing Joanna's words while handing over the vase.

The charity woman's cheeks grew pink. 'Goodness me, how clever of you.'

He shrugged. 'I know someone who used to collect it. Mind if I go early for my lunch hour by the way?'

Simon liked to have his lunch hours early if possible. It was the best time for Lydia to speak and it wasn't as though he could talk to her at home. Already, since their meeting, they'd fallen into a pattern. He'd call her when she got up after lectures, depending on what her day was like. They'd talk about everything from what was on the news or whether the other had read a certain book. Their similarities were incredible.

Quickly, he strode up to an empty bench and hoped no one else would sit next to him. His fingers moved unfamiliarly over the new mobile which Claire had helped him buy after his horrible experience at the first shop.. It still seemed strange not to queue up inside and enter his pin number. 'Lydia?'

'Dad!'

The sound of her voice filled him with light. 'Dad!' he wanted to yell out at the young girl who was pushing her child past. 'Did you hear that?'

'Are you OK, Dad?'

'Great. Great.' He stood up and began striding along the street. 'I'm just on a lunch break. What are you doing?'

'About to go into the library. Listen, may I call you tonight? Only I've got this essay to finish.'

'Of course. Of course.' He was so happy that it made him repeat everything twice. His daughter couldn't talk to him because she was going to finish an essay in the library. Ben could take a leaf out of her book.

'Talk then! Bye.'

Wow! He felt on a high; as though he was climbing that frame in the playground he was walking past right now. Just look at that kid. Entranced, Simon stood and watched a little pink-track-suited girl scramble up the blue plastic steps of a slide. He could imagine Lydia doing that as a child. Suddenly, the force of what he had missed out on, hit him like a concrete wall.

Slowly, Simon walked back towards the charity shop. He hadn't nearly had his full lunch hour but he felt more comfortable inside the shop, tidying up and putting right what others had simply left as a horrible mess.

'You're a gem, Simon,' said the charity woman when she came into the back at the end of the day. 'Our takings have almost doubled since you arrived. And just look at the floor! You've washed it for me, bless you. Thank you!'

The glow was so good that he decided to walk home instead of waiting for the bus. It was nice being appreciated.

'*You men,*' scoffed Joanna. '*You're all the same. All you need is for some woman to pat you on the back and you're putty in their hands. You were exactly the same with Caroline-Jane.'*

That reminded him. The letter he'd written to her was still in his pocket along with the original one from Lydia. It was very innocuous. Just a simple thank you for everything she had done.

'Go on then, post it,' said Joanna. *'It can't do any harm. Hang on. What's that motorbike doing on your drive? It's got an L plate on it too.'*

Claire met him at the door. He could tell from her face that she was as unhappy about the bike as he was. Ben had been going on about driving lessons but this was even worse.

'Hiya, man! Surprise, surprise!'

What? Simon did a double-take as Spencer's face loomed up over Claire's shoulder, grinning and doing a thumbs-up. 'You don't mind, do you? I mean you did say to look you up. Don't look so worried, man. I haven't walked out. I got my tag date early.'

Simon looked from the bike to Spencer and back to the bike again. 'Where are you living?'

He made a funny face. 'I was going to this hostel but it was full up so I wondered if you and your missus could put me up for a bit. Won't be for long. Just till I get on my feet, like. That *is* OK, isn't it?'

Chapter Fifty-one

'You should have said no!' Alex reached out and grabbed her hand as though trying to shake the import of what he'd been saying, into her. 'You must see that, Claire. Why should you open your doors to a petty thief?'

She interrupted him, using the opportunity to extract her hand. 'Cannabis dealing, actually. He stole to fund his habit. That's the phrase, I believe.'

Alex's eyes grew brighter as though he was running a temperature. 'Even worse. What on earth has Charlie said about his son living under a roof with a drug addict?'

Claire pushed her plate of pasta away. They were sitting in a Bella Italia just off Covent Garden. She'd suggested it, knowing that thanks to the Peckham Rolex, Simon wouldn't be in the area. 'I haven't told him actually and besides, Spencer doesn't do drugs any more. He promised. Anyway, I thought it might help Simon to have him around.'

Alex spluttered. 'Claire, please. Think about what you're saying. You've got enough on your plate with a husband who can't find any work and a son who's already been to three schools in as many years.'

Her hands gripped the red napkin under the table and began ripping it into several tiny pieces. 'That's not my fault.'

Alex shook his head. 'We know it's not.'

'We?'

Alex coloured. 'Rosemarie cares too but she's embarrassed; doesn't know how to handle the situation.'

'And you do?'

She made the mistake of putting her hands out on top of the table now to find another napkin to shred. Instantly, Alex's hands came down on hers again. This time she found the warmth surprisingly comforting. 'I'm doing my best, Claire. I'm sorry for you. It seems to me that you've been caught in the middle of all this and – I know this sounds mad – but if Joanna was alive, I'm pretty sure she'd want someone to be looking out for you.'

Joanna? 'But you hardly knew her.'

'She was a woman, Claire. Like you and like Rosemarie. Call it the chivalrous side of me but I don't like to see any woman in a mess that is no fault of her own. Besides, I feel responsible for introducing you to Simon in the first place. Now please tell me that you're going straight home now and telling this Spencer to pack his bags.'

She looked around for her bag which had slipped to the floor. A piece of paper had fallen out, reminding her that she'd been meaning to get in touch with the name below. 'I don't know, Alex. I really don't. But it's lovely that you care.' She stood up. 'That means a great deal to me.'

The text message came just as she got on the train at Waterloo. *Thank you for your words just now. You mean a great deal to me too. A x.*

The kiss seemed just a bit too familiar. Hang on. There was another text message.

Am free tomorrow if it's not too short notice. How about the reference section in the central library by the main desk? Martha.

Yes! Excitedly, Claire tapped back an affirmative. She should have got in touch with this kindly-sounding woman before but somehow with everything that had been going on, she hadn't had time. Now, with hindsight, she realised she should have made time. An organisation for wives whose men had been Inside or just come Out, was exactly what she needed. She could hardly wait for tomorrow.

Claire opened the door to the sound of the vacuum cleaner. Simon was vacuuming again! It was all he did when he got back from the charity shop – that and his stupid childish

360

drawings which were messily propped up on the kitchen table against the wall, leaving blue and red smudges on the wall. She'd have to get that off or they'd lose their deposit.

'Hiya!' Spencer waved his hand in greeting. He was sitting on her sofa with his feet up on the coffee table and a bowl of Cheerios on his lap. 'Had a good day, man?'

Alex's words came back to her. 'I'm not your man, Spencer. I'm your hostess or so it would seem. Have you seen Ben?'

'Nope.' Spencer was staring into his bowl of Cheerios as though he had lost something. 'Come to think of it, I have. That's right. He was going to take that dog of yours out for a walk.'

That was something.

'Simon's been cleaning,' added Spencer unnecessarily. 'Thought he might be a bit better now he's on the Out.'

She stopped at his words. 'Was he like this Inside, then?'

Spencer nodded, slopping some of the milk and Cheerios onto his blue track suit. 'Sure, man. The others used to tease him but the doctor said it was 'cos it helped him feel in control.'

Alarm bells were ringing now. 'Doctor? He saw a doctor?'

'Nah. He wasn't really a doctor. We just called him that 'cos of his glasses. They were made of wire and made him look all brainy. But he'd seen enough quacks in Broadmoor to know what he was talking about.'

This was scary. Ever since he'd got out, she'd been asking her husband to get a check-up but he'd refused.

'I've made dinner, by the way,' called out Spencer.

'Really?' Instantly she felt guilty. 'That's nice of you.'

'Yeah.' Spencer got to his feet, swaggering towards her. He was wearing a thick gold chain round his neck and he had a bulge, she couldn't help noticing, below the drawstring of his jogger bottoms. 'Pot Noodles. Curry flavour. It was Simon's favourite when we was Inside.'

That night, Claire dreamed Simon was vacuuming her body. The nose of the Hoover was exploring her breasts, taking each nipple in turn and forming it into tight peaks in the suction.

Then the hose moved down and inside her. Gasping, she woke to find her husband fast asleep with his back to her. For a moment, she had thought he had taken her while asleep. Slowly, she ran her index finger down the top of his penis.

He stirred and turned towards her, pulling her body towards him. Wordlessly, he stroked her inner thighs, making her damp so that when he sat astride her, looking down in the dark, she felt sick with desire. A different woman from the one during the day. He too was different as he silently threw aside the sheets, aware (as she was) that Ben was on the other side of the wall and Spencer on the sofa in the sitting room below.

Two different people at night. It was the only way to survive. Yet when she woke in the morning, the space next to her was empty save for an imprint and she could already hear the urgent hum of the vacuum cleaner before he set off for 'work'.

Confused, Claire woke Ben for school and then dived into the shower. It was cold, which meant that Spencer had got there first. He'd even used her shampoo!

'Where's your friend?' she said with the emphasis on 'friend' as she flew downstairs to make sandwiches for all three of them for lunch.

'Gone to meet someone.' Simon was wearing a suit which she hadn't seen before.

'Have you got an interview?'

'No. Why?'

'You're wearing a new suit.'

He looked down as though his body belonged to someone else. 'That? It's from the charity shop. We often wear our lines to encourage buyers.'

Claire wondered if she'd heard him right. 'Lines? Buyers? This is a charity shop, isn't it?'

He frowned. 'We prefer the phrase 'ecological finds' to 'charity shop' and, before you ask, I washed the suit before wearing it. Please don't cut the bread like that. It makes the next slice uneven.'

This was getting out of control! 'Are you feeling well,

Simon?' she asked gently.

'Well?' He frowned. 'What do you mean?'

'I just think it would be a good idea if you had a check-up like I suggested before.'

Carefully he lined up the squares of bread, holding the knife over it as though he was measuring the line. 'There's nothing wrong with me, Claire, although if you're worried about health, you might like to investigate Ben's room. When I was cleaning his computer screen yesterday, I found a packet of condoms underneath the keyboard.'

Somehow Claire got through a day of teaching. If it wasn't for the meeting with Martha, she'd have gone straight home and tackled Ben. She also ought to ring Charlie. Condoms were definitely a subject for a father.

The reference library, Martha had said. Well she was here but there was no sign of a woman looking for someone else; only the dark-haired woman on the other side of the reference desk who was smiling at her.

'Claire?'

She stumbled over her words. 'I hadn't realised you worked here.'

'Sorry. I thought I'd explained.' She stood up, extending her hand. Her grasp was warm and reassuring. 'I'm just about to finish my shift. Shall we go to the café next door? It makes great coffee!'

Over the next hour or so, Claire discovered that she was not alone in this strange world in which she had found herself. 'Our charity tries to help families who have been broken up by prison,' she explained. She had kind warm hazel eyes, reminding Claire of her mother, long dead. 'All the statistics show that prisoners who stay in touch with their families when they are Inside are far less likely to re-offend.'

Claire thought of Spencer who didn't have any family to speak of now his own mother was back in jail.

'We run informal drop-in centres so women whose men are Inside can come and talk about any issues that are troubling them.' A pair of understanding hazel eyes fixed on Claire. 'You sounded rather troubled on the phone, if you don't mind me saying.'

Without meaning to, Claire found herself pouring out her heart about Joanna (the guilt); Simon and his obsession with cleanliness together with his reluctance to get paid work; and Ben who was probably sleeping with his girlfriend.

'He's how old?' Martha asked and even as she said it, Claire could see what she meant. Ben was doing what many young boys of his age did and at least he was taking precautions.

'The tidy thing is another matter.' Martha was taking a notepad out of her bag. 'I've got the names of some psychologists that I promised. As for this poor woman who died – Joanna, isn't it – have you thought of trying to talk to her family?'

Briefly, Claire explained about Hugh and his earlier vendetta against them.

'But it's all right now?'

Claire nodded. 'Seems to be apart from the fact that it's his daughter who is sleeping with my son.' She gave a hoarse laugh.

'What about you? How are you coping?'

'I have my painting. It's my escape.

Briefly she thought about Charlie whom sometimes she imagined she was still married to and Alex whose over-friendly texts unsettled her. No, she couldn't tell a stranger everything.

'There's one important thing I would say, for what it's worth.' Martha was leaning towards her. 'And that's to tell this guest of yours that you simply haven't got the room to have him. I know that seems cruel but you've got enough on your plate as it is.'

Claire nodded. 'Thank you. You've put into words everything I've been thinking. I don't know how you do it.'

Martha touched her arm lightly. 'That's because I've been through it too.'

'Really?'

'We all have to have some kind of experience before we can

be volunteers,' said Martha in a soft voice as they went out onto the street. 'My son was Inside for ten years.'

Ten years?

'He stabbed someone when he was high on heroin.' Martha smiled sadly. 'It was a colleague at his bank. You might have read the headlines. It was about five years ago?'

'Did he live?'

Martha's voice dropped. 'The victim survived but my son gassed himself in his car the week after he was released. He just couldn't cope.'

Claire struggled to find the right words. 'I'm so sorry.'

'Thank you.' Martha bent her head in gentle acknowledgment. 'That's why I would urge you to go home and look after your husband. And if that means getting him to a doctor and throwing out his friend, that's part of the caring process. Trust me on that.'

When she got home, Claire found they had not only eaten before her, judging from the open tins of baked beans on the side, but had scoffed their meals in front of the television.

How could Simon insist on being so tidy, yet slob out on the sofa like that with his 'friend' and Ben. Spencer was telling yet another story. 'So there we was, after nicking the dosh, dressed in suits so the pigs would think we was businessmen like and all the time we had thousands of pounds stuffed in our briefcases!'

Ben's face was a mixture of admiration and horror. 'Didn't they get you to open them up?'

'Nope, son. We just walked past them like and got back to this geezer's house where we took our suits off. Then we went shopping.'

Claire sat down, aghast. 'You went shopping after you'd done a robbery?'

Spencer grinned. 'Yeah, man, 'cos then we could prove on CCTV that we'd been out shopping round the time of the robbery.'

'But the timing wouldn't have matched.' Simon's voice was in lawyer-mode. 'You committed the crime earlier.'

Spencer grinned. 'We was quick, man. We was in that

shopping centre ten minutes after. ''Sides, they couldn't prove nothing.'

'You couldn't have spent it all!' Ben's voice was almost a squeak. 'Where did you hide it?'

Spencer's face was glowing with the attention. 'In the washing machine, man. When the police searched this geezer's house, it was the one place they didn't think of looking.'

'Clever,' murmured Simon.

Claire jumped up. 'It's not. It's stupid. And you're stupid too, Simon, for not realising that we shouldn't be talking about this kind of thing in front of Ben. It might give him ideas.'

'Come on, Mum!'

Simon turned his face towards her. 'Give him ideas,' he repeated coolly. 'We wouldn't want that, would we Claire? Tell me. Where have you been tonight? Why are you late?'

Claire was horribly conscious of three faces staring at her. 'I was seeing a friend,' she murmured.

'And what about yesterday when you had to go up to London for a "work meeting"?' He placed an added emphasis on the two words. 'Did you go anywhere else?'

Claire felt her body burning. 'What are you talking about, Simon? What's got into you?'

He gave her a cold look. 'I could ask the same question about you. Excuse me, everyone, but I am going to bed early. I have an early start for work and I am planning on meeting my daughter afterwards.'

'C'mon you two. Cut it out.' Spencer was looking like a worried kid. 'By the way, Si, got a book I can read? I've really been into my stories since you got me started.'

That night in bed when she moved towards him, seeking reassurance, he turned his back. 'Don't touch me,' he hissed.

In the morning, she found him asleep on the carpet.

Ben woke after finally dropping off in the early hours. He didn't want Mum and Simon to row. Cold arguments when people didn't say much to each other, but just looked, were the worst. Poppy agreed with him on that.

They'd also agreed that he would tell his mum about Rosemarie's name on the CD cover but, after last night, he wasn't sure.

Then his mobile rang, firstly the alarm to remind him to get up and then Dad calling. 'Just wanted to check you're coming down this weekend.'

Part of him wanted to say no but, if he did, he wouldn't see Poppy. 'Did you and Rosemarie have an affair, Dad, when you were still with Mum?'

There was a silence. Not a very long one but enough. 'What makes you ask that?' His father's voice was sharp. Ben suddenly got frightened, remembering the raised voices when he was smaller.

'I just wondered.'

'Of course we didn't. I never want to hear that sort of talk again. Do you understand? Now are you coming down this weekend or not?'

Ben agreed, allowing his father to talk him through the travel arrangements. But all the time he was talking, his fingers were closed over the CD cover and the message from Rosemarie to his father which was dated the year before his parents had split up.

Chapter Fifty-two

It has come to our knowledge that you recently wrote to one of our tutors, Caroline-Jane Smith. We would remind you that it is not permissible for ex-offenders to contact members of staff ...

Carefully, very carefully, Simon tore up the letter in small strips; each one measuring roughly the same size. He then opened a kitchen drawer in which he had been storing supermarket bags since his return. Each one was neatly folded into small pasta-like shapes. Undoing one, he dropped the pieces of letter inside before tying it with a knot and placing it in the kitchen bin.

'Keep painting,' Caroline-Jane had said on that final day of his paperchase. 'When life gets too much, bury yourself in your canvas.'

She'd made him feel like a professional! At school, he'd loved messing about with paints but art in the sixth form hadn't been an option for the Oxbridge set. Yet at leavers' prize-giving, Simon – despite his clutch of trophies for Latin and History – had envied the tall, gangly boy with long thin fingers who had received the art award and was on his way to St Martins.

Prison had helped him realise a forgotten dream. But now the letter from the prison authorities made him ashamed.

'You're being too hard on yourself,' Joanna's voice was soothing. *'No one's in, right now. Spencer's out, doing goodness knows what, and Claire is teaching. Ben is having phone text sex with Poppy in his bedroom so what's to stop you?'*

She was right. Delving into his jacket pocket, Simon pulled out the paint set he'd found at the charity shop. It was almost new! Inside, were all the colours he wanted: cerulean blue and geranium pink and olive green. There was even a sketching pad with two brushes …

'Wow, man, that's really good!'

Simon looked up with a start, realising it was already dusk outside. When he'd begun, it had been precisely four minutes past four. Time passes when you're painting, Caroline-Jane used to say.

'Real good!'

Spencer's breath smelt of beer and fags. 'What's your painting about, man? I mean, it's good, like I said, but I don't really get it.'

Simon glanced at the swirl of colours he'd produced without thinking. 'I don't really know, to be honest. It's as though something just guided my hand.' He took in Spencer's maroon suit with trousers that were too big. 'You're looking smart.'

The boy shrugged. 'Just felt like it. Got it off a mate. Thought it might come in handy for a job interview if one came up.'

So he really had turned over a new leaf.

'Listen, man. I'm just going out for a bit again.' He flicked Simon's shoulder playfully like he used to do Inside but somehow it didn't seem so right now. 'If anyone comes looking for me, can you say you haven't seen me?'

Simon's heart sank. 'Spencer, I can't do that. Besides, you've got a curfew, remember. You can't go out now.'

The boy was shifting from one foot to the other. 'I've got to, man. I'll explain later. OK?'

When Claire came back half an hour later, her face tightened when she saw him still clearing up his paints. 'What's for dinner?' she asked, without commenting on his canvas.

With a jolt, he remembered that he'd promised to cook. 'I'm sorry. I forgot …'

'Too busy doing other things, I see.' She cast another look at the blur of pink and green. 'It will have to be pasta again. You'd better tell your friend that dinner will be ready in twenty minutes.'

369

Her bossy tone was really getting up his nose. Couldn't she understand that when the urge took you, you simply had to paint? 'He's gone out,' he said shortly.

'Doesn't he have an ankle bracelet, like you?'

All right, rub it in.

Claire began chopping onions. 'Just so long as he doesn't get us into trouble. Otherwise, he leaves. OK?'

The following morning, Spencer still hadn't returned. Should he call the police? Claire glanced at the empty space on the sofa and declared she was going to be late again tonight.

Simon didn't even dignify that with a reply.

Besides, he was having a day off himself. His probation officer had given him special permission to visit his daughter in London. Even better, she didn't know. He couldn't wait to see the surprise on Lydia's face. He already knew she didn't have lectures on a Thursday so he planned to take her out to lunch. Nothing fancy because he only had twenty quid in his pocket from the money Claire had given him. Just somewhere where they could sit and chat like a real father and daughter. Simon's heart swelled with pride at the thought as he carefully placed Lydia's address in his jacket pocket.

Two hours later, he was still looking. I live in Hampstead, she had told him, but this postcode was more Kilburn. There were loads of greengrocers selling vegetables he'd never heard of. There was a fair smattering of electrical shops too with faded SALE stickers in the window.

Last week, he knew from the news, that a bomb had been found near here. Thank heavens it hadn't gone off. Some splinter Islamic group had claimed responsibility and Simon was aware that a couple of people walking past were giving him suspicious looks. Maybe it was the beard. Or perhaps it was because Joanna wouldn't stop nattering.

'Please be quiet!' he called out in exasperation and a woman coming towards him crossed to the other side.

Picking his way through the vegetable peelings littering the pavement, he found himself coming up to a huge high concrete block of flats which had boarded-up windows. Surely his daughter didn't live in a place like this? She'd be better off in halls, like he had been. Simon's mind flickered back to Oxford, his beautiful high-ceilinged room and the dining room echoing with academia and lavender wax.

But, yes, here it was. Simon checked the writing on the slip of paper and the scrawled sign outside the flats. The third floor. Might as well wait for the lift.

'Don't work, mate!' called out a girl, her voice echoing across the concrete. She was wearing a very short black skirt over pink leggings and, somewhat incongruously, a red flower in her hair as though on holiday. 'You have to walk.'

He followed her up the stairs, trying not to look straight ahead. Didn't she realise how much leg she was showing?

'You stalking me, darling?'

She turned round, a half-smile on her face, and he could see now that she was older than he'd thought. ''Cos if you are, I'm full up today. Might fit you in tomorrow, though!'

Simon felt a hot surge of embarrassment sweep over him. So she was *that* kind of woman! 'Actually,' he spluttered. 'I'm looking for someone.'

'Yeah?' She had stopped now on the third floor, standing, her legs provocatively apart. 'They all say that. Who are you looking for then?'

'Lydia,' he spluttered. 'Lydia Mitchell.'

He'd expected her to say that he didn't know anyone by that name and then he could just go home because clearly there'd been a mistake. His daughter wouldn't live in a place like this. But this girl in the pink skirt and black leggings was pointing to a paint-chipped door. 'Lydia lives there. But don't disturb her. She's working.'

He felt relieved. 'Probably got an essay to finish.'

'Essay?' Her eyes twinkled. 'Client, more like.' Then she looked him up and down. 'You from the police or summat?'

'Actually,' he said quietly. 'I'm Lydia's father.'

The girl's voice hardened. 'No you ain't. She doesn't have one. What do you want with her?' Her voice rose. ''Cos if

371

you're trying to hurt her like the last one did, I'll call the police myself.'

Like the last one did? Simon began to shake the door handle, rattling it violently. Whoever was in there might be accosting his daughter. He had to get her out.

'Shut up,' someone shouted from the upstairs landing. 'I'm trying to get some kip here.'

Then the door opened. It was Lydia but not as he had seen her before. This Lydia had bright red lipstick and heavy black mascara. She was wearing a dressing gown revealing a flash of bare leg.

'Dad?' Her face froze. 'What are you doing here?'

As she spoke, a much older man came out, nodded at Simon, and walked quickly down the stairs. 'I've left something in the toilet,' he called up.

Simon felt sick. He must be referring to the money.

'You'd better come in,' said Lydia quietly, ushering him in through the door.

He looked around it, a nauseous feeling in his stomach. On one side was a sink, heaped high with plates of noodles and baked beans. On the floor, by the sofa, was a mattress where the sheets lay rumpled, reeking of sex.

Lydia scooped them up, threw them in the corner and put on the kettle. 'Coffee?' she asked, as though none of this had happened.

'I thought you were doing a degree.'

'I am.' She measured a spoonful of granules into a mug. 'But it's expensive so I have to fund myself.'

'But this …' He waved his hand around, unable to say the word 'prostitution'.

'Lots of students do it.' She set the mug down by him and together they perched on the edge of the mattress.

Her matter-of-factness shocked him. 'It's not safe!'

'It is if you use precautions.'

He stood up again. 'Why don't you come back and live with us?'

She smiled and for a second, he could see her mother all

372

those years ago. 'That's really sweet, but it's not practical. You've got a wife and a stepson to look after.'

'But you're my daughter!'

'Listen.' She spoke as though he was the child. 'I've managed all these years without you. It's good to have met you, Dad, but I don't need you to tell me what I can and can't do. I've had to be resilient because of what has happened to me and you've got to be the same now. I know it was tough inside prison – I've got friends there myself – but you're out now. If you don't act more responsibly towards Claire and Ben, you might lose them. Get it?'

More responsibly? What did she mean?

'This charity shop stuff. You need to bring back money. It's been tough for Claire and I don't want to see her ending up like Mum without a man. Get it?'

He thought about it all the way home on the train. Lydia had promised to come round for dinner the following week. In the meantime, he would try and get a proper job even though the prospect of being turned down at interviews terrified him.

That shortness of breath feeling was coming back too. Distract yourself, Spencer always said. So he picked up a newspaper that someone had left behind. There was a photofit of one of the men who was thought to be involved in the bombing. Simon took a second look. It vaguely reminded him of someone. But who …

By the time he got off at the station, he'd decided to take Lydia's advice. He needed to listen to Claire more instead of seeing her constant criticism as nagging.

Then he stopped. Standing on his doorstep was Charlie! Bloody hell. The bloke had his arms around Claire. He was trying to kiss her.

'What the fuck are you doing?'

They both turned towards him. Claire's face was rigid with shock. 'It's not what you think,' she began.

'Yes it is.' Charlie faced him full on, his chest puffed out as though he was a peacock protecting his hen. 'I've been trying to

373

persuade Claire to leave you and come back with me. She's told me all about you, Simon. You've gone crazy with your obsession for painting and your need to make everything tidy. You don't deserve her.'

Simon turned towards his wife. 'Is this true?'

She was crying. 'Yes and no. I'm …"

He cut in, taking in the bags that were already packed by the door. 'You're going now?'

She nodded. Only then did he see that Ben and Slasher were already in the car. Flinching, he felt her cheek on his. 'I'll call you,' she whispered. 'All right?'

Inside, the house was horribly quiet. No one was there. Not even Spencer. Simon moved towards the understairs cupboard where he'd hidden his painting set. Slowly, one by one, he undid the top of each tube of paint and squirted the contents down the sink, taking care to clean the stainless steel afterwards. Then he sat down and ripped up each sheet of sugar paper until the bin was full.

It was then that the doorbell rang. They were back! He flew to the door, taking in the orange and black figure looming up at him.

'Simon Mills?'

He nodded.

'We're looking for a Spencer King. We have reason to believe he is staying here.'

'Not any more. He was but …'

'Mind if we search your place, sir? We have a warrant.'

Silently, he nodded. Another man in an orange and black jacket swarmed in, together with a dog not unlike Slasher in appearance.

'What are you looking for?'

Even as he spoke, he knew the answer.

'Substances, sir. Can you tell me where Mr King slept?'

He pointed to the sofa, watching as they searched it. Nothing. And then he remembered.

'I was in prison with the man.'

The officer nodded. 'I know, sir.'

'He told me some things. After he had taken … taken stuff, he would sometimes hide it in the washing machine.'

'Can you show me where yours is, sir?'

They swarmed towards it. There was nothing in the drum but the dog was sitting, perfectly alert.

'What about the filter?' suggested Simon. He got down on his knees to unscrew it. Instantly, a gush of water came out. The officer put his hand in, grimaced and then pulled something out.

It was a small white package.

The officer's eyes narrowed. 'Any idea where we might find this old friend of yours?'

Oh my God. It was coming to him now. Not where they might find Spencer. But to the terrorist's face in the paper …

Chapter Fifty-three

She hadn't intended to leave him. Not really. But something that Martha had said, kept haunting her. *'Not all wives stick with their men when they come out. Sometimes you have to go.'*

She'd gone on to say other things too; about people changing, both on the In and Out. In fact, Martha said all the things that Claire had been thinking for so long but been unable to tell anyone else.

Then Charlie had phoned to make arrangements for picking up Ben. He was in London, he said, so it wouldn't take much of a detour to pick him up and take him down to Devon for the weekend.

'Alex has told me about your guest,' he said in that tight angry way she remembered so well. 'I'm not having my wife and son in the same house as an armed robber!' She'd felt a pang at the way he still referred to her as his 'wife'. In one way it was quite reassuring ...

When he'd arrived to pick up Ben, she'd been ready to tell him that although she was grateful for his support, she owed it to Simon to stay. 'He's not well, mentally.'

'So get him to a doctor.' He touched her arm briefly. 'Look, why not come with us now, just for the weekend. I'll book you into a hotel if you like.'

The prospect of two days without Simon's irrational behaviour was tempting. 'All right,' she said, gratefully. 'Thank you.'

And that was when he had bent down and kissed her cheek. It was just a swift action; almost one between friends. But he had chosen the very moment that Simon had walked up the road and seen them.

Her husband would think she'd gone for good. He'd panic. Do something stupid. Claire looked out of the car window as they headed for the motorway. 'Please drop me off,' she heard herself say sharply.

'Mum!' Ben's voice came from the back. 'I want you to stay.'

Charlie nodded as though to say 'See?'

'Don't go to a hotel,' he added quietly.' Ben needs you close. You can have my room. I'll sleep on the sofa.'

Claire hadn't thought she'd get any rest but she fell into a deep slumber. When she woke in Charlie's bed, she reached for her phone. No messages. Was Simon all right?

Martha had warned her about the guilt.

R U OK? she texted. No reply. Maybe if she had a shower, something would come through. Making her way into Charlie's en suite, she looked around curiously for signs of a girlfriend. A feminine bottle of shower cream, perhaps, or maybe a woman's shaver.

But there was nothing. Nor was there a message on the mobile when she came out.

Simon was probably cross with her – just as she would have been if he'd caught her kissing another woman on their doorstep. It wasn't like that, she wanted to say. Please. Give me a chance to explain.

'Are you decent? Charlie was knocking on her door. Quickly, she slipped into her jeans before opening it. She watched him take in her appearance: damp hair, just a bare trace of make-up on her face.

'Just wanted to check you've got everything you need.'

'Actually, I could do with a hair drier.'

'Sorry.' He grinned. 'This is a bachelor flat.'

Over breakfast (delicious croissants from the bakers round the corner apparently), Charlie casually suggested a trip on the boat. Ben, who'd got up surprisingly early, beamed. 'Can we bring Poppy?'

Claire glanced at Charlie with a 'what-do-you-think?' look.

'No harm in asking her, provided her father's happy.'

'Dad, she's seventeen!'

'Exactly,' said Charlie almost happily. 'And your mother and I can both remember what that was like. Can't we, Claire?'

He continued to make little references like that all through the weekend. Chance remarks about how they had done this and that and what it had been like when Ben was little. It brought home the fact that they were a real family. When Charlie gently reprimanded Ben for something ('watch that rope, son'), it didn't seem out of order because Charlie was his father. Unlike Simon.

Step-families were so complicated, but add another ingredient like prison and they became virtually impossible, thought Claire.

As for Poppy, she had really blossomed since she'd last seen her in London. Such a lovely girl, with a gorgeous tumble of blonde curls, and green eyes that stared right at you. No wonder Ben was besotted. Perhaps she looked like her mother, Claire pondered. Yet she'd noticed that whenever the subject of mothers came up, Poppy neatly skirted round it.

'Where does Poppy's mother live now?' she asked when the girl had gone to the loo below deck.

Ben made a 'shh' noise. 'Sort of. I can't say right now. She doesn't like talking about it. Just relax, Mum. Chill out. '

So Claire did because it had been a long time since she'd had the luxury of a whole day off without anything to do. The mobile didn't have any reception out here on the water but she knew that Simon would be painting his ridiculous primary school stuff on the kitchen table and Spencer would be watching television in the sitting room, his dirty feet up on her coffee table.

That night, they all went out for a Chinese. Charlie seized the opportunity to talk about her prison book while Ben and Poppy held hands under the table. 'Sounds like a great idea,' he enthused as though forgetting how he used to complain when she painted at weekends so he could look after a small Ben.

Suddenly she found his hand covering hers and squeezing it. 'I'm really proud of you, Claire. Always have been. I'm sorry I didn't show it enough.'

She looked across to Poppy and Ben who were in a world of their own. 'I hope you show your feelings more to your girlfriend now.'

He looked away. 'Actually, Claire, I finished the last relationship a few weeks ago. Would you like to know why?'

It would be so easy to say yes. Then she knew he would tell her that he still had feelings for her and she would say … what, exactly?

'Excuse me.' She stood up. 'I've got to go to the bathroom.'

She flew up the flight of stairs and into the Ladies, to check her mobile messages. Still nothing. When she dialled Simon's number, it went through to answerphone. But what if she changed her settings so her number didn't show up on his screen?

'Hello?' Simon! Her ploy had worked!

Quickly, she cut him off. So he *was* rejecting her calls. Anger could be healthy, Martha had said. Better to show emotions than bottle them in.

Very well then. If Simon wanted to play silly games, so could she.

By the time they got to Sunday, she wasn't sure if she wanted to go back. It had been so wonderful to see the sea again and immerse herself in Devon's slower, politer pace.

'I should have popped in to see Jean,' she remembered.

'Maybe,' suggested Charlie deliberately as he carried her bag to the door, 'you'd like to come down next weekend with Ben.'

He wanted to re-claim her gently! It wasn't an unpleasant thought. When you'd been together for years – and had a child together – you couldn't just throw someone away.

'Mum.' Ben sounded nervous. 'I want you to borrow this.'

Charlie was frowning. 'Your mother doesn't like jazz.'

'I do now!' Ella Fitzgerald had been one of Simon's

379

favourites and she'd got to like the music. She turned over the disc to read the lyrics titles and then stopped.

To my darling Charlie with all my love. From your Rosemarie.

It was dated the year before they broke up.

'Ben,' she said in a voice that wasn't hers. 'Can you just give Dad and me a minute to have a talk?'

'It was *her*,' she hissed. You had an affair with Rosemarie – my so-called friend.' She tried to hammer at him with her fists but he grabbed them, hurting her.

'Stop! You're a bastard, do you know that?'

He nodded, his colour drained. 'I'm sorry. I can't tell you how many times I've regretted it.'

'How long did it go on for?' Above all, she needed the facts. 'How long were you sleeping with her for?'

'Two years.'

'Two *years*?' When he'd first said the word 'two' she'd expected it to be followed by months, not years. 'But that's awful. Disgusting. Terrible.'

'I know.' His voice had changed now and become clipped as though he was trying to distance himself.

'But she introduced me to Simon … Of course! To keep me out of the way so she could carry on with you.' Another thought struck her. 'Please tell me you're not still seeing her.'

Charlie shook his head. 'We finished just after Simon went to prison. I felt it wasn't right any more. Joanna's death really shook me.' He reached out his hand to touch her. 'When I thought about how it could have been you in the car, I realised how much you still mean to me.'

She shook off his hand. 'Don't touch me.'

'Then listen. Please. I was waiting for her to leave Alex but she kept putting it off. After Joanna, she was ready to come to me because 'life had to be lived for the day' as she put it. But by then I'd changed *my* mind.' He stopped and then added almost proudly. 'She was furious that I still had feelings for you.'

She could scarcely take it all in. 'You've messed up so many lives! Mine, Ben's, Alex's …'

He broke in. 'But you've seen what we can be like as a family; this weekend has been great and we can do it again. I don't expect you to leave Simon in the lurch. We'll get him some medical help and then we can start our own lives all over again.'

She stood there, unable to say anything.

'Ben would like it.' His voice was soft. Almost hypnotic. 'Don't you think we owe it to him?'

Ben was in his room, one ear against the door. Quietly, so they couldn't hear the bleeps, he rang the number.

'Hello?'

'Simon. It's me. Ben. Are you OK?'

'Why?'

His stepfather's voice was suspicious and no wonder.

'We were worried about you. Mum hasn't been able to get through.'

It was a bit of a guess but he'd seen her check her phone enough times.

'I've been busy. Where are you?'

'At Dad's.'

'Both of you?'

'Yes.'

There was a sound at the other end which sounded like a snort or someone blowing their nose.

'You'd better get back then, hadn't you?'

'Listen, Simon. It's not what you think. She doesn't want Dad – she wants you but you've been acting like a complete prat. You've got to go back to the person you were before.'

There was a silence. 'I can never be that person again, Ben. You're too young to understand.'

But he could! When he was with Poppy, he felt like a completely different person. Adults could be so stupid sometimes.

'I'm just telling you that Mum still loves you. It's up to you to sort your own lives out.'

Another silence.

'Are you staying down there?'

'No. Mum wants to come back.'

'Then tell her that I'll be gone by the time she's here.'

Ben's fingers felt sweaty on his mobile phone. 'Where are you going?'

'It doesn't matter. But just in case your mother thinks I'm doing something wrong again, you can tell her that my probation officer knows about it.'

Chapter Fifty-four

Luckily the police seemed to believe him when Simon insisted that the white powder had had nothing to do him and that, no, he didn't know where Spencer was. He didn't add that Spencer had also taken a pile of novels from the sitting room; something that made Simon smile wryly to himself, despite the circumstances.

They also said they'd follow up his hunch about the man in the paper. 'I've just remembered,' he'd gasped. 'It was one of the youths in the Multi-Faith Room back in Freetown. I interrupted them during my paperchase.'

The policeman had looked him up and down. 'Don't take this the wrong way sir, but your lot all look alike, don't they?'

Talk about being racist. But if it helped to catch a terrorist, the slur wasn't important. Meanwhile, he had to think about himself. He and Claire weren't together any more. And the worst thing was that he'd brought it on himself.

Practicalities. Think practicalities. It was the only way to keep sane. He'd find somewhere to live in London. That's what he'd do. A hostel, maybe, so the house money could go to Claire. He owed her that.

As for Spencer, he felt thoroughly let down. He'd trusted the boy; helped him read; given him a bed; and now he'd repaid him by doing exactly what he'd been put in prison for. 'You're lucky,' his probation officer had said grimly, 'that the police believe you knew nothing about it.'

Meanwhile, Winston had been caught at a bus stop and was now in custody waiting for his case to come up after being turned down for bail. What a waste. All those fine words which he'd come out with about turning over a new leaf, man, had come to nothing.

She'd stay in the rented house, Claire told herself, until Ben finished his A-levels. At least that way, his schooling wouldn't be interrupted again. Simon's sentence had already done that enough times.

Meanwhile she'd carry on teaching at the college and with her own work. There was talk already of a second book with Max; their publishers seemed to think that the first, which was due to be published in three months, would sell. 'Prison stuff is Big,' her editor had declared delightedly. 'You've hit just the right time.'

Simon might have found that funny. But she had no way of telling him. His phone always went through to voice mail and she had no idea where he was living. If it wasn't for Martha to talk to, she'd go mad.

'People who come out of prison,' the older woman had said soothingly, 'can be like wounded animals. They need a quiet space to lick their sores. With the right help, they feel strong enough to come out again.'

Claire had tried to give him that help, she told herself, but he'd made it so difficult! Maybe Simon might 'come out again' as Martha put it. Or maybe not. In the meantime, she owed it to Ben to get on with their own lives and create some kind of stability.

As for Charlie, she wanted nothing to do with him apart from necessary communication about Ben. She wasn't even angry any more about Rosemarie; instead, she felt a relief that the jigsaw pieces were finally falling into place.

It was when Simon was still in the house, shoving stuff into his rucksack before Claire got back, that the mobile flashed.

Lydia, said the screen.

'Dad?'

They hadn't spoken since that last time when he'd been so shocked by her 'career choice'.

'Are you all right?'

'Are *you* all right? Something's wrong, isn't it?'

384

She knew him already even though they'd only met a few times. What greater vindication could there be that Lydia was his flesh and blood? Simon felt his heart swell with pride and love.

'Claire and I have split.'

'Dad.' The reproach slapped him in the face. 'I told you to give her an easier time.'

He zipped up the rucksack. 'It wasn't just me. It was her too. I ... I caught her snogging her ex.'

'Oh.'

Exactly. 'So I'm leaving to give her some space.'

'Where will you go?'

She sounded like a worried mother.

'I've found a place at a hostel. In Earls Court.'

'You don't need to do that!' Her voice had an excited edge. 'You could come and live here, Dad, with me!'

A flash of dirty concrete walls with young girls and dirty old men scurrying down the stairs, came into his head. 'That's very kind, Lydia but it's not really practical is it?' He gave an embarrassed cough. 'I'd be in the way of your clients for a start.'

'I've stopped.'

'What?'

She gave a shy laugh that reminded him so much of her mother. 'What you said, Dad, shook me up a bit. I'm absolutely skint, mind you, but I'm making do just about. Besides, it's giving me more time for my studies. They think I might be in line for a first!'

That was amazing! He himself had got a 2:1 which had disappointed his mother. 'Just as well your father isn't here to see it,' she had said.

'I'll get a job,' he said suddenly, pushing the image out of her head. 'Anything. I don't care what. I'll pay part of the rent and we'll be fine.'

'Really?' The excitement in Lydia's voice was wonderful to hear.

'That would be fantastic! There's only one bedroom though

385

so …'

'I'll sleep on the sofa.'

'What about your tag?'

Simon glanced down at his right ankle where there was a slight mark, indicating its former presence. 'The Peckham Rolex? It's gone. I don't have to wear it any more, according to my probation officer.'

Lydia's voice was getting higher, the way her mother's used to. 'That's brilliant, Dad. We'll celebrate. When can you get here?'

'Couple of hours, maybe.'

Someone was knocking at the door. There was a gas van outside. Next door had had a leak last week. Just their luck if it was their turn, though he hadn't smelt anything.

'Hello?'

He took in the uniform just as the man's arm headed for his nose. 'Stay out of stuff you don't belong to, Mills. Or we'll get you. Got it?'

And then everything went black.

Ben's voice was sleepy from the back. Slasher had fallen asleep too and was snoring. 'Where are we going, Mum? I thought the motorway was that way?'

It was.

'I've got someone to see first before we go home.'

It had only been two hours since her row with Charlie over Rosemarie. In fact, it hadn't been so much of a row as a clear, cold statement on her part that she was going now and wouldn't be back.

'Can you wait in the car?' She glanced back at Ben. There was no answer. He'd fallen asleep – or was pretending to – his head buried in Slasher's coat. For all his grown up behaviour, he was still a child, she realised.

'I won't be a minute,' she whispered in case he was shamming.

There was only one other car in the drive; a silver Audi.

'Claire!'

Rosemarie's face was shining with shock. Even as she stood there, two tiny tell-tale circles of red on her cheeks grew before Claire's eyes.

'I expect you know why I am here.'

'No.' She shook her head. Too firmly. 'I don't.'

A strange sense of satisfaction flooded Claire's body. 'Charlie hasn't rung you, then?'

The circles of red grew bigger and her eyes took on a wary look. 'Why would Charlie ring me?'

'Don't pretend, Rosemarie. I know about you both!'

Claire had never ever hit anyone but it was all she could do now not to slap her old friend's pretty made-up face. 'For years you were sleeping with Charlie when we were still married! I even cried on your shoulder when I found out he had another woman, never guessing it was you.'

Rosemarie leaned against the door, shaking. 'Please come in. I don't want people to hear this.'

'No.' Claire let her voice rise. 'On the contrary, I want everyone to hear. When Joanna died, Charlie broke it off, and that's why you wouldn't have anything to do with me. It wasn't just because of Joanna and me becoming a social pariah. You couldn't bear the sight of me because I reminded you of what you couldn't have.'

Rosemarie was trying to shut the door now but Claire put her foot between it and the step.

'He told me,' hissed Rosemarie, 'that he'd made a terrible mistake. He wanted to try to get back together with you. It wasn't fair! Not after everything we'd gone through. That's why I threw the brick ...'

Claire gasped. '*You* threw it? It wasn't someone from the village? You broke my window and scared us out of our home?'

'I hated you.' Rosemarie's eyes grew small and piggy. 'I hated you because you had what I wanted even though you had got another husband.'

'And what about poor Alex? Does he know about this?'

Rosemarie laughed wildly. 'Poor Alex! Didn't you know?'

Claire a cold shiver of premonition. 'Know what?'

'About him and Joanna.' Rosemarie's eyes were sparkling now with malice. 'They were in love.'

It was too much to take in. 'Did Hugh know?'

Rosemarie snorted. 'Of course he did! Why do you think he got so drunk at your place on the night of the accident? He was pissed off. And why do you think he tried to grab the steering wheel? He wanted to kill his wife – and he didn't care who else he murdered in the process.'

Chapter Fifty-five

His bloody nose and the bruise above it were too obvious to hide.

'What happened, Dad?'

Simon hadn't wanted to explain – the fewer people involved, the better. But Lydia had insisted. 'The bomb, the other week,' he began. 'They ran a photofit of the suspect in the paper who looked like someone in the prison. So I told the police. Someone must have split on me because after I spoke to you, a man called, pretending to be the gas man, and socked me one; telling me to keep out of business that didn't affect me.'

Lydia's eyes were open wide. 'You've got to report it.'

'No.' He reached out his hand and pulled her towards him awkwardly, giving her a half-cuddle. It was the first time he had touched her, this girl who was as young as some of his previous girlfriends. 'I'm not doing anything that might threaten your safety. Suppose they came here?'

She shook her head. 'I'm ready to risk it, Dad. Blimey, you did meet some oddballs in prison, didn't you? First Spencer and now this.'

He had to laugh. 'You wouldn't believe it. It's another world in there and frankly, I'm beginning to wonder if I can ever escape.'

Lydia clapped her hands as though she was in a schoolroom. 'Come on then. Why don't we unpack your stuff and you can settle in.'

Of course, everyone thought he was a dirty old man at first. It took weeks before Simon stopped getting knowing looks from the woman on the floor above who came back from work every morning at 6 a.m., tripping in her high heels. Even Lydia's friends took some persuading before they finally accepted he really was her dad.

'It's because you look young!' she teased him. They were walking to the park which had become one of their favourite Saturday lunchtime activities. They'd feed the ducks and buy ice creams even if it wasn't the weather for it. All the things, Simon told himself that he would have done if he'd been around when Lydia had been little.

'We *were* young, your mum and I, when you were made,' he replied, watching a family group walk past. It was made up of a youngish lad in jeans and a hoodie cuddling a woman who simply had to be at least fifteen years older. She was pushing a buggy and there was a toddler running ahead.

'See,' said Lydia sharply. 'Families are different nowadays. They're not neat and conventional any more and that's fine. That reminds me. Have you heard from Claire recently?'

Simon thought of the letter he'd received from her last week in her distinctive ink handwriting and MK postal stamp. He'd shoved it in his jacket pocket, not wanting to open it in case it burst this bubble of happiness he was in now. Besides, the letter would only be a string of excuses about why she couldn't cope any more and she'd be right on every count.

She and Ben were better off without him.

'Money isn't everything.' Lydia was kicking a small stone as they walked on. She was wearing dance shoes this morning with thick black leggings and a pink T-shirt that matched her alice band. The effect was ridiculously naive. Simon's heart lurched every time he thought of those dirty men crawling over her, just so she could finance a degree. 'I mean, don't get me wrong. I know you've been really generous giving her the cash from the house but there are more important things.'

He could remember her mother saying the same thing. She'd had a similar attitude; it was all coming back. During his brief friendship with Francoise, it was obvious that she knew her own mind. No surprise, therefore, that she'd chosen to bring up a baby on her own.

'Lydia, darling.' He stopped as a man went by and looked at

them curiously. 'Lydia, love,' he tried again. 'I thought I knew it all at your age too. So did your mum. But trust me. I messed up Claire and Ben's life – not just with the accident but because I married her, knowing she still felt something for her husband. That's why it was so fast. I was frightened she might go back to him. At least this way, I am giving her some breathing space so she can decide what she really wants to do.'

Joanna's voice tinkled with amusement. '*And do you really think she might choose you?*'

'Shut up,' he growled.

'Shut up?' Lydia took his arm worriedly. 'You've gone all weird again. Stop it. Please. You're scaring me.'

They sat down on a bench and he tried to claw back the normality of their conversation before Joanna's interruption. But Lydia wasn't having any of it. 'Are you hearing those voices in your head still?'

He should never have told her.

'You are, aren't you?' Her young face was creased with concern. 'I told you, Dad. You need to see a doctor and if you don't book yourself an appointment, I'm going to do it for you.'

'Very well.' He knew he sounded like a sullen child.

'Good.' Lydia was running after him now as he got up and walked. 'I know you think I'm nagging but it's for your own good, you know.'

Desperately, he tried to change the subject. He nodded his head towards the fast food restaurant they were passing. 'Fancy a veggie burger?'

That was the other easy thing about living with Lydia. They were both non-meat-eaters although she'd been veggie from birth. Her mother, he remembered now, had been one of the first vegetarians he'd come across.

'OK.'

He pointed out a window seat and joined the queue. It was then that he saw the poster.

Wanted. New recruits. Good pay. Hours flexible. Apply to manager.

Ten minutes later, he returned.

'You were ages.' Lydia looked up from her mobile where she'd been furiously texting.

He put down the tray in front of her. 'I've been enquiring about a job.'

Then he told her about the notice and speaking to the manager who happened to need someone urgently. He'd had to tell them about his record of course but the manager's brother had done time and, providing probation approved, his application would be seriously considered.

Amazingly, it all went through – far more smoothly than he'd thought. Simon felt humbled by the manager and his probation officer who genuinely wanted to give him a chance.

Funny. When he'd read about people being employed at fast food places, they all moaned about the routine. But he loved it. It stopped him thinking. Wrap the burger. Turn over the chips. Tip them neatly into the cardboard box. The rhythm was so soothing. By the second week, they'd upgraded him to front of the desk.

He earned a fraction of what he had done as a lawyer but somehow he got more satisfaction from his pay slip than he had ever done before.

At lunchtime, he went for a wander round the shops. Sometimes he met up with Lydia although she spent most days in the library. Once he saw a boy who looked like Ben and he called out. But then the youth turned round. It surprised Simon how disappointed he felt.

Every now and then he touched Claire's letter inside his jacket pocket, just as he had once touched Lydia's. So long as he didn't open it, he could carry on being brave and allow Claire to pursue her own life. If he ripped open the envelope, he was scared he might ring her.

'*You're getting worse,*' tinkled Joanna. '*When did you say the appointment with the doctor was?*'

Next week. He'd already been to the GP who had listened to him carefully for all of five minutes ('Next time, Mr Mills, it would be better if you booked a double appointment') before

392

referring him to a psychologist. They couldn't make him go. It wasn't as though he had done anything wrong.

'Big Issue,' called out a street vendor. 'Big Issue!'

Simon stopped, searching his pocket for some change. Several of the men went on to sell the magazine when they came Out; apparently they had to buy them out of their own money. They might not make their fortune but it gave them a job; a purpose to the day.

'Thanks, mate.' The man was looking at him with sharp, bright eyes. 'Don't I know you from somewhere?'

Bloody hell! It was a friend of the Coin Man – the one who had to toss a coin before he could make any decision.

'No.' He pulled up his jacket collar as though to shelter himself from the man and his past. 'I don't think so.'

'Yes I do!' The man was grinning. His teeth were discoloured. 'You're that nutter that kept talking to a dead woman all the time, aren't you? Spencer told me. He said you were crazy, man; really crazy.'

Simon began to walk faster. People were looking or was that his imagination? As soon as he reached the park, he sat down and tried to breathe.

'*Go back to your job,*' said Joanna quietly. '*The routine will calm you down. If I were you, Simon, I'd keep our appointment with the psychologist. I think we both need it.*'

The psychologist was a kindly bear of a man who wore a brown tweed jacket like his father used to. His office was at the back of a big London hospital which made Simon hope that, if anyone saw him, they might think he was going in for a more 'normal' medical complaint.

He listened carefully to Simon's story, nodding every now and then and making notes. 'Quite a story,' he said finally. 'One that could happen to almost any of us.'

Really? He thought about his father and what he had omitted to tell the psychologist.

'Do you know anything about cognitive behavioural thinking?'

'Not much,' admitted Simon although, come to think of it, they'd had a book in the library called *Cognitive Behavioural Therapy for Dummies*. The title had intrigued him.

'It's a good book.' The psychologist was nodding again. 'But I'm going to teach you a couple of ways now to re-programme the way you think about events. There's also something else I want you to consider.'

Simon listened. At first it seemed like a crazy idea but then the more he thought about it, the more it made sense.

'Just one more thing,' said the psychologist as he left. 'Consider opening your wife's letter sometime.' He glanced at Simon's right pocket. 'It's funny how doing something that you're scared of can make you stronger.'

'How did you get on?' asked Lydia.

She'd made noodles for dinner. It was a Tuesday night when they both sat down in front of the television and watched a series that he and Claire used to watch before the accident. He wondered if she was doing the same now.

'Fine.'

'Did it help?'

He nodded.

'Don't want to talk about it then?'

'Not really.' He picked at his noodles. 'I've taken the day off tomorrow. There's something I've got to do.'

She reflected on this. 'Want me to come with you?'

'No thanks.' He smiled. 'But it's good of you to offer.'

Joanna had been buried in Harrow. It was where she'd come from apparently and where her own mother was buried. She hadn't wanted to be cremated. He knew that much from Alex who had been his go-between and found out the necessary information. His 'friend' had sounded surprised when he'd contacted him and only agreed, or so he said, because the psychologist had suggested it.

Simon got on the Metropolitan line, which he wasn't very familiar with, and then walked from Harrow Station up the hill.

It was further than he thought. Joanna's stone was, Alex had said, in a new cemetery not far from Northwick Park Hospital.

It took him a while to find it.

Joanna, wife to Hugh. Stepmother to Poppy.

The bald inscription surprised him. Almost like a reflex action, his hand closed around the envelope in his pocket.

'*Go on,*' sang Joanna. '*Open it.*'

Gently, he knelt down and placed a bunch of freesias on the turf. 'I'm sorry,' he whispered.

'*Just get on with it!*'

All right. All right.

Rosemarie told me ... thought you should know ... hand on the wheel ...

Simon read and re-read Claire's letter.

'*See?*' tinkled Joanna. '*I said you shouldn't have felt so guilty. Hugh wanted to kill me all along.*'

But why?

'Ask him yourself.'

Only then did he see the figure sitting on the wall. 'I can't believe you have the gall to come here.' Hugh's voice came out in a growl.

Simon thought of the email that the psychologist had encouraged him to send, asking Hugh if he'd meet up. 'You said it was the only place you'd see me.'

Hugh scowled. 'And why did you want to see me? To say sorry?'

Simon's mouth was dry. 'Actually, yes.'

Hugh's eyes pinned him down. 'If it wasn't for you, she'd still be alive.'

Simon handed him the letter. 'I'd like you to read this. I hadn't opened it when I asked you to meet but I think you should see it.'

Hugh made to flick it away but then stopped and took it. Silently, his eyes went down the page.

'It's true.'

'What?'

Hugh shrugged. 'Joanna was having an affair. I'd found out

that night, just as we were leaving. I saw Alex kiss her when he went to get her coat. I'd had my suspicions of course; it was what my first wife had done as well. '

Simon felt sick. 'But to try and kill her …'

'I told you. I was drunk. Didn't know what I was doing. Just saw red. You were messing about getting lost and I grabbed the wheel. At that time, I wanted her to die for what she had done. It was only afterwards that I realised how selfish I'd been.'

He began to weep. Huge crocodile tears? Or real ones?

'But you let me go to prison for it!'

Hugh raised his head. 'Yes. I did. What else could I have done?'

'Told the truth?'

He shook his head. 'Grow up! There are times when telling the truth can get you into more trouble. My punishment is knowing that I contributed to Joanna's death. Yours is knowing that you were at the wheel, over the limit. And nothing can ever change that. Deal with it.'

Chapter Fifty-six

Nearly two months had gone by now and Simon still hadn't replied to her letter. What had she thrown away? Supposing he was ill?

Then Lydia had emailed. 'Dad's fine! Seems to be liking the fast-food place – think it's the routine that keeps him going.'

It had been a surprise when Lydia had contacted her through Facebook. She thought it was important, so she said, to keep in touch and, besides, she wanted to know how Ben was doing.

That had touched Claire.

'I know Dad cares too,' the girl had added. 'About both of you. Whenever I have a bit of a heavy night out, he says he didn't realise how tough it was to be a parent.'

Too little, too late, thought Claire. If her husband cared so much, he'd pick up the phone.

Clearly he'd decided to get on with his own life so she would do the same. Like Simon, she'd fallen into a routine. Two days a week at the college. Three days on her own work – the publisher wanted another book. Constantly making sure that Ben didn't do anything daft. Thank goodness he seemed to be settling into his course. When she looked into his room to check, he was nearly always at his computer, Slasher at his side.

As for Charlie, the only contact she had with him now were short texts about their son. To think she might have gone back to him if she hadn't found out about Rosemarie! She'd thought of having it out with Alex but what was the point of yet another disagreement?

Besides, the mentoring scheme was taking up all her extra time. It gave her a real buzz! It had been Martha's idea. 'You seem to be levelling out,' she'd commented. 'Let me know when you feel ready. I've got a new woman who's got in touch.

397

Her husband's gone Inside for fraud. She could do with someone to talk to.'

But didn't she need some training? 'It's a four-week course,' replied Martha smartly. 'We have a trainer from Relate and there's me. You'll be doing just what we have. Listening to people just like I've been listening to you. Not making judgments. Helping them deal with practicalities like not getting house insurance. You'll be good at it. I know you will.'

That was how Claire found herself agreeing to meet a woman called Joyce in a café at one of the new shopping satellites that had sprung up just outside the centre. Joyce turned out to be older than her voice suggested on the phone. She appeared rather aunt-like in a soft lilac cardigan and a shoulder bag that she clutched as if it might run off without her.

'I didn't know Keith was in trouble at all until the policed turned up.' Joyce needed no encouragement to talk. 'Keith didn't seem surprised. That was the weird thing. It's as though he'd been expecting something. We'd been married nearly forty years. He was going to retire soon and we were saving up for a cruise.'

Claire could guess what was coming next. 'I wanted to go down to the police station with him but he wouldn't have any of it. He wouldn't let me go to the trial either.'

So he'd wanted to hide the facts from her.

'He got three years for fraud which apparently means eighteen months.' Joyce addressed her bag now. It was black and shiny. 'That was back at Easter. Now I'm just trying to live one day at a time.'

Claire nodded. 'It's the best thing to do. Do you visit him?'

'Every week. But I hate it. The others … they all seem different.'

She could remember that so well! 'If you start to talk to them, you might find a kindred spirit. Try and find an officer to talk to as well. They mean well, on the whole.'

Joyce looked doubtful.

'And do something that you didn't do before. A hobby. Something that might distract your attention.'

'A friend has asked me to help run her shop with her.' Joyce gave a rueful smile. 'She's one of the few friends who's stuck by me.'

'Good! Take her up on it. It will stop you thinking so much.'

Joyce squeezed her hand. 'Thank you. The worst thing is wondering what it will be like when he gets out. I always thought of him as being totally honest.'

Claire wavered. 'You may never trust him again,' she said honestly. 'But don't think about that now. Concentrate on the day to day, as we said before.'

That night, while Ben was upstairs doing his homework and she was working on more sketches for the book, Claire was unable to get Joyce out of her head. Fraud would be a very difficult thing to come to terms with. At least Simon had been honest. He'd made a mistake but it wasn't a calculated one.

Her phone vibrated on the desk, indicating a text had arrived. It was Lydia.

Check out this. One of Dad's paintings has won something called a Koestler Award. It's going to be in an exhibition.

The Koestler Awards? What were they? Going on Google, she found they were a series of prizes given to men and women in prison, secure units, or psychiatric hospitals for all kinds of artistic achievements. There was a list of winners including Simon who had won a bronze! Lydia was right. There was an exhibition open to the public on the south bank. Should she go along?

Her phone blipped again. *Dad's going on the Wednesday in the first week. He's told me so. Just thought you might want to know in case you don't want to bump into him.*

She would go then. On a different day. It would be part of her closure.

'Mum?'

Reluctantly, she put down the charcoal.

'Can Poppy come up this weekend?'

'Thought you were going down to Dad's.'

'He's going away.'

399

She felt an unreasonable pang of curiosity. Clearly it hadn't taken him long to move on again, just as it hadn't the first time.

'That's fine as long as her father knows about it.'

'He does. He's being really nice now. Even bought her a car!'

How could Hugh let his seventeen-year-old daughter drive after everything that had happened?

'You can't let that affect everything, you know, Mum.' It was as though he was reading her mind. 'She's a safe driver.' Slasher, by his side as always, made a small noise as though agreeing. 'When can I have lessons?'

Never, she wanted to say.

'Dad said he'd pay for them if you agree.'

That was typical! Suggesting something that he knew she'd be unhappy about. 'We'll see. When is she coming up?'

'Saturday evening, I think.'

Better make sure she was back from the exhibition by then. She needed to be around if those two were under one roof. She turned back to her painting. 'I'll cook something nice for supper if you like.'

'OK.' He was staring at the drawing. 'I like that. It's just like Slasher, isn't it?'

'Yes,' she said abstractly, still thinking about Charlie going away and the lack of news about Simon. 'It is.'

Claire spent ages deciding what to wear for the exhibition. Jeans were too casual but a dress too formal. In the end, she plumped for a pair of white trousers and a long flowing jersey cardigan. As she headed for the building on the south bank, she was surprised by the number of people streaming in.

'Non-alcoholic punch, ducks?' A deep-voiced, tall woman whose dark tresses brushed her shoulders, beamed at her. She was wearing purple and had a badge on her chest, proclaiming her name to be Georgie.

'Thanks.'

She looked around. The walls were covered in canvases displaying huge coloured images, both in paint and fabric.

400

There were sculptures too, and framed poems. That one over there looked like an excerpt from a life story. '*When we grew up, we had to decide whether to be a bank robber or a drugs dealer ...*'

'Know any of the exhibitors, do you ducks?'

'My husband actually. Simon Mills.'

Suddenly she found her hands being clasped by this woman's. 'Was he at Freetown?'

She nodded.

'Me too!'

That couldn't be right. 'But it's a man's prison.'

Georgie made a face. 'Unfortunately, ducks, it was the only option.'

It was beginning to dawn on her now. Georgie, who had those painted eyebrows, was actually a man!

'Great bloke, your Simon. Not sniffy even though he's posh. Used to talk about you and your son. Ben, isn't it?'

She nodded, unable to get a word in edgeways. 'He was a Listener too. Hey, Coiny!' Georgie grabbed a man who was passing. 'This is Simon's missus. Say hello.'

The man opened his palm to reveal a coin. He turned it over, nodded and then put his other hand out in greeting. 'Hi. Your husband was kind to me. Is he here?'

Claire bit her lip. 'He's coming on another day.'

Georgie frowned. 'You two are still together, aren't you?'

Oh dear. 'Not exactly.'

The Coin Man was looking upset too. 'Heads we look at his paintings and tails we don't.'

What did he mean?

'It's tails.' Georgie spoke with a smooth, kind voice as though he was reassuring the man. 'That means we can show her. Please, Claire, this way. That's the governor over there, by the way. Decent chap. Now, what do you think of this?'

Simon's painting had something! Something that the kitchen table paintings hadn't. This was a woman. About the same height as her and having similar hair. She liked the way the colours melted into each other.

'Excuse me,' said a rather beautiful woman, gliding up. 'Someone told me that Simon Mills is your husband.'

Claire didn't like the way this woman used her husband's name so familiarly.

'My name's Caroline-Jane. I'm the artist in residence and your husband was one of my students. He was often talking about you. You're an artist too, aren't you?'

She nodded.

The woman's eyes softened. 'He was always saying how proud he was of you.'

Was he?

'He wrote to me, you know, when he got out, to say how much he appreciated our workshops. I wasn't allowed to reply because it's against the rules so do tell him that I appreciated him getting in touch and that I hope he continues to paint. He's got a good eye for colour.'

'Tell me,' said Claire suddenly. 'I have to ask you this, so forgive me. Did he have a crush on you? Only he used to say your name in his sleep sometimes.'

The woman flushed. 'You have to remember that men fantasise in prison. It's all they have, sometimes.' Her hand rested lightly on Claire's. 'But he didn't stop talking about you. It was obvious that he loved you.''

Claire's heart lurched. Really? Yet he had also changed so much …

'It's not easy for the men when they are released.' Caroline-Jane seemed to guess what she was thinking. 'They are so cocooned in prison that it is hard for them to adapt to the outside world.'

'Why do you do this job?' Claire blurted out 'Do you get a thrill from working with men who have done terrible things?'

'No.' Her companion flushed again. 'Why don't we sit down?'

She led the way to two empty chairs. 'I started,' she said in a low urgent voice, 'because my own marriage broke up. Until then I was a freelance artist but that wasn't enough to bring up two small children.'

Claire suddenly liked this woman. 'I know what that's like.'

There was relief in Caroline-Jane's smile. 'Thank you. Now let me introduce you to Governor Number One. 'He's always keen to meet families.'

Ben knew Mum would be out all afternoon. It had been in her diary. Poppy had driven up early from Devon but just as they were making their way upstairs, the doorbell had gone.

A scruffy short man, whose bright eyes seemed to be darting everywhere, was standing at the doorstep.

'Where's Mills?'

Something in the man's face made Ben put on the security chain. 'Why?'

'He's got my dog. Said he'd look after it till I was Out. Well I've got my tag now so I want him back.'

Ben's hands tightened on the door. 'Slasher's not here. He's gone out. With my mum for a walk.'

The man's face creased in disbelief. 'Thought I heard a dog bark when I was waiting for you to answer.'

'That's next door's. Come back tomorrow, can you?'

'I'll give your mum an hour, sonny. No more.'

'Quick,' whispered Ben. 'We've got to sneak Slasher back to Devon. I can't give him back.' Ben's voice came out in a choke. 'I just can't.'

'So you see,' the governor was saying. 'Winning a prestigious award makes the men feel good about themselves. It can also help them discover latent talent.'

She could understand that. Some of these paintings were really amazing! 'Your husband was a very interesting man,' the governor continued. 'His was a very sad case. Still, at least he has a family to come back to. If offenders don't have anyone to come out to, it can so easily go wrong again.'

He obviously didn't know.

'Well, I must circulate.' The governor was shaking her hand. 'Nice to meet you, Mrs Mills.'

As he turned to go, she heard her phone bleep. The message

would have to wait. She needed to look round the exhibition one more time.

A car shot past so fast that it rattled Poppy's little car as she waited at the T-junction. Her view was obscured by Slasher sitting on Ben's knee. 'I can't see.'

'There's a motorcyclist at the bend.' Ben tried pushing the dog on the back seat but he refused to budge. 'It's clear now. Go. No. STOP.'

Chapter Fifty-seven

It was all right to go to the exhibition today. Claire had gone last Wednesday. Lydia had said so.

Someone's got to be in touch, she'd declared in that slightly haughty tone which, again, he could remember from her mother. She was probably right. He just didn't want it to be him.

'I'm going on the tube,' he announced when Saturday came.

His daughter's eyes lit up. 'Really?'

'Really,' he replied, more to reassure himself. Since moving to London, the crowds had made him panic. But because he refused to go back to the consultant, Lydia was helping him face his fears; just as he was slowly learning that it didn't matter if things weren't always in the right place.

When he reached South Bank, after being buffeted by weekend shoppers, he wanted to cry with relief.

Incredibly, the exhibition had been mentioned in *The Times* arts page that very morning. It had given him a real buzz to know he was part of it. It was a buzz that he would have liked to have shared with Claire.

'*Whose fault is that?*' whispered Joanna.

Simon gave his name at the door to an awkward looking man, handing out badges. He glanced at his programme, wondering where his painting was and then, as he moved round to the left, he suddenly saw it.

It looked different on the wall. He could see lines that shouldn't be there. Colours that he would now change. He'd enjoyed it more, Simon realised, when painting it.

And then he saw her. His wife! Talking to the governor. Her hair had grown into a longer bob but her voice was the same.

'Claire!'

She turned.

Both her face and that of the governor's registered surprise.

It was Caroline-Jane.

'I'm so sorry.' He wanted to sink into the ground and replay the last five seconds. 'I thought you were my wife.'

They both looked sorry for him. 'She was here a few minutes ago, Simon.'

But she had come last Wednesday. Hadn't she? Of course! His daughter had done this on purpose. She wanted them to meet.

'She's very nice.' Caroline-Jane was speaking carefully. 'We had quite a chat.'

He flinched as someone patted his shoulder. 'Hello, ducks! How are you doing?'

It was Georgie, although a sleeker Georgie in skinny tight black jeans and glossy hair tied back in a ponytail.

'Fine, thanks.' He forced himself to sound like everything really was fine. 'What about you?'

'Great, ducks, great.' He tossed his ponytail. 'I'm back on the books now.'

Books?

'My old model agency. They took me back. Listen, I met your wife. So did Coiny.' Georgie tittered. 'Had to toss a quid of course before he'd allow himself to talk to her but luckily it was tails. She's really nice – mind you, I see what you mean about the resemblance to our Caroline-Jane.'

Simon grabbed him. 'Is she still here?'

Georgie made a wide sympathetic face. 'You've just missed her. Said she was taking the tube. Hey, aren't you going to stay to see the rest of the exhibition?'

Simon was already striding across the hall. 'Later. I'll come back later.'

Of course, it was daft. What was he going to say that hadn't already been said? Prison had changed him and it had, by proxy, changed her too. And yet ...

'Claire! Claire!'

He could see her now, striding ahead. He ran faster. 'Claire!'

She looked back. Her face went from shock to relief. 'Simon!' She ran towards him, waving the mobile in her hand. 'I've just had a message from Ben. Slasher's owner has turned up, wanting him back so he and Poppy are taking him back to Devon. But they're not picking up the phone. What are we going to do?'

We! She had said *we*. Simon clung to that, as they took the train back to MK. He would need to deflect the dog man.

'What was he in for?' Claire asked.

He crossed his fingers and muttered something about fraud. No point in scaring her. Instead, they talked about Lydia; each smiling as they realised she'd set them up.

'Try again.' He gestured at the phone in her hand.

'I just have. It's still not picking up.'

It took just over an hour to get back to the house. 'Someone's on the doorstep. Look.'

'Wait there.' He put a hand on Claire's arm before striding up to face the music. 'How did you know I lived here, mate?'

Dog man spat on the ground. 'Spencer told me. That boy of yours said my dog would be back by now. Where the fuck is he?'

'I don't know,' said Simon truthfully.

'You playing games with me?' The man took a step towards him. 'I asked you to look after my dog while I was Inside. Well I'm Out early now and I want him back. Shitting hell.'

At first, Simon thought the expletive was directed at him but then he spotted the police car, stopping on the other side of the road.

He turned back to the dog man but he'd scarpered.

'Excuse me.' The policeman was walking towards him. 'I'm looking for a Mrs Fraser.'

Claire had been hovering closer than he'd realised. 'That's me. At least it was.'

'Do you have a son called Ben Fraser?'

'Yes!' Claire was grabbing the policeman's arm. 'What's happened? Please. Tell me quickly.'

                          *   *   *

'It's my fault,' Claire kept saying, as the nurse led them past a
trolley containing a grey-faced elderly woman with a drip. 'If
I'd stayed at home today, this wouldn't have happened.'

He squeezed her hand tightly. 'It will be all right. They said
Ben was lucky.'

'*But what about Poppy?*' whispered Joanna who'd gone very
quiet.

'But what about Poppy?' whispered Claire.

The nurse took them into a room off to the left of the
corridor. There were two beds. Ben was in the further one.

'Mum! Simon!'

He looked bigger than when Simon had last seen him – he'd
filled out and there was a painfully adult look on his face. 'I'm
so glad to see you.'

Slightly embarrassed, he patted his shoulder. 'It's all right,
you're safe now.'

'But Poppy!' Ben's voice came out in an anguished cry. 'Is
she all right? No one will tell me. And what about Slasher?'

Claire glanced at him and then looked away.

A vision of the car came into his head. Hugh's hand on the
wheel. A car. A glass cobweb. Deathly silence.

'Poppy's critical,' he said softly. 'And Slasher ...'

He left Claire with Ben, once the boy had calmed down, thanks
to the sedatives which a nurse gave him.

'*Coward,*' sniffed Joanna.

No. It was giving them space. Simon glanced round the
waiting room. There he was, just as the nurse had said.

'Hugh?'

'*He'll punch you!*' said Joanna excitedly. '*I know him! Why
do you think I always wore long sleeves?*'

'Hugh? Can you hear me?'

He was lifting his head now. Simon was shocked. Hugh's
eyes were red with grief and his face was crinkled and grey.
Reaching out, he clutched Simon's collar and for a moment,
Simon thought he was going to strangle him. Then he pulled

                              408

him towards him and placed his head on his shoulder. He stank of whisky.

'Poppy's being operated on right now. But if I'd told the truth, none of this would have happened. I'm being punished. I'm so sorry.'

Joanna snorted. *'For God's sake. NOW he's sorry? Listen, Simon, there's only one place here that's going to help. Take a left and a right. It's signed clearly enough.'*

The hospital chapel was empty apart from one woman at the back who singing softly to herself. Memories of the prison chapel, its gloriously lit stained glass window and wooden pews came back into Simon's head.

'Do you want to tell me exactly what happened that night?' he said quietly, sitting next to Hugh.

Hugh was still now. 'I tried telling your wife some time ago when we met for coffee. But I'm afraid I lost my nerve and chickened out.' He drew a deep breath. 'Joanna said she was leaving. She said there wasn't anyone else but I suspected there was.' He gave a small laugh. 'My wife wasn't brave enough to do things like that on her own.'

'Bloody cheek!'

Simon ignored her. He was getting better at that, he'd noticed.

'So I hit her on the arm with a shoe just before we went out.'

'That's not all! Ask him about my dress.'

'Her dress ...' began Simon hesitantly.

Hugh gave him a sharp look. 'I suppose she told Claire, then.' He sighed. 'All right. She had to change into long sleeves to hide the bruises.'

'See! See!'

'I still don't understand.' Simon was looking intently at the Virgin and child statue on the altar. The plastic madonna looked very peaceful, considering the stories she must have heard here. 'Why did you still come to our dinner party after the argument?'

Hugh sniffed. 'She insisted and that's when I got suspicious.

I guessed she wanted to see someone. In fact, I thought it might be you.'

'*Me?*'

Hugh made a wry face. 'But as soon as I was introduced to Alex, I felt the energy between them. They were like dogs on heat. Surprising no one else noticed.'

No wonder Alex had turned a cold shoulder on him after the accident. He blamed him for the death of the woman he loved. My God, he realised with a start. That anonymous note he'd got in prison. It hadn't been from Hugh. It had been from Alex.

'So you drank too much that night to numb the pain?'

Hugh nodded. 'My first wife made a fool of me and now Joanna was doing the same. I could have strangled her, right there in your car.'

Something wasn't making sense. 'But she spoke so fondly of you. Kept calling you 'darling'.'

Joanna's voice reverberated with laughter. '*That was just a front!*'

Hugh looked away. 'It was just a front. She kept saying she should never have married me although, ironically, she got on quite well with Poppy.'

Simon was still trying to get his head together. 'So you honestly meant it before, when you said you wanted us to crash?'

'Yes.' Hugh was staring straight ahead. 'I wanted her to die and I wanted to die and I didn't care who else died in the process.'

'But you let me take the blame! If you had told the court that you had interfered with my driving, they might not have sent me to prison. I'd still have my wife. Still have my job.'

'You see?' Hugh's hand was tugging at his lapels again. 'I've ruined your life and I've ruined Joanna's. There's no point in going on.'

'*Yes there is.*'

Joanna's voice was so soft that he could barely hear her.

'Yes there is,' he repeated more loudly.

'*If I can forgive you,*' whispered Joanna, '*you can make a new start.'*

The Virgin Mary's plastic face beamed innocently. The woman in the pew across the aisle was singing louder now.

'If I can forgive you,' he said quietly, 'you can make a new start.'

Hugh's grip tightened. 'Can you do that?'

He nodded. 'Yes.'

Hugh put his arms around him with a whiff of whisky and cigarettes. Then, over Hugh's shoulder, Simon saw a doctor in a white coat at the door of the chapel, waiting.

411

Chapter Fifty-eight

Ben limped along the corridor towards Poppy's ward. It had been a month since the accident – only another week until the plaster would come off. He hadn't been able to take Slasher for his usual walks but Simon had done that for him. He was glad Simon had moved back in. Mum was much happier.

'You're late!' Poppy beamed up at him from her bed. She looked less pale than last weekend.

'Sorry.' He made a face. 'Coursework. Mum made me do it first.'

'Quite right!' She patted the side of the bed, even though the nurses kept telling him to sit on the chair.

Quickly, before anyone went past, he leaned down and kissed her. She tasted soft and warm.

'You two up to it again!' The nice bustling Irish nurse was on duty, thank goodness. She was all right. 'Make the most of it, if I were you. There's nothing like young love, is there Mabel?'

Mabel was a sweet old lady in the bed opposite Poppy. Ben would often go over and have a chat.

'How are you feeling today?'

'Great.' Poppy's eyes sparkled.

That was one of the things he loved about her. She was always bright. That's why he knew she'd pull through, even when Mum and Simon had said she might not make it. People like Poppy didn't die.

'In fact, I've got some news!'

'They're letting you out!'

'Not so fast! They've moving me. Down to a hospital in Devon where Dad can see me. Don't look like that. He says you can come and stay at weekends.'

412

He nodded, trying to hold back his disappointment. This hospital was so much closer and, besides, Dad had a new girlfriend so he might not want him there.

Poppy was stroking the inside of his palm. 'Just another year and then I'll be able to join you!'

Poppy's eyes sparkled and he felt a funny lurch inside. They'd both agreed to go to one of the London universities. Then they could get a flat together and, as Poppy said, see what happened. He couldn't wait.

'How's Slasher?'

He nodded. 'Great.' There was a pause as they both remembered that terrifying moment when the van had plunged into the side of the car. The left had been clear. But the right hadn't.

'It's incredible really,' said Poppy softly.

Ben nodded. 'He was just sitting there apparently, by the side of the road, waiting for them to get us out.'

They'd said this before but they still needed to say it again, every now and then to reassure themselves.

'No sign of his horrid owner?'

Ben laughed. 'Simon says he was so scared by the police car that he reckons he's scarpered for good.'

'That's good.'

He nodded. 'So is this.'

And then he kissed her again.

'How's Simon?' said Poppy a few minutes later.

'OK.' That reminded him. 'He's taking his driving test again. It's what you have to do after ...'

He stopped.

'Poor Joanna,' said Poppy quietly. 'She didn't deserve it.'

That was true.

'Simon reckons she'd want us all to get on with our own lives now.'

Poppy nodded. 'Reckon he's right.'

There was another bomb that week. This time in Knightsbridge. It injured three but killed no one. A miracle, said the headlines.

Simon read the paper as he ran back up the steps towards Lydia's flat after being at the hospital. When he got to his daughter's door, her face was streaked with tears.

'Two men … two men …' She was sobbing so much that he could hardly understand her.

'Who? I don't understand.'

She was clinging to him and he tried to comfort her, patting her on the back. 'Two men. They knocked on my door and said that if you said anything, we'd both be dead. Dad, you've got to do something, don't you see? This is your chance. You say you ruined Joanna's life. Now you can save others.'

They took it very seriously. Yes, they could guarantee protection although Simon knew they were promising something that couldn't be delivered. So he repeated what he had told the policeman already. He thought he recognised the man from the photofit. He had been in the Multi-Faith Room with two other boys his age and they had been chanting.

The man from the special forces stiffened. Chanting what?

Simon shook his head. 'That was the weird thing. It wasn't a prayer. It was like a rhyme that my grandfather used to tell me when I was a boy. It was in Urdu.'

Could he write it down?

He'd forgotten some of the words but then when he reminded himself of what was at stake, some of them came back.

The man from special forces seemed excited. He didn't say as much but Simon had the feeling that it was some sort of code; maybe an indication of where they would strike next. Meanwhile, said the special forces man, they would find a safe hiding for his family 'just in case'.

'No.' Simon had already discussed this with Claire and Lydia and Ben. They all felt the same. 'We're staying put. We're fed up with change, all of us. We're not running away from anything, any more.'

'Are you sure about that, Mr Mills?'

And as he spoke, Simon realised something. Maybe now

was the time to stop running from the other thing too. Picking up the phone, he made an appointment for the psychologist.

'Why don't you tell me the story from beginning to end,' offered David. He was sitting next to him. None of this patient versus doctor across the desk, Simon noticed.

'You'll think badly of me.'

'Does that matter?'

'Funnily enough, yes.'

'Simon, I don't judge people. We're all guilty of something. Now fire away. It so happens my next patient has cancelled. So we've got all morning.'

He had been nearly eighteen. A boy in the smart set had invited him to the party. It was to be held in the school grounds to celebrate the end of A-levels. He was told to bring 'some gear' if he had it.

'Gear?' questioned Simon, wondering if he meant spare clothes or possibly snacks stolen from supper.

'Cannabis, stupid,' said the boy. 'Or anything else.'

He should have said no then. He'd never done drugs but had been swayed by the fact that the smart set – the in crowd – had included him. So he'd climbed out of the dorm window along with the others and threaded his way through the rugby pitches and then the cricket ground to meet the girls. Alice was going to be there. Alice, whom he'd already met through joint debates at the girl's school and who, her blonde hair swept back in a hairband, had made it quite clear that she would like to see him again.

But that night, Alice didn't have a hairband on. She didn't have much on at all by the time he arrived. One or two couples were already at it in the bushes, stark naked. She handed him what she called a spliff and for a while, they sat and snogged.

Then she'd taken his hand and silently led him into the bushes. Simon could hardly believe his luck. Fumbling with his trousers he eased himself on top of her. Oh my God. Oh my God.

415

But then she screamed. Simon thought she was screaming at him to go on. He certainly didn't think she was screaming at him to stop. Or maybe she was. Maybe it was because she had heard the teacher coming. Suddenly he was being thrown roughly onto the bracken.

'It wasn't my fault,' Alice kept saying. 'It was him. He raped me.'

Simon stopped, looking across at David.

'Go on.' The voice was neither sympathetic nor disapproving.

His father was called to the school of course. Simon was to be expelled immediately. But he was lucky. Alice's family had taken legal advice and been advised not to press charges. Simon's father had driven him home, shouting at him all the way. 'Disgrace to the family. Don't know how you can live with yourself. Don't deserve your place at Oxford.'

He was still shouting when they pulled up outside the house. And that's when it happened.

Simon stopped.

David waited.

'My father got out of the car and fell. Just like that. Straight onto the gravel. They said later that it was instant. A heart attack. Brought on by stress.' Simon's voice came out coldly. It was the only way of coping. 'Of course my mother blamed me.'

'Just as you did yourself?' suggested David.

Simon nodded. 'I never forgave myself. It took me a long time to ask a girl out again after that and when I did, I never allowed it to last. I always made sure she meant "yes" ...' He stopped, conscious that this sounded horribly crude. 'But I also refused to allow myself to get emotionally involved.'

'Until you met your wife?'

'Exactly.' Simon allowed himself to relax. 'She was different. She was damaged just as I was. I wanted to mend her.'

'But you couldn't find complete happiness because ...'

Simon was beginning to understand David's technique now. He would give him part of the sentence in order for him to

416

finish.

'... I was convinced that I needed to be punished. Don't you see? I had killed my father. But I'd been allowed to get away with it. So when I killed Joanna, it was right that I should be punished. That was why I pleaded guilty.'

David's voice was low. Steady. 'And now you know you're a father yourself, do you still believe you were guilty of your father's death?'

Simon was silent.

'Do you?' David persisted.

'I'm not sure.'

'Consider this. Think of that time when you discovered your daughter was working as a prostitute. What if the shock or your medical history gave you a heart attack and you fell down dead. Would you blame Lydia?'

'No.' Simon didn't even need to think about that.

'Exactly.' There was a look of triumph in David's face. 'So I suggest that you allow yourself the same treatment. Put your memories in a box, Simon. Tie it up with string and place it in a mental vault. Give yourself permission to get on with the rest of your life.'

SIX MONTHS LATER

Chapter Fifty-nine

He was late. Claire lay awake, trying not to let monkey thoughts take over. That's what Lydia called them. She was into tai chi and feng shui and goodness knows what else. Some of it helped. Some of it didn't.

So much had happened in the last three years. Simon. In and Out. Ben, now doing his A-levels. Poppy, finally walking. Hugh. Max, who had even come to visit in the hospital. Her mind went back to those terrible early days after the accident.

Who was this coming towards them? Claire peered down the hospital corridor disbelievingly. Mrs Johnson? And Max?

'Thank you for coming.'

She flung her arms around the older woman who in turn, hugged her back. It felt good; rather like being comforted by a youngish aunt.

'Max told me, my dear.'

Confused, Claire turned to him, taking in her former landlord's slightly abashed look and foppish hat pulled firmly down over his eyes as though worried that someone might see him here. 'I saw it on Facebook – as a writer, one has to keep up nowadays with the youth of today, you know. Is the boy going to be all right?'

Had he forgotten how he tried to cheat them both out of her royalties?

Anger and fear made her snap. 'What is to you?'

To her surprise, his face crumpled. 'Got quite fond of you both, I did. In fact, the house has been very quiet without you both. Look, I'm sorry about ...'

'Max,' said Jean, putting a warning hand on his arm. 'This isn't the time or place.'

He nodded, like a small boy who'd been rebuked. 'Of course not. I just wanted to say that I'm afraid I let my ambition get in the way of my better nature. It takes an accident to make you put life in focus, doesn't it?'

'Yes,' said Claire quietly. 'It does.'

He made a face that made him look surprisingly vulnerable. 'I'm afraid, as my sister has pointed out in no uncertain terms, I'm just a crusty old bachelor who'd got too used to thinking about himself.'

Then somehow she found herself putting her arms around him for the simple reason that it seemed the right thing to do.

A few months later, rather astonishingly, their book– *The Day My Dad Went To Prison* – made it to the Bestseller List, leading to a contract for a series. *When Mum Got Out* was commissioned for the following year. The advance wasn't huge but, as Max pointed out, it sent out a message. Prison could happen to (almost) anyone.

But there was, thought Claire as she tossed and turned in bed, still so much more to come to terms with. Simon's part in catching the men behind the bombing. Alex and Rosemarie moving to France but still inexplicably together.

And now this. This final test.

Six hours earlier

The instructor handed Simon a piece of paper. He glanced at the Pass certificate, nodded briefly, and then got back into his car.

He waited until it was dark. Then he drove to Beech Cottage. This is where he needed to start, to end it all.

'*Left,*' Hugh had roared.

He was going past the exact spot right now. Why wasn't Joanna saying anything? Simon slowed to a stop by the edge of the lane and then wiped his palms on the side of his trousers. He needed a break.

Simon booked into a Travelodge to get some rest. After setting the alarm for 4 a.m., he rang Claire. It went through to answerphone.

He woke before the bleep, keen to get off. Wide awake. As he drove smoothly and slowly along the motorway, he saw ambulance lights flashing ahead at the Winchester turn off. Simon waited for the usual sarcastic comment from Joanna, along the lines of: *'There's some other poor soul, killed by a careless driver.'*

Nothing.

In his head, he said a silent prayer. It seemed to make sense to have a faith now. It gave you something to live by.

As he drove, Simon's mind drifted back to the conversation he'd had with Hugh, after Poppy had pulled through.

'I want to help,' Hugh had said. 'Tell me how I can make it up.'

That's when he'd told him about his idea. 'It's difficult to find a job when people come Out,' Simon had explained. 'People are scared of employing men who have criminal records. '

Hugh had nodded. '*I* wouldn't.'

'But what if we started an employment business for people who have a record?'

'No one would employ them!'

'Some people are willing to give second chances.'

'Could work, I suppose.' Hugh's voice was gruffly conceding. 'Might get a grant for it too. What would you call it?'

'Inside Out,' said Simon promptly.

'OK. I'll put up the funding but only for a year. If it's not self-sufficient by then, we shut it down.'

'It's a deal,' said Simon.

'But you'll need to drive again.' Hugh eyeballed him. 'If you want me to get over my demons, you've got to get over yours.'

And that's exactly what he was doing.

Nearly there now.

When he'd moved back in with Claire again, a few weeks after Ben's accident, they'd decided to stay put. Ben liked his college. She had her teaching. At some point, they agreed, they'd move back to the sea. Maybe near Jean.

'It's not the house you live in, it's the person you live with,' Claire had said. She was right.

Now, as Simon looked up at their window, he could see the curtains were still closed. Quietly, he slid the key in the lock.

Slowly up the stairs. Past Ben's room where Slasher looked up from his bed, grunted his approval, and then nestled down back into Ben's chest. Into their room.

Claire had her back to him, her beautiful naked shoulders rising slowly up and down below the duvet, like the back of an elegant violin.

Peeling off his jeans, he slid in next to her, breathing in her smell and holding her from behind.

'I'm home,' he whispered. 'I'm home.'

For more information about **Jane Bidder**
and other **Accent Press** titles
please visit

www.accentpress.co.uk